Praise for *The Matchmakers of Minnow Bay*

"Fans of Jennifer Weiner, Mary Simses, and Jennifer Close will adore this clever and witty story of self-reinvention and the power of clarity."

—*Booklist*

"A funny story about second chances at romance and life and is a great summertime read."

—Amy Phelps, *The Parkersburg News and Sentinel*

"I loved this book! Fresh and devastatingly funny, *The Matchmakers of Minnow Bay* is romantic comedy at its very best."

—Colleen Oakley, author of *Before I Go*

"Sometimes you read a book that hits all the right notes: funny, charismatic, romantic, and empowering. *The Matchmakers of Minnow Bay* is that book. I loved it in every way!"

—Amy Reichert, author of *Luck, Love & Lemon Pie*

"Filled with witty dialogue and an unforgettable cast of characters, *The Matchmakers of Minnow Bay* is a complete charmer."

—Anita Hughes, author of *Santorini Sunsets*

"Harms weaves together a small town and big dreams into a delightful and heartfelt tapestry of friendship, love, and getting what you deserve, in the way you least expect. I was hooked from page one, then laughed out loud and teared up while reading—exactly what I want from romantic women's fiction."

—Amy Sue Nathan, author of
The Good Neighbor and *The Glass Wives*

"Kelly Harms has once again written the kind of characters you want to be friends with—funny [illegible] flawed—all set against a charming canvas of s[illegible]

[illegible]*ge*

"*The Matchmakers of Minnow Bay* is a glorious read, full of heart and humor. Lily is the kind of character you'll root for to the end, and the delightful residents of Minnow Bay will keep you chuckling with each turn of the page."

—Darien Gee, bestselling author of *Friendship Bread*, *The Avalon Ladies Scrapbooking Society*, and *An Avalon Christmas*

"A world so real and so inviting that you absolutely will not want to leave. *The Matchmakers of Minnow Bay* proves that a little small-town meddling never hurt anyone and that, sometimes, it takes a village to fall in love. Kelly Harms has done it again!"

—Kristy Woodson Harvey, author of *Dear Carolina* and *Lies and Other Acts of Love*

"*The Matchmakers of Minnow Bay* thoroughly entertains as it explores friendship, flings, and finally finding yourself. Harms tells the story in a funny, fresh voice ideal for this charming coming-into-her-age novel."

—Christie Ridgway, *USA Today* bestselling author of the Beach House No. 9 and Cabin Fever series

To Allan Harms,
1945–2014

The Matchmakers of Minnow Bay

KELLY HARMS

Thomas Dunne Books
St. Martin's Griffin New York

To Allan Harms,

1945–2014

This is a work of fiction. All of the characters, organizations, and events portrayed in this novel are either products of the author's imagination or are used fictitiously.

THOMAS DUNNE BOOKS.
An imprint of St. Martin's Press.

 Printed in the United States of America. For information, address St. Martin's Press, 175 Fifth Avenue, New York, N.Y. 10010.

www.thomasdunnebooks.com
www.stmartins.com

The Library of Congress has cataloged the hardcover edition as follows:

Names: Harms, Kelly, author.
Title: The matchmakers of Minnow Bay : a novel / Kelly Harms.
Description: First edition. | New York : Thomas Dunne Books/St. Martin's Press, 2016.
Identifiers: LCCN 2016002480 | ISBN 978-1-250-07061-6 (hardcover) |
ISBN 978-1-4668-8094-8 (ebook)
Subjects: LCSH: Man-woman relationships—Fiction. | City and town life—Fiction. |
Mate selection—Fiction. | BISAC: FICTION / Contemporary Women. |
GSAFD: Love stories.
Classification: LCC PS3608.A7493 M38 2016 | DDC 813/.6—dc23
LC record available at http://lccn.loc.gov/2016002480

ISBN 978-1-250-13046-4 (trade paperback)

Our books may be purchased in bulk for promotional, educational, or business use. Please contact your local bookseller or the Macmillan Corporate and Premium Sales Department at 1-800-221-7945, extension 5442, or by email at MacmillanSpecialMarkets@macmillan.com.

First St. Martin's Griffin Edition: August 2017

10 9 8 7 6 5 4 3 2 1

Acknowledgments

Thank you to:

Holly Root, for making me start this, and Laurie Chittenden, for making me finish it.

Tom Dunne and Pete Wolverton: the ne plus ultra of publishing, and Katie Bassel and Melanie Fried for being indefatigable.

Hatch Art House, Art Beat of Hayward, and Absolutely Art of Madison, for setting my mind awhirl with the sublime beauty of the Midwestern landscape. The Art Institute of Chicago, for setting my heart on fire with the sublime beauty of everything else.

Kris Adams, Jennifer Ferreter Sabet, Abbie Foster Chaffee, Kelly Hilyard, Mrs. Emil Hoelter, Ms. Tina Juntunen, Amanda Maciel, Kimberly Megna Yarnall, Sara Naatz, Kelly O'Connor McNees, Barbara Poelle, Anna Rybicki, Ellen Shanman, and Cricket Stevens Gage: these incredible women are my Minnow Bay Village.

The Harms family: Claire, Doug, Kris, Roger, Sally, and Griffin, I love you.

PART I

Time Transfixed

TEN YEARS EARLIER

"I think I've looked at this one too much," my best friend Renee says to me as we come around the corner and find what I suspect is Magritte's most annoying piece. It's got the same strong lines and supreme confidence of his most famous work, *The Son of Man*, the fancy guy with the bowler hat with a green apple floating in front of his face. But the subject matter of *Time Transfixed* is very different—a flat fireplace in a streamlined drawing room, with the perspective angled from lower-left corner to upper right, so you know the room is a room, not a box. And of course, the ultra-black locomotive made out of a steam pipe thrusting out of the fireplace. Like it's . . . you know.

"Yeah, me too," I agree. "Or maybe the idea of *Time Transfixed* is just not sitting well with me right now," I say. It is the day before art school graduation. Four years living with my best friend and making art and looking at art and eating, sleeping, drinking up art, and tomorrow it is all over.

Time is most certainly not feeling very transfixed.

"Magritte preferred a different translation for the French," she tells me. "Something about stabbing time with a knife. It's a lot more aggressive, more active that way."

"I wish I could stab time with a knife."

"No, you don't."

"Easy for you to say. You're going off to law school after graduation. Law school, Renee. You're going to be a lawyer, and make tons of money, and wear suits." I pause at that. "Have you really thought this through?"

She laughs warmly at me. "Of course I have! It's going to be great. I love arguing. And you don't *have* to wear suits unless you're in court."

"Do you even own a suit?" I ask her.

She laughs. "Just the one I bought for the interview. And it was separates so I don't think it counts. Don't worry, Lily. I'm still me even if I'm going to be a lawyer. Law school won't change the fact that I don't wear pantyhose."

"When will you sculpt?"

Renee shrugs. "There will be time. Or I can always set it aside for a little while, come back when I'm more inspired. It hasn't really been as fun for me since . . . well, since I started planning my future."

I look at her sideways, thinking, *That is what you get for always worrying about your future.*

"I don't think you'll survive without your art."

Renee tilts her head at me, looking away from the Magritte for the first time. "Or maybe that's more you than me. You need to be covered in paint every hour of every day. You are the one who's talented. You're the one with the passion."

"You're talented! You have passion!"

"Remember what they said to us at orientation freshman year?"

"No," I say honestly. "Something about reporting date rape?"

"Besides that. They said, if you can do something besides art, you should."

I open my arms in question. "Well, that's everyone, though. I can do lots of other things. I can sort of play the piano. I make a good espresso. And a good martini."

"They meant do any other *job*. They meant if your soul wouldn't die from not making art, don't make art."

"I think that's a lousy litmus test," I say. "Soul death is kind of an extreme bar to set."

"And yet for you, I think you meet it. You are destined to do this." She gestures at the museum, as though I am supposed to end up in a place like this. When, much more likely, I'd be lucky to get paid to paint the side of a barn.

"So I'm destined to be poor and tortured for at least the next fifty years, and you, my best friend in the whole world, are destined to sue people for a living?"

Renee smiles mildly. "Well, that's what I'm hoping."

I gesture to the Magritte. "I am the fireplace. All out of whack and stagnant. And you are the locomotive, doing useful things and plowing ahead."

"Actually, I think the locomotive is supposed to be his penis."

I snort. "You think everything in art is genitals."

Renee shrugs. "It isn't?"

We laugh. But my laugh is melancholy. Four years in art school together. Four years living together as best friends, telling each other everything, seeing each other at our absolute worst and absolute best. How can it be over already? How come time isn't just a little more transfixed?

"There's room for you to stay in my apartment any time you visit," I tell her. "It's such a sweet place; you're going to be so jealous."

"I'm just jealous that you don't have to live in South Bend, Indiana, for the next two years. Promise you'll visit every weekend you don't have to work." Renee grabs my hand. "I can't believe we won't be living together anymore. I don't even know how that's supposed to work. About seventy-five percent of my clothes are actually your clothes. I'm going to have to go shopping. Promise when you come you'll bring your Seven jeans for me to wear?"

"Of course. Me, tequila, Seven jeans. I won't even call first."

"Perfect. See, things don't have to change that much. It's only a few hours in the car. Plus, I'll have all those law school hotties rounded up for you to date."

"You are *the* best friend, Renee. Let's trade keys tomorrow before the ceremony starts."

"If you haven't locked yourself out before then," Renee says, speaking of my truly extraordinary ability to trap myself out of cars, dorms, studios, and apartments.

I ignore her. "And then when law school is over you can move in with me."

"I might meet someone, you know," she says vaguely. "Fall in love. Move to the suburbs."

"Don't even joke!"

A shadow crosses Renee's face. I work very hard not to see it. It feels like the shadow of the locomotive. "Anyway," she says eventually, "you think you'll still be in that apartment in two years?"

"Renee, I am going to die in that apartment. In eighty years they will find me in there surrounded by bad paintings, half-eaten by cats. And you know what? I'm pretty okay with that."

"Well," she says, turning on her heels and making for the Miró. "As long as you have a plan."

One

TEN YEARS LATER

"Getting evicted is the best thing that could have happened to me."

I am trying to be convincing. I am keeping the tears at bay like a champ. Now I force a closed-mouth smile for punctuation.

"Well, that's insane," says my oldest, best friend. We are sitting at the coffee shop sixteen stories below her office. She looks good, for her, for right now, the place in her life that she's in, which is one that is not overmuch concerned with how she looks. Still, good. I am sure I do not, with my paint-stained yoga pants and puffy eyes. I'm a crier, a private crier, and I have been exercising that muscle quite a lot since I came home early on New Year's Eve and found yellow seal tape around the edges of my apartment door.

In public, and we are in public right now, I try to be tough. I admire tough women, like Renee. Her toughness can be mistaken by some for rudeness. It is toughness. In another life, in another universe, she could have been a dynamite soccer coach. Or a bouncer.

Renee says, toughly, "The best thing that could happen to you is that you move according to your own timeline and your own terms, without a bad credit reference and a looming deadline."

Today, as raw as I am, the toughness feels rude.

"Yeah. You're right," I say. "But this is the *next* best thing. It's a sign from the universe saying, 'Get on with your life, Lily.' "

"It's a sign saying, 'Pay your bills on time,' more likely," she says with a sigh. "Where will you go?"

I look at her long and hard. She is wearing a navy pantsuit. The suit is pressed and clean and fits funny. There is a lime green scarf involved, running under the collar of the jacket, maybe intended to soften the look. It does not look like something my oldest, best friend would wear if a gun were pressed to her temple, but I think that about her outfit every time I see her lately. I think, *Who is this person?*

And now I wonder again, is there any chance in hell she will go along with this plan of mine? Her grand and stately home in the near west suburbs has room for me. It has room for a flock of me's. There are four bedrooms up and one master down and a huge finished basement, which she and I refer to as the pleasure dome, that is divided three ways: a mom cave (for scrapbooking. Scrapbooking! My oldest, best friend, scrapbooking!), a man cave, and a children's playroom. That playroom alone is twice as big as my old apartment and has three times nicer things in it, if you are the sort of person who believes that handmade, hand-dyed all-natural wooden educational toys are nicer appointments than a beat-up IKEA platform bed and upcycled shelving. I am that sort of person. I would rather sleep on a yoga mat on her playroom floor, cooking all my meals on her charming switch-operated pellet stove and eating off of compostable children's tea sets, than spend another night in my old apartment where my life and choices have grown stagnant and dusty.

That is not true at all.

I want to stay where I am. I've been in that apartment for ten years now. Since the summer after I graduated from Northwestern. It's an ancient two flat with good bones and good light. It is small and noisy, but so am I. There was never any reason to move.

Now there is a very good reason. Three months ago my landlord told me to find a new place because she was going to sell to developers. I did not find a new place, or look. I still had ten months on my lease. Then I missed a rent payment, in December, when Christmas gifts always get me a hair behind. Just a hair. I paid her later, midmonth. Late-month, really. Not the same as not paying at all, I don't think. But she says it is. She wants me out by next week.

A suspicious person might think that my missing that one isolated payment was my landlord's opportunity to cash out of that particular rental investment. That evicting me for one three-week-late payment is morally iffy and, probably, telling me to leave within seven days is legally iffy as well. I try not to be a suspicious person, though.

I would also prefer not to be a homeless person. I look across the table at Renee. Her face is suddenly wide and unfamiliar to me. We have been best friends since freshman year of college, and that feels like a long time to me. We've been through a lot.

"Do you think—" I begin.

She knows right away what I am about to ask and cuts me off. "You know what I wish," she says, and it is not a question. "I wish I could just offer you a bedroom at our house. Wouldn't that be nice? I'd love you to come stay with us for a while, God knows I could use the help with the girls. If only I had the room. Chicago real estate is so hard," she concludes.

"I know," I say, nodding. "It's hard." We both turn our heads to gaze out the windows, at the snowy, windy, gray Chicago January. As bleak as it is, it is better than looking at each other.

If I were a suspicious person I would think that maybe Renee does have plenty of room for me. Room upon room upon room for me to choose from. It's just her and Nic and Natalie and Natasha in there. The girls sleep in the same room. In the same bed even. That leaves approximately thirty-five bedrooms available for guests and/or evicted oldest, best friends.

"I know the house is big compared to your apartment, but with two little kids running around it shrinks fast. We need one bedroom open at all times in case the nanny needs to stay over. That's part of our agreement with her so we can use her at night, you know. And we need the guest room with the en suite for Nic's mother to visit. I can't have her on a sofa. She's hard enough to deal with when she gets a good night's sleep."

"I know," I say. I do know how hard she is to cope with, how jealous and possessive she can be of Nic. Before they married, Renee and I used to refer to her as the deal-breaker. "I totally understand."

"And we're still trying for a boy. You know. Keep your fingers crossed. And then it will be a full house."

I cross my fingers obediently, but . . . a baby takes nine months to arrive. I just need a couple weeks. Does she think I'm looking for a place to crash indefinitely? Maybe if I clear that up.

"I totally understand, but I so wish it were possible, even for a very short time." I say the words "very short time" a bit louder than necessary. "I never get to see the girls anymore. Or you. We're just all so busy. And it would be so nice to have a home base for a couple of weeks so I can find a decent apartment instead of just having to move into the next available dump I can find."

She looks at her hands. They are showing her age, I think, uncharitably.

"Have you asked Mitchell?"

I take that as a firm no. I wish, not for the first time, that I had never dated stupid Nic Larsen, future husband of my best friend. I have not so much as been invited to dinner at their house since he made a crass but complimentary joke about the caliber of our college-era sex life. Renee was pregnant with Natasha at the time and did not take it well. Now she simply cannot keep us far enough from each other, though the idea of cheating with my best friend's husband is odious, and Nic himself is also odious.

"I don't think Mitchell is in a position . . ." I begin. Then I give up.

"You asked him and he said no?"

I shake my head, embarrassed. "I haven't asked him yet."

"What? Why not?" she asks.

"I know what he'll say. He'll say that it would muddle our professional relationship," I say softly.

Renee rolls her eyes. "This is what you get for sleeping with your boss."

"He's not my boss, you know that. He's my gallerist. We have a partnership. And a relationship. Two separate things."

"But not the kind of partnership or relationship where you can ask to move in with him."

"His place is too small anyway," I say. His place is not too small, not by a mile, but I want her to hear how ridiculous her own excuse sounded.

And maybe she does. She purses her lips, but doesn't respond to that, saying instead, "Have you tried Daniella?"

"Daniella moved to Seattle last year," I say. "You should see her Christmas card. She loves it there."

"Hm. I must have gotten deleted from her list."

"I'm sure that's not it," I say. Though I am actually surprised Renee was ever on Daniella's list. We were all best of friends at Northwestern, but Renee and Daniella grew apart, rather passionately, after graduation. "Probably she doesn't have a list. You know her, she probably just sends the cards to whomever she saw on Facebook that day."

Renee laughs a bit at this. "Seattle is perfect for her. Fast and cool but still removed from reality."

I cannot help but nod. That is Daniella to a T. In college we all believed she would be the one to go all the way with her art career. Now she's a freelance graphic designer who makes a killing when she works, but doesn't work very often. She drinks a little more than seems prudent, and doesn't make art anymore, and plays weird mind games with men. Whenever I call her she is either out of breath or slurping dashi. I imagine most of her days are spent running long distances on foot to ramen noodle shops.

Renee is insightful, to sum up Daniella so well even though they probably haven't been in the same room since my last birthday party. She has always had a gift for seeing people, knowing them through and through in an instant. As a result, she always knows just what to do, which way is up.

Which is why I ask her what she thinks I should do next about housing. If she can't take me in, maybe she has a better plan.

"I think you should sue, honestly," she says casually, sipping her flat white.

"Sue Mitchell?" My brain doesn't compute.

"Don't be ridiculous. Mitchell is the best thing that ever happened to you. I think you should sue your landlord."

I roll my eyes. Renee is a divorce lawyer—she thinks everyone should sue for something.

"I'm willing to bet your lease clearly states you have thirty days to leave the premises—that's the law. But even beyond that, I'm not sure she *can* boot you for being late with rent one time. So either you're not telling me the truth about your payment history or she's evicting you illegally." Renee recrosses her legs and checks her phone and then adds, "Probably it's a little of both."

I nod, though I was telling her the general truth. I've bounced a couple of rent checks over the decade I've lived there—I'm a visual artist, for God's sakes—but none in the last two years. Other than that, I've kept up to date. It's the first bill I set money aside for whenever I get a sale.

Still, it's a moot point. "I'm not going to sue. You know that."

Renee nods her head and rolls her eyes at me. "Good old Lily. Never one to put up a fight."

I decide to take that as a compliment. "Any other ideas?" I ask her.

Renee pretends to think for a moment. "If you ask me, and you just did, it's time to get out of Chicago. No offense, but you can't afford it here. Not the way you live. I bet you're in credit-card debt up to your ears, or you would have paid your rent with a card advance. Am I right?"

I bite my lip. She is a *little* right.

"And what good does it do you exactly to stay here? Your apartment sucks, your day jobs always suck, and now that you've got a good relationship with a gallery you don't need to be here to schmooze with the art people anymore. Go live in the outer suburbs and see Mitchell on weekends."

I am speechless. Stunned. Chicago is my home. I've never lived anywhere else.

I think Renee sees my face crumple up a bit, because she softens her tone and takes my hand across the table.

"Lily. Honey. You're so talented. Your art sells well, and for a lot of money, for what it is. Go somewhere you can live on that and keep making your beautiful art. Meet new people. Get your feet under you. Be a grown-up, just a little."

"But all my friends are here," I say. And I think, *Really, Lily?* Daniella's gone a year now. Kat, Corie, Risha, all married with children in the suburbs, their art careers waiting quietly off to one side while they live their other lives. Their *real* lives. And Renee, my best friend, actually telling me to go farther away from her than I already am.

"I know," Renee says, nodding sympathetically. "It's hard to make a change."

"Especially when you never wanted a change."

Renee exhales. Puts her phone down. "Well, that's the thing about you, Lily," she says sadly. "You never want anything to change."

My heart sinks. I know what Renee is talking about. Not just about my decade-long residence in my crappy apartment, or the five-year stint as a barista at the Starbucks across the street, or even the way I paint the same subjects again and again, over and over, in morning light or nighttime, from the left and then the right, and then straight on again. She is talking about her and me. About how she has moved in new directions that don't include aging friendships with thirty-two-year-old fiscally unsound visual artists.

We have nothing left to talk about.

"No, you're right," I say lightly, but I take back my hand. "I'm working on it. And now there will be change, no matter what, right?" I say in a falsely chipper voice. "Who knows what the future holds?"

But Renee only raises her eyebrows. It is as though she is saying, "I know what it holds. And I am not impressed."

. . .

The Helms gallery was, for a brief time, my favorite place in Logan Square. Now it feels like the principal's office. It is sandwiched between a taxidermy shop and a bespoke handbag designer, and, because of Mitchell Helms's particular brand of high/low taste, it seems to actually tie the two neighbors together. I text Mitchell when I'm five minutes away so he knows to expect me. He tells me to come straight upstairs.

Upstairs is an iron spiral staircase in the middle of the second gallery that leads to a little glassed-in loft where Mitchell oversees his kingdom. Downstairs there are assorted staff members to greet me, but after the most cursory of hellos, I climb up the stairs, clang, clang, clang, and surface at the foot of his large chrome and glass drafting desk. When he turns toward me, I feel that *thing,* that thing I always feel around Mitchell. Renee calls it chemistry, but I know it as something else. I feel like I am wearing too-high heels and a too-short skirt and a too-sheer blouse. The effect is at once intoxicating and uncomfortable.

"Lily," he says on an exhale. He has this way of saying my name like he invented it. My imaginary heels grow higher. Then he looks me over and says, "You're empty-handed."

Inwardly I cringe. I have been avoiding, at all costs, letting Mitchell discover how stagnant my painting has become over the last few months. Every two or three weeks I've been dusting off something old from my stash and passing it off as a new work. But I haven't even done that lately. When was the last time I showed him something "new"? It must have been before Christmas.

"Nothing?" he asks me, a little sadly.

"Nothing," I admit. "I'm sorry, Mitchell." His eyes look genuinely concerned. I think he must know something is wrong. For a moment, just a fleeting one, I consider trying to tell him about how I've been painting the same thing for the last six months, over and over again, unable to get it quite right. Sometimes I have gotten lucky and made something I like, and sometimes I have even given something to Mitchell to sell. But mostly I am treading the same waters over and over again, day in and day out.

"Lily, don't apologize to me. This is how it works. Sometimes inspiration comes, sometimes it doesn't."

I exhale. He's right, of course. It's never how it's worked for me before, but nothing has really been the same for me since my art started to sell. Maybe I just need to tune out some of the pressure.

"The only thing is," Mitchell continues, "people are asking."

Or, maybe I need more pressure.

"I don't want a long fallow period to depress your stock."

Mitchell is always talking about my artwork like it's an offering on the Dow Jones. I cannot imagine trying to do what he does—to balance some kind of business acumen with the tastes and whims of buyers and the egos and frailty of the artists. As a particularly frail artist myself, I don't know what I would do without him.

"Something new is coming," I lie. Then I remember why I'm here. "However. I'm having a little issue with my studio. It isn't helping the situation. I have a favor to ask."

"Hm?" Mitchell steps out from behind his desk at last. He towers over me at six foot something. My imaginary heels are starting to totter. "Wait," he says. "Come here. I forgot to give you something."

For a moment I dare to hope he's got some kind of check for me. Maybe I lost track of a quarterly payment? Forgot to cash something from months ago? But when I get closer he puts his arms around me, pulls me in for a quick peck, and then goes back for a real kiss that I feel up and down my spinal column like a cold wind off Lake Michigan. When he pulls back he shakes his head at me and says, "I can never get over the way you smell. Like cured acrylics and candy."

"I need to stay with you for a week," I blurt out. "I'm being evicted."

Mitchell drops his hands from my arms. "How can that be?"

I don't care to explain the whole situation. "It's complicated. I, um, I have to be out in a week."

"Well . . ." He waits a long time. I can see the wheels turning as he goes shopping for an excuse. "Of course you can stay with me," he says.

"Really?" I start. I was being too pessimistic. My heart sort of twists up, relief mixing with surprise mixing with something else . . . maybe just a tiny shred of apprehension.

"At some point. Of course," he says. "Not now, though, Lily. Not when we're working together professionally too. You know that's not good for us. It's too confusing. You painting, in my house, you'd have no privacy to work, I'd have no perspective on your work, it would muddy the waters."

"I know that. But it's kind of . . . almost . . . an emergency," I try.

Mitchell takes me by the waist and leads me to one of the armchairs that face his desk, sitting himself down and then pulling me to him. I feel like a child, even though I am thirtysomething. "Let's table this discussion for later," he says. "Someday you'll be too big a star to keep down in my galaxy here." He waves his arms to indicate the gallery spaces below. "That's when we'll talk about the next level between us. Now is the time for you to focus on your work."

"But I won't have any place to work," I say, feeling petulant.

"But of course you will," Mitchell says. "Just because I'm not going to catch you every time you feel like you might be falling, that doesn't mean you can't catch yourself. And won't you feel better when you do?"

I shrug. "I guess," I try, wondering if he's caught me mid-plummet lots of times and I just haven't noticed.

"You will. I promise." Mitchell brushes something off my face and presses his lips to my cheek. "I have to get back to work now, but listen, we can talk about this later, right? Maybe after this show this weekend. It's killing me. I can't focus on anything else. This artist is completely outside his own mind. But the works . . . It's going to be spectacular if it doesn't fall completely to pieces." He laughs. "I could say the same thing about you, Lily."

He could, I think. But it would be nice if he didn't. "I'm not falling to pieces," I say aloud. "Or if I am," I add quietly, "it's nothing new."

Mitchell smiles at me as he takes his place back behind his desk, his crow's-feet appearing, his eyes positively twinkling at me with a lack of concern. "And I wouldn't have you any other way."

Though it is only 4:00 P.M. when I leave the gallery, I stop on the way home at Red or Dead, a wineshop that specializes in red varietals. I positively love this store. They sell one or two Chardonnays and some good Champagnes, but if you go in there demanding a Riesling they politely suggest you go fuck yourself.

The shop is owned by Annie and Jo, two of my friends from college who are living, breathing proof that some college relationships do last forever. Came in majoring in sex, left engaged to each other. Married November 20, 2013, the day Illinois legalized gay marriage.

"Hi, ladies," I say when I see that both are working today.

When they see me they both start grinning. "Guess what we got each other for Christmas!" Annie sings out before the door is closed behind me.

"New glitter nail polish?"

Annie stretches out her fingers and Jo laughs. Their nails match, both purple with pink sparkles. Not for the first time I imagine my version of their evenings together, painting nails, watching *True Blood,* making out. I twist with envy. "Besides the nail polish," Jo says. "Look up!"

I look at the ceiling. "What?" I say after a moment's inspection.

"Oh my God. Aren't artists supposed to be observant?" Annie asks. She points at the space between the copper ceiling tile and the brick fireplace at the side of the store, next to the South American reds.

"Oh oh oh," I say. "You didn't!"

"We had to!" Jo cries out. "We couldn't let anyone else have it. It's too beautiful."

My heart swells. It's one of my paintings, one that was for sale at Mitchell's gallery downtown. It's a night landscape—the view from my apartment window. Two hauntingly beautiful Chicago buildings, a sidewalk, a storefront. A private, quiet kiss I saw one day when the lights were on late in the store and one partner was leaving the other behind. Half the work is in movement—cars, stoplights, people, hands—and the other, buildings and row upon row of wine bottles, still like stones.

"You shouldn't have spent so much . . . I mean, I would have given you a piece if I knew you wanted one."

"But not that one. It had to be that one," says Annie.

"Was it a fortune?" I am not always privy to the pricing of my art at the gallery until after it sells. *If* it sells. Frankly, once it's in Mitchell's hands, I think of each piece of art as gone forever, never really knowing where it all goes next. I wish I could know, could even have some say, but if I were any good at pricing and marketing, I would be a gallery owner, not an artist, and therefore have no need to sign what Renee calls a "draconian" gallery agent's agreement. But, as Mitchell is happy to remind me, our professional relationship relies entirely on trust. *Trust and autonomy,* that's what we always say. That's how we make it work. Right?

"No, no, not a fortune," says Jo. "Okay, maybe a tiny fortune. So worth it, though. Most of our customers have noticed it right away. And the insurance assessor thinks we made a good investment."

"You have to insure it?"

Jo says, "Girl, aside from that case of '63 Bordeaux that *someone,*" she levels a glare at Annie, "ordered four years ago, this is the most valuable thing we own."

I smile and blush. "You have very expensive tastes, Annie."

She laughs. "Unfortunately, I seem to be the only one in Chicago who is willing to spend for the finer things. At least in the wine department. In the art department we very nearly missed out on this piece."

"Really?"

"Really. While we were there for the showing someone came in asking about it. Said she saw it on some art blog that morning. Another day and it would have been gone."

"Wow." I go to great lengths to stay off of the art blogs. I even blocked a few of the URLs on my browser. This is a fickle business and I don't need editorial chatter in my head when I'm trying to work. But I am honestly surprised this quiet landscape is getting any kind of special attention from the media. I've painted similar ones for the last six months, and Mitchell has actually passed on a few of them. All the same view, pretty much, though never looking much the same on the canvas. I think I'm working something out. Well, I hope I am.

"Wow," I say again. "Maybe I should buy one of those fancy bottles you were telling me about."

Jo shakes her head at me. "You absolutely may not. That wine is not going to be swigged out of a juice glass on my watch."

"I could use a coffee mug instead. I think there's a clean one in my cupboard right now."

Annie looks faint. "How about we find you something wet and red in the $15 price range."

I shake my head at myself. "You know my tastes so well." They pick out a wine and tell me things I should notice about the bottle. I tune them out until they tell me what it costs. Affordable enough to leave room on my last working credit card for a couple nights in a suburban hotel and some groceries.

"Should we add a sliver of brie and some honeyed figs?" Annie and Jo are brilliant enough to sell a few good cheeses, chocolate truffles, and dried fruits in a case by the register. By the time you've tasted two or three bottles to find something you like, the cheese is pretty much a done deal.

"Maybe more than a sliver," I start, thinking of the credit cards and the eviction and the weird reality that though my art is selling, I won't get a check from my gallery until the end of the next quarter. April 15th. It's January 2nd. I have to be out of my apartment by the 7th.

"I have some bad news," I blurt out.

Annie and Jo both swivel where they stand. "What is it?" they ask almost in unison, as if neither hears the other start to speak. I look from one woman to the other and then to my painting, which has been shown so much love here, which I can come see whenever I want to be reassured that someone truly looks at my artwork, that it is more than just wall filler for Wall Streeters. I change my mind. "I'm a fraud. That art is worthless," I say, instead of telling them about the eviction.

They both laugh gaily and my heart breaks. "Tell it to the appraiser. In the meantime, I think we'll just leave it up and keep loving it all the same."

When I get home I have arms full with the bottle of wine, cheese, figs, and several empty wine boxes bound up in twine from the shop. I live lean, so they should be enough for all my fragile possessions. The clothes will fit in my two suitcases. The paints, pastels, and brushes already have huge Rubbermaid bins to call home. The canvases themselves will be the only real logistics problem.

In the past, whenever I finished a painting I was proud of, I would take it, by hand, to Mitchell's gallery, in a big black Hefty bag. If he liked it, great. If he didn't, the painting and I would come back together on the L.

This means I have a small but formidable stack of rejected canvasses that I like too much to paint over. I usually work large, so we're talking about four-by-six-foot pieces, unframed, in stacks against the wall. I've never hung any of my own works—that would be too vain for words—but I do put my favorites face-out. You know, for when guests come over. In case they want to admire me, just a bit. That's not vain, is it?

I contemplate the sum total of my adult life. The art will fit in my hatchback, with the suitcases, I think. That means the rest has to go into storage or into a new place asap. *A new place.* When I look around at my battered thrift-store pots and plates—the same things I took with me to college, by and large, I think maybe it would make more sense to start fresh. If I had any money to start fresh with.

Still, most of this is not worth the cost of storage, and since I won't be able to afford first and last months' rent until after April, what doesn't fit in my car doesn't have a place to go. I pour myself a juice glass of wine and start dividing the keeps and the giveaways.

As my body works on sorting, my mind works on my next steps. I could go home. My stepbrother and his wife live together in my parents' house two hours west of here. Charlie runs our dad's Dairy Dame and Carrie does the books. We have a muddled history. Before Carrie, Charlie needed constant handouts to stay above water. Every time I had a dime, he asked for five cents. But Carrie is the opposite, responsible to the point of rigidity. I should be grateful to her for stopping the hemorrhaging, but now Charlie and I hardly have reason to talk at all. Whenever I call, the first words out of his mouth are always, "Who died?"

Even so, they have to take me in on account of me being family. But Carrie will expect me to work behind the counter to pay my way. I can just imagine what Mitchell will say about his girlfriend selling milkshakes and slushies. I suppose I just won't tell him.

I won't need pots and pans at my brother's house—or my dignity—but Charlie and Carrie will need some warning. Three days should do. I have five more days in this place, so that gives me maybe two more days to think of a better plan, and, if I can't, three days to gird my loins that I am moving home.

What will I need for five more days? I am no kind of cook. In half an hour the room is down to a microwaveable bowl for soup, a mug, a spoon, and my bread knife. Four cabinets and three drawers of silverware, dishes, gadgets, and Tupperware is whittled into one solitary box. What doesn't fit, goes to the curb.

The fourth and final drawer in my kitchen is where I've stashed "important" paperwork for the last decade. Basically every time I have a tax return or health insurance statement or paid credit card bill, I put it in there. I can probably throw away half of it, if I just sit down and face the pile. One glass of wine into the packing process, I can think of no better time than now.

I refill said glass and make myself a little plate. Good bread from the bakery, topped with cheese and fruit. It is, with a spread like this, impossible to feel poor. After savoring a couple bites standing up, my food and wine and I sit down together on the kitchen floor for a spell to deal with the mess of my life.

Twenty minutes later I find it.

It's in a manila envelope—the same one it came in ten years ago. It says:

State of Nevada, IMPORTANT, OPEN IMMEDIATELY

and the minute I see it I think, *Oh no.* Like I'm watching it on YouTube, I remember that day, the day that envelope came. I had been back from Las Vegas for a month, and the whole ridiculous trip was already a distant memory. Renee and Nic's wedding was the very next day—so it must have come on a Friday. Back then I waited tables on Thursday nights at a long-defunct club renowned for its uptown martinis and downtown waitresses. Almost all of us were artists, waitresses, or novelists. Or wanted to be. The owner told me to look "edgy, but no tattoos." I've always been more Nashville than Flatbush, but he seemed happy enough with that.

Bartime was 3:00 A.M., but we didn't always go home. There would be these boys there, boys just waiting for the last call to bring out the big guns. I was twenty-two and nursing a bit of heartbreak—my best friend, after all, was marrying my college sweetheart—and the boys seemed so helpful to my healing process, with their ready cash, easy confidence, and total disinterest in commitment. The other girls were all just the same as me, happy to party, as lovely as they were ever going to be and with no place to be in the morning, if you didn't count long-held promises to ourselves to finally start working on the audition monologue, or first chapter, or gallery scene. We didn't.

This is all to say I was hungover that Friday when the mail came. It was signature requested. I signed the green slip in a fog and went back to bed. When I woke up again later, I opened the envelope with the same knife I'd used to butter a piece of toast—I can see the butter stains on the envelope now, brown with age—and peered inside, groaned, and went back to bed for a second time. I don't think I even ever took the paperwork out. My God. I am colossally stupid.

I pull it out now. The cover letter is on the stationary of the State of Nevada, Clark County. There is a little seal at the top and under that it reads:

RE: petition for annulment of Benjamin Hutchinson-Lily Stewart marriage

Supporting Evidence Needed

And then there is a simple request: that I provide a copy of my birth certificate, as well as the enclosed signature page attesting that I am in good mental health, not pregnant, and am not requiring further action or assistance from the county or the state on the manner of maintenance payments or fiscal settlements. And at the bottom it reads:

Failure to provide said documents in a timely manner constitutes dismissal of this matter and continuation of the marriage.

I set down my juice glass of wine heavily.

It would have taken fifteen minutes, maybe thirty, to track down these documents, notarize them, and mail them back. But I never did. I never replied at all. Never sent in these small, easy documents to finish the annulment. I saw the paperwork, thought, *Oh lord, not now,* and put the manila envelope into my "to do" drawer in the galley kitchen in my new little apartment, knowing I could handle it after the hangover passed, after I was a bridesmaid in my best friend's wedding the next day, after I spent thirty minutes holding her bouquet so her hands were free for my ex-boyfriend's ring. I would do it first thing Monday. Monday, June 7th.

Almost ten years ago.

Oh God.

I have been married for the last nine and a half years. To a man whose last name I only learned when I filled out the original annulment paperwork the day after we said "I do."

A man I haven't spoken to since.

Two

First, I close the drawer. Maybe I could just leave the contents behind. Move away and forget the whole thing for another ten years. Or a lifetime.

Then I open it again. Study this guy's name. Benjamin Hutchinson. Ben Hutchinson. Ben Hutchinson. Almost without thinking, I open the Facebook app on my phone and type his name into the search field.

There are thirty results. Bens and Benjamins and Benjis and Benazirs. Some have no photo. Most do. On my tiny screen they all look strange to me. I start sorting through the results, ruling out high school boys, college kids, a couple old guys who are indiscriminate with their privacy settings and throw around lots of emoticons. Five of the Bens are hyper-private: artsy nature photos for their cover, impossibly zoomed-in pictures of their hands or eyes or in one case, mustache, as profile pics. I think back to that night in Vegas. It was so long ago. Even if I had a lineup of police mug shots, would I be able to find this guy's face? He definitely had dusty blond hair. Or light brown. Dark brown? No. His eyes were . . . eye-shaped. He was definitely a man.

So that narrows the field. He was a man, and he had hair, which was lightish, so he's probably Caucasian, or part-Caucasian. Maybe I could sketch him? I stand up and find a sketch pad on the little table I use for extra counter space and, while I'm at it, I pour myself another glass of wine. A big glass. A fortifying amount. Then I draw the edges of a face, with a strong jaw, high cheekbones, long lashes, lightish hair. The rest is a blank for a while. Finally, I remember his nose. Broken at the bridge, and set just a millimeter to the left of where it must have started out. And his smile that leaned in the other direction. God, no wonder I married this guy. Even eyeless, the man in my picture is hot.

I go back to Facebook, this time on my laptop, where I can get better intel, and start looking harder, sleuthing around to every single Ben-something Hutchinson in America and beyond. There are three guys he definitely *could* be. One is married—he's married!—in Utah. He could be a bigamist, thanks to me!

At least it's Utah, I tell myself as I drain the last of my wine. According to HBO, they should be used to this sort of thing.

But more investigation proves that Utah Ben Hutchinson is not my guy. My Ben Hutchinson was older than me by a few years. This one graduated from high school ten years ago. He's thirty at best, even if he was held back. I'm thirty-two.

The next Ben Hutchinson contender has a real photo up, and he's blessedly unattached, at least according to Facebook. He looks blondish, and he's not ugly, though he's no match for my sketch. He lives in Durham. *I would not marry this man, would I?* I ask myself as I look at his incendiary political posts all over his friends' pages. When I see that his favorite movie is *The Fast and the Furious: Tokyo Drift,* I start aggressively looking for proof that it is not him. I know my Ben Hutchinson lived in California when we met. Has this guy ever lived in California? Not that there is any Facebook record of it. It's probably not him.

If it's him, I need to get this annulment fixed pronto. If it's not him, I scoldingly remind myself, I still need to get this annulment fixed pronto. I pour myself one more teeny tiny glass of wine.

The last Ben Hutchinson has to be him. This one is the most private of the bunch. There's only a picture of something red on his profile picture, and his cover is a panoramic picture of a blimp. I click on the profile pic and zoom out to try to achieve some kind of resolution. Okay. It's the Stanford Cardinal. It's a football helmet with the Stanford Cardinal symbol on it. I remember the guy from Vegas liked football. Blimps fly over football games. Stanford is in California. Is this my guy? This must be my guy!

Under "About," it shows that he is engaged. Shit. Lives in Berkeley. Is an attorney. Double shit. My guy was definitely not a lawyer, at least not openly, but he had ten years to go to law school since I saw him last. Wouldn't a lawyer have noticed if some girl he married on a whim in Vegas never finished her annulment paperwork? Maybe that's why he became a lawyer. To be able to personally find me and nail my ass to a wall.

No, that's the wine talking. One would not need law school to nail my ass to the wall. I am insanely easy to find. I'm on Facebook both as myself and with an artist's profile. I have a respectable number of likes on my artist page, most of them probably art bloggers who blab about everything. All the Vegas guy would need is my name and some recollection of our conversation about the inexplicable popularity of Dale Chihuly and he'd find me.

But he hasn't found me. Does he know? I look at the one Facebook photo of this Ben Hutchinson that he has let slip through his privacy filters. It's a row of guys, arm in arm, in front of a stadium. More football. He's hefting a beer joyously, in a can, and giving the camera a thumbs up. Even with my art-school expertise with Photoshop I cannot seem to get a good look at his face. All I see is blondish hair, a good jawline, and a thumbs-up.

So this is my husband, I think, a little sadly. He's engaged. A lawyer. In Berkeley. I need to find him quickly, and explain what happened, and beg for his forgiveness, and hope he'll be relieved that it all happened before he tried to get a marriage certificate. I can hope it's nothing more to him than a little blip on his radar, a funny story. Tomorrow, when I wake up, first thing in the morning, I will send him a PM and explain the whole situation and offer him free art for life if he just helps me finish this annulment and doesn't press charges for wrongful being-married-to-him-ness. I'll do it tomorrow early, when I'm perfectly sober and alert, before I have time to screw things up worse: 6:00 A.M. I set the alarm on my phone with the following memo: "wake up and smell your bad choices."

I send a text to Renee reading: *fucked up badly. Call me tomorrow?*

And another to my stepbrother: *any house guests this weekend? I could use a place to crash—strictly short term.*

And one more to Renee: *no need to worry.*

And one more to my brother: *and by short term I mean a couple months.*

And finally one more to Renee: *you can worry a little but, really, I'm fine. But also, a little bit married. xo. This is Lily btw.*

Then I haul myself to bed, phone on the kitchen floor, Attorney Ben Hutchinson of Berkeley, California, mostly forgotten, $15 red wine making up the majority of the contents of my veins.

That night I dream of Ben Hutchinson. The real one, not the Facebook version. The guy I met in Vegas. The one I married. I see him more clearly in my dream—even remember the shirt he was wearing—and see myself too. Short dark hair flipping up at the ends, thick mascara, all arms and legs and a revealing dress I bought at a teen mall store. The dream stays factual at first. I am in Las Vegas for Renee's bachelorette party. Renee looks like a giant Mr. Potato Head, but she is still Renee, thanks to dream logic. I'm her maid of honor and still feeling a bit on edge about helping my best friend plan her dream wedding to my ex-boyfriend. She wants a Vegas Girls' weekend, I plan a Vegas Girls' weekend. She wants a spa day, sushi dinner, and Neil Diamond tickets followed by swanky casinos, I deliver on those things. And really, all things considered, we have a very good time. But yes, it hurts to be in the front row of the audience for what was, I thought, going to be my show. My wedding. My bachelorette party. My husband.

It is at the blackjack table in the Venetian, both in the dream and in real life, that I meet Ben Hutchinson. He is wearing a Shins T-shirt under a well-cut suit jacket and winning hand after hand after hand. I watch him for a few rounds from across the table—I am not playing but just watching Renee lose a lot of her own money while enjoying the free drinks—and then I stage whisper to one of Renee's friends—I can't even remember who—something rude about him. Real me has stifled the memory of what I said that night—it's too mean to admit, even to myself—but dream me knows my exact words: "Hey, look at the dot-com douchebag killing it over there. I wonder if he's one of those computer geniuses who can count cards."

I say it really loud. Everyone hears. The dealer hears. I shit you not, it takes less than a minute for two floor security guys to come over and ask to buy Ben Hutchinson a drink. At the bar way over there. And they are not really asking.

I feel terrible. I look up at him and give him the biggest wordless *I'm sorry* a girl can give when she's had three shots of Cuervo and is on hour eighteen of orchestrating the best weekend of someone else's life.

In response, he smiles just a little, that crooked smile, shakes his head, and nods to his spot at the table, where rests a fortune in chips. "Keep my streak going," he calls to me and then is led away.

My stomach jumps into my neck. The pile of chips is enormous. This guy just left a few hundred—no, thousand—dollars in a pile to be watched over by a complete stranger who just called him a mean name and then got him accosted by casino security. And he wants me to gamble with it?

I think that's what he said. And so does the dealer. She has already dealt me my first card. I sit down anxiously and take a look.

The table is, thank God, just $20 bets. A fortune to me, chump change for this guy. I slowly, as slowly as humanly possible, start losing his money. Every time the bet comes to me I wait as long as I can possibly stand to make a decision, just to try to slow the hemorrhage. Everyone at the table looks annoyed at me. I keep asking stupid questions and trying to distract the person to my left into slowing down too. To this day I'm not entirely clear how the rules of blackjack work. But I just keep plugging away.

Then, about a hundred bucks down, with me sweating bullets about if he'll make me pay him back, and how will I ever come up with a hundred bucks after spending everything I had to throw this party in the first place, I hit blackjack. I don't even notice until the dealer tells me. The whole table cheers for me and the dealer pushes over a huge stack of chips with her fancy chip shover. And Renee glares at me. And then I feel a tap on my shoulder and it's a waitress with a drink for me "from the guy over there." The guy over there is Ben Hutchinson, and he is sitting on a bar stool with his two new best friends in the world who are now slapping him on the back and laughing uproariously at his jokes. When he finally does look over at me, he mouths, "Lucky girl!"

And I do feel very, very lucky. Ben Hutchinson, I learn soon, is indeed a dot-commer, though he doesn't seem as douchey as I thought at first glance. He first tells me he's a programmer, but in time I peel it out of him that he *was* a programmer, and now he's a developer—and then a drink later it turns out he *runs* a development company, and I start to get it that the boy is pretty successful and maybe a little smart too. He cashes out his chips—more fun to make it than to lose it, he tells me as though he knows from some experience, and starts calling the fistful of bills they give him "our winnings" and says ridiculous things with a twinkle in his eye that I find irresistible. Things like "What should we spend our winnings on? Shoes? Jewelry? A nice suite upstairs?"

Believe me when I tell you the boy has game. I tell him laughingly that I'm not that kind of girl, and he sobers his expression a bit, looks me right in the eye, and slowly, softly, cups my face in one large warm hand. "The best ones never are," he says. I swear I hear the sound of my panties hitting the floor.

I am just getting to the part where a Vegas wedding comes up in our conversation when I wake with a start. There's some sort of commotion in my kitchen. It almost sounds like a pigeon got in. That happened a couple years ago—it flew in through the chimney and scarred me for life. Now whenever I hear a sound in my apartment, my first thought isn't rape or murder, it's rabies.

I grab the broom I keep under my bed for just such an occasion. I jump out of bed with a thud and stomp to the light switch and flick it on, then come around the corner brandishing the broom and shouting, probably for my own benefit, "Get out of here, Mr. Birdy! This is my house!"

And I hit Renee in the face with the soft part of the broom.

"Oh my God," she shouts. "Oh my God, Lily! You are a psychotic crazy person and I fucking hate being your friend!"

She looks tired and stressed. I know she doesn't mean it, mostly. "I thought you were a bird. Sorry! Are you okay?"

"You hit me with a broom."

"It was the soft part of the broom," I say.

Renee looks so mad I am afraid to say more. I can tell she is doing the kind of deep breathing they teach you in birthing class.

"What the fuck, Lily. What the fuck?"

"Well, you broke into my apartment," I say in my own defense. "I wasn't expecting you."

"You weren't expecting me? You sent me, like, three insane text messages in the middle of the night and then stopped answering your phone. What did you expect me to do, exactly?"

"I did?" That's right, I did. But why? "What about?"

Renee's eyes leave their sockets for a moment. "Fuck you, Lily. Fuck you. I'm leaving."

"Wait, no! Hang on. Did I tell you to come over? I honestly can't remember. There was some wine and a bit of crying . . ."

"You didn't have to tell me to come over. You told me you had an emergency and you were married. I thought you had been sold into white slavery."

"So you rushed over in the middle of the night?" I am so touched. Maybe I was wrong about our friendship wilting.

"Christ, you basketcase. It's not the middle of the night." She turns open the mini-blinds, and sure enough, it's not dark out there. "It's eight A.M. I'm on the way to work. I worried about you last night and decided I better come check, is all."

"Oh, Renee. I love you. That is so sweet." I rush to wrap my arms around her.

She responds with more deep maternal breathing, but eventually hugs back.

"I'm so glad to see you," I tell her, now that I've fully woken up. "It really did feel like an emergency last night—I was packing up when I found out I'm accidentally still married to that guy I hooked up with at your bachelorette party, remember him? And he's engaged now so I've got to go make this right, and I wasn't thinking straight and imagining all these terrible repercussions but truly it should be okay—probably just a phone call and some kind of processing fee. And then I passed out and forgot all about it."

Well, not really all about it, now that I start remembering my dream. "And my phone was in the kitchen."

"I know," Renee says. "I called it on my way in here. I could hear it buzzing on the linoleum through the so-called door I jimmied open with my credit card. This place is such a dump, Lily. It's good you're moving."

"That's what I was saying to you yesterday!" I agree.

She shakes her head like I'm the crazy one. "I'm going to work now," she says. "If you need help getting unmarried, you know where to find me."

"No, wait! I need your legal beagle skills to help me find this guy."

"You don't know where *your husband* is?"

"No idea. Some rough guesses, but nothing for sure. I do know his first and last names, both."

"Well. No wonder you guys got married, with that kind of intimacy." She heaves a sigh that would be appropriate for, say, when your husband's just surprised you with a boat or your kid brings home a stray dog. "Get dressed. I don't have any clients until ten. I've always said a divorce lawyer's office is the best place to find a husband."

Besides the police databases, subscription search engines, and private investigators Renee has at her disposal as a litigious and well-compensated divorce lawyer, she also has another asset: she can Internet stalk way better than me. This, I suspect, comes from lots of practice. On her office computer, I show her the Facebook page for Ben Hutchinson, Attorney, and she clicks three times and gets to the spot where it says, "Engaged to Dani Ricthers." One more click and we see Dani Ricthers.

"Are you one hundred percent sure this is your guy?" she asks archly. Dani Ricthers is a gorgeous man in black eyeliner and frosted blond hair. If they lived in Tulsa instead of Berkeley, Dani would be Danny, but a man this fabulous has no place in Tulsa. There's a picture of him posing with his fiancé in his cover shot—probably an engagement photo. They are hand in hand, Ben Hutchinson's head resting on his future husband's shoulder, absolute adoration in both pairs of eyes. Dani is a blond god in very tight jeggings. Ben is six inches shorter and fat, and also, distinctly swarthy.

"Maybe not him," I concede. "But then where the hell is my Ben Hutchinson?"

"Maybe he doesn't use Facebook. What happened when you googled him?"

Googled him? Huh. Why didn't I google him? I stifle a laugh at myself, knowing Renee will not find my Internet quirkiness amusing.

"You didn't google him."

"Not even on our wedding night," I try.

Renee just raises an eyebrow, sighs, and shakes her head. "You didn't google him."

"Google's not so great. Back when we got married, they didn't even have Google."

"Yes they did."

"Whatever," I shrug. "Let's google him! Great idea! Scootch over."

Renee does not scootch anywhere. She elbows me off the keyboard and clicks over to the landing page where Google's logo is presently a celebration of Frida Kahlo's eyebrows.

.0046 seconds later we have found my husband. And he has a Wiki.

> ***Ben Hutchinson,*** *37, is the Silicon Valley millionnaire who graduated from MIT and then moved west to start his own app develop-*

ment company, Freep Inc., specializing in so-called freemium games such as Rural Route, GemBash, and Panda Roll. Called "The Genius Who Wasted Our Time" by The New York Times, *Hutchinson and his games have been met with a combination of devotion and loathing from players. After selling Freep Inc. five years ago, he retired to spend more time with his family.*

"Retired?" says Renee. "It says here he's thirty-seven. Who the fuck retires at thirty-seven, I want to know?"

"My husband, apparently. Holy shit, Ren. I knew at the time he was a programmer from California. He didn't say anything about having a million dollars. But then, it didn't really come up either."

"Are you sure this is him? A guy like this would notice if he had a wife on the books, don't you think?"

"I'm not sure. Can we find any photos?"

There are no photos on Google Images, just stills from the games he created.

"Where does he live now?"

Both of us read the Wikipedia entry again. It doesn't say. We click around Google a bunch. Nothing else. No website, no social media, no nothing.

"God, he's mysterious."

"Probably explains why he's not on Facebook, though. Those games are the worst. Can you even think of the hate mail he must get?"

"Playing them is totally optional," I say, though I have never downloaded any such game out of fear. I generally think of my phone as the enemy. Playing games with the enemy would just be silly.

"Sort of. I mean, once you get hooked on GemBash, it's like, thirty hours of your life down the toilet while you wait to get more free Sparkle Points."

"I guess you could pay for them," I suggest unhelpfully.

"I've thought about it, believe me. And plenty of people do, apparently, if he has all this moola."

"Had," I say. "Easy come, easy go. We spent a lot of cash that night in Vegas, and if that's his style then he's probably broke by now, same as me. Anyway, money didn't seem to mean much to him."

"Money means a lot to anyone with a lot of it," she says. "So if you're hoping for a piece of whatever's left, then I think you've got a fight on your hands."

"Renee! Don't be ridiculous. I just want to find him and get unmarried. No muss, no fuss." But even as I am saying that, I am thinking, *Wow.* Not so much that I want this guy's money, but that I want to make out with this guy a little. He was so, so hot in my dream last night. I remember how he made me feel in Vegas so long ago. Beautiful. Special. I was trying to have fun at that bachelorette party, but underneath it all I was miserable. I still loved Nic, or at least a part of me did. I was so angry at Renee for dating him in the first place, much less marrying him, much less making me be her maid of honor. And I was mad at Nic for proposing to her when he had told me only a year earlier that he wasn't the marrying kind. I felt betrayed, and terribly alone, passed over, and then there was Ben Hutchinson, stroking the side of my face and saying nice things about me. Was it all wishful thinking then? Was he as cool as I remember, or was he any port in a storm?

The problem is, it's ten years later, and my life is not so different, stormwise. If anything, it's worse. I'm ten years older, dating a man who doesn't always take my calls, about to be evicted, and the friend I sacrificed so much for back then treats me like I'm a troublesome teenager now, not her oldest and closest confidant. It wouldn't be the worst thing in the world to have someone stunningly gorgeous and stupid-rich caress the side of my face before sweeping me off my feet for a night.

A knock at Renee's office door wakes me from my daydream. It's her paralegal. Renee stands up and gestures to her Aeron chair. "I've got to go bill some hours. Stay here and track this guy's address down. When you find him, I can send him something formal on our letterhead telling him you need to renew the annulment filing. Easy as pie."

I nod. "That sounds perfect. Thank you. You are really saving my ass here."

"As usual," she says. She sounds incredibly bored with me. "I'll be back in an hour. Try to find him by then, because my afternoon is booked solid. Oh, and if you have extra time, would you grab me my latte from downstairs? My assistant is out today, and I'm dragging already. The girls don't sleep anymore unless they're in bed with me—us. I have to be refueled every couple of hours or I fall asleep standing up."

"Of course. Thanks, hon. And sorry I'm so psychotic."

"You're not psychotic," she says on a beleaguered sigh. "You're just messy. Your apartment, your hair, your life. Just messy."

At first I am obedient. I google and google and click and click, looking for some hint as to where Ben Hutchinson might have gone after "retiring" in his early thirties. There's nothing. Then I start looking for the family mentioned in the Wikipedia entry. The family for which he retired. Might he be (illegally) married? But then there'd have to be a wedding announcement online somewhere. Weddings are a big deal. I don't care how private a guy might be, someone in his life—his bride, his mother, even more likely his mother-in-law—is going to take out a wedding announcement.

There's nothing of the kind, and it's a relief to be reassured that I'm not responsible for any bigamy-type issues. I look more closely at his bio. It says he went to MIT, so I search for his name plus "MIT" and find an archived piece about him in the student paper. Bingo. It has his hometown in the copy. Minnow Bay, Wisconsin. Never heard of it. Maybe I could find a family member in Minnow Bay and track him down that way.

A few more clicks and I learn there are roughly four million Hutchinsons in Minnow Bay. They all have superbutch Wisconsin Man names like Justin and Thad and Gus. No Bens whatsoever. I am getting the idea that my Ben is some kind of Internet privacy freak. No Facebook, no Twitter, no Instagram, no personal details on his Wikipedia page, no way to find him . . . online, at least. Who doesn't have at least a Facebook page? Animals, babies, and the dead.

Could he be dead?

I really don't want my newfound once-rich and possibly still-hot husband to be dead. I keep looking, focusing my lens on this quaint-sounding North Woods town where Ben grew up. It has a cute little Chamber of Commerce website with pretty lake pictures and a map that shows it is about five hours' drive from Chicago, three from the Twin Cities, four from Milwaukee, and—as though it counts as a real city—two from Green Bay.

There's a guy named Hutch Hutchinson who pops up on the chamber site a couple of times; I find a bar he owns at 44 River Street in Minnow Bay that the "About" page says he bought for $500 cash and a taxidermied Northern Pike in 1962.

I love it.

"Hutch" has an entry on whitepages.com too. According to that, he lives at 44½ River Street, which I'm guessing means an apartment above the bar. It's 9:30 A.M. by now so I pick up the phone and call the number.

"Yello," says someone who is just old and creaky enough to have bought a bar in 1962.

"Hey, Hutch," I say, putting some familiarity in my voice. "Is Ben there?"

"Shit, no, why would he be? Is this Kristine?"

"Ah, no, this is Lily," I say vaguely. *Who is Kristine?* "I thought . . . he might be downstairs."

"At 9:30 in the morning? You must be thinking of his brother."

I laugh, as though I know what that means. As though I know he had a brother, or what his brother would be doing in the bar at this hour. But I do know that there's a Ben Hutchinson in this town, now, thanks to good old friendly Hutch. My pal, Hutch.

"Isn't he at the high school?" says my new friend. "I thought they went back today."

"Oh," I say. "Of course. I thought they didn't start up until next week. Thanks!" I hang up before he asks me anything else. Dammit, this isn't good. Is *this* Ben Hutchinson actually a high school student?

I pick up the phone again, call Minnow Bay High, home of the

Stormin' Sturgeons. I guess minnows aren't scary enough? "MBH," says the admin who answers.

"Is Ben Hutchinson in today?" I ask. I'm not sure what a school is allowed to say about a student, but it's worth a try.

"Yep," says the admin. "But he's got the kids in the lab right now. I think it's AP Comp Sci. I can get him if it's an emergency."

"He teaches computer science?" I blurt. Well, I guess I was right about the money being gone. I wonder why he's not still in California, making more crappy time-wasting games, instead of toiling away on a teacher's salary in the back of beyond.

"Who's calling, please?" the admin finally thinks to ask.

"Oh, I'm sorry, this is an old friend of his." Sort of true? "I just haven't spoken to Ben for a while and lost his cell number." More true, if by lost I mean left it on a nightstand in the Venetian ten years ago.

"Ah. Okay. Well . . . I can take a message? I'm pretty sure he doesn't want me giving his number out. You know how he is."

I think of Renee's marching orders to get an address. "Actually I was just looking for his home address. I'm running a little late on Christmas cards this year"—totally true—". . . and I was kind of hoping to get to the post office this morning and realized I didn't have his address filled out yet . . ." And . . . that's a full-on lie.

"Um . . . would it be okay if he called you back?"

"That's so sweet," I start slowly. "But I'm sure you've got lots to do. I'll just send him an e-mail. Thanks!" Another quick hangup. The poor people of Minnow Bay. When I find Ben Hutchinson, I'm going to tell him what nice people he has in his life and apologize for being rude to half of them.

Wait, no. I'm not going to tell Ben Hutchinson anything. My attorney-slash-best-friend, Renee, is going to send him a carefully worded letter, in care of the high school if need be. He'll be pissed that I screwed up, but then it will be fixed quickly enough and we'll both move on. I'm never going to see him again. Which is no big deal because I haven't given him a moment's thought for almost a decade. I click back over to the high school home page and start writing the school mailing address on one of the four million yellow legal pads that coat Renee's desk: 95 Lake Street. According to the map on their website, Lake Street intersects River Street a few blocks down. I can just imagine Hutch's little bar with it's snappy website, and Ben, walking over after work to see his dad—or grandfather, maybe?—to help him get it online. Ben probably lives in another little house on River a few more blocks down the way. Maybe one of those small-town old Victorians, big and rambling and storied? Maybe he has a staff party there every Christmas, makes mulled wine and everyone brings chips and salsa and they let off steam and talk smack about the principal and a few people always dance and at least one spur-of-the-moment coupling sneaks out five minutes apart pretending they left alone.

Maybe he has a spare room where I can crash until April.

"You are like no woman I've ever met before," Ben told me back in Vegas all those years ago.

"Should I take that as a compliment?" We were sitting in two red velvet seats, side by side, in an empty Cirque du Soleil theater in the Venetian sharing a bottle of Champagne. It was, Ben had told me, the only place it gets dark in all of Las Vegas.

"You should," he said. "You seem to be impervious to money and success. As far as I can tell my winnings tonight only made you nervous."

"Hah!" I said. "God, thanks a lot for noticing."

He shook his head. "A lot of people are not impervious. Ever since I moved to California, I've wondered if anyone really is."

"Is Silicon Valley really as bad as all that?" I asked him.

"Maybe it is, or maybe it's me. I have bad taste in women."

"Exhibit A," I said, gesturing to myself. "You should watch out for the self-depreciating ones."

He frowned at me. "In the past I've mistaken *pretending* not to care about money for actually not caring. And yet I do feel pretty sure that you are not pretending."

"You can be sure of that. I just graduated from art school. That's basically like taking a vow of poverty." A vow that, so far, I was taking very seriously.

"Are you a good artist?"

I thought about that question for a moment in the cool dark theater. "Yes. I think so. But I have a commercial failing."

"What's that?"

"I paint the same thing again and again. I think it might get me into some trouble, from a sales perspective."

"What do you paint?"

"Sides of buildings."

"You're a muralist?"

I laughed. "No, I paint pictures of the sides of buildings, onto canvas, or sometimes rice paper. I like the way sides of buildings look."

Ben just looked at me hard for a second. "Oh yeah. You are going to be poor for the rest of your life."

I laughed. "See? I'm pretty okay with it, though. I have amazing friends, even if they are being kind of inconsiderate right now. Decent family. Good teeth. The sort of stuff money can't buy."

We were quiet for just a moment. Neither of us was drinking anymore. The Champagne was there more for permission than inebriation.

"Here, this is why we had to come in here."

He pulled out his Blackberry—it was ten years ago, and tech guys had Blackberries—and added a little square attachment that plugged into the headphone jack. Then he fiddled with the device a bit, and points of light appeared all over the ceiling. First, I thought, *Disco?* Then I realized: Stars.

"Wow."

"You're from Chicago, right?"

"Right."

"This is what the night sky would look like from Chicago tonight, if you could see stars there, which you can't."

"That's really cool."

"I made it."

"Really? What's it called? I want to buy it."

"You can't. Not yet. I only finished coding it yesterday."

"It will sell like hotcakes," I tell him.

He shook his head a little sadly. "No, it won't. People use their Blackberries for work. They don't like to be distracted. They want to pay for hardware that makes them money, not makes them happy."

I nodded knowingly. "I don't think they like to pay for art, either."

"And yet you still make art."

"And you still make stars."

"Mostly I make operating systems that will be obsolete by the time I go to bed at night. It's a little soul-killing."

"As long as you take a few moments for stars now and then, your soul will stay alive."

Quiet fell over us. Ben changed the star setting to California, then Vegas, and the shift was almost imperceptible. He turned something on that makes lines appear in the constellations, then fidgeted again and large moving points of light appeared—the planets. We just looked up for a while. Both of us were draped over our seats, legs kicked against the row in front of us, heads gaping back. I remember now how I imagined I could feel the bubbles of the Champagne rising up from within me to my head and pop, pop, popping pleasantly in my brain. Maybe I was a little drunker than I realized.

"Grasping." He said after a long period of quiet.

"What?"

"You're not. Grasping. That's what it is about you."

"Oh. Thank you. I guess I never thought about it."

"And you're beautiful."

I have never been able to hear those words. "Not really—" I started, almost reflexively, maybe because I wanted him to elaborate.

"Oh yes," he obliged. "Beautiful eyes. Beautiful hair. Beautiful lips. Beautiful, ah . . . stuff below your neck." His eyes darted around my body then. And when I inhaled deeply, he stared a bit. My mouth went dry. My chest pressed upon my lungs. I knew that feeling. The feeling

I would get just before I pounced. I've been known to pounce from time to time.

But this time I waited. He did nothing. We were frozen. I couldn't take it.

"I can't decide if you're actually a bit shy under that ridiculous suit, or if this is all part of your amazing game," I told him.

"You should take off my suit and find out."

I nodded. "That answers that."

"Sorry to disappoint," Ben said, not even slightly sorry. "But I'm not shy." He turned his shoulders toward mine and looked at me hard. I remember how I could feel his eyes on my eyes, then on my mouth, then on my eyes again. "I'm a gentleman, but I'm not shy." He was a gentleman, or had been thus far. Suddenly, the way he was looking at me was not at all well-mannered.

"I'm not always a lady," I told him, and I reached out and pulled him by the lapels, so close I was almost talking into his mouth.

"Show me," he said, and like it was nothing, he was hoisting me over the armrest and onto his lap.

God help me, I did.

I shake myself out of the memory and back into Renee's office. Whew. Ben Hutchinson. How did I ever forget *you*?

I think of the men since him. It's been ten years. There have been a lot of men. A couple of serious relationships, but mostly not. I don't like change. Things derail fast when guys ask me to make any change—to move in with them, to meet their families, to travel. And then there's Mitchell. Mitchell has never asked me to do any of those things. Sometimes I wonder if he ever will.

Renee wanted coffee. She wanted coffee in exchange for writing to Ben Hutchinson so I wouldn't have to face him directly. I grab up my handbag and log out of everything I'd logged into on her computer. She'll be back here in ten minutes, and I will be too. I'll just go grab us both coffees, and then we'll draft that letter, and send it to Minnow Bay High School, and I will go home to finish packing and moving my stuff into my brother's house in the far west suburbs and never give Ben Hutchinson another thought. Never see him again or know what he became or feel that insanely powerful desirability I saw in his eyes again. After all, I haven't even thought of it in ten years and certainly haven't missed it in my relationship with Mitchell.

Unbidden, Renee's words start buzzing around me. *Mitchell is the best thing to ever happen to you.*

It's time for you to leave Chicago.

I fucking hate being your friend.

Everything about you is so messy.

I shake my head to stop the onslaught. She was overreacting. She's just sleep deprived. Really, this whole marriage nonsense is no big deal. Just a blip in the landscape of my life. Finding a new place to live on a shoestring—that's my real priority. Not this little paperwork snafu from a decade ago.

I close Renee's door behind me. Onward, not backward. That should be my new mantra.

But I am not quite ready to move onward. I rush back to Renee's desk, grab the address, and print out driving directions to Minnow Bay, Wisconsin.

Three

Minnow Bay, Wisconsin, in January is cold as hell. Wisconsin always is. The last time I was up here in the winter, it was because Mitchell was dragging me to Door County to taste wines. All due respect to Door County, but when I want to taste wines, I go to the wine shop across the street from my apartment where they sell wines from such exotic places as Napa and Bordeaux and the Willamette Valley. I do not go to a place where they have goats on the roof and paint their homes green and gold and boil whitefish in a pot with corn and call it dinner.

Still, Mitchell and I had a lovely time up on that trip, whenever we were indoors. Outdoors was beautiful and icy and a wasteland. I took pictures of it and painted from them when I got home, but beyond that, my recollection of winter in Wisconsin was of a hat, hood, and scarf, all wrapped and cinched up so I was viewing the world through a tiny, down-lined tunnel. A very cold tunnel.

Minnow Bay in January is colder still. There is a harsh blowing wind, probably coming off some lake somewhere. These North Woods people and their lakes. And there is snow up to my knees everywhere. The roads themselves are that brownish gray sludge of snows thawed and refrozen, but the rest of the world is white, white, white. White coating the trees. White on the roofs. White in the corners of every window, door, alcove, or nook. Icy, pure, colorless white.

My car is parked in a diagonal spot in a row of diagonal spots that line both sides of this street. The car is jam-packed, completely solid, with my belongings. Just the sight of them makes me long painfully for my old apartment. My furniture was picked up by Goodwill this morning—even they didn't seem too excited by some of it—and all but a few of my books went to the Friends of the Chicago Public Library. What is left is art supplies, canvases, and clothes. Apparently I wear a lot of leggings. I have half a suitcase of just leggings and yoga pants.

And, because I am a human, I kept a few sentimental things I've accumulated over the years. Photos and precious things, the necklace Mitchell bought me to celebrate my first show, and my mom's ring. Those things, and the art stuff, and the canvasses, and the clothes, and me; that is all in the world that fits into my beat-up, twelve-year-old hatchback. And that's fine. Bringing more than that to my brother's house would surely be an imposition. I don't want to impose. I don't even want to go. But if I must, I want to stay as invisible as possible while I'm there.

I turn my head back to my car now. It is quickly being covered in white itself. It is snowing big fluffy flakes right now, and it is positively beautiful, and probably snows like this every single day, if the crowds are any indication. No one here has stayed home by the fire to watch the flakes today. The streets and sidewalks are bustling with people. People going into the markets and the shops, and driving who knows where. People in bomber hats and brightly colored parkas and Sorel boots that lace up to their knees. People who are not afraid of a little cold.

I am afraid. I dart to a three-story brick building with an elaborate facade. Pull open the world's heaviest door. Feel a burst of warmth and brightness and hear, oh thank you lord, hear a fire.

"Welcome to the Minnow Bay Inn. You must be Lily."

My heart melts on contact. Oh, Minnow Bay. You sweet, sweet little place where the only lodging in town has just one reservation.

"Hi," I say to a beaming, soft blond woman about my age, with a round baby face and big blue eyes. "It's cold," I add, gesturing to the spot where the door is sealing itself shut against the storm.

"Really? It was warm when I ran out this morning. Must have taken a turn."

I purse my lips. It didn't take a turn, I'm quite sure of it. I am just a weenie, and she's too polite to say so.

"This is beautiful," I say, gesturing to her lobby. It really is. I don't normally go in for chintz, so most bed and breakfasts make my eyes bleed a little, but this is the idea done right. Intensely feminine, but not cluttered or dusty or bland. Baby blue cabbage rose wallpaper over a chair rail, white bead board below, faded woven carpets. Cream velvet couches grouped around the white brick fireplace. A hearth crowded with handwritten notes and postcards and snapshots in mismatched frames. A round bowl on the table full of fresh white roses that must have come rather dear at this time of year. Round gilt frames around really pleasing portraits of who knows whom, and a truly amazing crystal chandelier hung low and glowing dimly even at 3:00 P.M.

"Oh," says the innkeeper. "I'm so glad you like it. Your room is in much the same style, only whiter still."

"Whiter? Don't let me have a bottle of red wine in there."

The innkeeper laughs. "Don't fret. Stainmaster is my best friend." She pulls out a leather notebook and presses it open to a page marked by a ribbon. Even the sound of her hand sliding over the vellum pages is soothing. "Shall we check you in?"

The innkeeper's name is Colleen, and she's a lifelong resident of Minnow Bay and sole proprietor of the Minnow Bay Inn. She lives in the attic and is available at a moment's notice, should I need her, she adds. I give her my last good credit card. She gives me a tour. There's a little round dining room with another stunning chandelier and more lovely portraiture. The table seats six, and there are three guest rooms up the grand tapered staircase. "Just the right size for good service and lively conversation," Colleen tells me. My room, just up the stairs, is white, ecru, and rich mahogany in color scheme, with enough soft pink—a pinstriped bolster, a border on the rug—to make me feel like the prettiest princess at the ball. On the landing above the stairs there is a little pod-style coffee maker and a fridge stocked with white wine, Perrier, and Izze sodas. Heaven. I wish I could live here. I tell the innkeeper so.

She laughs, a round laugh with a flattered little peal at the finish. "You can, sweetie, at least for tonight. Make yourself utterly at home. What do you need to be comfortable?"

"You mean besides the whirlpool tub and the gas fireplace in my room?"

"Besides those. Do you have dinner reservations?"

I give her a wry look. "Do I need them?"

"Not in the slightest. But we like to pretend. Now, for dinner tonight. The bistro across the street really is amazing, not just for Minnow Bay, but for anywhere. The steak frites on the winter menu are the whole reason I have to wear yoga pants all January long." I give her a skeptical look. She is dressed like a Ralph Lauren model who tarried too long in Land's End. Perfectly fitted denim, a marled fisherman's sweater, rich brown leather boots. "And there's a good coffee shop, too, with a lovely bakery, and the brew pub across the street does a killer fish fry on Fridays and Wednesdays. I've got a town map downstairs, not that you'll need it, that tells you where everything is and what's open this time of year. The shops, the bookstore, the winery."

A winery. Delightful. "What else is there to do around here?" I ask her, feeling I may have some time to kill.

"Besides skiing, you mean?"

"Uh, yes. Besides skiing."

"Ice fishing, of course. That's the biggie."

I grit my teeth. "I'm not sure I'm the ice fishing type. I nearly lost a toe to hypothermia between here and the parking lot."

She smiles and shakes her head slightly. "You will get used to it, fast. Do you have any warm clothes? That is what will really make it easier on you."

I shrug. "I thought I *was* wearing warm clothes."

"Show me your gloves."

I pull out my leather gloves, lined in a thin layer of cashmere. A gift from my father at high school graduation.

"No," is all she says in response. "Go down the block to River Street Outfitters. Get good gloves, a serious hat, and some wool socks. That coat will do," she says about the shearling jacket she hung up for me back in the foyer. "And a gaiter."

"A gaiter?"

"Something to keep your neck warm."

"And then I'll be ready for ice fishing?"

"No. But then you'll be ready for walking back to the inn from the outfitters. It's a start."

"I'm utterly unprepared for Minnow Bay, Wisconsin, aren't I?"

She laughs. "Honey, the only way to prepare for Minnow Bay, Wisconsin, is to come to Minnow Bay, Wisconsin."

"Well, then. Here I am."

"And soon you'll never want to leave."

I keep my thoughts on that matter entirely to myself.

Here is what I have on when I lay eyes on Ben Hutchinson—my *husband*—for the first time in ten years: my dark brown shearling jacket buttoned up to my throat, a white down-filled bomber hat lined with gray-brown faux rabbit fur with the earflaps down, a Möbius scarf looped around and around and around my neck until it's a little puddle I can rest my chin in, and the most ridiculously soft, warm, comforting mittens the world has ever known. They are camel-colored wool, with thrumming—which means, apparently, that though the outsides of the mitts are itchy knitted yarn and the palms are soft undyed leather, the insides are a bed of fluffy unspun wool, leaving me with the feeling that I'm putting my hands directly into the winter coat of a lamb. The friendly guy at the outfitters showed me all kinds of techno fabrics and gloves that you can leave on while you use your phone, but when I spotted these mittens all was lost. "You'll be warm and dry," he told me, "but you can't do much."

I can manipulate the latch of the Minnow Bay coffee shop door, though, and I do, and as soon as I walk in I smell cocoa powder, melted butter, rising yeast, and oranges.

And, to my great surprise, I see Ben.

The coffee shop is crowded. It seems to be doing a steady business in chocolate croissants and plain coffee, the kind dispensed from airpots set in a row with little hand-inked signs stuck onto them with masking tape. "Highland Roast." "Crisp Winter Blend." "Downtime Decaf." Down the row are three flasks of milk, a honey bear, and some sugar dispensers. Then there are small round tables, with people in various states of bundlement, some peeling off layer after layer, some pulling them back on, some sitting still in their hand-knit scarves and watch caps, and a very few who are warm enough to be down to their indoor clothes. Ben is one of those people. He is wearing a flannel shirt, gray with a tartan plaid, rolled up to his elbows, and glasses—he definitely didn't wear glasses in Vegas—and sitting alone reading something on a tablet. He is eating a chocolate croissant. There is a flake of pastry by the corner of his mouth.

I stare for a while, my heartbeat slowing down, my mouth growing dry. There is no mistaking him for someone else, and there is no doubting he is the same man I married, and there is no denying that he is as handsome as I remembered. His face is ten years older. His jaw more defined, stubble darker, skin creased in three places by his eyes. His hair is the same golden brown but styled with much less attention. It is a bit longer now, and shaggier, and blonder on top, and his skin is a bit more weathered, and I wonder if he spends more time outside in the arctic chill of the North Woods than he did in mild Santa Clara County.

Maybe he feels me staring because he looks up, and I feel my lips part slowly, as though caught, and my heart starts to speed up again, like maybe this is *it*. But it is not it. He just gives me the world's most innocuous smile and looks back at his tablet. He has no idea who I am.

"Can I help you?" asks the teen girl behind the counter. I order a chocolate croissant—who am I to buck a trend?—and a latte. All I have to do, I tell myself, is get a cup of something and go ask him if I can sit down. Just introduce myself, and bring him up to speed. Hope he doesn't get angry. Hope he's glad to see me.

"How about coffee," the barista helpfully counters, gesturing to the airpots.

I tear my eyes away from Ben. "Thanks, but I'm feeling like something richer."

"Richer than a chocolate croissant?" she asks.

This strange turn in conversation finally causes me to look at the young server for real. She is tiny, pint-sized even, with bleached-white bangs and light purple braids going down both sides of her head, and is dressed in what can only be described as a juniors-section muumuu. It is floral, and horrible, and she has belted it with what looks to be an actual length of rope. Under it is a pair of mukluks covered in road sludge. She is giving me a very, very stern look. Daring me to push the issue. For some reason, I take that dare.

"Don't feel like making a latte?" I ask her. Five years at Starbucks tells me making a latte is really easy, unless the espresso machine is clean and you don't want to get it dirty before closing. Could it be clean at, what, 4:00 P.M. on a weekday?

"I don't feel like it," she says mildly. "Plus we don't have an espresso machine."

I crane my head. "Isn't this a coffee shop?"

She narrows her eyes. "I guess you're new here. Welcome to Minnow Bay." The words could not be less welcoming.

"So . . . Okay . . ." I say patiently, though this is the first time in my life I've been to a coffee shop with no espresso maker. "No espresso, no latte. I get it."

"Good for you. Do you want coffee?"

"Sure."

"Here's a to-go cup."

I look at the nearby tables. Everyone else seems to be drinking from ceramic mugs.

"Actually, I think I'll take it for here."

"Are you sure?" she asks, not skeptical; rather, disappointed.

I look over at Ben. He is not seeing any of this. Just as well.

"I'm sure."

"Fine." She reaches under a counter and produces a real mug. "He's not interested in you," she says, as she puts back the cardboard cup.

"What?"

"Mr. Hutchinson. He doesn't go for city girls."

I nod, just once, very slowly. I wonder what it is about this look that screams city girl, now that I'm wearing fifty dollars' worth of quilted down and polar fleece. "I see. Good to know." I take the mug, maybe a bit aggressively.

"Whatever," says the girl. "Don't believe me. I don't care. But you're wasting your time."

I start to open my mouth, to set this hideously dressed and probably lovelorn teen straight, explain that her "Mr. Hutchinson" and I go way, way back, and once upon a time at least, he *did* go for *this* city girl. And how.

But before I can, my phone rings. I think it will be Renee, reading me the riot act for vanishing, but it's Mitchell. Mitchell, my actual boyfriend. The brilliant, influential gallery owner I am seeing. Who has no idea where I am, or that I am probably not going to be back in town for his latest opening tomorrow night, or that I am, for argument's sake, married to someone else.

That Mitchell.

The phone still ringing, I look back to Ben. He is paging on his tablet, oblivious to me, and laughing at something he reads there. His laugh is inaudible, but it warms up his eyes. I could go over there and tell him what I did, screw up his day, and then go home tomorrow and move in with my brother, and still make Mitchell's opening with time to spare.

Or, I could enjoy the cuteness of this little northern town for another night. Check out that bistro. Catch up on my rest. I wonder if the B&B has cable. I *love* cable. I put my phone back in my pocket. "You know what?" I say at last to the girl across the counter, "I'll take that coffee to go, after all."

"Good call," she says, sounding unmoved. "Trust me, you never had a chance."

I nod. "You're probably right. Thanks for the heads-up."

The B&B does have cable, I discover, when I get back to my home away from, um, evicted home. There's a reason I can't have cable myself, besides the fact that I can never afford the bill. I cannot stop watching the most insane shows. There's one where preschool girls dress up in sequins and go into beauty pageants. It's an hour long. Snuggled into my princess bed with croissant crumbs dusted over my chest, I watch several episodes in happy horror.

Then, around eight, I go to the bistro and have the steak, which really is amazing. It's seared to almost the point of crunchiness on the outside, and meltingly red on the inside. The fries are thin, tender, salty, and the aioli that goes with them is bright but not pungent. Down over the top of the steak is a tangy arugula salad dressed with lemon, and each bite of spicy salad makes the next bite of steak taste as delicious as the first.

When I get back to the B&B I talk to Colleen for a while, show her my winter garb, and she brings out lemon butter cookies and chamomile tea. Her guileless demeanor and soft Irish features balance out her beautiful ballerina's posture and long limbs. She is an avid cross-country skier and, when I look at the way her faded sweater clings to her collarbones and outlines her shapely arms, I want to be one too. I can tell winter visitors are rare here, because she seems happy to entertain me as long as I will linger, and takes requests for breakfast. I request more lemon cookies.

I go to bed early, for me, and wake up late, and go to the big bay window with the set-in seat, and kneel on it facing the street and yet more falling snow, and let myself feel purified by Minnow Bay. Maybe Renee was right. Maybe Chicago isn't the right place for me anymore. I could move here, fall in love with my already-existing husband like in a romance novel, become the wife of a high school teacher, learn to ski.

Except I don't want to do any of those things. I want to go back to my apartment in the city. I want to go over to Mitchell's apartment and watch fantastic foreign films and drink good wine and be inspired by his other artist friends who are always dropping by and saying brilliant, sophisticated things. I want to wander through the shops in Lincoln Park with Renee, and linger at Red or Dead for an hour with Annie and Jo, and go to the gallery's beautifully catered events, and keep painting that view out my apartment window until I finally get it right. In other words, I want things the way they were a week ago.

Out the window, something catches my eye. It's a yellow Lab, bounding off-leash down the street. The color of his fur is beautiful against the snow. Like he is made of snow himself, part dog, part polar bear, carrying a bloodred leash in his mouth with no one holding the other end. I reach for my camera without taking my eyes off of him.

The windows are soundproof but I know the dog is called when I see him halt suddenly. His body turns toward the east and his rump immediately finds the ground. His head is high, and one ear is cocked. I snap a photo. Maybe this is what my recent series is missing. I've tried people and snow, together and separately, but never dogs and weather. Never anything quite that color of creamy custard.

The dog bounds up again. Runs in a circle, then drops down on his belly and rolls in the snow. When he comes right side up again, his fur is whiter, coated with snow, those hard sticky iceballs that will stay frozen in his coat until he is inside again. His tongue lolls out, and his tail wags maniacally. I snap more photos. Then he trots back the way he came, until his leash is picked up by his master and the spell is broken. As it should be, I remind myself. I'm not here to make art.

My plan today is to go hang around the high school, find out when Ben's prep time is, and talk to him then. It's a safe public place for both of us, but, assuming he has a classroom of some kind with a door, it still has elements of privacy that will allow him to keep this private business private. And privacy is key. I've seen *Northern Exposure*. It doesn't take meeting a teenager in a muumuu for me to understand the power of gossip in a tiny town like this one. Gossip is probably the official town sport. In fact, though I try not to be overly cynical, a loud voice in my head does suspect the cuteness of this town is a mirage. How could a little place like this stay afloat if it were made only of aw-shucks northerners doing good for others and shaking hands in church? It's probably all fueled by frack-sand money, or racist, or populated only by urban expats running away from the real world, chasing a fantasy that doesn't really exist. Not that I would know anything about that.

Still, Colleen, the innkeeper, seems like the real deal, friendly, mellow, genuine, and straightforward. In some ways she reminds me of Renee before Renee became a downtown divorce lawyer and got fed up with my antics. Colleen hasn't asked once what I'm doing here or why I came alone. My car jammed full of belongings has been parked in her lot for almost a day and she's asked me nothing about it. She seems comfortable taking me only on what I'm happy to share myself. Face value. It's nice.

Cupping a travel thermos of coffee from Colleen and dusting off lemon poppyseed muffin crumbs from a hurried breakfast, I walk out into the snow and wind and down the street to the high school and around in circles and up and down stairs and past oodles of curious students until I find the computer lab. And, like it is all meant to be, my husband is sitting in there completely alone, door closed, in sight of the window. The whiteboard on his door says, "Office Hours, Please Knock," and I knock.

Ben looks up. Today he is in another flannel shirt, a blue and yellow one. Over the flannel is a tie, and all of this is worn with faded denim jeans. He looks so North Woods it hurts. What became of that slick Silicon Valley millionnaire I met in Vegas? Through the inset window I see him mouth, "Come in" and give me a friendly, curious wave.

When I step into the room I feel it right away. An aura of calm, of stability, of infinite patience. It seems to be radiating out of his eyes. This. This is why I married him that night. This is why the teen coffee shop girl is in love with him. This, and his green-gold eyes and thick eyelashes and broad, broad flannel-clad shoulders. "Hi," I start. It comes out on a little sigh. Oh lord. I have more in common with Junior Miss Muumuu than I thought.

"Hi," he says. His eyes are searching mine, then my face. There's no attempt to mask the confusion. But it's confusion, not displeasure, not disdain, just confusion I see. "Ben Hutchinson," he says at last, rising from his chair and extending a hand to shake. "Have a seat."

"Thanks." I take his hand and give it a little jostle. "I hope I'm not interrupting?"

"Of course not. But . . . we've met, right? I . . . I'm embarrassed to tell you I've forgotten your name."

"It's Lily. Lily Stewart. But there's no way on earth you could have remembered me. I couldn't remember you, frankly, until I looked you up."

"Lily . . ." he mumbles. Then his eyes widen. "Las Vegas Lily?"

"The very same," I say, forcing a meek smile. To my alarm, I feel all the calm and patience wash out of the room. The man looks positively panicked.

"Oh. Whoa."

"So you remember me, then," I say, hoping to lighten the mood. But I am getting pretty panicked myself now. Why is he looking at me like that?

"Well," he says and there's an interminable pause, and he takes an enormous breath, and lets it out very slowly. "Yes. Of course. A bachelorette party. You were the maid of honor." He runs a hand over the stubble of his chin.

I nod. "That's right," and wait for the penny to drop.

"That was quite a wild night," he says, slowly shaking his head. "And it was a long time ago . . . And we . . ." Ah, here we go.

"Yeah. We did. Ten years ago, to be exact."

"Are you . . . ? Did you . . . ? Am I a father?" he squeaks out.

"What? Oh god, no. Oh my god. You . . . we . . . we were careful. Jeez." I can't help but laugh at his terror.

"Oh, thank God," he says on a monster exhale. His head tips back and he looks at the ceiling and I swear he actually mouths a prayer. "I know we were smart, but my brain just went there because, well, why else would you be here?"

"You really have no idea?" I ask.

"None. Nostalgia? Soul-searching? AA?"

"Guess again."

There's a pause and then he says apologetically, "I'm sorry, but can you just tell me? My next class starts in two minutes." He looks to his classroom clock, then to me, then to his phone. "I'm sorry to be so rude, but how did you even find me? No, wait, first tell me why you're here. Then explain how you tracked me down. No, wait." he looks at the wall clock again. "There's no time."

"I'll be quick," I tell him, because I don't think I can get the guts up to do this again. "First, I googled you. And secondly, we're married."

He opens his mouth to say something, but no words come out. Instead he stares at me blankly for so long I start to sweat. Profusely. Eventually, after what feels like five minutes of solid silence, I dig in my handbag and foist over the notice from Las Vegas County. He takes it, reads it, and looks up at me.

"Well," he says at last. "So we are. Wow."

"We're coming up on our ten-year anniversary," I say jokingly, though I can't imagine why I am joking right now. He grimaces and I do too. "I'm sorry. It's not funny. I screwed up badly a long time ago, and I'm here to fix it."

Another long silence. "I . . . am . . . a little . . . flummoxed," he says slowly. He is choosing his words so carefully, so kindly.

"Of course you're surprised. And your students—" I gesture to the door, where it looks like about thirty acne-marked faces are pressing up against the door.

"They're here. Okay. So, I've got to teach this class."

"Yes, I understand. I'll go. I just wanted to let you know that I'm on it, and I'll get it taken care of. I have a friend who's a lawyer—"

This seems to make him snap out of it. He shakes his head quickly. "No. No, that's—I mean, yes, but—" he takes a deep breath. "Listen, this is a private matter. Come to my house for dinner tonight." He quickly jots something on a scrap of paper. "Come over around eight. We'll figure it out between the two of us, right? No big deal. No lawyers."

I take it gratefully, feeling like it is more than I could possibly have hoped for given the circumstances. "That's so . . . yes, of course. Yes, I'll be there."

"Good. Perfect. Uh . . . looking forward to it." He seems to have largely regained his composure. "Let the hordes in on your way out, would you? They'll be dying to grill me the second you leave."

"Of course. Good luck. I'll see you . . . tonight?"

"Tonight. Turn left at the giant carving of the bear."

Four

When Ben told me to turn at the giant carving of the bear, I probably should have understood that when directions like that are necessary, you will be in the deepest, darkest woods imaginable. At 8:00 P.M. in mid-January in the frozen north, the sky is darker than dark, full of stars, just five minutes outside town. There is only a waning moon for light. If there are street lights, they aren't on. My car's headlights are the only illumination in any direction, and they light up only a small cylinder of snow falling on pavement. I can still see the yellow lines on the edges of the road, and I stay just to the left of them, and drive as slowly as I can safely drive until I find the bear. It is indeed giant, and lit up by a spotlight.

In Minnow Bay proper, I'd seen a store dedicated to selling just these types of log carvings, made, I have to imagine, with chainsaws. Eagles, fish, bears, the occasional Super Bowl trophy. But nothing on the scale of this. I imagine the lumberjack who'd endeavored to make this fearsome, violent statue. The bear is more than life-size, ten feet tall probably, with his forearms up high and claws bared but his elbows tucked in close to his body, as the medium of log carving requires. His mouth is open in a silent roar.

I start to wonder if Ben Hutchinson has lured me here to kill me. I imagine my mangled corpse dangling from the bear's mouth, and a sign below painted in blood: "This is what happens when you don't do your annulment paperwork!"

With this likelihood in mind, I pull over—or I think I do: there aren't even yellow lines painted on this new road, and the newfallen snow makes the shoulders indistinguishable from the ditch—and text Renee the address Ben gave me. She writes back, "???" and I reply, "Where to send the police if I mysteriously vanish after tonight." And quickly she texts back, "Good to know!" And then about sixty seconds later, "Srsly, txt when safe, k?"

"OK," I punch back and then put the car into drive. In three minutes I'm on a winding road that services a lake and the homes set deep in between the woods and the lake.

These are not fishing cabins. Each estate is grander than the one before. No wonder he's broke now, I think, taking in one million-dollar estate after another. I hope he has a good mortgage rate. Or maybe he paid cash. Either way, it's the sort of neighborhood that doesn't come cheaply.

The houses I'm passing are largely dark. It's a seasonal community, I suppose. Wealthy Chicagoans who come up for summer weekends, and snowbirds currently scooting about Arizona until the thaw. Though desolate, what I can see is appealing. None of the vaulted front alcoves and gabled four-car garages that speak of a housing development popping up overnight like in the area where I grew up. This lake, its homes, they're mixed in age and they're all different, starkly different. Each, I imagine, was built *for* a family, a particular set of people, who fell in love with this particular body of water. And because the trees are leafless right now, and the thick forest is nothing more than a black bar code stamped over my view, I can see the large, open, bean-shaped hole in the growth past the houses that must be the lake. I see the skinny moonlight bouncing off the white white white of the snow that stretches in every direction, that lays itself down silently on the thick ice day after day.

I take a gentle curve slowly, circling the lake counterclockwise. The snow is growing more treacherous, or I am growing more intimidated. I am only going twenty-five miles an hour, though the last speed limit I saw posted was forty-five, but it is so hard to see anything here even that feels too fast. Soon, I fear, I will have made it all the way around the lake and be back at the bear. But, to my great relief, around the bend I can just make out three houses in a row, and they are all lit up. One, a rambling brick ranch, has twinkling, icicle-style Christmas lights still blinking a week into January. I can't imagine going to all the trouble of hanging lights for the two or three cars that might pass by on any given night. Immediately, I like the people who live there. There is a dimly lit wooden sign, nailed to a tree right by the mouth of the driveway, that reads "Grandpa's Hide-A-Way." And a snow-covered Santa hat festoons the curve of the G. I make a mental note to run to Grandpa's if Ben comes after me with a knife.

The next house is a rustic-looking A-frame, a true lodge rather than a house, with big logs stacked upon each other forming the siding. It's rich-looking and speaks to me of woodstoves and heavy woolen blankets and the scent of leather. I imagine a graying anesthesiologist, his slick, slender wife, and four blond children, each in various stages of affluent ennui, sitting around a big-screen TV with iPhones at the ready. This is the sort of place I can picture for Ben Hutchinson, but their wooden sign reads only "Van Holden" in dignified script.

The last in this row of winter neighbors must be the house I'm looking for. It is imposing, dark, and hyper-masculine. Ugly, even. The side facing the road is peeling brown wood slats and garages, no windows, and it seems to be only one story, maybe one and a half. The road has risen a bit, so this house must be set into the hill, with some kind of spectacular lake face that only the people who really matter get to see. I suppose it makes sense, but still, pulling up to this home after seeing one beautiful well-loved property after another is a bit disorienting. There is no cute wooden sign, no landscape lighting, just a low red-fire number that catches my headlights at the last second. This is it. I turn in to the long, barely plowed and certainly unpaved driveway, and pray for traction.

I get up the driveway by staying in well-worn tracks, and park in front of the garage, but I do not get out. It's hard, from my car, to tell even where the front door is. To the left I finally discover an awning and a small shoveled pathway in the snow. I pull my bomber hat down low around my ears against the windy chill, and tromp through new fallen snow to a nondescript door, and think, *Does someone actually live here?* The closer I stand to the house the scarier it seems. The wood siding is rotting in a couple of places, patched up with aluminum in others. There are icicles everywhere, including in the doorframe. There is plywood nailed over the window of the door.

Should I knock? Or should I turn around and go home?

I knock.

"Sorry for the mess," Ben Hutchinson says even as he opens the door and gestures inside. I step in right away—I'm so cold, I forget my manners—and take everything in. Ben, tall, blondish, striking in his now-untucked flannel and worn denim. As hyper-masculine as the house. But with a much nicer facade. And then the house. Egad, the house.

This is no million-dollar house with a beautiful lake face to offset the modest approach. The land might be worth something, but the house itself is a dump. As ugly as it looked from the outside, it is worse inside. Half of what I see is just walls stripped to the studs and then draped in plastic sheeting. The other half is a Formica and wood-paneled 1970s nightmare. Behind Ben I can see through the framing all the way to a back bedroom, and I can tell it's a bedroom only because it has a mattress on the floor.

"Let me take your coat," he says. I hand it over a bit warily. Does this place have heat? Then I bend down to slip out of my boots, but Ben shakes his head. "You'll want to keep your shoes on." Never has a sartorial advisement seemed so ominous.

The livable bits of the house seem to be concentrated toward the lake side, and that's the direction Ben leads me. There the walls have drywall at least, but no paint, no molding, no nothing. Measurements or diagrams are written on every wall in thick contractor's pencil. I also see a shopping list written on a wall near a table, unless "bagels, milk, cream cheese" is a secret builder's code. Near a counter that might once have been a breakfast bar, there's a doodle of a maze. Stuck to an exposed stud I see some Christmas cards, pushed in with thumbtacks. So that's the décor.

And then there is the furniture. Well, furniture is sort of an overstatement. In the main room of the house there's a card table, an old one with a drooping middle, with three folding chairs around it. There's a vile-looking black leather sofa that I pray I won't be expected to sit on, and propped up on a wooden fruit crate, a large flatscreen TV and various blinking video devices.

And that's it. Mattress, couch, card table, TV. My riches-to-rags hypothesis about Ben is confirmed. I find myself feeling strangely relieved.

I do smell something rich and warm cooking in the kitchen, and hear lovely music playing, something acoustic and rhythmic and maybe Brazilian, but beyond those touches of home, I would describe this place as uninhabitable.

"Make yourself at home," he says warmly while I am taking all this in. I look down at the floor, wondering, *Should I sit?* I am standing on a piece of wet, filthy cardboard that seems to be serving as protection for subflooring.

"The secret is to not look too closely," he says before I can ask. "You're right in the middle of a construction zone."

"I see that," I say, and I hope it doesn't come out snappily. It shouldn't. I mean, since when do I care one whit how someone lives? I had cinderblock bookshelves in my apartment. And I wasn't doing construction, so I had no excuse. "You're in the middle of a remodel?" I ask, to try to soften my tone.

"You could say that. I guess that implies that I'm actually working on remodeling."

I smile with what I hope is compassion. "I assume it would be hard to work on much in the middle of winter."

"Harder still when I don't know what I'm doing. I bit off more than I could chew when I moved into this house. I saw all this potential and forgot that I would be the one tasked with bringing that potential to life."

"I get that," I say, thinking again of my fantasy life, where I get control of my finances, command respect from my friends, get some vague semblance of commitment from my boyfriend, and am left in peace to make my art without getting evicted.

"Anyway, I think by spring I'll have a better handle on what to do next."

"That's a long time to live without walls."

He smiles. "I live alone. What do I need with walls?"

As if intending to make a liar of him, a knee-high brown-and-white mutt wanders into the living room. The dog is fluffy and rotund, maybe part basset? Definitely part spaniel. He makes for that horrible leather sofa and hops up. I think again of the yellow Lab I saw this morning, purebred and dignified. The rugged log-hewn lodge I passed on the way here. Those are part of the North Woods life I could have imagined Ben Hutchinson would have. Not this.

"I see you're not entirely alone," I say with a smile. "Who's this?"

"Oh, this gentleman is Steve. Steve the dog. He doesn't need walls either. He needs little more than space to bound in and a wrecked leather sofa. And the occasional slice of roast beef."

"Nice to meet you, Steve," I say. Steve inclines his head. He's ridiculously cute for someone quite as wild looking as he is. He almost makes me want to approach the sofa.

"Here," says Ben, and goes into his jeans pocket and pulls out a hard little dog biscuit. "He'll love you forever."

I take the biscuit and slowly approach the pup, sidestepping a wrench, a stack of two-by-fours, a case of beer in cans. Ben trails behind me and I hope he is not seeing his house through my eyes. My heart goes out to this man I know so little about. In glitzy Las Vegas the stars were all out for him. Here in the North Woods, it seems his star has fallen.

When I get near the sofa, fluffy, gentle-looking Steve knows something is up. His tail starts to thump on the couch and then he can't lie down anymore and sort of pops up on all fours, like a trundle bed. I give him a little smooching sound, kiss kiss, and he flies down off the couch and to my heel. "Steve," I say, "sit," and he does. "Lie down," I add, with an open hand pressing toward the floor in that universal dog language, and he does that too. I lean over and give him the treat and a good petting and he gobbles it up and then looks up at me for instructions and I say, "Good dog," and he releases and goes back to the sofa, chomping all the way.

"Now, that's a gentleman," I say to Ben. He is watching me, his head inclined in much the same expression Steve the dog gave me a moment earlier. As if to say, "Hey, who's this, and what's she all about?" I wish I had some sort of milkbone for Ben too, to break this ice.

Ben straightens up. "I hope you're not making a contrast between me and my roommate?"

I blush. "Well, no. I guess I remember you being pretty polite too." I think of his hand on my face, so gentle. How he asked again and again, "May I kiss you here?" and waited to hear an answer as he moved from neck to collarbone to the crease between my breast and my ribs.

"Oh, good. I'll have to take your word for it, though. My recollection of that particular night is a little shaky."

"Ah, of course. That makes sense." Because I must have been one of many. Getting married on a whim was probably, hopefully, unique to me. But meeting and sleeping with strange women in Vegas may have just been Ben's average Saturday.

"I mean, I do remember you, and getting married. But . . . why?"

He is looking at me hard and I try to see myself from his point of view. I haven't changed much since then, added maybe five pounds and grown my hair a bit. Even then I didn't think I was his type. I'm not really anyone's type, small, compact, plain-featured. Still. He hit on me, back then.

Lightly, I say, "I was probably wearing a lot more makeup that night."

"That's not what I . . ." his voice trails off. I think that's exactly what he meant. There is a moment of long silence. Uncomfortable silence. Awkwardly, I lift my gaze to the corner of the room, where I see that there is a jigsawed hole in the ceiling with a coax cable dangling out of it.

Finally, I speak. "I guess the way I remember it, it was kind of a dare. We had just . . . you know. And we probably should have gone our separate ways. But it was really, really late, and you said something about an all-night breakfast place and I was so hungry, and then it was right next to that chapel, and we watched people come and go and it looked so fun . . . like a stunt, a lark, you know. You said it would be the perfect revenge on Renee—the friend getting married—to beat her down the aisle. And I was feeling a little vengeful."

"That's right," he says slowly. "It was my idea."

I nod. "I was going to say that, but I was trying to be tactful."

He sighs. He is not happy. I feel terrible. "I need to work on tact, clearly," he says. "I'm sorry. I'm just . . . I've been taken by surprise. It's not often that I revisit that part of my life."

I nod, thinking again of his Wikipedia entry, wondering how he went from self-made millionnaire playboy in the Valley to high school teacher and crappy cabin owner in the darkest tundra.

"I'm sorry to bring it all back up," I say.

He pauses a moment and then says, "There's something you should know, Lily. Things are different now. I'm not that same person you met back then."

"I understand." One only has to look at this house to understand.

"I don't do that stuff anymore. Things on a whim. Stupid things. I don't sleep with strangers or stay out all night drinking or blow a grand on a meal."

"Of course not," I say. "It was ten years ago."

"Ten years of marriage," he says. He isn't looking at me.

"I'm sorry, again. For screwing up the paperwork."

He gives sort of a bitter laugh. "Are you, really?"

Lost, I look at his face. It's set in this weird, hard way, a way that almost scares me. "Yes, I am sorry."

He says nothing. My mind goes blank. I am so uncomfortable. The room is cold. My host is cold. I want to be anywhere but here. I want to get this over with and go home to Chicago. I want to go back in time before I knew about this marriage, far enough that I pay my rent on time and never have to open that kitchen drawer.

"I brought a salad," I blurt, after the silence becomes more than I can stand.

"A salad?"

"To eat, with dinner?" He invited me over to dinner, didn't he? I call back the memory of Ben's classroom, the conversation we had there. He was so much warmer there. Like a different person.

Just then his phone rings. It's sitting on a sealed cardboard box next to the sofa that seems to be in service as a coffee table. It has a few water stains on it, from sweaty beer cans, I imagine.

"I have to take this."

Though Ben Hutchinson has no way of knowing this, since we met in a time before smartphones, nothing makes my skin crawl like choosing a phone call over an in-person human being. He falls several rungs in my estimation just by scooping up his cell and answering it while still facing me. Then he just walks away from me, muttering into the phone a little, but mostly listening.

My eyes follow him as he walks through the framing sideways, getting farther and farther away from me. Finally he winds into a real hallway and disappears into a room with an actual door. It must be a bathroom. He is gone for a long time.

While I wait, I do not sit, or take the grocery bag of salad fixings into the kitchen, or even set down my purse. I just stand there, impatient, and ignored, and getting a little angry. I find I don't really like this version of Ben Hutchinson that much. Didn't like him even before he took that phone call and vanished. He runs very hot and cold. Makes me feel quite unsteady on my feet. When I remember that night in Vegas, I remember someone warm, funny, and attentive. Someone who could have had anyone, but chose me.

But maybe that was not really how it was. Maybe my memories of Ben Hutchinson have been whitewashed by time. Maybe coming up here, abandoning my real life, real boyfriend, real friends, to track down a fantasy of the past, was a mistake.

The door opens.

Ben rejoins me in the room wordlessly. Sets the phone down on the cardboard box again. I look into his eyes. They are cold. I can't imagine I ever had sex with someone who could look so cold. But I did.

Time for me to apologize and get out.

"Listen, I am really sorry about this," I say quickly, and now there is more truth to those words. Now I *am* sorry to be here. "I was pretty disorganized when I got home from Vegas." That is a misleading statement, designed to make it sound like I have my shit together now, which I don't, but I don't particularly feel like laying my weakness bare before this guy anymore. "And I misplaced that notice, stuffed it in a drawer, probably in a frenzy to tidy up before someone came to my apartment."

Ben looks unimpressed. "And then ten years went by . . ."

"Well, yes. It was a junk drawer. Full of random things I never look at. I never would have looked at this, either, but then I got—I *decided* to move"—I can't bear to tell him about the eviction—"and I found it while I was packing. That was only two days ago. I came as soon as I found out where you were."

"And you did that how, exactly?"

"I told you, I googled you."

"I spend a lot of money on Reputation Defender. Google should have been a dead end."

I make a face. "Maybe you should ask for your money back. I googled you plus MIT and found your high school affiliation. I called a bar in the same town owned by a guy named Hutch. He gave me the name of the school. It wasn't exactly CSI."

"So you invaded my privacy and the privacy of my family."

My mouth falls open. What is this guy's problem? I stare him down. "You're being kind of a dick about this. The whole thing is an innocent mistake. One I'm trying to fix."

"Trying to fix it would be sending your paperwork to a clerk of court in Vegas. Letting them worry about contacting me."

I stand in dumb silence. "I guess I could have done that, yes. I was trying to give you a heads-up. Reach out and apologize in person. I thought—"

"You probably thought you were winning the lottery," he says, crossing to that card table, where a laptop is open and a stack of paper sits nearby. "When you looked me up."

"What do you—"

"That was my lawyer on the phone." He helps himself to a folding chair but doesn't offer me one. I have been standing this entire time, I realize. He sits, leaning back, legs open wide, arms folded, in that awful masculine power position men seem to learn in high school. "When you came into my classroom this morning I thought, pretty girl, wild night, botched paperwork. No harm, no foul. I was just relieved not to have fathered a child. But my lawyer just gave me a much different picture of what I'm up against. You're a sometime painter with virtually no work history. You've just been evicted for past-due rent. You're in credit card debt up to your eyeballs. You find out who I am and think it's your big payday. After all, we've been married all this time. Half of my earnings over the last ten years belong to you now. Is that what you think? Think you will come up here, get me in the sack, and then demand alimony for life? Is that why you consulted with a divorce lawyer one day ago?"

"Consulted—I don't—What are you—How did you—" I'm so mad and disoriented I can't complete a thought. I keep interrupting myself. "I'm not a sometime painter," I say at last. "Fuck you."

"Get off your high horse. I know a con job when I see one. And I've seen plenty. My lawyer assures me I owe you nothing. Not one red cent. I don't know what promises your second-class divorce lawyer pal made you, but let me assure you, if you press this issue, I will counter-sue for invasion of privacy and intent to defraud—"

"What the hell?" I interrupt. "What's wrong with you? I'm not trying to steal your precious fortune. Christ. You think anyone in her right mind would want this shithole anyway?" Nice, Lily. But I am hurt, and surprised, and I can't stop myself. "I don't know who you think you are, but let me assure you, I am *more* than happy to walk away from you and never ever, ever, ever speak to you again. Where do I sign?"

Ben Hutchinson, Dot-Com Douchebag, looks taken aback.

I sneer. "Stop looking at me. You're making my skin crawl with your icky greedy grabby suspiciousness. Nice way to go through life, jerkwad. Is everyone out to get you? Steve here just waiting until you turn your back for a second so he can eat all your roast beef?" Steve, sweet innocent Steve, thumps his tail at the mention of roast beef.

Unrepentant, Ben inclines his head toward his so-called front door. "You'll have the paperwork first thing tomorrow morning."

"Good."

"I better have a fully signed copy in my hands by sundown tomorrow."

"You'll have your copy. Oh, and I brought you something. A little souvenir for you. To remember me by." I reach in my back pocket. Tucked there is a worn beer coaster from that night, something else I found in that stupid kitchen drawer. It's from the all-night Beer 'n Eggs joint next to the all-night wedding chapel next to the all-night tattoo parlor next to the all-night dry cleaners. It's written on in a fine-tipped Sharpie, the kind of pen I always keep in my sketchbook, which I always keep in my purse, even now. The handwriting is blocky and masculine. Ben's.

It reads:

> *Prenuptial agreement for Ben Hutchinson and Lily ~~Something~~ Stewart*
>
> *1.1.1. What's mine is mine, what's yours is yours.*
>
> *1.1.2. That's the entire prenup.*
>
> *1.1.3. This is legal because we the undersigned say so.*

And then there are our signatures, and the date, scribbled drunkenly at the bottom of the coaster. It had made me laugh at the time. Seemed like such a funny joke. I had suggested the so-called prenup in the first place, reminding Ben that one day I was going to be a famous artist and he wasn't getting a piece of it.

What a joke.

What an asshole. I throw the coaster on the ground as I'm yanking my coat off its nail, rushing out the front door and into the cold before

I can get it slipped over my slumping shoulders. My parting words surely would make no sense to anyone but me, but I say them anyway. "I should have just gotten a tattoo."

And then I'm gone.

Five

Though I want to be Renee, to be tough and righteous and unapologetic all the time, I am not. I cry in the car on the drive back to town. And it takes forever, because I get lost, and there is too much darkness, and too much snow. I hate this godforsaken town in the middle of nowhere. I hate that I came here, that I spent my last dime on gas and lodging and these stupid mittens that are impossible to do anything in. Why did I buy these mittens?

The next morning comes hard and bright. I stay in my bed past breakfast and when I come down, Colleen is nowhere to be found. Dinner last night was regret and a banana from the fruit bowl on the dining table, so I'll have to visit the café for some sustenance. In the North Woods, I am learning, a bright piercingly sunny day in winter means bone-chilling cold, and today is very sunny. I practically run across the street, ignore the sneers of the angsty teen barista-with-no-espresso-maker, and huddle in a corner as far from the door as possible, clutching my bottomless coffee like it is a firstborn child.

Ten minutes in, I see that there is no one else in the shop, and so I carry one of the airpots back to my table. Now I don't have to get up for the thirty refills I'm anticipating needing before I can muster the will to pack my bags, check out of the B&B, and supplicate my stepbrother for mercy.

The girl behind the counter comes over twenty minutes in. I think she's going to want the airpot back, but instead I see that she is holding something. A scone. Lemon. My absolute favorite.

"Here," she says. "You look like shit."

I should take offense but I doubt she's wrong, and I want that scone. "Thank you. How much?" I've got about six dollars and fifty cents left in cash. The card I am using to settle my bill today at the B&B is off limits, and the others are maxed out, so it's cash only until I get to my brother's.

"It's a pity scone," she says. "The cost is, you have to hear me say, 'I told you so.'"

I sigh. "You were so right. He's a total asshole."

The plate with the scone, which the barista is still holding, suddenly whooshes out of my grasp. "Hold on now. You take that back. I giveth, I can taketh away."

Rather than retract my statement, I dart my hand out and take the scone right off the plate before she can pull it farther out of my reach. "How old are you?" I ask her around a delicious mouthful.

"Fifteen," she says with pride. "I have my learner's permit."

"Well, I've been driving since before you were born. And in that time I've learned how to spot an asshole when I meet one." Oh, if only that were true.

"You're wrong," she says. "You just don't know him as well as I do."

"And how well is that, exactly?" I ask, suddenly wondering if asshole is the wrong word, and statutory rapist is a better fit.

"Oh, get off it. Not that I don't wish," she adds wistfully. "He told me I need a boy my own age. But look at them," she says, gesturing out the huge windows to a scene of three teenage boys, who, rather than be caught dead in a hat or proper winter wear, have their jackets open, their bare hands stuffed in their pockets, their shoulders shrugged up high, and their faces set in miserable coldness. "They're morons."

"Yes, they are. But I'm not sure it gets any better as they age."

"It has to. Or I'm going to die a virgin."

I consider this girl. I know her. A misfit in high school but not a true loser, not a victim of bullying or gossip. An unrequited crush on an idolized teacher, a menial job for spending money, the confidence that she knows everything, the satisfying illusion that she doesn't belong. She'll go on to be some sort of silly major at a liberal arts school miles from home. Eighteen more years of unrequited crushes, bad jobs, a few better outfits, and she's me.

"No one's dying at the moment, virgin or otherwise. What's your name?"

"Simone."

"Simone?" I ask with eyebrows raised. This girl could not be less of a Simone. She's more like a . . . Gertrude.

"Whatever. Your name is Lily. What does that even mean?" I notice that she is sitting down uninvited, leaving the register unmanned. I can't decide if I want someone to come in and give her something to do or if I actually want her company.

"A lily is a flower," I say. "That's what it means. Flower. And how do you know my name?"

For this I get only a wry grin. "You're from Chicago," she says in answer. Again she sounds wistful.

"Yes, and I like it there," I say. "It's big enough that you can visit for a day without everyone learning your name and life story."

"Oh, I don't know your life story," she says. "I only know that you are a landscape painter and you went to art school at Northwestern. You have a brother in the suburbs. You've never been to the North Woods before. You drive an old foreign car with a small dent on the rear passenger side. And you had a date with Mr. Hutchinson last night."

I blink. "That's about it. Jesus." I honestly don't remember telling any one person in Minnow Bay all those details. It must be a carefully compiled composite from every interaction I've had since I arrived.

"Don't take it personally. It's not that you're interesting. Just that this town is dull."

"Um, thanks. But you know, it's actually not so bad here," I say, though I can't wait to leave. "The restaurants are good, there's some nice people, it's quiet . . ." And it's a frozen wasteland occupied by horrible Ben Hutchinson.

"Yeah, I'm sure I'm going to super-duper appreciate all that stuff when I'm like, sixty-five. In the meantime can I come live in Chicago with you?"

"No," I say. And then, to soften the blow, I add, "Chicago is expensive. And big."

"I don't care if it's expensive. At least there, people will understand the way I dress."

I look at what she's wearing today—a purple maxi-length sweater dress that I'm pretty sure she knit by herself. Baggy and misshapen and so, so purple. More purple than her hair. It's horrifying. "Well . . ." I drift off, unable to think of anywhere outside a circus where people will understand the way she dresses. "You could go to college in Chicago. There are lots of good schools."

"I'm not going to college," she says quickly. "I'm going to be a professional party planner."

I look at her for a few moments open-mouthed. Then I see just the hint of a smile. It is the first she's given.

"I believe you're messing with me . . ." I say.

"I'm messing with you. My parents have a dairy farm. I'm going to be a dairy farmer."

"Don't you go to college for that?"

"Not if your parents teach you everything."

"Oh. Huh."

"Yeah, exactly. Shoot me now."

"My dad owned a Dairy Dame. Doesn't make me a restauranteur."

"Dairy Dame is not a restaurant."

"That's not the point. Though it *is* a restaurant. It's a delicious restaurant that puts gravy on everything. I'm saying, you can do something different if you want to."

"That's only because your dad isn't an authoritarian dictator."

I pause for a moment, thinking of letting it go. But because I am warming up to this strange Simone, I tell her, "Actually, my dad was totally like that while we were growing up. Which is probably why I didn't want to go into business with him. The fact that someone as strong-willed as you is even considering going to work for your parents tells me they might not be as bad as you say."

She gives me an approving nod. "Yeah. They're actually pretty okay."

"Meaning, they want you to be happy?"

"I guess so."

"So if you figure out what it is that would make you happy, then they'll probably support you in that." I think of my mother. The day I told her I wanted to go to art school. Her happy tears that I had found my passion. She hadn't told me yet, about the test results.

"Probably . . ." she says, but her voice is noncommittal. Like she doesn't quite believe me. Or doesn't quite like me. "Oh. Oh, shit. Go hide behind the counter."

"What?" I furrow my brows at her. "Why?"

"Mr. Hutchinson. He's headed this way."

"Are you just trying to get rid of me?" I ask. But I crane around and sure enough there's a tall, parka-clad figure approaching from the other side of the street. "Shit. I do not want to see him, Simone."

"I know. So go duck behind the counter and wait for me to distract him. You can get a to-go cup while you're back there."

I sigh, but eye the counter. "This is ridiculous."

"Are you kidding? Every girl he's ever dated has hidden behind that counter at some point."

"Whoa. Really?"

"No. But you do really look awful."

"Thanks," I say. "But I don't think I'm bad enough to turn him to stone." I stand up with steely resolve. Cram the last big bite of scone in my mouth. Top off my ceramic mug of coffee and put my coat on, slowly, deliberately. "I'll bring back the mug," I tell her. Then I walk to the door, reaching it at the exact moment Ben Hutchinson, Douchebag, reaches the other side. He pulls it open and then steps back with a start when he sees me.

"Lily," he starts. "Lily." But I hold my hand up so that it blocks his face from my line of vision.

"Step aside," I tell him, and then barge through the door, leading with my hot coffee, wishing I was the sort of person to accidentally spill it on him. Then I turn around and put one finger in his general direction. "FYI: You may never talk to me again. Good-bye."

And then I march over to the B&B with my head held as high as the minus-ten-degree temperature will allow.

Fueled by coffee and righteous indignation, it takes me all of ten minutes to pack up what I brought with me into the B&B. I can't find my phone, and after crawling around on the floor looking, and being dazed at how clean Colleen keeps it under the highboy dresser and bed, I remember I was texting with it in the car last night. Hopefully it can withstand arctic temperatures, because I definitely owe Mitchell a phone call. I glance at the clock on the nightstand. If that FedEx package from horrible Ben Hutchinson comes soon, I can probably make it to Mitchell's gallery opening tonight. He loves me to come to the openings. Some small, cynical part of me thinks he likes being out in public with me more than he likes being together in private. Not because of my looks, nothing to do with that. But because I am a living embodiment of his ability to discover artists. A pet project of his. I think of the way he takes me shopping before really important events, "treats" me to days at the Red Door to get my curls blown straight. I like my hair curly. The whole charade kind of pisses me off.

As quickly as they came, I push those ungrateful thoughts out of my mind. I am me, no matter how my hair looks, and it's me he wants to be with. Besides, can I honestly say I don't love the way his face lights up when I've cleaned up well? The way he introduces me, with great pride, to all the most important people in the art world? The way I would probably be answering phones at Renee's firm by now if he hadn't decided to feature my work at his gallery?

And hasn't he stuck by me as I've toiled in creative paralysis, painting the same scenes over and over again, powerless to break through the block?

I should check out of the inn. Get the bill settled, pack up the car. Then, the minute the FedEx truck arrives, I can sign, return, and get back to the city. I can sleep over at Mitchell's tonight, and then go grovel to my brother tomorrow after the opening. Perfect. Do something nice for my boyfriend and avoid my fate for one more day. What could be better?

I head downstairs and start hunting down the innkeeper.

She isn't in the dining room, the foyer, the parlor. She isn't in the kitchen, which I've never set foot in until now and find is small but lovely and clean as can be. There's no note by the door or on the table about her whereabouts. I wonder if she's upstairs and I missed her. Maybe she's making up another room for a reservation. I hope so. I find I really like this woman, and am hoping her inn does well.

She's not in another guest room. The other two doors are standing open, showing variations on the theme of white opulence, though I still like my own room best. She must be in her attic apartment. Did she say anything to me about it? No, she didn't. I figure I can just climb the stairs and knock on the door. If she's not there I'll have to just cool my heels and hope she and the package both show up here soon.

But at the top of the stairs, there is no door. I find I'm standing right in the middle of her private quarters. I'm about to turn around when I hear a friendly voice, figure it's Colleen greeting me, and let my eyes scan the room for her.

It's one of those vast but awkward open-plan third floors with a narrow hole for the stairs right in the middle and slanting ceilings in every direction. To my left there are two lovely dormers facing the street with pretty wavy glass windows. The dormers are fitted with window seats, which are topped with plush cushions, and draped with soft-looking cream throws. One is stacked with books, the other is a perch for a pretty long-haired cat dozing in a small sunbeam. Across from that seat on the alley side of the house, I see a bed, a four-poster paean to femininity, perfectly made up with a quilted silk duvet and pillows of every size and shape, and yes, a well-loved plush bear. I imagine Colleen, like me, reading *A Little Princess* far too many times as a child.

The carpet is a thick white wall-to-wall, and over the carpet she's used rugs to create a few little zones within the big open space. The effect is lush, plush, squishy, and soft. There's a TV in a corner in a pretty armoire, and a yoga mat is spread out in front of it. I see lamps of every size and shape so long as their main descriptor is "pretty," and a loveseat so smooshy and inviting that, though I know I am intruding, I can barely avoid the urge to try it out. There's a little nook off the bathroom door with a tea service and kettle and a tiny dorm fridge set into a cabinet. And, on the other side of the stairs on the south end of the house, there are two French doors, closed, and behind them I see the seated back of the person I'm looking for.

She's on the phone in her office. Not talking to me, and with no idea I'm here. I've intruded on her sanctuary. I turn to leave, but when I'm only three stairs down, my eyes catch on something curious. A closet door, wide open, affording me a perfect view of its contents.

Baby stuff.

An infant car seat, the bucket kind, with the handle, with a lemon-yellow polkadot cloth cover. A white Jenny Lind crib, unassembled, leaning against the back wall. Hangers upon hangers of white, yellow, and green baby clothes. Some kind of bouncy seat in the same colorway as the car seat, and crib linens covered with pale yellow giraffes neatly washed and folded.

What am I looking at here?

I hear Colleen's voice rising on the phone. It's some kind of dispute. She's getting upset. What would she think if she turned around and saw me staring at what has clearly been tucked away in an off-limits closet for a reason? And listening in on some private conversation? After she's been nothing but lovely and accommodating for my stay?

I retrace my steps back downstairs as quickly as possible. Pose myself as casually as I can on the velvet sofa and stare in the general direction of the fireplace. Pull a magazine off the coffee table and prop it on my lap. Wait for Colleen to come downstairs while I try to comprehend whatever I just saw.

Six

She is downstairs within minutes. I cannot stop myself, I look to her tummy. It's flat as a board. And she's single. We talked about it at breakfast yesterday. No question. She said there were no eligible men in Minnow Bay. At the time I thought of Ben, but now I understand why he wasn't in the running. Because he is a jerkface. Is she planning a big baby shower at the inn for some local mother-to-be? But then why was that gear all opened and washed already? I am about to ask her when she clears her throat.

"Excuse me," she says to me and, instead of her normal warm tone, she sounds brittle. Did she catch me snooping? "Miss Stewart. A word."

"Lily, please," I say warmly, and stand up. "I was just thinking about you. I'm done with the room and ready to return my key, but I've still got to turn around a package from FedEx. I'm not in your way down here, am I? Do you have any idea what time the express delivery usually comes?"

"Your Visa," she blurts. "It's no good."

Momentarily, I am taken aback. But no, I gave her the card with plenty of room on it, didn't I? The one I was saving up for January bills.

If not, I just need to switch out cards. I laugh, as though this has never happened before. "No wonder you looked so dour. Don't worry, it's a mistake. Probably my fault. Did I give you this Visa?" I dig in my handbag, and provide the right card.

She looks from the card to me. "I've just been on hold with the card company for the last hour, and though they will not give me any particulars, they tell me your borrowing limit has been reached."

"What? I know that card is still good. I have three hundred dollars left on there. I haven't used it since . . . well, at least not for a week . . . And besides, you swiped it when I checked in. Maybe you accidentally swiped it twice?"

Colleen shakes her head. "Every time a guest checks in, I put a hold on their card for $100. It's kind of an arbitrary amount, not quite enough for one night in the summer, but more than enough in the winter. Mostly it just tells me if the card is valid and protects me in case of room damage. I don't run an actual charge until checkout."

"Just a hold?"

"Just a hold."

I puzzle over this. "But then, if the hold went through okay, how can they say there's no money on there?"

She sighs mightily. "They accepted the hold two days ago but later in the afternoon some automatic monthly debits came through that took precedent to my hold. A credit hold is not the same as a credit guarantee, Visa tells me, unless I upgrade my vendor status to the Silver level." She shakes her head. "I can barely afford the level I'm at now as it is."

Oh. Oh dear. Automatic monthly debits. Of course. "Hang on a sec," I say, and reach for my phone to look at my bank statements. But of course my phone is in the car. The *phone.* The phone *bill.* "Crap," I say. "I'm very sorry about this. I seem to have forgotten about the autopay on my wireless bill." I am utterly mortified. Now would be a good time for me to suffer a stroke, or some other debilitating medical emergency.

"Do you have another card?" Colleen suggests hopefully.

Eyes cast downward, I shake my head.

"If you have a valid driver's license, I could accept a check," she tells me.

I can't answer. Instead I start to cry.

"Oh, for Heaven's sake," says Colleen.

"I'm sorry," I snivel. "I'm such a mess, I'm sorry." I start fishing for a tissue in my bag.

She puts her face in one hand and sighs dramatically. It's Renee all over again, after all. "It's okay," I hear her say. "Well, it's not okay. You do have to find a way to pay me. I can't afford to—"

"No, of course not," I say quickly. "I mean, I will. I'll borrow the money. My stepbrother . . . he can lend me the money. Lord knows I've bailed him out a hundred times. It's just . . . I'm so very sorry. This is very embarrassing."

She looks like she wants to strangle me, but says, "These things happen."

I cough and try to swallow my tears. "I'm having kind of a bad week," I blurt. "I keep screwing things up. I'm a disaster. I got evicted, and I've been accidentally married for ten years, and I . . ." I dissolve into snotty tears. "I can't even get a divorce right. And now I've stolen a hotel from a very nice person . . ." I cough and sneeze at the same time.

Colleen gives me a wan little smile. "So far, the hotel remains in my possession," she says. "Come on into the dining room. I have no idea why, but I'm compelled to make you a cup of tea instead of turning you upside down and shaking you dry."

"Because you're a nice person," I wail, as though it is the worst thing in the world.

"Too nice. But you still owe me a lot of money."

"I know. I promise you, I will pay you back." How, though? She leads me into a dining room chair and puts a box of tissues next to me. They are the soft, lotiony kind. Which makes me cry harder.

"I'm not always this awful," I say when she reemerges with a whistling kettle and two mugs. I can tell she does not believe me for a second. A train wreck is as a train wreck does, as my mother would have said. "I have a nice life in Chicago. I was mostly solvent until recently. Well, not solvent. But I kept up with my bills. Things just got a little out of hand at Christmas. And I didn't have a very good third quarter for sales so I started out a little low. I only missed one stinking rent payment. I've lived in that apartment my whole adult life," and I'm back to unintelligible crying. She sits, patiently, waiting for her tea to steep and for me to stop crying.

"I wish I could tell you not to worry about it," she says after a little while. "But it's a small inn, independent, in a friendly little town. I've never had anyone stiff me before."

Of course not. I am public-enemy number one in Minnow Bay, Wisconsin, now. "I'm so, so sorry. I will borrow the money," I say again, thinking as I do, *Will my stepbrother lend it to me?* Renee? Mitchell? Maybe Daniella—she owes me far more than that from her shopping habit over the years. "I'll call someone right now to give you a card number. It's just, my phone, it's in the car. I'll just run out and . . ." I trail off, thinking of what that must sound like. Like I'm going to attempt a runner. "Actually," I amend, "here are my keys. It should be on the passenger seat."

While she runs out to the lot behind the inn, I stare into my tea and self-flagellate. The tea is sweet-smelling and the color of an overdyed red Easter egg. I can't drink and cry at the same time, so I drink. Try to get my composure. Try to figure out how I'm going to come up with a couple hundred dollars.

After a moment she's back. Wordlessly she hands me my phone. I'm so mad at myself. I'm so embarrassed. And then I look at my screen and see four missed calls and realize I forgot to call Renee back last night, to tell her I'm safe. She's going to be livid. And then I'm going to hit her up for my hotel bill? Oh, shit. Shit, shit, shit. I call my stepbrother.

I go straight to voicemail. "Hey Charlie, it's Lils. I'm sorry, I realize this is going to piss you off enormously, but I need to borrow some money and it's an emergency. Not a lot," I say, and then look at Colleen who mouths, "One seventy-five."

"Two hundred bucks is all I need," I say into the phone. "The thing is, I need it, like, today. I had to travel up north. It was an emergency. God, I'm sorry. Just. I *will* pay you back. Call me."

"He didn't pick up," I say needlessly. "I'll try a friend."

Daniella doesn't answer. Probably sleeping something off. I leave another message. Same for Renee, only in this one I start by apologizing profusely about not texting her last night and then segue into apologizing profusely about the money. Now I'm down to Mitchell. Mitchell, who answers on the third ring.

"Oh, thank God," I say into the phone when he picks up.

"Lily, my love," he says. His voice is calm. Always calm. Always adult.

"Mitchell, I have never been so glad to get you on the phone. I need a huge favor."

He laughs. "And I thought you were just calling to hear my handsome voice."

I try to force a smile into my voice. "Well, always that, you know. But ah, I'm in a pinch."

"Same pinch as you were in on Tuesday?"

Tuesday. When I found out I'd been evicted, and asked if I could crash with him. "No, no." This couldn't be more embarrassing. Well, I could be doing all of this in my underwear, like a bad dream, but beyond that, this is as humiliating as it can get, I hope. "I seem to have overextended myself financially."

He laughs again. I am not in a position to be hurt, but I'm hurt nonetheless. "Mitchell, I know what you are thinking. I just need some help. A one-time thing."

"Lily," he says. "Beautiful, brilliant Lily. You *don't* need help. The fact that you're convinced you do is why you keep getting into these situations."

If he only knew, I think, remembering Ben Hutchinson's expression at the coffee shop this morning. "No, I really do need help. I owe this innkeeper in Wisconsin two hundred dollars and all my credit cards have been maxed out. All I need is a tiny loan."

There's silence on the line. Then, slowly, scoldingly, he says my name again. "Lily. Honey. You know you can't do this to me, professionally speaking. It puts me in such a difficult situation. What will I tell all the other artists I represent when they come to me for advances on their quarterlies, if I give one to you just because you're my girlfriend?"

I flounder. "I'm not asking for an advance from my gallerist," I say, though, wouldn't that be nice? "I'm asking for a loan from my boyfriend."

He sighs loudly into the phone. "That's even worse. Bringing money into a relationship that's supposed to be about passion, and connection, and trust?"

I prop my elbow on the table and sink my face into my hand.

"Lily, the best thing I can do for you right now is say no. You will thank me later. Now, will you be home from, ah, *Wisconsin,* in time for the weekend opening? This artist is so demanding. She will take it personally if I don't bring you. You're like a signal to the art world. A signal that I am excited enough about something to get you excited too. People so admire your taste."

I pick up my head, defeated. "I'll try," I say.

"My dear, if you only understood how capable you can be, when you put your mind to something. I wish I could make you see that."

I wish he could make me see $200. "Thank you, Mitchell," I say glumly. "See you."

"See you shortly!" he calls cheerily. And the line goes dead.

I look up at Colleen. She is looking back at me with pure, painful pity.

"I will find someone," I say. "Just—don't worry. I'm not going anywhere."

She sighs deeply.

"I mean, I will leave. Once I've paid you. Which I will do. Soon."

She shakes her head. I can tell she does not believe me. But still we both sit there. "Where will you go?" she asks.

I take another gulp of tea. "I'm going to go stay with Charlie. My brother. Stepbrother, actually. He lives in our dad's old house in the suburbs. Where I grew up. He kind of owes me after a lifetime of me bailing him out of trouble and covering for him to Dad."

"It's a long drive down there. The forecast tonight is not good."

"I know," I say, shaking my head. "I saw a paper at the café. I was supposed to be gone by now. But I was waiting because . . ."

At once she remembers the FedEx package and snaps her fingers. "The package you mentioned. Let's go see if it came." A minute later she returns, holding a slim, legal-sized express envelope. "Maybe there's cash in here?" she says. She's being so charitable. It almost makes me feel worse.

I smile meekly. "I sincerely doubt it. Still, I'll understand if you want to hold on to it. As collateral."

She looks at me curiously. "Don't get me wrong, I do need that money. But I'm not going to hold your mail for ransom. Even if I wanted to, I think that would be totally illegal."

"So's credit card fraud," I say.

"I don't think you meant to defraud me. Did you?"

I shake my head. "I totally didn't. It was an accident. I'm doing a lot of accidental defrauding these days. You and Ben Hutchinson can have a good laugh about it. Someday. I hope."

Colleen looks surprised. "*Benji* Hutchinson? Hutch's son?"

"I think so. I've been accidentally married to him for the last ten years."

Now she looks genuinely stupefied.

"That's why I'm here. Once I sign whatever is in there," I gesture to the FedEx package, "we'll be divorced and I'll never have to see his stupid jerk face again."

"He's a really nice guy actually. I mean, he's a friend. A great teacher too. And he built out my website for free."

I let my head fall back against the high back of the upholstered dining chair. "Of course he is. Of course he's a decent guy, a friend of yours, a mensch. I'm the problem."

She looks at the walls, the furniture, anywhere but at my face. Then she says, "I hope you're not offended when I say you seem to be having a sort of rough couple days."

I bring my chin back down and scan her face, unable to tell if she's being serious. Then I break into laughter. "I'm not offended. I'm touched that you put it so nicely. In case I didn't mention this, I got evicted from my shitty apartment and then found out I've been accidentally married without knowing it for ten years. In those years, I have desperately and fruitlessly attempted to date, marry, and procreate with several of the worst human beings who have ever walked the planet. I have lived like a college student, wracked up crippling credit card debt, slept on a futon, and watched friend after friend leave me behind for husbands and families, while waiting for my latest boyfriend to make even the slightest commitment. All while I have, completely unbeknownst to me, been married to the Nicest Most Attractive and Wealthiest Man in America who is polite to everyone in the universe except for me.

"And," I go on after a breath, "after a humiliating and utterly degrading reunion with said man, I am trapped in a hyper-quaint bed-and-breakfast in the middle of nowhere with absolutely zero dollars and no clean underwear. You, my friend, are the queen of understatement."

Colleen puts her hand to her mouth, maybe in shock, but more likely to conceal laughter.

I wave my hand dismissively. "No, no, it's okay. Have a laugh. I owe you much more than a laugh at this point."

So she does. Her laugh is silly, giggly, and contagious. Soon I am laughing too. Because what else is there to do?

"You're telling me you're married to Ben Hutchinson?" she finally gets out. "That's not so bad. He is hot."

"And a wonderful teacher, and probably also a Nobel Prize winner, and a genius, and a zillionnaire. Oh, and he threatened to sue me for um, I can't even remember what, last night. All the things you can sue for."

She lets out a few more giggles. I put my face in my arms, crossed on the table, and pretend to weep dramatically.

"Okay, we're going to figure this out," she says. "Your brother's good for the money, right? So we can take that stressor off the table?"

I think for a long moment, thinking of something. Something that came to mind while I was sitting on the velvet sofa, staring at the fireplace, wondering about the closet full of baby gear with no baby to go with it. "I have a better idea. If you're open to it."

"I'm listening," she says.

"I'm a painter," I tell her, though I'm sure she's already seen the canvasses in the back of my car and figured out as much. "I think I'm a decent painter. I mean, I sell well. My stuff is worth something. I can show you a gallery statement, show you what they charge, how there's a waiting list for my works . . . Or you can google me. Here:"

I hand her my phone, open to a browser window. "L-I-L-Y S-T-E-W-A-R-T," I spell aloud.

She types it in, and looks at the results. Hopefully she's getting some nice articles from the glossies, and not just the occasional blogger who calls me a talentless hack. "Wow. Very impressive."

"That space," I say, gesturing to the wall above my pretty little white brick fireplace. There's currently a gilt mirror there.

"The mirror is beautiful," I say, "but it's round, and the fireplace is arched, so the area looks too smoodgy."

"Smoodgy?"

"There's no structure, no straight lines. Like an igloo, or a hobbit dwelling. Too whimsical, when taken with the rest of the house." Colleen studies the space and I press on. "And there's no saturated color. White white white, round round round. If you move the mirror to the hole over there," I indicate the long empty space above the buffet in the dining room, "then you fix the emptiness over there, add curves to the dining area, make the narrow space feel bigger with the mirror, right? But then you have a hole over the fireplace which is basically like, design suicide, right? I'm not an interior decorator, but visual artists do look at this stuff."

"Where are we going with this?" she asks me.

"I have something. A landscape. It's perfect for that space. I know contemporary art's not your bag, but it's representational. It will fit in here okay. Actually, as soon as I came into that room on Thursday I thought of it. But saying something then seemed rude . . ."

She smiles warmly. "It doesn't seem rude now?"

"Well, probably it is. I'm so sorry. But it's yours. The painting. I know it's worth at least twice the money I owe you. I'm not just bragging; my stuff really does sell."

She twists her mouth into a thoughtful expression, and looks again at the iPhone screen, at the search results. "I guess I could take a look," she finally says.

"Yes! Yes, just look. Then decide." I hop up and, leaving the phone and the FedEx package and even my coat, I dart out into the freezing cold to fetch the painting.

"Here," I say when I'm back in the warmth, and thrust a paper-wrapped canvas toward her. "It's yours now. It has to be here. It just won't work anywhere else." Even as I am speaking I realize how true this is. Even if I find a way to pay her back with actual money, I will always want the painting to live here.

"Is it okay to, um, take off the paper?"

I laugh. "Well, it will definitely look nicer if you do." She and I pull off the kraft paper, her hands moving gingerly, as though she might accidentally ruin the whole thing, and mine less so, eager for her to see my work.

"There." I spin it around for just a second, and show it to Colleen. Her eyes open wide. It is a landscape of a long, periwinkle-colored horse stable. A stable and a sky and one horse. That's all it is. Yet I am indescribably proud of it.

There is no depth whatsoever, and very little detail, so that you have the feeling of looking at something directly head on, standing in that one magic spot where all lines lead straight backward. But I've done shade work, in the rich blue side of the stable, in its joints and corners, that tells the viewer that it is spring, overcast, still cold, and early in the day. We know the sun will be moving high in the sky again soon for the first time in so long. We know animals will be out today, chittering. We know the warmth will make slicks of sweet-smelling mud.

The dark roof of the stable is a sort of green-brown, and it does recede a bit, the slightest nod to perspective, and then the sky is a hazy gray-blue that melts away into a few patches of leftover snow, here and there. I wanted to make the dreariest spring colors somehow cheery and inviting. I somehow knew it was destined to fit in a room of florals and velvet, before I'd even seen the room itself.

Colleen stands perfectly still, frozen and staring at the painting. I go to the fireplace and heft the mirror down. Carefully, I take it to the dining room and prop it against the wall. When I come back into the living room I find her clutching my painting with both hands. I know the look on her face, and I am supremely flattered by it.

"It was the horse," I say, as I gently take the canvas from her and hang it, frameless, where the mirror had been. She still says nothing, but stares. Just to the left of that purple-blue stable is a dark, dark brown horse, not actually a brown at all, but a bay, with that rich chocolate mane. It is nearly monochromatic nose to tail but for a white blaze. The horse wears a saddle, but the cinch is loosened. Under it the light cream color of a blanket shows through.

In my imagination, the rider, who I did not paint, is getting her grooming tools after a muddy morning ride. A stiff brush to run all over the horse's dusty body. Ointment for any spots the saddle rubbed wrong. A pick to clean the hooves. An apple, maybe? Or a carrot? I wish, not for the first time, that I had learned the horse's name.

"I'm not really a horsey person," I tell her. "This horse tells me about something else, though. I was doing some country work. Cooped up in Chicago too long, last March, and then there were a few days of warm weather, that false spring you get where you suddenly remember that not being cold is a possibility."

She nods. "I love and hate those days equally."

"Me too. I regret them being over even as they're happening, even as I'm rushing outside in a barn jacket and rain boots and breathing wet air."

She smiles. "I know exactly what you mean."

And then it hits me. I know why I wanted her to have this painting. Why I liked her instantly, why it's been so easy to chat with her over breakfasts. Why I was so embarrassed when my card was declined. Why she made me think of Renee. "Your mother's gone, isn't she?"

She starts, and looks away from the painting for the first time. "What? How did you know?"

"Mine too. Partly it's the house. You have a lifetime of fine things in here, a lifetime longer than yours. Like the coatrack," I say, pointing toward the hand-bent wooden coat tree in the foyer. "From a distance, it could be from Restoration Hardware. Only from up close do you see that there are no joints." Or the antique lace pillows in her bedroom, I think to myself. The Hull vase in the hallway.

"No one has ever commented on that before," she says.

I shrug. "And partly it's just knowing. When did you lose her?"

"Six years ago. This was her mother's house before her. So it's two lifetimes' worth of stuff, actually."

I smile sadly. "Mine was in college. She offered to leave me everything at the end, but I didn't want it."

Colleen nods. "I understand. Taking it would have made it real."

"Yes. That, exactly. So she sold it to an auction service. Prepaid the rest of my tuition."

"Oh, wow. What an amazing gift. Better than stuff."

"Yes." I turn to her. "But it, uh, didn't exactly motivate my stepbrother to return my calls, as you can tell."

She gives me another of her gentle smiles. "There are days I'm glad to be an only child."

I smile back, matching her compassion as best I can. I can only imagine how hard it can be to grieve a mother all on your own. "Your father?" I ask.

"He lives four doors down, all by himself. I'm trying to get him to date. Are you interested in older men?"

I laugh. "He can do better."

She laughs too. "Well, he's not much into art. Your father?"

"He divorced my mother and remarried a third time when I was still in high school. Lives in Arizona. Didn't even come to the funeral."

She shakes her head. "Some men walk away so easily," she says. I think of Colleen's closet. The tiny carefully hung onesies in a row. Did someone walk away from that?

"It's strange," I say. "I can barely leave even when I'm evicted."

She gestures around the room and says, "Case in point."

Relieved to be able to laugh about this, I plop back down on the sofa. "Kick me out at any time."

"I will, but first, tell me about the painting." She comes over to the wingback next to me, settles in, and trains her eyes on the stable, the horse, the sky.

"Right." I remind myself that she hasn't said if she wants it yet. "The painting. March. My mother died in March." Out of the corner of my eye I see her absentmindedly rub a hand over her cheek, and I imagine the touch she is recalling. A kiss? At the end, my mother was too weak for real hugging, but she never stopped touching us, moving the hair from my face or pulling lint off my brother's shirt. "The day I painted that, I couldn't stay inside anymore. I put everything in the car and went west, past the suburbs, almost to Iowa. As I drove I watched the developments fall away in my rearview mirror, and started taking photos." I think of that strange, softly lit day. Probably the last time I was artistically inspired, and it was nearly a year ago. "It was the beginning of a series, my first rural one ever. I got so many lovely barns—I love really flat buildings and what could be flatter than a barn?—and then I heard a story about something interesting on the radio and pulled over to listen."

What *was* that story on the radio? I don't even remember. It proved not to matter at all. "That's when I noticed the stable. I watched a woman in her forties come in from a ride. I watched her dismount, and then show this horse a kind of firm tenderness it understood. She handled the horse so lovingly and spent so, so long cleaning him and putting his tack away. An hour, maybe? I watched the entire thing. It was a strange process, I thought. I'm not really sure what she was up to but she seemed to be doing more than necessary. She was babying the horse. Like . . ." I stop myself, check Colleen's expression out of the corner of my eye. Her lips are pressed together like she is swallowing something scratchy.

"When I painted this I had a whole story in my head. About a woman living alone with her animals, three hours from the city, living comfortably and joyfully and yet with a kind of wanting I can understand. Like you can be discontented and happy at the same time, somehow? Like such a thing is possible. That's what this picture is about."

She is silent for a while. Finally, in almost a whisper, she says, "I know about that."

I quietly stand up and straighten the work over the fireplace, though it wasn't crooked at all. It's just that I want to give Colleen my back for a moment. In case she needs me not to see her. "I didn't sell this painting because it wasn't right for the series. It wasn't right for the series because it was right for your B&B. See?"

"Thank you," she says. "I love it."

"I still plan to pay you for the nights I stayed. This is a gift to apologize for the inconvenience I caused."

"It's so beautiful," she tells me.

"It needs a frame, I'm afraid."

"I have a good friend in town who owns a gallery. She'll frame it for me."

The gallery I saw on the walk to the outfitters. It looked so inviting. I should have gone in, but it would have felt like a betrayal to Mitchell. Gallery people are so possessive. I think of how he'd feel about me giving this work away, and then decide he wouldn't care. He didn't want to sell it himself, after all. He passed on the entire series. Said it wasn't in keeping with my urban aesthetic.

I look at the painting one more time, whisper a good-bye to it in my heart, and let it go. "If it's all right with you," I tell her, "I'm going to do that paperwork I told you about and get going. I'll leave my brother's number and address so you know how to find me. The check will be in the mail."

"It's okay," she says. "Your bill is paid in full. More than in full. I've never been so moved by a piece of art before."

Wow. "My goodness," I say. "I don't know what to say. Thank you."

Colleen dismisses my thanks and looks at her watch. "Actually, it's getting too late to drive all the way to Chicago. Why don't you stay another night, on the house? Tomorrow the roads will be plowed. It will be much safer."

I pause, silently. I think of last night, driving through all that snow down the winding dark roads of the North Woods. Then I think of Mitchell, with his thousand-dollar suits, unwilling to spot me two hundred dollars in an emergency. Maybe he should have to wait one more night to see me. "Really?" I ask Colleen. "Are you sure?"

"I'm sure. Go back upstairs and unpack. Deal with your divorce—or whatever that's about—in private. I'm taking this over to my friend now so she can be jealous of me and I can get it framed."

"That's really amazing," I say, flabbergasted. "Thank you."

"Strangely enough, I feel I am the one who should be thanking you," she tells me.

"You're wrong about that, but I'll take it. I'll take whatever help I can get right now."

She smiles widely at me. "Well, now you've got me."

Seven

The next morning, I trot down the stairs of the Minnow Bay Inn feeling incredibly restored. It's utterly illogical, because my best friend's not taking my calls, my boyfriend is "very disappointed" that I may miss his opening, and I am, thanks to a grilled cheese at the diner for dinner, down to my last three dollars. But I must have gotten used to the quiet here because I slept like a baby last night, and I am very much looking forward to another of Colleen's epic breakfast offerings, and I am still feeling touched by the way she responded to my art yesterday. It has made me feel like, at least in this one respect, I can go back home with my head held high. Or maybe I just have a spring in my step because I am clutching a prepaid FedEx envelope with my completed annulment filing inside it, and will soon be putting Minnow Bay and Ben Hutchinson far behind me for good.

But when I get to the dining room I find Colleen sitting on a chaise reading a paper with her feet up, and no breakfast in sight. "Aha!" she says when she sees me. "I was hoping you'd come down soon." She takes in my still-wet hair and a pretty embroidered tunic I picked out this morning. "Wow, you clean up nicely."

Sweet woman. "The secret is that spa shower in the room. I'm cleaner than I've been since my baptism. That, and the restorative food. Speaking of which, what's for breakfast?" Wait, what did I just say? "Oh my God, that was so rude. I'm sorry. I cannot believe I just demanded food from you after all you've done. Your cooking is too good; it's made a beast out of me."

"Don't apologize! It's a B&B. That's a very reasonable question. The answer is, today I am forced-marching you across the street for brunch, my treat, at our wonderful local brew pub, where you can have a Bloody Mary that will change your life, and killer market scrambles, and they will put hollandaise on anything if you ask them to. I hope that's okay by you. It's hard to get myself all amped up to cook a big breakfast for one patron in the dead of winter," she says. "And, to be honest, I have someone I want you to meet over there. Plus, a Bloody Mary does sound amazing. I love drinking my vegetables."

"Me too! But who is this mystery someone? It better not be Ben Hutchinson."

"It's not, I promise," she says.

"Well then, let me get my handbag."

At the River Street Brewery, Colleen and I are seated at a high four-top right by the big storefront windows. A warm vent between us and the windows keeps the winter at bay, but there is something about January brunch in Wisconsin that speaks of leaving our scarves on, and we do. Moments after we place our Bloody Mary orders, the door opens with a whoosh and in walks a pretty woman with chin-length black hair and a trim white parka, belted at the waist. She sees Colleen and me and comes straight over.

"There you are!" she cries. This must be our special guest. "Did you tell her yet?"

"Tell me what?" I ask.

"I don't know how you can keep secrets the way you do," the woman says to Colleen. "I would have blurted it out the minute I laid eyes on her."

"Blurted out what?" I ask again.

Colleen pats a chair next to her and says to me, "Lily Stewart, meet Jenny Cho, Minnow Bay's own artist-wrangler and gallerist extraordinaire."

Jenny nudges Colleen. "You forgot town councilwoman and deacon of the church, dummy."

"Yeah, yeah. Jenny runs ArtWorks, the biggest summer art festival in the North Woods. She consults for major collectors and she's kind of a huge deal—"

"Ignore her," Jenny says. "She's only sucking up to me because the festival keeps the inn booked solid for the entire month of July."

"That, and she's my best friend," says Colleen.

"Oldest friend," corrects Jenny. "River Street Bloody Marys are my best friend. Did you order me one?"

Just then our server arrives with our drinks. We both ordered bloodys, my "Regular" arrives with celery, three olives, and a perfect hint of spicy heat. Colleen's is "Salad Style" with a veritable pickle plate sticking out of it on skewers. Both come with tiny glasses of beer on the side. "What's this?" I ask.

"That's your beer back," Jenny says as she helps herself to one of Colleen's dilly beans. "Chris, can I get mine briny?"

Chris shakes his head. "It's vile, is what it is," he tells her, but leaves to go make whatever vile thing it may be.

I look from my Bloody Mary to my tiny glass of beer in confusion, but decide to let it go. "So, what is it you're going to tell me?" I ask.

"It's about the painting," Jenny says. "Colleen brought it over to me last night. I plotzed."

"Good plotz or bad plotz?"

"Bad plotz, for me," said Colleen. "I can't accept it."

My face falls.

"It's not what you think," she says quickly, over my groan.

"I thought you liked it yesterday. Crap. I have no idea how I'm going to pay for my nights at the inn now. My brother called last night and told me that he wasn't allowed to lend me any money. He said Cammie—that's his wife—thinks lending is bad for family relationships." I seethe at the memory. Suddenly when I'm the one who needs help, there's a policy? "If you ask me, being an embittered prick isn't good for family relationships either, but I didn't say that to him."

"Maybe you should have," Jenny says lightly. "Maybe your brother needs to hear another perspective." I look at her with an arched brow, wondering what she thinks she knows about me, and what she learned from the Minnow Bay Grapevine. "Anyway, you don't need to worry about the money. Like, for a nice long time."

"Excuse me?"

The waiter, Chris, returns right then. He is holding a regular-looking Bloody Mary, a tiny glass of beer, and an oyster on the half shell. Jenny takes it right out of his hands and throws it down like she was born and bred in Maine. Chris looks sick.

"Have you seen Jenny's gallery yet?" asks Colleen. "It's just beautiful."

"Thanks, Coll," she says, once she's swallowed and chased. "God, I love oysters."

"Chris is right," says Colleen. "Shellfish before noon goes against God's law. I think she does this just to gross me out. But bad taste in seafood aside, she shows some very important artists, not that I can remember their names to save my life." She pauses and Jenny supplies a few. I'm impressed. There are even a couple of names that Mitchell couldn't get a meeting with to save his life. "You wouldn't guess this from the dead of winter, but Minnow Bay is an art lover's haven," she adds. "Jenny is so, so good at her job, can match a patron and an artist like some kind of cultural yenta. Anyway, I showed her your work and . . ." She gestures to Jenny to deliver the good word.

"I want to sell it," Jenny announces. "Please say you'll let me. I'll be sure it goes to a good home. For a very good price."

I turn to Colleen, startled. "You want to sell your painting?" I'm surprisingly hurt.

"Sell *your* painting," she replies. "I can't accept it. It's too valuable. But once Jenny places it, and any others you want her to handle, you'll have enough money to pay me back, get an apartment, hell, get a lawyer if Ben's attorney is pushing you around. Not that that is any of my business, and really, Ben is a nice guy, and wouldn't—"

"Wait, go back," I say. "What exactly did Jenny think this painting was worth?" Jenny is now pulling some of the celery out of Colleen's drink and chomping it down with gusto. Luckily there are three more stalks remaining.

"Well, you know," she says as she smacks Jenny's hand away from her cornichon. "She looked up some of your past sales."

"I only have a very large ballpark so far," Jenny says around a mouthful of veggies, "but I think I can appropriately ask as much as fifteen thousand."

I am taking a drink of Bloody Mary just then, and Jenny and Colleen incline their heads toward each other as I begin to choke on it.

"Fifteen? Thousand? Dollars? American?" I am sort of cough-wheezing and shaking a bit.

"I'm confused," says Colleen. "You've sold several other paintings, and a few have even changed hands on the secondary market. You said something about a gallery in Chicago?"

None of this is making any sense. I don't think most of my work sells for fifteen *hundred* dollars. That kind of money is more than I net on an entire *series* of paintings, more than I make in two quarters of sales. And secondary sales? I've only been selling my works for a couple of years. Even very hot art needs longer than that to appreciate.

Why would there be a secondary market? Unless my works were selling for far less than they are worth . . .

And then the penny drops.

"Mitchell," I say on a low hiss. "It couldn't be . . . could it? He wouldn't."

"Uh . . . ?" says Colleen.

"My boyfriend. My gallerist. The guy I asked for money yesterday. Dammit. I knew something was up. I just—nothing was making sense anymore. I should have asked how to read those earnings statements. Dammit! I need another drink. And pastries. And a bowl of ice cream."

"Slow down," Colleen says, though I do appreciate the way she is waving Chris over even then. In her sweet but take-charge way, she orders another round of drinks, cinnamon rolls, millionnaire's bacon, a big salad, and scrambled eggs with chives to eat family style. "Okay," she says when Chris departs. "Tell me everything, from the beginning. Who is Mitchell? What is the deal?"

I clear my throat. Take a deep breath.

And here is what I tell them:

Mitchell is the most recent one of three serious relationships I've had in my life. The first was Nic, who dumped me and married Renee within a year. Then there was Travis, who crashed at my place for two years but never paid a dime of rent. He told me he was working to become an artist, but all the time we were together, he never made any actual art. He left me for another barista at the Starbucks where I worked. She had some "sick piercings," he told me.

"And then there was Mitchell." Jenny and Colleen exchange a meaningful look when I say this.

"What about Ben Hutchinson?" asks Jenny, and I can't help but notice the entire brew pub has gotten noticeably quiet.

"Ben Hutchinson is a blip," I say, hoping my voice is loud enough to be heard by any interested parties. "A bug in the system. Anyway. Mitchell is, without a doubt, the most impressive man who's ever looked at me twice. Fifteen years older, tall, lean, bright eyes, beautiful suits, and impeccable style. He came on to me, picked me up, actually, at a opening at his very important gallery. Of course, I didn't know it was his gallery at the time. I was—still am, apparently—clueless about the business side of things." How could I let myself be so naïve? How could I just give up the reins of my life so easily?

I go on. "The artist's work that night was eye-burning and allegedly brilliant but really just plain ugly, and when Mitchell asked me what I thought, I had already had two glasses of free wine so I answered that I needed to close my eyes for a while and feel terrible about what I'd just seen. He laughed, and, I shit you not, when he laughed his eyes flashed like something out of a romance novel. Even then I knew I might be in trouble."

I take a long pull from my drink and press on. "Our first date was this swanky restaurant I could never have afforded in a million years. I was already dazzled when we got to the front door, but when the hostess treated him like royalty and escorted him to a little private alcove and the chef came out to say hi, I realized what I was dealing with here. This guy was Somebody. Travis, the couch guy, occasionally took me out for falafel, but that had been about the extent of my wining and dining up to then." I shake my head, pushing out that other exception—Ben, in Vegas. "I probably shouldn't have been so impressed by Mitchell's flash and dazzle, but I was. By the bottom of the best bottle of wine I'd ever tasted, I was hooked."

Mitchell Helms, I learned that night, owned that gallery in Logan Square where we had met, and represented artists I had looked up to my entire life. He traveled widely and well, and knew how to have, and enjoy, the finer things in life. There have been times when I've worried if I was part of that. That collector's mentality. But what if I was? He wanted someone young and gifted on his arm, and I've been so flattered to be that someone. He truly believes in my art, after a fashion, and has connected me with mentors who made me into more than I'd ever thought possible. He's encouraged me to stick with it when it seemed, time after time, that I was destined to be nothing more than a deluded barista with an apartment full of my own rejected canvases.

So I suppose it made sense that, in return, I have let myself be toted around: his brilliant, young artist girlfriend, rife with unrealized potential.

"No offense," says Jenny, "but that doesn't sound like love."

"I guess it isn't," I reply. "I thought he did love me. But if you're right about the painting, then I'm wrong about him."

"Oof," says Colleen. "I'm so sorry."

"I don't know why I should be surprised," I say dryly. "I'm having kind of an off week."

"When did he start representing your work?" Jenny asks.

The answer to this question is heart-piercingly painful. "I found out he cheated on me. Just a one-time indiscretion; the girl—she was younger than me—she came to my apartment and told me because she was trying to break us up. It was a big awful scene. Anyway, he apologized and it never happened again, but it was right around then that he offered to represent me at the gallery. I had made a little breakthrough the month previous with a small series of three works, and he suggested he take it on and see how the public reacted. I figured it was kind of a way to make it up to me. That he'd give them a shot and that would be the end of it."

"And they sold?" Jenny asks.

"They sold. At the end of that quarter, Mitchell sent me a check for $3,500, a bottle of Champagne, and a bouquet of flowers with a note reading, 'Congrats, beautiful, and welcome to the big leagues.' It was the largest check I'd gotten since my mom died, and my life changed. I was able to quit my day job and paint during good light instead of in stolen moments at night. To kick out my roommate and gain a dedicated studio. To splurge a little bit, or at least go out for drinks with my gainfully employed friends without going into hock. It took the sting out of the cheating, let me tell you."

"I'll bet," Colleen says. But we both know this is only partly true.

Jenny clears her throat. "So does he have an exclusive with you?"

I shake my head. "No, actually. He never actually asked for one. He doesn't like some of my works. Because they're 'off-brand.' Like the one I gave Colleen."

"But he's sold more than that series on your behalf?" she asks.

I nod. "He's acquired almost everything I've offered him over the last year and a half. A friend told me there's even a waiting list between series. And yet it's never been enough to live on. Jenny, you understand the realities of life as an artist, I'm sure. I thought this was just how it was for everybody who works slowly. I had no idea the paintings were worth more than he was telling me."

Jenny looks appalled. "Don't you read your gallery statements? Check the blogs? Insure your works?"

I shake my head. "I left it all up to Mitchell."

"But surely," says Jenny, apparently unwilling to believe just how stupid I am, "you saw how he priced your works at the gallery. Where did you think the rest of your money was going?"

I think of the inscrutable statements I once asked Mitchell to break down for me. He just made me more confused. "Commissions? Framing fees? Listing fees? Gallery fees? Events? I dunno. Hang on, I've got the latest statement on my phone. You tell me."

I scroll until I find one and hand the phone to Jenny. She takes a few moments to look at the document and then gives the phone back. "You, my new friend, are getting robbed."

"Are you sure?" I ask. "This isn't some line to get me to sign an exclusive with you?"

Jenny sort of snort-laughs and I can tell she's a bit offended. "This isn't the big bad city. In Minnow Bay, Wisconsin, honesty and relationships matter—my business isn't just who I sell to, but how I sell it. I pay my artists their sales less commission. And I don't sell them to myself and my friends for a third of their real value, and then resell them at auction for a huge profit."

"Is that what Mitchell's doing?" I ask. "Do you think?"

"It certainly looks that way," says Jenny. "Unless the works he represents for you are totally different than what Colleen gave me, and way worse, then Mr. Helms may have stopped screwing other women, but he never stopped screwing you, if you know what I mean."

I can feel my face turning bright red. "I will murder him." I am angry, but even more, I am ashamed.

"That seems reasonable."

"How could I let this happen? No," I say, before Colleen and Jenny can tell me what I already know. "Don't answer that. I know exactly how I let this happen. This is sort of a pattern for me. My friends, my boyfriends, my bosses, my brother, my dad. Even my stupid landlord!" I'm gaining steam, and my voice is rising from it. "This is what I do. I let people treat me terribly. Give them their way, no matter what I need, no matter what's right, as long as they're happy. They take what they want from me, but when I need help, they don't want to 'complicate our relationship.' People I love, even people I don't love. Even assholes I only met once ten years ago!"

I cannot believe this. And at the same time I can *completely* believe this.

"Holy shit!" I very nearly shout, hands on head. "I'm having an epiphany!"

"I told you the Bloody Marys were good," Colleen says.

"I've gotta go," I say, and hop off the bar stool. "Innkeeper," I point to Colleen, "the painting is yours."

She opens her mouth to protest but I wave my finger violently in her face to shush her. "But I need another night at the inn."

"Of course," she says. "A week, a month, as long as you need, but—"

"If you sell it," I tell her, "I want the change. But if you keep it, it's yours. And you," I turn to Jenny. "If you want to show my work, I have three other paintings in my trunk from that series, similar to Colleen's, bigger too. Mitchell passed on all of them. I'll leave them in the inn for you. I just need a . . . um . . ." I shoot for the moon, "One-thousand-dollar loan that I can pay you back when one of them sells. That's okay, right? I mean, if you really think you can sell them for as much as you said?"

Jenny laughs. "I don't *think* I can sell them. I know I can. And I'm happy to give you the cash. But it's an advance on sales, not a loan. That's how I roll."

"Whatever," I say. "Just sell them, okay?" I push my untouched second drink away and pull on my hat.

Jenny looks absolutely gleeful. "I already have the buyers in mind," she says, but she is talking to my back. I am halfway out the door, buttoning up my jacket and pulling on my hat.

"Sorry to run out," I call out to my new friends. "I've got a FedEx truck to stop. No, wait." I run back to the table, grab the last piece of salty sweet bacon on the plate we were all sharing from, and cram it into my mouth. "Did you see what I just did there?" I ask joyfully. "I took the last slice of bacon. Without asking. I'm a new woman." And then I am gone.

PART II

The Key

TWO YEARS EARLIER

"I think I met someone."

Renee looks off at the distance like she didn't hear me. She is scanning the warren of second-floor Contemporary as though she's lost, even though, of all the halls in the Institute, this must be the one where we've spent the most time since it opened a few years earlier.

"What are you looking for?" I ask her.

"A bench."

"Opposite the early Pollock in the long room, I think. Are you okay?"

"Oh, sure. My feet hurt, is all."

Trailing behind Renee, I look down at her feet. It is high summer and I am wearing gold leather gladiator sandals I found at the Goodwill. She is wearing navy blue heels that look like they came from the Stewardess collection at Lord & Taylor, as I told her the moment we met up on the steps of the museum. "Wanna trade?" I ask her, when I catch up to her. Renee and I wear the exact same shoe size: 7.5 and just a hair narrow. For a long time, we shared shoes so fluidly that we weren't exactly sure which pairs belonged to which of us.

She looks at my ridiculous sandals. "Those don't exactly go with my outfit," she says, laughing. "Or yours."

"At least they're not the Slingbacks." At some point during junior year, we bought a pair of unbelievably painful black-and-white pointed-toe Italian slingbacks. We talked ourselves overbudget by saying that we could wear them to interviews, but they were absolutely crippling after about thirty minutes of wear. At one point I wore them across campus, staggered into the student union, and called Renee to come bring me a pair of flip-flops so I could walk home. After that, we kept the shoes but put them up on a high shelf and used them only to threaten the other roommate. As in, "If you don't wash that moldly hot pot right this second I am taking away all our shoes except the Slingbacks."

"I wonder what happened to those godawful shoes," she says now as she flops down opposite *The Key* and slips her pantyhose-clad feet out of her heels.

"Wonder no more. I still have them in a box in my apartment."

"No! You must throw them away. They are bad shoe karma."

"Bad shoe karma would be giving them to Goodwill and then having someone else try to wear them. I am keeping the world safe from the Slingbacks. It's basically a charitable endeavor."

"I wonder if you can get a tax break," she says dryly.

We fall silent. This room, of all the halls in the Institute, may have the highest wow factor. There's *The Key,* of course, which is huge, probably five by seven feet, and colorful as all get out, especially for a Pollock, with a palette of tomato and teal and about three different golf-course greens. This work, done on the floor, was the first step on the way to the drip works that made him so iconic, and it practically vibrates with anticipation of what might come next, though thanks to the clever curators of the Contemporary wing, you need only take a few steps to see the answer: one of Pollock's best action paintings, *Grayed Rainbow.*

And then in this very same gallery, Willem de Kooning's manic brushwork, the crayon madness of Twombly, the Lichtensteins and Jasper Johnses competing for oxygen, and then the Calder sculpture floating down from the ceiling and effectively trumping it all. And my personal favorite, Joan Mitchell's *City Landscape,* which does not look much like either a city or a landscape, and, despite its urban title, is awfully meditative. It's an oil on linen abstraction, sharp in places, almost muddy in others, with the tomato and teal palette not dissimilar to the Pollock we're staring at now, but no green to speak of. I miss it.

"Let's go stand in front of the Joan Mitchell and feel like talentless hacks," I tell Renee now.

"You go ahead. I never needed to be inspired by genius to feel that way," says Renee. "Plus, she's more your thing."

"I know," I say. "Mitchell says she's referential."

"Why would she say that about herself?"

"Not Joan Mitchell. *My* Mitchell."

"Hm," she says. "Wait. You have a Mitchell?"

"I don't know that I have him, but sort of, maybe. His name is Mitchell Helms. I think we might be dating."

"*What?* Why didn't you tell me you had a boyfriend?"

"Well, because I don't. I have a guy I am sort of dating."

"How long have you been sort of dating him?"

"It's hard to say because I couldn't really tell we were dating until we started sleeping together on a weekly basis. Which he's pretty okay at, all things considered."

"Oh, man. You're having sex. Oh, Lily. Tell me what it's like. I've completely forgotten."

"Not really?" I say, knowing once upon a time she and Nic were at it like rabbits.

"Oh, really. Do you have any idea how much sex the mother of a three-year-old and an almost-five-year-old has?"

"I don't."

"Zero sex," she tells me now. "And if it were between sex and a nap right now, I would take a nap."

"Don't say that. You don't mean that."

"In a heartbeat."

"Well," I say. "To be honest, on my end, if it's between talking art with Mitchell and having sex, I would probably pick the conversation."

"He can talk art?"

"Renee, you will never believe this: He owns his own art gallery. And it's legit."

"Whoa, get out! Well done, Lily! I always believed you could sleep your way to the top if you really applied yourself!"

"Oh, no. This has nothing to do with my work. He's never even seen my paintings."

"Well, you're just playing the long game. Soon he'll see how talented you are and the personal will become the professional," she says with a winning smile.

"I don't think so. We both agreed to keep that part of our life separate from, you know, the sex thing—or whatever it is we have."

"Hm." Renee looks skeptical. "Then what good is he?" she says. "If he can't jump-start your career?"

"He's very handsome," I tell her. "And smart. And he knows everyone in the art scene. And he's older. I really like him. I feel like he's too good for me."

"How much older are we talking?" she asks me quickly.

"A few years."

"A few ten years?"

"A few fifteen years."

"*Hot.*"

I shrug. Mitchell makes me uneasy. I have seen firsthand at parties that this guy could have any woman he wants. He has a way of making me feel so . . . honored to be the one he picked. To me, that doesn't spell long-term success.

"It won't last," I say. "I give it six months, tops."

"Nothing wrong with that."

"You don't think I'm wasting my life with this one?"

"Trust me," says Renee, sounding almost a little sad. "Someday you'll have two children in preschool, and you will long for the days you had six months to waste having good sex with a brilliant older man. Anyway, don't rule out something more meaningful just because he's older. A guy with a guiding hand and a solid bank account might not be the worst thing in the world for you. I mean, how much more of the art-fair-and-coffee-shop scene can you really take?"

I think of the misery of hustling for every single $250 sale. It's true. A little leg up in the art world might not be the worst thing in the world, if one thing leads to another.

"Or I could give up and go get a real job."

"I forbid it," says Renee. "Not yet. You're the real deal, Lily. Give this Mitchell guy a chance. If he's worth his salt as a gallerist, he'll see that too, and then you'll be on your way."

I sigh heavily. As Renee well knows, I've tried to crack the gallery scene. But I'm not a natural born schmoozer. I like to stay home and paint, or talk about painting. Gallery people don't talk about painting. They talk about the best places to vacation on St. Barts.

Maybe she's right. Maybe a schmoozer boyfriend is not the worst idea in the world.

"I think if you weren't in my corner I would have given up by now," I tell her, putting my arm around her weary shoulders. I don't feel worthy to Renee anymore, with her beautiful family, successful career, enormous salary, sensible shoes. I feel as though all I do is struggle, and all she does is flourish and yet, she still, for reasons I don't entirely understand, keeps meeting me here over lunch. Like Mitchell, she feels vaguely out of my league.

"And if you weren't in my corner," she says sweetly, "I probably would be napping in my office. There'd be drool on my laptop. I'd have forgotten sex or art even existed. So really, we're good for each other."

I smile, not sure if what she's said is true, but grateful for the words all the same.

Eight

Where I come from, the phrase "out of character" is definitely not a compliment. When someone does something "out of character" it means they go on a rampage and drink too much and get into a fight with a biker in a parking lot. They hop in the car and vanish for days, without telling anyone where they are going. They burn down the shed in their backyard.

What I do next is very out of character.

First I pop the hatchback of my car and throw, or practically throw, three of the paintings I find there into the entryway of the inn. Then I grab the FedEx package that is propped against the front door, just waiting to be shipped far, far away. Finally, I hop into my car, coax it to life, and point it in the direction of Lemon Lake. God, I hope he's home. If he's not I'm going to wuss out. But if he is . . .

I turn at the carving of the bear and wind past the mansions. In the light of day they are even more imposing, more regal, more glorious. The homes seem to suggest escape and solitude in the same breath as they promise large noisy family dinners and rowdy barbecues. Now, the bright snow-covered lake is glistening through the trees and beckoning to me, speaking of rosy cheeks and snow hares and the pleasing creak of ice freezing and refreezing in the undercurrent. I see a snowshoer out there in the far distance, with his big wide march, and closer in, a pair of turkeys romping in the snow. Angry as I am, I must concede, what I see is beautiful and beckoning.

Finally, Ben Hutchinson's house comes into view. If possible, it appears even smaller, even more ramshackle by day. It's long and skinny, and set so deeply into the hill that from the road it looks no bigger than a one-car garage. Scattered about the front yard are what I surmise to be fishing boats, under black covers, which in turn are under a few feet of snow. Near to the house is a huge rickety-looking woodshed, painted, inexplicably, hunter's orange. His neighbors must positively hate him. I pull into the drive, throw my car in park, and before the door is even opened I am greeted by a racing beast, ears flying in the wind, snow spraying in every direction.

I step out carefully and tell Steve firmly to sit. He does, though I can see it's killing him. Then I give him my hand to sniff and a good pet under the chin and he leaps out of his sit to greet me properly: snowy paws on my stomach, tongue on my face. "Hi, Steve," I say warmly. "How are you, buddy?"

"Steve, get down!" his master says. I muster a stony heart and pat the dog away. "It's okay, boy," I say to him sotto voce. Then I look up and see Ben Hutchinson walking toward me. He's wearing denim, flannel, and a down vest. He looks like a cross between Sasquatch and an Eddie Bauer model. He's holding something in his hand. A hammer, maybe? I grab the FedEx envelope off the passenger-side seat and square my shoulders in his direction.

"Hello, Ben," I say in my coldest voice. It's easy because it's so insanely cold out here.

"Lily," he replies with an equally chilly nod. "What are you doing here?"

"I came here to give you something," I say, waving the envelope in my hands.

He extends a hand, reaching for it as he comes my way. "Uh uh uh,"

I say. I rip open the zip pouch I sealed only an hour ago and grab the divorce papers out of the envelope. "Not so fast." I wave a finger in his direction. "You were really rude to me the other night. I made an innocent mistake and came all this way to correct it, and you accused me of all kinds of horrible things and treated me like crap. That's not okay."

Ben seems taken aback by this speech, and for a second I think he's about to apologize. Then the second passes. "What am I supposed to do when I find out I've been married to a complete stranger for ten years without my knowledge?" he throws back at me. "Throw you a bridal shower?"

I level my pointer finger at him like a parochial school nun. "You are still being very rude."

He inhales deeply, like I am trying his last nerve. I suppose I am. Too bad. He needs more nerves.

"You see this?" I ask him, gesturing to the annulment petition, which I have fished out of the envelope dramatically. "You know what this is?"

"Did you sign it?" he demands instead of answering me.

"I did. But I take it back," I say, and then, with a flourish, I tear the papers in half. It's all very exciting.

"What the hell!" he cries.

"I do not like the way you tried to bully me."

"Bully you? You're the one who trapped me in a marriage I never agreed to!"

"Excuse me, sir. You were there, fully conscious and in your right mind, when we got married in Vegas. You liked me well enough then. I was good enough for you then."

"I didn't say—"

"In fact, you seemed to really enjoy my company," I say. I feel outrageous saying this, alluding to a long past roll in the hay like a character from a 9:00 P.M. drama, but he hears my meaning and blushes enough to make me glad I did. At least I wasn't the only one who had a good time that night. "And then, afterward, when the annulment papers never came, I didn't see you noticing a problem and picking up the phone."

"I thought you were taking care of it!"

"I'm not your mommy," I say. Boy, he does not like that.

"If you were so sorry about what we did that night," I go on, "you should have made sure it was undone. But you didn't. Probably because you were already on to the next wild Vegas fling. So perhaps you should get down off your high horse."

"You don't know the first thing about me—" he starts, but I don't want to hear it.

"And you don't know me either, obviously, or you wouldn't have accused me of such nasty things. I am a nice person, and a decent human being, and I was just trying to do the right thing," I announce. "And I demand to be treated with basic courtesy!"

And then to punctuate this, I throw the shreds of paperwork into the snow.

"Here's your same-day delivery, jerkface," I tell him. I can regret the use of the term "jerkface" later. "You want a divorce? New policy: you'll have to be nice to me first."

"The hell I will," he says. "This isn't a team decision. I am not going to stay married to you, no matter what you think."

"Aren't you?" I say. "Because I asked Siri in my car, and she says there's a ninety-day waiting period for a divorce in the great state of Wisconsin. So unless you want to enjoy my wifely company from now until the spring thaw, you better change your tune really quickly. I'm not going anywhere until you do."

"Jesus Christ." Ben Hutchinson turns away from me for a moment, lets out a few choice words, and then turns back. "Of *course* I married a total lunatic," he says. "Of course. A city full of desperate women, and I get stuck with the one who is batshit crazy."

This stings on so many levels. First, I'm not crazy. I'm being a little crazy right now, but it's a justified kind of crazy. A long overdue kind of crazy. And second, he didn't get stuck with me that night. He picked me up. He wooed me. He is the one who suggested we get married "just to see what it would be like." And thirdly, I was not desperate. Outwardly.

"Okay, then, if that's how you want it," I say, and I summon my inner bitch—that voice that has always been there, shouting at me, saying, "Lily, it is not okay that your best friend stole your boyfriend! Lily, you should not have to be the maid of honor in their wedding! Lily, you must make Mitchell explain your sales statement to you! Lily, don't let some strange man from Nowhere, Wisconsin, push you around!" I summon her, and let her take over, at last, after choking her down for so very, very long. She is more than ready.

"I wonder how these extra months we stay married will affect my alimony payments?" I muse. "Of course, I had no intention of asking you for a penny when I first arrived, but I feel myself growing less and less reasonable by the second. I suppose you can talk to your five-hundred-dollar-an-hour lawyer about that. Take your time. As you so rudely pointed out the other night, I have nowhere to be."

"OH MY GOD," he says. It is only now that I realize he's not holding a hammer, but a hatchet. He must have been out here splitting wood for his stove. It makes me like him even less. If he's so rich, why can't he afford a stupid furnace like everybody else? "What do you want from me?" he demands.

"Just like I said. Some courtesy. A kind word. A polite gesture."

"I—I can't." He shakes his head violently. "I can't pretend to be nice to you," he says. "Right now I can barely look at you, I'm so mad." He clenches one fist, starts toward me, stops himself. "You're extorting me!"

"No, I am *threatening* to extort you. The extorting hasn't started yet. First I'm giving you a chance to get off with a smile and a friendly apology."

"I'd rather kiss a cobra." A tiny piece of Real Me pops up, speaks into my inner bitch's ear. It says: *This isn't right, Lily. Time to back down.*

I ignore it. "Suit yourself," I say, but I am backing away from him just a bit, telling myself it's about the axe he's wielding and not the guilt creeping in. "I'll be staying at the inn if you change your mind."

"Go right ahead. I'm calling your bluff. I'd rather stay married to you for the rest of my life than have to pretend you deserve a shred of my respect."

"Okedoke. Do you mind if I call you Hubby? You strike me as a 'Hubby' type."

"Get off my property," he replies.

"Oh, you mean *our* property? Surely you know that Wisconsin is a marital property state."

He takes a menacing step closer. "If you so much as—"

"I'm leaving," I say. "What would I want with this falling-down dump? Just know this: I have been walked all over for my entire life, and treated the way you have treated me by way too many people. And it stops today. Someone has to pay the price. Guess who that somebody is?"

"I'm going to lose my temper," he tells me.

"Oh, so this up till now, this has been you staying calm?" I say. He growls a little. I remember the hatchet. "Fine. I'm going. If you reconsider and decide to talk to me like someone worthy of your notice, you know where to find me. At the only hotel in town. The Minnow Bay Inn." I get back in the car, start it up, buckle in. As I do, I watch Ben Hutchinson throw down his hatchet in the snow with fury, and hear him let out a string of words that would make a lumberjack blush. He is mad. Mad, mad, mad. I have never, in my entire life, purposefully, intentionally, made someone mad before.

I've gone too far, I think as I pull out. And then, *I'm so incredibly proud of myself.*

Jenny and Colleen listen to the retelling of this story with the same expression on their faces as I must have had as I drove away. Agog. That's the only word. We are all three of us agog.

"Holy gumballs," says Colleen.

"You called him a jerkface?" says Jenny. And then, "Who wants more wine?"

We are sitting in Jenny's gallery, lounging around on the collection of low midcentury sling chairs that are scattered around the middle of the room. Around us on white partitions and walls, I see my works, but also several beautiful other collections. Some artists I recognize. Some are brand-new to me. All of them I would hang in my home, if the price tags didn't make my hair curl.

"A jerkface," I say, nodding. "I don't know. I was in the moment."

"Obviously," Jenny says. "I don't know what to say. I'm so . . ."

"Horrified," supplies Colleen. "You can't force someone to stay married to you."

"Obviously not," I say. "I know that. I just, after I heard about the paintings, and Mitchell, I snapped. I felt like I had to take a stand somewhere. And Ben Hutchinson is the person I stood on."

"Well," says Jenny. "That's crazy."

I nod, a little regretful, a little ashamed. To my left there are three severe portraits of stern-faced Scandinavian women painted with raw strokes and ashen colors. They look down at me reproachfully.

"But," Jenny continues, "I will say that Ben was incredibly rude to you, and you're right, you deserve better. And he can do better. I know you don't know him that well, but I think he's a great guy. Just incredibly, um . . ."

"Isolated," says Colleen.

"Like a hermit," finishes Jenny. "He came here under some really mysterious circumstances, about five years ago, and he just . . . stayed. Bought that rundown cabin on Lemon Lake, the abandoned clubhouse from an old dilapidated lake resort, and has been living in it like a squatter this whole time. I don't think it even has central heating."

"He's been in that house for five years?" I exclaim. I had figured he'd just bought it. How, I wonder, has he not frozen alive in there over four previous winters?

"Give or take. The whole thing was weird. I mean, town gossip has it he could afford a mansion on its own lake, but instead he buys a shack that everyone in the zip code was praying would be knocked down. Can you blame them? It's not even up to code for winter dwelling. I think he has been blowing insulation in retroactively, one wall at a time."

"I think you're right about the heating," I say. "He was out splitting wood when I showed up."

"Ooh. I think if I were in your shoes I would have just tried to make out with him," says Colleen.

"He's really hot," I say in agreement. "It is what it is. But he was really mean."

"You should give him a chance," Colleen says. "He's a very nice guy, deep down."

"That's exactly what I'm doing," I say. Jenny raises her eyebrows in silent dispute. "Well, after a fashion, I am."

"I think he'd be more apt to come around if he had the annulment papers in his hands," Jenny says.

"He'll have them soon enough," I say. "I can only sustain this hard-ass thing for like, ten minutes at a time. If he shows up and says he's sorry I will sign whatever in a flash."

"But what about giving him a chance, chance?" Colleen asks. "Obviously he's attracted to you, right? Because he married you once upon a time. Maybe he's been alone too long. Just needs a reminder of how to treat a woman."

I laugh. "Oh, absolutely not. First of all, I still have the satisfaction of dumping Mitchell ahead of me," I say. Because I want it to be true. Want to be the kind of person who will enjoy putting Mitchell in his place. But I think of how I feel right now, after doing the same with Ben. Lousy. It's just not my style. "Secondly, I am not going out with a guy who accused me of trying to rob him. Even if he didn't want to hack me to bits with his hatchet, which he does."

Jenny laughs. "You know, the more I think about it, the more I think I would have done the same thing in your shoes. I mean, look at that guy. He's great looking, smart as hell, and rich as an oil baron. If I had a chance to be married to someone like that, I'm not sure I would give it up too easily either."

"That's not what this is about," I say. "Not money or brains or looks. It's about respect."

"Maybe he'll claim his marital rights," says Jenny, ignoring me altogether.

"Ooooh," says Colleen. "How fun would that be?"

"You two have been in northern Wisconsin too long," I laugh.

Jenny nods emphatically. "She's right on that front," she says to Colleen. "We need more single people up in this town."

"Ones who live in heated homes, preferably," Colleen replies. "Who aren't married to complete strangers."

Jenny nods again. "Plus there's the Hutchinson factor."

"The Hutchinson factor?" I say.

"Oh, yes," says Jenny. "Ben Hutchinson is one of five Hutchinson boys, sons of Hutch Hutchinson, who is one of four boys himself, and then going through the branches of the family tree you get six more Hutchinson boy cousins, and a couple of second cousins too, and a few nephews even."

"Whoa," I say.

"Yep. Not one girl with the maiden name Hutchinson in this entire county. The word is that the Hutchinson X chromosomes don't swim. Only the Y sperm get through the gauntlet, and it perpetuates, down the line, fathers to sons to grandsons. For some reason, Ben's mom wouldn't believe it, kept trying for a girl, to the point that their fourth son is named, but not called under threat of instant death, Dana."

"Don't ever call him Dana," echoes Colleen, shaking her head.

"Let's see," says Jenny. "It's big brother Drew, then Ben, who is from Coll's and my class at Minnow Bay High, Connor, three years younger, Dana, the baby of the family, and Erick, the oops. We all just call Dana Doc."

"He's a doctor?"

"Yes, but probably only went to med school because we were all calling him Doc already."

I laugh. "And they all still live in Minnow Bay?"

"All but Connor, and he's not far off," says Colleen. "Which is surprising, because a couple of them seemed like goners for sure. In high school we knew Ben was stupid smart, and when he left a year early to get a leg up at MIT, we thought he was lost to us forever. But then he came back. Tall and strapping and fully grown with some kind of legendary Tech God status, and his serious hermit tendencies. Probably that was no small part of why he came back. Well, that and Erick."

"Erick?" I ask.

"The littlest Hutchinson, Erick, has always been, well, wayward," says Colleen.

"She's being tactful," interrupts Jenny. "Erick's several years younger than the other guys, a surprise long after Hutch had pulled the plug on trying for a girl. As the story goes, Mrs. Hutchinson got a gender determination ultrasound with Erick, and from then on he gestated in her disappointment. I'm not sure that's the real issue. I think the real issue is he's kind of a dick. He dated a friend of mine and left her brokenhearted. That's neither here nor there."

"So the entire population of single men in Minnow Bay are Hutchinson boys?" I ask.

"Exactly," says Jenny. "And the thing is, if you date one Hutchinson, the rest of them are off-limits forever. They are draconian about it."

"So you see, Lily," says Colleen, "Ben's all yours if you want him."

"Thanks, but I don't want him. I want to prove to myself that I can stand up for myself. If I can do this with a near stranger, then maybe I'll start trying it in my real life back home."

"Makes sense. Sort of." Jenny says charitably. "Anyway, it's fun to hear about. And we will be hearing about it quite a bit, I'm willing to bet. This town doesn't get a lot of good gossip-worthy marital standoffs."

"I'm not going to be the one to tell," I say.

"You won't have to be," Jenny replies. "Ben will tell Drew. He lives on the other side of Lemon Lake, just fifteen minutes away on snowshoes. Drew will tell Hutch ten seconds later. Hutch will tell the world. I estimate it will take about . . . thirty-two seconds before Simone Wajakowski bursts into hysterical tears over at the café."

We all turn our heads to the gallery's front bay windows, as though we'll see through them, across the street, to the café, to poor Simone's heart breaking in two. I tip my head back, feeling bad for my young barista friend. "Poor strange Simone. She's going to be so mad at me."

"I wouldn't eat anything she serves you for the next week or so," Jenny says, laughing.

Colleen gives me a wan smile. "Same at River Street Brewery. Chris was hoping he was a switch hitter. Maybe the bistro too. Aimee can really hold a grudge. Actually, half this town is either Hutchinson family or is half in love with one of the Hutchinsons," she says.

"But not you two?" I ask.

"I'm gay," says Jenny, and I start. She laughs. "I thought artists were supposed to be observant. And Colleen's got history with Ben's cousin."

Colleen nods a little sadly. "Mason Hutchinson. You think Ben is hot . . ."

My eyes get big. "Really?"

"Really."

"What happened?"

"Meh," says Colleen, so I guess she doesn't want to talk about it. "It's late. I've got a super-pesky guest at the inn right now, so I better get to bed."

"Me too," Jenny says. "This horribly demanding artist wants me to find buyers for her so-called 'pieces of art.' "

"She sounds awful," I say with a laugh, and we all head to our respective quarters. Colleen to her mysterious attic apartment full of tiny booties at the inn, Jenny upstairs where she keeps a small apartment above the gallery, and me to my pretty white-and-pink room facing River Street. Once there, I lay down on the butter-soft high-thread-count pillow, close my eyes, and slip into that wonderful dark deep sleep of a city girl in the country.

But I get only about twenty minutes of shut-eye before I am awakened by a noise. A racket, in fact.

It is the unmistakable sound of pebbles on my bedroom window.

Nine

Pebbles on the window. They creep into my subconscious slowly, taking some weird part in my dream, until I wake up all the way, and try to figure out what I'm hearing. There's silence, then another spray. Rat-a-tat-tat. I'm in a teen romance, I suddenly realize, though I have no idea who would be attempting to get me to sneak out of my frothy chintz bedroom to neck in the woods.

It's Ben Hutchinson, says my subconscious. *Dreamy!*

No, idiot, I say back to my subconscious, who is, apparently, thirteen years old. Ben Hutchinson hates my guts.

I get out of bed—ooh, how warm my bed was, how inconvenient teen romance can be—and pad to the window on tiptoes because the floor is too chilly to put my whole foot down. I pull back the gauzy curtains just as my admirer lets loose a handful of projectiles—I see now that it's a handful of loosely packed slush coming my way, which of course makes sense because where would someone get pebbles when the ground is covered in two feet of snow?—and they slop over the window, making it momentarily impossible to see out. Then ice and wet slide down out of the way and I see him. Okay, subconscious, you win this round. It is Ben Hutchinson, and he is dreamy.

He is waving sort of ridiculously. Obviously he wants me to come outside. I get that. I wave back noncommittally. I don't know if it's such a good idea for me to meet this guy in a dark empty street in the dead of night. In the Motive, Means, Opportunity department, this would be a perfect hat trick. But he keeps waving, and he is using both hands so I know for sure there's no axe. And he looks sort of beseeching. And cold.

I am wearing a white racerback tank top, a pair of well-worn blue cotton pajama pants, and nothing more. I'm not going out there. But I can let him in. I give him the universal "hang on a sec" finger, wrap a big gray cashmere cardigan around myself, and trot quietly downstairs, keeping my feet on the narrow carpet runner the whole way down to avoid frostbite. My, but Colleen does set the thermostat back at night, doesn't she?

I throw open the front door. The cold rushes in on me. I see Ben, standing back about five feet from the door, still looking up at my window, standing in a swirl of snowflakes, letting them land on his shoulders and cheeks undeterred. He looks a little startled at the sight of me so underdressed, but doesn't make for the door.

"I am going to freeze solid and then die if you don't get in here right now," I announce. And then I shut the door in his face to save a little heat in the microseconds it might take him to approach.

A heartbeat later he is peeking in, saying, "Is it okay if I come in?" and I nod violently.

"Hurry. You're letting all the fifty-degree air out."

He slides in. His jeans are snowy up to midcalf. Over his top half he has a lined flannel shirt that buttons up with snaps. It's navy blue plaid. Of course it is. Mountain-man standard issue. His blond hair is smushed under a light gray watch cap and he's got about a fifteen-o'clock shadow going.

"Where is your coat?" I ask him, as though that is the most pressing question his appearance presents.

"I was in a bar that doesn't rigorously enforce Wisconsin's smoking policy," he tells me. "I didn't want it to get smoky."

"Oh," I say. "So you're drunk?"

"No! Well. I'm not super-sober. I'm, like, forty-five percent sober."

"That sounds drunk to me."

He nods. "I think I'm exactly as drunk as I was when I suggested we get married."

"Oh," I say again. "Well. That's an excellent point of reference."

"I need to talk to you, before I get more sober," he says.

"How flattering."

"Go get your coat and boots."

"Are you crazy? No, I'm not going outside."

"It's not that cold out."

"Maybe not if you're full of scotch."

"It was just three Snowshoe Ales," he says. "And anyway, it's twenty-five degrees out there. No one is dying of exposure tonight."

"Wow, twenty-five degrees? I should have brought my bikini. Let's go huddle by Colleen's gas fireplace."

He shakes his head. "No, there's something I need to show you. And say to you. Come on, you can bundle up."

For reasons completely beyond my understanding, I go put on my shearling coat and the zillions of bundlements I've procured in Minnow Bay. I cram my icy bare feet into the soft, fur-lined Sorels. It feels like heaven. When I come back from the coat closet Ben looks at me and laughs. "Well, you'll be plenty warm in that getup," he says. "Come on."

Outside, now that I'm swaddled in fur and polar fleece and the wooly warmth of my thrummed mittens, I have to agree with Ben. It's not that bad. There's no wind, so the air just feels sweet and crisp and invigorating. The last of my sleepiness fades away. Our boots crunch crunch in the soft new snow and the streetlights turn it into fairy dust. "This is actually kind of pretty," I say.

"Minnow Bay looks good in white," he says. "And green too. And orange and red and gold for that matter. It's heaven on earth, and no one knows it, so it stays that way."

"Is that why you moved back here?"

"What? No. I moved back here because my mom was dying."

I swallow. Him too? Some of my resentment is instantly replaced by empathy. "I'm so sorry."

"Don't be," he says dryly. "She couldn't pull it off. She's still alive and driving us all bonkers."

I look at him, alarmed. Colleen is completely wrong about this guy—he really is the asshole I suspect him to be.

"I'm kidding. It was a miracle. She's in remission. But at the time, we didn't know how strong she was so we were braced for the worst."

"Oh," I say. I can't help but feel stung by his words. He has no idea about my mother, but she was strong too. As strong as anybody. Just not as lucky.

I try not to let this bug me. He doesn't know. If he did, maybe he wouldn't say it that way. Or maybe he would, I think, remembering the way he behaved last night in his cold unwinterized shack. Maybe he thinks he's not just better than me, maybe he thinks his whole family is better than my whole family. Maybe he went and got liquored up with all his four hundred brothers at the bar and now he's here to take me down another notch. Why else would he be here? I bristle. Without meaning to, my footsteps stop.

Ben gets a few steps ahead of me before he, too, stops walking and turns to me. "I'm sorry."

Ah, so that's what this is. I exhale. The apology I insisted on this morning. It's less satisfying than I imagined.

"It's okay," I say. Here it is. Time to give him the annulment. Time to go home.

"No, it's not. I had you investigated, remember? They told me about your mother. I'm so sorry. It's a terrible thing. Even the scare was the worst thing I ever went through."

"Oh, that," I say. "Thank you for saying that. Wait, not thank you. Un-thank you! You had no right to have me investigated!"

Ben lets out a huge sigh and starts walking again. "Look, Lily. When we met ten years ago, I was something of a . . . ah . . . a player. I had just sold my first multimillion-dollar company, and I was too young to know how to handle all that money. I was reckless and impulsive and thought I could behave like I was in a music video all the time. I was surrounded by people who behaved the same way, who never ran out of money or women or drugs, for that matter. I got taken in."

"That's not my fault. That doesn't make me an automatic suspect."

"You have to understand. You caught me on a weird night. I had just had a falling out with someone I had trusted, someone who was using me. When I picked you up in that casino I thought, I don't know, I guess I thought it would be a nice distraction. When I talked to you and realized how guileless you were, well. I got taken in again."

"I certainly didn't mean to 'take you in,'" I say, offended.

"Exactly. Do you remember your expression when the check came after dinner? How you snatched it out of my hands and nearly fainted dead away at the total?"

"It was $250 for two people!" I exclaim. I remember that moment perfectly. I still feel a little stressed thinking about it.

"You were so freaked out and worried about how we would pay for it. You made that joke about us having to wash dishes, but you weren't really joking."

"I was twenty-three and up to my earballs in debt paying for that stupid bachelorette party."

"And that's the other thing. You were selflessly, without complaint, throwing a budget-busting bachelorette party to celebrate the marriage of your best friend to your ex-boyfriend. And you weren't whining about it much either. In fact, you seemed genuinely happy for them."

"I was. I mean, I am. They have two kids now." *And no time for me,* I think to myself.

"But you had clearly been dicked over."

"I tried not to think of it that way. But yeah." I guess I had been a little dicked over, if I had to put a label on it.

"So I guess what I'm saying is, I knew these things about you, even if I'd forgotten them in the ten years following. Knew you were not avaricious, knew you were selfless. Liked that about you enough to think it would be fun—and harmless—to let the romance of the night carry us away. But because you were part of a time in my life when the other people around me weren't anything like that, I grouped you with them when you showed up here last week."

"This is your apology?" I ask. "It's not very good."

He groans. "Come on. I'm trying here. This is kind of a weird situation. Not black and white, I'm wrong, you're right."

"Which is why I drove up here, hat in hand, to try to apologize," I say. The things about me he just listed off, those are good things, not liabilities. The sleazeballs he surrounded himself with aren't my problem, my inner bitch reminds me. "And I did apologize, a real apology, not some bullshit context lecture while being dragged through the freezing cold. Where are we even going?"

He turns to face me, takes my gloved hands in his, and looks me dead in the eyes. My heart stutters, the traitor.

"Lily," he says. "I'm sorry. I'm sorry about treating you like a criminal since you arrived at Minnow Bay. I'm sorry I was so suspicious and questioned your motives. I'm sorry I sicced my lawyers on you and sorry I had you investigated and invaded your privacy."

I nod, wordlessly accepting what he's said. There. That's better. That actually feels kind of satisfying.

"Will you please divorce me?" he asks.

"I will," I manage to squeak out.

"Thank you. Now look."

I break from his stare to look in the direction he's turning. It's a river. Of course, we've traipsed behind River Street now, and here is the titular river. But it's no ordinary river. It's a long crooked clearing in the tall maples, meandering off in both directions, about fifteen feet wide, with ice and snow coming about three feet shy of closing the whole thing off. The narrow still-liquid channel down the middle rushes fast, burbles beautifully, freezes and melts itself over and over against its edges. River stones glisten underneath. And I can see all of this because of two low long paths of very dim warm light, one on each side of the water, glistening a beautiful frosted warm yellow from underneath the snow.

"It's so pretty," I say.

"Here," he says, handing me his phone from his pocket. "Tap anywhere."

On the screen is a round rainbow palette of color, the same you'd see in Photoshop or while making a desktop background. I tap on the blues and watch as, slowly and magically, the lights on the river in front of me turn from yellow to pink to lavender to, finally, the soft gray blue I touched on the phone's screen.

"Everyone within city limits can download this app," he tells me. "I made it so you can come out here anytime, and make the lights fit your mood, your occasion. Set them to a loved one's birthstone. Celebrate National Wear Red Day, or Black History Month, or St. Patrick's. Look." He reaches over and swipes to the left, and a keyboard pops up. "You can type in a message and the app translates it to Morse code." Upside down he taps out, I M S O R R Y, and I watch as the lights, one by one in order, switch to what looks like a random pattern of dark and light. "and then you go to Google Earth," he says as he navigates to that app, "and you can see it on the satellite."

Stunned, I look from his screen to the river and back.

"That's amazing," I say. I think, *He's an artist too.*

"Thank you. I did it because the city council was planning to put in ugly concrete railings on the town side. Block off the beautiful river. Drunks were coming out at bar time and giving themselves hypothermia. It happened three times, and one of them almost died. They had to do something to make the border clearer in the winter."

"So you designed this," I say. "And gave everyone who lives here the tool to control it?"

"That's right. The only thing they can't do is turn it off from sundown to dawn."

"It's brilliant."

He shrugs. "It's an elegant solution to a real problem. That's all I've ever wanted to make. And I wanted to show you. I'm not a dick. I was a dick. For some reason you agreed to have a one-night fling with me when I was a dick. So, yeah, you have reason to think the worst of me."

I remember a moment, after we'd cashed his chips. When he pressed the money into my hands and called them "our winnings," and then asked if he could borrow fifty bucks, and I laughed as though it were truly my money and said, "Sure! Take a hundred!" and he did, dashing off and returning five minutes later without a word.

How Renee, not knowing what I had done with the rest of my night, had conversationally mentioned the following day that the dot-commer I had gotten in trouble had returned to the blackjack table to tip the dealer—the one who called her pit bosses on him—$100 in cash after I had left.

Snow falls down on the space between us. I see some of it in my eyelashes, and in his. It's beautiful and crystalline and as far from Las Vegas as a pair of strangers can get.

"But you'd be wrong," he finishes, "if you think the worst."

Unable to speak, I nod instead. I think maybe I was wrong.

"Tonight, let's leave it on your blue."

He reaches toward the phone in my hands to set it. I don't let go. He looks up at me and I follow suit. My lips part. For a moment, a long moment, I think we are about to kiss.

Think that, and more to the point, want that.

Then, mercifully, the moment passes. He looks down, and my fingers release the phone.

"Your hands will get cold," he tells me, eyes locked on the screen.

I nod and shove them back into the mittens. It is only then I realize that I have been holding my breath.

Ten

Though I don't wake up the next morning with Ben Hutchinson in my bed, I feel as guilty as if I had. Yes, we stopped short of a kiss last night. And yes, technically, Ben is still my husband. But, on that same technicality, Mitchell is still my boyfriend. Things are all happening in the wrong order. The cold up here is making me crazy. I'm like one of those Mount Everest climbers who succumbs to the weather and slowly loses her mind, but with men.

I've got to get home and get back to my real life, while there's still one to get back to. As if to reinforce this, my phone chirps at me. A text message from Mitchell. Actually, three messages: He misses me. He needs me there. He wants to know what I'm working on.

A vengeful growl rises up in me. Now that this ridiculous marriage snafu is cleared up, it's time to go home and tell Mitchell to go to hell. Maybe I'll drive straight to his gallery and tell him off there.

Or . . . Maybe there will be customers when I arrive.

Maybe another artist.

Maybe someone from the media. Yikes.

Who am I kidding? I hate making scenes. I should just do this on the phone. I snatch it up and tap his picture in my favorites menu a bit aggressively. The phone rings twice and then he picks up.

"Baby," he starts.

Just that one word and I'm reinvigorated. "Do not—"

"I have something huge to tell you," he says, before I can start my tirade.

"Oh, you do, do you?"

"I do. Your whole life is about to change. Are you ready to be in a museum?"

My heart stops. It just plain stops.

"What are you talking about?"

"Now, before you get too excited, we're not talking about a main collection. But it's still pretty great. I submitted one of your Clark Street series to a traveling art curation company. They borrow from private collections, do topical shows for smaller museums . . ."

"You've got to be kidding me." This is not how I expected this conversation to go.

"This is going to change everything for you, Lily. I know you've been struggling. Stuck artistically for months on the same subject, and then losing your apartment like that in the blink of an eye. But this is proof that I've been right about your talent all along—you know I've never stopped believing in you, no matter what you've been showing me. And now it's paying off—your stock is going way, way up."

I say nothing. What can I possibly say? My inner bitch is just as stymied by this news as I am.

"Say something. Are you there?"

"I . . . it's . . ." I need to fire him. That is what I must do. He's been screwing me over on my sales.

"There was a time, not so long ago, before we met, when you didn't think you'd ever hang in a gallery, much less a museum. A museum, Lily! Think of that."

I think of that, but it's almost beyond my understanding. He's right. I vividly remember life before Mitchell, how hard I had to hustle to sell even a single painting. He came into my life and believed in what I could do, and gave me my first break. And now this. My wildest dream.

"What museum?" I finally think to ask. "Did they say?"

"Well, DePaul University is a maybe, here in the city. Or it could end up in Smart," he says, referring to the stunning collection at the University of Chicago. "They don't know who will take it on until they build out the entire exhibit."

"Smart? No." I think of the Judy Ledgerwood painting at the top of the Smart Museum stairs. Three enormous rows of color: green, then hot red, then dusky blue, covered in a vivid geometric print that seems to rock across the wall, to drop like plinko balls from the blue sky to the green earth. You look away and the red negative is burned into your retinas, so you look back, and before you know it an hour of this has passed. How could my work have any place among that kind of mastery?

"It's a real possibility," says Mitchell.

This is *beyond* my wildest dream. "I don't know what to say."

"Say you'll come back soon, Lily. I missed you on Friday. We haven't been apart on a weekend since we met."

This is not remotely true, but I can't help but be touched by the sentiment. What is true is that I have spent many, many content Saturday mornings over the last two years propped up in Mitchell's bed, drinking good French press coffee, nibbling on bagels and lox, reading art sections side by side.

How can that man be the same person who ripped me off? My resolve is fading. I can feel it draining away.

"It's just that I . . ." I attempt.

"And I want you to come into the gallery and see how this achievement will affect your sales. We'll do a special event for you. Your prices will go through the roof. Let me tell you one thing, the days of being evicted are behind you now."

My brain wrestles with this information. Fact one: Mitchell got me into a museum exhibit. Fact two: He's the reason I'm broke. Poof—my brain overheats. There's got to be a reasonable explanation for all this.

Could it be that Jenny was wrong about the value of my paintings? It seemed so tempting to believe her at the time, that I was worth all that money, that my present straits were not entirely my fault.

What do they say, though? When things seem too good to be true, they usually are?

"You're with me on this, aren't you, Lily?" I hear him ask me. "You seem so distant all of a sudden. I thought this would be good news."

"It is, it is," I tell him. "It's really good. It's just that . . ." I summon up all my courage. I have to get this out. "I met a gallery owner here in Minnow Bay. She thinks my work is worth more than you've been selling it for—"

"And she's right," he says quickly. "I've been sitting on this news since last week, hoping to tell you in person. The market is adjusting fast."

"But she said that you, uh, that you were . . ." I try to find the nicest euphemism for "screwing me over."

But Mitchell saves me from myself midsentence. "Oh, I get it. Oh, Lily," he says. "Lily, Lily, Lily, you're so sweet and naïve. Sometimes I worry that you're going to be devoured in this business."

Well. He's not alone in that.

"You're experiencing that burst, that flash of light that happens when your career begins to ignite. Strangers start telling you incredible things. People offer to sell your art for more than is actually possible, just to get you to sign with them. They'll tell you you're being taken advantage of, promise you all kinds of crazy money, even give you advances just to ensnare you before you can think it over." My eyes drift to the $1,000 check Jenny slipped under my door yesterday, sitting across from me on the pretty vanity table. Gulp. "I never asked you for an exclusive representation agreement, Lily, because I trust you. Because I know you can see through all that. You can see through that, can't you?"

I think of my rural series of paintings hanging in Jenny's gallery right now. Have I made a colossal mistake? Betrayed the one person who believed in me from the beginning?

Panic sets in. I've got to get back to Chicago. I can leave the paintings I already showed to Jenny. Let the chips fall as they may.

"Mitchell," I start, slowly, fighting the rising fear. "I gave her a few works. From that rural series that you passed on. Nothing you wanted to sell. I had no idea what to believe, and I've been needing money so badly . . ." My voice drifts away into regret.

There's a long quiet pause on the phone.

Then, "It's okay, Lily. I get it. You were feeling lost. Hurt even, about me wanting to keep our relationship on an even keel while you go through this apartment thing."

Is that all this is? I wonder. A misunderstanding that I accepted as fact because my feelings were hurt? I feel like such a fool. "You don't mind? You're not mad?"

"Of course not. It's a new market, this, where are you? Wisconsin? A market that might lean toward those unsophisticated pastoral scenes you mentioned. Maybe this woman you stumbled on, with her little vacation art shop, maybe she can place one of them and give you some pennies from heaven. I can't imagine the buyers up there are all that discerning, so who knows. Worth a try, right?"

"Right," I say slowly, setting aside the backhanded compliments. More misunderstandings just waiting to happen. "I mean, I always give you first look."

"And aren't you glad you do? Now that you're a big fancy exhibiting artist?"

I smile. I love the way that sounds. People will see my paintings across the country! Or at least one of my paintings. This is what I've always wanted, since I first stepped into the Art Institute as a child and fell in love.

"I am so excited," I tell him. "Thank you, Mitchell. Thank you so much."

"Baby, you can thank me in person. You're getting home soon, right?"

"I promise," I tell him. "As soon as humanly possible."

I levitate down the stairs. A quick delicious breakfast with Colleen and then I'm out of here. Probably—hopefully—never to return to this judgement-destroying place called Minnow Bay ever again. I think of what Mitchell told me. Jenny seemed so trustworthy over Bloody Marys yesterday, and she's Colleen's best friend, and Colleen seems trustworthy too. But this entire town is like a fun-house mirror. Everything looks so perfect and dreamy and impossible. *If it's too good to be true . . .* I remind myself.

Thankfully, Mitchell's right, no real action is necessary. I can let Jenny take a shot at selling those discarded paintings without much risk, considering he didn't want them, and she's already made such a big investment in me. If she can't unload them, I suppose I'll owe her back her advance, but by then, if Mitchell's predictions prove true, my stock will be way up; $1,000 won't break me like it would now. It won't be the difference between a decent apartment in the city or quitting painting to work at my brother's Dairy Dame in the distant suburbs. The relief courses through me.

"You're in a good mood," says Colleen, who bustles out to the dining room moments after I arrive. "What's up?"

I realize I am actually whistling. I think for a moment of telling her about the museum acquisition. But it puts me in a weird position with Jenny, I realize. Actually, I put myself in that position, by rushing to conclusions about Mitchell. But I don't need to exacerbate things.

"It must be the good accommodations," I say with a smile, and she smiles back.

"Or maybe the late-night walks in the snow?" she asks.

I'm suddenly embarrassed. "You guys don't do privacy in this town, do you?"

"Well, I wouldn't go that far," she says. "But if we want to avoid speculation, we don't do it by making a racket as we tromp off into the bad weather with handsome gentlemen."

"Fair enough. I hope I didn't wake you with my tromping?"

"Not at all," she says mildly. "I was having trouble sleeping anyway."

I think of the stack of books I spied by her bed the other day. One was *The Mayo Clinic Guide to a Healthy Pregnancy.* Could she be pregnant? She sure isn't showing. But being single and pregnant might explain why she couldn't sleep. And why her coat closet is a Babies R Us warehouse.

"Everything okay?" I ask before I can stop myself from prying.

"Oh, sure. Thanks for asking, though. Some nights my little attic apartment is just a little too quiet, or something."

"Well, a constitutional in the freezing cold did seem to greatly improve my night's rest, if you ever find yourself in that situation again."

Colleen smiles. "I'll keep that in mind, though I suspect having a Hutchinson man to gaze upon is the real trick."

My shoulders slump and I heave a mighty sigh. "This town. There are eyes everywhere. My secret's out."

"It was never in. When I went to buy the paper this morning, Simone Wajakowski said Richie Meier saw you and Ben in the alley behind River Street while he was locking up the bookstore, and he told Andy Kielholtz at the diner ten minutes later, and he went straight to Hutch's bar to spread the news, and Davie Barnes told Simone when he brought the egg delivery to the café."

"I cannot *stand* it."

"Jenny's on her way over for a debriefing."

I shake my head violently. "There will be no debriefing. It was a polite and dignified conversation. I'm signing the divorce papers, um, again, and mailing them posthaste. Then I'm headed back to Chicago."

"What?" says Colleen, genuinely shocked. "Why are you going back *there*?"

I smile at her. She is sweet to take such an interest, but hardly unbiased. "My life is there. And my boyfriend, which is why I'm not eager to relive my, ah, polite and dignified conversation."

"Your boyfriend the art gallery dirtbag?"

I shake my head. "I think that was the Bloody Marys talking. I just got off the phone with him. This whole affair is nothing more than one big misunderstanding."

Colleen levels me with a look that I find very intimidating. "A . . . *misunderstanding*?"

"Uh huh."

"That he has consistently defrauded you on the sales of your artworks over the last two years?"

I hold my tongue. I can't possibly tell her what Mitchell told me about other galleries saying whatever it takes to sign me. It would hurt her feelings and malign her best friend. "I think, maybe . . ." I trail off, try out some words in my head. "Jenny might have slightly overestimated the value of my work . . ."

Colleen presses her lips together. "Hmm," is all she says.

"The truth is," I continue, a little desperately, feeling every bit as naïve as Mitchell suggested earlier, "I don't really know my way around the business side of art dealing. I have to trust the people I work with, and trust my own instincts about what I'm worth—"

"Hmm," says Colleen again, before I've finished talking. Then, without another word, she picks up my empty coffee cup and saucer and backs into the swinging door of the kitchen and pushes her way through, leaving me to sit out here and ponder her opaque response.

Well, there's no better way to ponder than over a bowl of citrus salad covered in sweet candied lime zest. I help myself to seconds from the bowl on the buffet and wait for whatever delicious main course Colleen's whipped up.

But when the kitchen door finally swings open again, it's Jenny, in an ankle-length down coat, a big gray handknit scarf trailing behind her.

"Oh, hi Jenny," I say as casually as possible. "Going to be another cold one?"

She is silent as she unwinds and unwinds the scarf. Then she slowly takes off the coat and makes a production out of hanging both garments on the coatrack. Finally she pulls a chair out right next to me, too close, even, and sits herself down dramatically.

"So," she says, with a tiny twist of her eyebrows.

"Good morning," I try again.

"You're going back to Chicago?"

I nod. "As soon as possible. I mean, after breakfast." *Colleen is still in there cooking breakfast, isn't she?* I wonder. Or did she just walk out on me when I told her I was going back to Mitchell?

Jenny stands up, very deliberately. She goes to the sideboard and pours herself a cup of black coffee, and slowly, slowly, adds three sugars. Then she sits down at the table even closer than she was before.

"I want you to stay here a bit longer," she says. I notice it's not phrased as a request.

I smile nervously. "That's very sweet, but I have a life waiting for me back home in Chicago."

"It's a stupid life," Jenny tells me.

I cut her a sharp look. "Well, it's my life, stupid or not."

"Where are you going to live?"

"I'm going to rent a new place. I mean, if you're still comfortable with my taking the advance you gave me—"

She waves her hand dismissively, as though discussing the dispensation of a thousand bucks is beneath her. "And Mitchell Helms?"

I cough nervously. "I was wrong about him. It was all a big misunderstanding."

When she says nothing in reply, I fold like a five-dollar umbrella. "He got me hooked up with a traveling exhibition company," I blurt. "It's going to change everything. I'm going to have works in a museum exhibit!"

Jenny leans back in her chair and takes a long sip of hot coffee.

"Hmm," she says at last.

"Oh my God. How are you not impressed by that? This is my wildest dream, coming true!"

She raises her eyebrows. "Lily, Coleen and I have discussed this at some length, and we think you should not return to Chicago."

I blink at her. "What, and stay here in Minnow Bay?"

"That's right. Not permanently, at least not at first. But for a few weeks, until you have time to see where this thing with Ben Hutchinson is going."

"What thing with Ben Hutchinson?" I say, feeling like I've fallen into the Twilight Zone. "There is no thing. As I'm sure you've heard from six different people by now, we shared a civil discussion last night by the river. That's it. No 'thing.' I have a boyfriend back in Chicago, and Ben and I have a divorce pending. That is all that is between us."

"I heard your discussion looked *extremely* civil," she says.

"Is that all you heard from what I just said?" I ask, my voice rising. "Nothing about the boyfriend or the divorce?"

She waves her hand again, just the same way she did when I brought up the advance. "You seem a little high strung. I think another week relaxing in the North Woods would do you good."

It is hard not to snort at this. "Are you going to break my legs if I try to leave?"

"Probably not," says Colleen, as she reappears at the door with a quiche—oh, sweet heaven, it smells like bacon and mushrooms, and it's warm from the oven. "But we might withhold breakfast."

I am grateful for the lightening of the mood. Jenny is pretty intimidating when she wants to be. "You wouldn't be so cruel," I tell Colleen, trying to sound breezy.

She puts the quiche on a trivet right between me and Jenny. The warm smoky smell wafts straight to the back of my throat. "Wouldn't I?" she says. And then, before my greedy eyes, she serves up an enormous slice for Jenny, another for herself, and then pulls the pie plate and server out of my reach.

"I'll crawl over the table and eat it with my fingers," I say, not even remotely joking.

"Just stay for one more week. Ben is such a good guy," says Colleen. "But he is a bona fide hermit. As far as we can tell, he hasn't gone out with a single eligible woman since he moved here five years ago. You're the first one. We want him to be happy and, more to the point, we like you. Can't you hang out and see if there's anything there?"

"I really can't," I say, and as I speak I realize I genuinely regret saying no. When was the last time one of my friends back home expressed some actual endearment to me? Or set me up with a friend of theirs, for that matter? "Minnow Bay is charming, and you've been delightful hosts, but Mitchell needs me back in the city. And I need to get back to my real life."

"Such as it is," says Jenny dryly.

"Such as it is," I say to shut her up. "Now, slice me up some quiche before I drool on myself."

She and Jenny exchange a long, meaningful look. It makes me genuinely nervous. Then, finally, Jenny reaches over to Colleen and puts her hand out for the pie server. Colleen passes it to Jenny, and Jenny passes it to me. "Eat your quiche. I've gotta go," she says, though there is still an untouched slice of quiche on her own plate. She scoops up her plate and fork in one hand, and offers me her other hand for a good-bye shake. "Best of luck to you in Chicago, Lily. Make sure you leave a forwarding address so I can mail you a big fat check when I sell those paintings for you."

"Of course," I say. "And if you can't sell them for as much as you hoped, it's no hard feelings, I promise."

She raises her eyebrows. "I'll keep that in mind," she says blithely as she walks out with Colleen's dishes still in hand. "Take care, now." She does not sound like she cares if I drive off a bridge into a flaming pit of lava.

Colleen and I watch her go quietly. "You let her just wander off with your place settings?" I ask Colleen, after I chew and swallow the most perfect creamy, fluffy bite of shiitake and bacon quiche.

"She's not going far," Colleen says, unconcerned. "How's the quiche?"

"You know how it is. Stunning. Perfect. I want to eat it every day for the rest of my life."

"Wait until you see what I'm making tomorrow," she says, apparently undaunted in the face of reality.

"Believe me," I tell her. "There's a real part of me that wishes I could. But the rest of me, the adult part of me, knows I've done what I came here to do. More. I dealt with Ben—and no, that's not what the kids are calling it these days—"

"That's exactly what I was going to say," she laughs.

"Somehow I had a feeling," I laugh back. "Anyway. I *dealt* with Ben, and I got to meet you and some of the other lovely if slightly eccentric citizens of Minnow Bay, and had some of the world's best breakfast food, and avoided my problems for a few days. And, on top of all that, I found a home for a few homeless paintings, including one of my favorites," I say, gesturing through the arched opening to the fireplace mantel. "And now I'm going to drive home to Chicago, find a nice apartment near my old one, go apologize to my boyfriend for thinking the worst of him, pay down a few credit cards, and maybe have a glass of wine to celebrate my divorce-from-the-husband-I-never-knew-I-had. I've got a pretty full docket."

Just as I'm finishing this speech, Jenny comes back holding a now-empty plate and wearing a smile that looks almost deliriously smug. "If all these delightful-sounding plans involve driving that little hatchback of yours anywhere, you may have to reconsider," she says even as she's serving herself up a second slice of quiche and sitting back down as though she never left. "Apparently we're not the only ones who think you should stay here. Destiny seems to have provided you with a nail in the left rear tire."

Eleven

She's right. My tire is flat. All the way, can't even drive it to the service station flat. And I don't have a spare. The car didn't come with one when I bought it secondhand, and I figured if the point of a spare is to be able to put it on and drive to the tire store to get a real tire, then it was pointless to have one, since I have no idea how to change a tire.

"I think we better call Hutch," says Colleen when she sees the extent of the situation.

"Wait," I say. "Hutch, Ben's dad Hutch? The guy with the bar?"

"That's him," she replies.

"Why?"

"To get you a new tire."

"Does he sell tires?" I ask, mystified.

"No, but no one else does either. Not in Minnow Bay. However, Hutch goes to Duluth on Sunday to get stuff for the bar, and he can pick up a new tire for you at Sears. Lot faster than waiting for someone at Hutchinson Auto to order one."

"Hutchinson Auto?" I ask, sort of sadly.

"Hutch's brother's place."

"Ben's uncle," I say in defeat.

"Well, it used to be. Erick works there now, when he can be bothered to show up."

"Let me guess. Erick Hutchinson."

"Yep. Ben's youngest brother."

"I hate this town."

Colleen just laughs. "Do you want me to call Hutch, or not?"

With a mighty sigh I confess. "I was hoping to just sneak out of town without having to face Ben again. After last night."

Colleen looks a little hurt on Ben's behalf. "You didn't even want to say good-bye?"

"I very nearly cheated on my boyfriend of two years last night, Colleen. I made a mistake. A series of mistakes. I need to stop the hemorrhaging."

Colleen locks eyes with me. I'm a little ashamed, but I try not to avert my gaze.

"Fine. Look, I'll call the bar, tell Hutch it's my car that needs the tire. Then, when he gets here, I'll tell him the truth and persuade him to keep his lips zipped. Hutch isn't a gossip, but his bar is . . . conducive to discussion. Even at nine A.M. on a Sunday, someone is usually coming and going."

"Thank you, Colleen," I tell her. "I really appreciate it."

"You're going to have to stay inside if you don't want to run into Ben or someone who knows Ben."

I nod gratefully. Any more cable TV might kill me, but it's only an hour or two.

"It's going to be at least half the day before he gets back."

Or half a day. "That's fine. I mean, it has to be, right?"

"Unless you want to pay for a tow to Duluth," says Colleen. "How badly do you want to get out of town?"

I think that question over.

"I don't know," I finally answer. "Will the bistro deliver those steak frites?"

She smiles. "I can arrange that. And um, hey. Since you have to stay today anyway, I am wondering . . ."

"Yes?"

"I have a little favor to ask. Nothing big. Won't take more than an hour, two at most. It would mean a lot to me."

"Of course. I owe you at least two hours for helping me get this tire fixed. I can't believe I didn't notice it was flat before now. I must have driven over something on the way home from Ben's yesterday. It's the damnedest thing."

"Hm, well," Colleen says cryptically. "These things happen! About that favor."

"Anything," I say. And then, within minutes, I am filled with regret.

Crazy Simone Wajakowski, coffee pourer, bad dresser, gossipmonger, and Ben Hutchinson groupie, is also a wannabe artist, it turns out. Her mother, Marina, knew Colleen's mother well, back in the day, when they were kids. Marina actually babysat Colleen for a couple years while Colleen's mother worked outside the home, and she was a huge help to Colleen during the funeral, years later. Colleen is giving me all this background as she's walking me down the alleyway behind Lake Street, behind the inn, and the theater, and the market, and then Jenny's gallery. There, in a converted garage, Jenny has built a beautiful, light-filled studio for guest artists. It's chilly, but normally it's only used by resident artists who come during the summer and show their works at the art festival. Jenny has installed a little pellet stove that currently lays dormant, and otherwise not concerned herself with HVAC or insulation.

"Welcome to the Lake Alley Studio," Colleen tells me as she pushes closed the door. "It takes about twenty minutes to warm up."

"I think it is colder in here than it is outside."

"Nonsense," says Colleen. "The windows, though, let in a lot of drafts. And the skylights are even worse. Drew Hutchinson installed them when he was still in school, using only reclaimed materials. He was still learning. He's much better now."

"Let me guess. Ben's brother."

Colleen smiles and nods. "Very good. So I'll go back to the inn and make you a nice big thermos of hot coffee, you keep feeding the stove, and Simone will be along in a couple minutes. All she needs is a little informational interview. Someone to talk to about the artist's life, maybe take a look at her technique. Give her some pointers. She'll bring all the paints and stuff you need. Brushes or whatever. Jenny keeps them in her basement. I guess they freeze if you leave them in here."

"I'm going to freeze if you leave me in here."

"Nonsense," Colleen says again. "Happy art-making, or whatever it is you call it! See you in a couple!"

She is perky as she slips out. Giving absolutely no indication of what, exactly, I have just signed myself up for.

The studio warms up. The stove makes a pretty sound and a soft glow, and that, plus the skylights letting in a low winter's sun, makes for beautiful light. It's cast onto interesting sketches hung with gallery wire around the perimeter of the room. Discards from artists past. I have never been invited to be an artist in residence, but my professors in college told me about the prospect of being installed in a place, living for free, like a pet, a novelty, a circus act. It sounded lovely to me.

The subject matter of many of the sketches is uninspired. This does not surprise me—my own sketches are probably pretty uninspired too. Much of my work is about color, and what I do with a soft gray pencil on thick white vellum isn't really the point. The point of a sketch is to have a conversation with yourself about what you see, and what you don't see, in the world before you. I like being in this room surrounded by other artists' personal conversations. It's like eavesdropping on moments long past. Unfinished moments. Each sketch is a cliffhanger. How did that field of sunflowers pan out? Is it motel art? Or something more?

There's a drafting desk near the stove. Sort of automatically, I sit down at it. Find an open, empty sketchpad. In the right-hand drawer there's a pretty dark green pencil tin, and inside, eight gradated graphite pencils. I take out pretty, rich 9B and find it already sharpened. I soften the tip with spit and pressure and then start to draw.

When next I look up, it's because the garage door is opening with a mighty racket. In an instinct left over from junior high, I quickly close up the sketchbook. Then I remember it's Simone coming in, see her in a pink parka and ludicrous orange faux fur trapper's hat, and open it up again. I was right in the middle of something. She can set up while I finish.

"Sorry it took me so long to get here," she says, laden with Rubbermaid tubs of art supplies. "I was afraid you would be gone. I brought coffee."

"It didn't take you that long," I say, still distracted. Then I feel a pang of hunger. "Wait, what time is it?"

"Noon," she says.

I start, and drop my pencil. I've been drawing for hours. I lost track of time while working. When was the last time that happened?

"Did you bring any food? I haven't eaten since . . ." I trail off, thinking of the interrupted quiche. Damn.

"No, but I can text Colleen. She said she would pack you a sandwich."

"Perfect. Thank you," I say. I hope Colleen will know to come get me when Hutch gets back with that tire. I promised to help Simone and all, but I've got places to be. "Ah, so, Colleen tells me you're an artist."

"No," says Simone as she unloads her ephemera. "You're an artist. I work at a coffee shop."

"Those things are not mutually exclusive. I worked at a coffee shop for five years. Of course, I knew how to make a latte."

"I know how to make a latte too," she tells me. "I just didn't like you."

I take a long, cleansing breath. "Fair enough. But you like me now?"

"No. Not exactly. But I need help."

"Wow. How can I resist that kind of flattery?"

"Colleen said you were stuck here anyway. What else do you have to do?"

I think of the sketchbook, which is now full to brimming with my own translations of all the landscape sketches in the studio, and then at the Rubbermaid bin of paints, sponges, rags, and brushes Simone is setting up. I could be painting, I think. The thought is so unfamiliar that it almost startles me.

"Do you ever do portraits?" Simone asks, when I don't reply.

"I did. In art school. I make landscapes now."

"I make portraits. I want to get good enough to get into art school."

"Instead of being a dairy farmer?" I ask gently.

"In addition to being a dairy farmer."

"Well, then, you need to practice a lot, every single day." I feel like a huge hypocrite. I practice, sure. But just as many days, I simply stare futilely at a blank canvas for hours, hopeless at ever feeling inspired again.

"I do," says Simone with an arrogant flip of a purple braid. "The thing is, I'm stuck."

I sigh and let any illusion of authority fall away. "I may not be able to help you that much, then. I'm stuck too. I've been stuck for months."

"On what?" she asks, handing me a thermos of hot coffee, which I find is already lightened perfectly the way I like it.

"On a certain subject. I have been painting the same view out of my apartment window for the last six months," I admit.

"Whoa, that's really bad," she says.

I pointedly drink my coffee instead of replying.

"Is it something you're not seeing?" she asks.

I look up from my coffee.

"I . . . yes. Yes, it is something I'm not seeing." When was the last time I really talked to another artist about process, I wonder? Since Renee quit sculpting all those years ago? And how did this teenager so quickly narrow in on a problem I've struggled with for months?

"What aren't you seeing?" she asks.

I think back. "Well, if I knew that, I wouldn't be stuck. The whole thing just doesn't make any sense," I admit. "When I started painting this particular view, it was because I was seeing so much." I think of Annie and Jo, their stolen moments at the wine shop, always devoted to either fighting or making up. The couple with the new baby who perambulated by my window at the same time of morning every morning in one direction, and then just the dad returning with the stroller ten minutes later, after seeing the mother off to work, and walking so much slower, and with a sort of heaviness. The old woman who did her dishes in front of a window facing mine, who laughed to herself while washing up dinner alone every night.

"But then, I kept painting that view, and ran out of things to see that I hadn't seen before. Or ran out of new ways to see them. So then it was just sun moving across windows. Or weather. And then, finally, it was just the same thing I painted the day before. For weeks, months, I've been going on like that. I think I see something new, but then there isn't anything new on the canvas when I'm done."

Simone nods at me. "Yep, that's my problem exactly. So how did you fix it?"

I shake my head at her. "What made you think I did?"

"So you're just not working anymore?" she says, horrified.

"Well. I don't really have a studio right now, and I—"

"What is this, if not a studio?"

"This is a garage. An unheated garage in northern Wisconsin."

"Seems warm enough to me."

That's true. It's warm and, dare I say, cozy now. And the light is truly quite pretty. "I only just learned about this place today, and I'm heading back to Chicago as soon as I get a new tire. Hutch is in Duluth right now."

"No he isn't."

"Do you contradict me just for sport, I wonder?"

Simone only shrugs at me. Then, after a moment's pause, she says, "You have to understand, I'm in love with Mr. Hutchinson."

Heavily, I sit down at the drafting table. "He's too old for you, Simone."

"No," she says wistfully. "I'm too young for him."

I smile sympathetically. "The end result is the same."

"I know. But I still don't want him to end up with you."

"You don't need to worry about that. I have a boyfriend in Chicago."

"Colleen says he's the worst."

"Colleen doesn't even know him!"

"She thinks you should stay here and be with Mr. Hutchinson."

"I think," I start, and then stop myself and try again. "Colleen may not totally understand." And then, because we've left reality so distantly behind us that I'm actually a little lost, I say, "Why don't we limit the conversation to the subject of art?"

"This is about art," Simone tells me. "See?" Then she pulls out her sketchbook. It's a big one, eleven by seventeen inches. Tucked inside are watercolor works in colors as garish as Simone's clothing. Each is a different representation of Ben Hutchinson.

I know I shouldn't be surprised. I really shouldn't. But I don't know what to say to her. I can't think of a single thing.

"Oh, Simone."

"Are they any good?" she asks me.

The thing is, they kind of are. But I remember being Simone. I remember being so incredibly needy for feedback for my art, and what made me strongest as an artist was the way I didn't get any. Not good, not bad. Creating in a vacuum, as I did while I was her age, made me learn how to do it for my own joy, not for applause and validation.

And then creating for money zapped all that away.

I am about to tell her this when there's a knock at the side door. It's Colleen and Jenny.

"Lunch is served," Colleen trills happily. "How are you fancy artists doing in here?"

"Ooh, it's so warm," says Jenny. "Don't you just love a potbelly stove? So atmospheric."

"Hello, ladies," I say. "We were just, ah . . ." I look out of the corner of my eye as Simone quickly shovels her watercolors back into her sketchpad. She has the same instincts to hide everything she's not a hundred percent happy with. I fear it may be a sign that she's the real deal. "What did you bring us?"

"Sandwiches and bad news," says Jenny, with undisguised glee in her voice. "Hutch didn't go to Duluth."

"What?" I look to Colleen. "I thought you were going to call him hours ago."

"I did," she replies with nonchalance. "But it's snowing up there something awful. Safer to go tomorrow. I made brie, arugula, and apple on seeded baguettes. Yum."

I ignore the growl of approval from my stomach. "But I need to get back to Chicago today."

"Why?" asks Jenny, unwrapping the most tempting-looking sandwich and taking a huge mouthful for punctuation.

"Because I . . . Mitchell is . . ." She hands me a sandwich while I'm floundering, and my willpower vanishes. "You guys, this town is like the island from *Lost*."

Colleen giggles. "There's better food. I brought Pellegrinos and a nice warm lentil salad too. Tonight when you're done in the studio, we can all head over to the brewery and have the fresh-caught walleye. With wild rice soup on the side."

I can't help but laugh. It is a defeated, confused laugh.

"We can sit in the back room, not talk to anyone. The Hutchinson boys will all be busy with their mom's Sunday dinner."

I pause long enough for Jenny to try to close the deal.

"One more night won't kill you," says Jenny.

"It may kill me," says Simone.

"Oh, shut up, Simone. You think she's cool too."

Simone just shrugs.

I think for a moment. What can I do? Rent a car? Take a train? Hitchhike? All my other options seem unreasonable and reactionary. I have to stay here.

"Do you do this to everyone who comes into town?" I ask them. "Keep them here against their better judgment for days on end?"

"Only in January," says Jenny, turning for the door. "See you at dinner."

That night, after a wholly pleasant dinner with the girls followed by hot cocoa at the inn, Jenny and Colleen go off to their quarters with yawns and talk of busy Mondays ahead. My brain is full of the sketches in the studio and some kind of unrest I'd rather not contemplate. I go up to my room, read for an hour, brush my teeth and wash up as though I'm going to go to bed, watch some bad cable, read some more, and then finally, after all that, admit that trying to sleep would be fruitless. Out the bay window, the most beautiful lacy flakes of snow are falling. I go downstairs and pull on my boots and coat and slip out the front door.

Ben is standing on the other side, staring right at the place where the the door swung out. I jump back an inch.

"Oh my God, you scared me," I say when I finally get my breath back. "What are you doing here?" He looks lost. Like he forgot where he lives.

"Where are you going at this time of night?" he asks, in lieu of an answer.

I was planning to go back to the river, to see Ben's lights again, play with the colors a little, and maybe take some photos for future sketching. Rather than tell him that, I just shake my head. "I don't know."

"I don't know what I'm doing here either," he says. "I was walking Steve at the house, and then I was putting him in the car and driving to town, and then I was here trying to figure why I wanted to see you so badly. I've been standing here, at this door, for ten minutes now."

I shake my head again, trying to unhear what he just said. "It's because of the snow," I say, at last. "It's so pretty tonight." I force myself to step out of his gaze so that we are side by side, our backs to the front of the Inn.

We both stand there in the portico, stupidly staring at the flurries for a long moment. Then Ben turns away, back to me. "Do you remember what we did, after? In Vegas I mean?"

For a moment, I don't. I shake my head. "I don't think so." But then I do remember. "Wait. Yes."

"The pen."

I nod. "Actually, I think it was an eyeliner."

I remember the stupid all-night wedding chapel. I remember leaving the chapel a little drunker than we came in, and making a bunch of clumsy allusions to consummating the marriage, and then Ben suggesting that we go someplace. Where did we go? To the pool. The over-the-top Italianate pool set into the courtyard of his hotel.

The sun was coming up. I was starting to get tired. We curled up together on one large chaise, pulled off to the side a bit, maybe to give us a view of the sunrise, maybe to block off the view from the hotel. Ben saw my eyes getting heavy and said, "No, no, Lily. Don't go to sleep yet."

"Ben," I muttered. "It's so late."

"Stay awake a little longer."

"I can't. I am too full of wedding cake."

"If you fall asleep now, our night together is over."

This made me peel my eyes back open, and tilt my head up at Ben carefully. Think about what he'd said.

"Ben, I just assumed . . ." I began. "I mean . . . this is fun." I pressed my lips to his for emphasis. "So fun. But it has to end sometime." I made my voice as gentle as I could. "I'm flying home soon. Like, in a few hours."

"No, I know that. But you know that thing, that weird phenomenon of really wild nights where you don't realize you're even drunk until you've fallen asleep? And then you wake up with a start and you're like, *Oh no, what have I done?*"

I nodded hesitantly, unsure about where he was going with this. Feeling suddenly very vulnerable, considering he'd already seen me naked. Twice.

"I don't want that for you," he said then. "I don't want you to have that feeling about tonight."

In the chaise, I rolled my lips together. I remember how much I wanted him to kiss me right then. I remember leaning into him in that half-drunken way, and him turning, suddenly, and jumping up out of my arms.

"Do you have any paper?" he had asked me out of nowhere.

"Paper?"

"Paper and a pen? You're an artist, right? So you travel around with a sketchpad?"

I couldn't help but smile at that a little. In fact, I usually did travel around with a sketchpad at that point in my life. But I showed him my tiny baby blue clutch and said, "Where would I put a sketchpad in here?"

He paused, then sat back down next to me, close again, and I wished he would just wrap his arms around me and let me sleep. "What about a pen, though?" he asked.

"Hmm," I said on a yawn, and opened the clutch for him. Inside we found my credit card, my ID, eight dollars in cash, the silly coaster contract from the diner, and a kohl-colored eyeliner. "I must have lost my pen," I announced.

"That thing," he said, pulling out the eyeliner. "Is it expensive?"

"No," I admitted. "It's from the drugstore. Three bucks, maybe?"

"Okay, so we just need something to write on." His eyes moved around some more. The pool, which was officially locked at that hour, was so clean and austere. No fluttering receipt in a corner. No stained cocktail napkin under a chaise. "Here," he said at last, and took off his sport coat, revealing his worn short-sleeved T-shirt. "Right here."

He turned his arm over, palm up, exposing a flat, broad plane of forearm. On it, he used his finger to draw an imaginary box, three by five or so, and said, "Make me a sketch."

I felt just a tiny bit of the tiredness slip away. "What do you want me to draw?"

"Anything. The side of a building. That's what you make, right?"

I nodded. "Sometimes the fronts of buildings too."

"Okay. So you have a range."

"Give me your arm," I said. I took it firmly in my left hand, craning it a bit into a comfortable position for me. Then I slowly traced the outline of the canvas he had made for me, not with the eyeliner but with my own finger, thinking of the planes of his arm, the way the black would look on his skin, my workspace made of his body. The feel of his skin on my finger was warm and charged—it seemed to electrify and settle me at once, like the moment after a good bolt of lightening.

"You can see it. It's already there, right?" I asked him after a few moments.

"What is?"

With the eyeliner I traced a curve of a vein, an outline of a muscle, until there was no way to miss what I had seen. "Here is the place where you fell asleep after . . . we . . ." I let my voice trail away. Rather than look back up at him, I drew the legs on the too-stark hotel-room platform bed, the sheet that had been tangled around me that I'd pulled away in my attempt to get a better view. He had fallen asleep almost midsentence on that bed, and I had thought, then, that perhaps our night was already over. And so I had, in that moment, with the sheet wrapped around my middle, climbed back far enough to the bottom of the bed to get a good view of him sleeping, to write the memory on the backs of my eyes, because that was what I always did when I saw something beautiful.

"And here is where I fell asleep," I said, drawing my outline toward the crook of his elbow, as far from his sleeping form as I could go. "Curled up, over here, just out of reach."

"You fell asleep too?" Ben asked me then. Now, all these years later, I remember how he had curled his hand over my drawing hand, leaving me nowhere to look but in his face. "After I did? In my room?"

"I did. So, you see, I already had my chance to be filled with regret. If I was going to be filled with regret."

"And you married me anyway," he said then, in that chaise by the pool in Las Vegas, as he pulled me in closer.

"And I married you anyway," I say now, aloud.

The Ben Hutchinson of now, of Minnow Bay, Wisconsin, of ten years later, says, "You remember."

The snow keeps falling. The pool in the desert could not be farther away.

"I'm leaving in the morning," I tell him.

"You're here now."

"Steve's in the car," I say, incredibly off balance.

"Do you want me to go?" he asks back.

"I think that . . ." I begin, wanting to say something about Mitchell and my life in Chicago, but he is already turning away from me.

Somehow in all that snowy silence, we have gotten very, very close together, and now, when I am only just noticing it, he is pulling away.

"Ben, wait," I say, and take his arm. Where is his coat? Why is he in nothing but a fleece hoodie?

He turns back and, as he does, he gently takes my hand off his arm and puts it on his chest. Then he looks down at me, and I look up at him. My chin tilts up to follow my eyes.

And, thank goodness, he understands why. He leans down and in, closer and closer, and then at last his lips are finally touching mine.

Twelve

The next day it is still snowing. I lay as low as I can in the morning, refusing to let myself wade into the paired black holes of confusion and want that lie at either side of my consciousness. At breakfast, I don't even ask Colleen about Duluth—it is obviously way too treacherous on the roads—and, mercifully, she doesn't ask about Ben. We make plans to meet up for dinner at the bistro, and then go our separate ways. I don't know if she is on to me, and I don't care to find out. The newfallen snow acts like a protective layer over my memory of the night before, sealing it off from the real world.

Simone and I work side by side in the studio that afternoon. Aside from sighing a lot, she makes a decent enough studio partner. Then, after dark, she looks at her brass pocket watch—no idea where she found a pocket watch or why she is wearing it when she has no pockets—and announces that it's time for dinner. I'm about to remark that, though I may seem old to her, I still don't eat dinner at 5:00, when I realize it's 7:30. The day is gone, I am still in Minnow Bay, and have made absolutely no effort to leave. But I have made my first start at new work in weeks. And it is not of the view out my old apartment window.

It is a painting of something I've actually never seen. A sketch made by an artist long gone, of a field of yellow wildflowers in front of a barn. The flowers hold no interest for me, but the barn, the field, the invisible line between ground and petals and sky; *that* has captivated my imagination. The sketch must have been made in late summer, but the big fluffy clouds depicted in the sketch are the white of bleached cotton, midsummer clouds, out of place, clumsy. I have no use for them, and puff them away. In their place is the hottest sky I can imagine, the kind that will burn up the flowers, dry up the prairie beneath, harden the soil, and fill the air with dust.

I labor at some length over that certain scorching blue that I can only vaguely remember here, in the face of the cold bitter winter. It is blue over blue over blue, but not bright, just intense. It gives you the impression that to look at it is to stare at the sun. It is angry, and bored, and rude. It is the thirteen-year-old-boy version of blue. I get the right base at last when I mix cadmium yellow light, an obnoxious neon, with enough red that I have the burnt umber that will engage my existing blue without dulling it down.

The process of making this particular color will be unrepeatable, but I won't need to repeat it because, though I've never given it much thought before, I now realize that my particular August blue sky is not a horizon-to-horizon solid, but rather a spot, the spot directly opposite the sun, the place where the color is stacked most deeply to your eye. From there, things go just slightly grayer, and then, finally, at the instant the sky meets the field, there is nothing but the smoky blur of heat overflowing out of the ground. But that's all work for another day.

"You didn't get much done," says Simone when she looks at my four-inch square of hot blue sky.

"Didn't I?" I reply. I am trying to be the wise mentor. The Mr. Miyagi of painting.

"No," she says without pause. "You didn't. Have fun tonight."

"I'm not leaving yet. I have a ton of cleanup to do."

"Nuh-uh. Jenny pays me to clean up for artists in residence, do other odd jobs around the gallery. It's how I can afford my brushes."

"You work a lot of jobs," I say. "The coffee shop. The gallery. And you have school too. Doesn't leave much time for milking cows."

"I do it in the morning," she says, entirely missing my point.

"Sounds like hard work."

"I'm not afraid of hard work," she says quickly. "Listen." She wipes her hands on her pants. "If you let me work with you, I'll be the best mentee you ever had. I'll try anything, study whatever. I'll mix paint for you, clean up, get here early to heat up the studio, whatever you need. You'll actually have more time to work, not less." She looks at me with her heart in her eyes. "Please," she says.

"Simone," I start. I cannot look back at her, with all her hopes bound up in me this way. "I think we've gotten our wires crossed. I'm going back to Chicago tomorrow as soon as I get my tire fixed. I'm not going to be able to mentor you. Now, if you do move to the city for art school, you should look me up—"

"What? You're just going to leave me like that?"

"Simone, you don't even like me. I'm screwing up your long game with Ben Hutchinson."

Despite herself, she smiles. "Well, that's true."

"Not that you should have a long game with him. He's way too old for you."

"He's not too old for *you*."

"I'm really not sure what you're cheering for here."

"I just want him to be happy."

"He'll be just fine."

"Are you sure?"

This stops me. Is there any reason, whatsoever, to think that Ben Hutchinson will be affected in any kind of long-term way by my arriving here, divorcing him, and then making out with him in a snowstorm?

No more reason than to think he'd be affected by getting married in Vegas on a dare.

"I'm sure," I tell her. "You sure you're okay with the cleanup?"

"Yep. See you later. Or not, I guess." She shoos me off and heaves up a Rubbermaid bin full of brushes that need cleaning, following me out and locking the door behind her. "Say hi to Ben for me."

"What?" I ask her, but she's already halfway to the gallery.

Maybe because I haven't had much to eat all day and my thoughts are consumed with French food, it is not until I get to the bistro's front door that the penny drops. *"Say hi to Ben for me."* This is a setup. Colleen inviting me out to dinner so casually, saying she'd meet me at the restaurant? As soon as I walk into the bistro, it will be Ben Hutchinson and a good bottle of wine in an otherwise empty restaurant, with candles burning low and romantic music playing. Maybe some Hutchinson brother can play the violin, I think drolly.

Well, I can beat them at their own game. I stop in my tracks, reverse course, and head to the inn instead. Dollars to donuts, Colleen will be in there humming "That's Amore" to herself. Nice try, ladies, I think smugly. I'll just order a pizza or something, and hide in my room for the rest of the night. Ben can eat alone.

But when I walk in the front door, I realize how grievously I've underestimated Jenny and Colleen. Ben Hutchinson is sitting in the front parlor, staring at my painting over a roaring fire.

At first I think I can back out the way I've come. But Ben is already standing up before I am more than halfway turned around. "Lily?"

I freeze. This is incredibly awkward. Is there still time to pretend I didn't hear him? I reach for the doorknob, trying to act nonchalantly deaf.

"Um, Lily? I'm pretty sure you can hear me," he says.

I turn back around.

To my chagrin, Ben is even cuter today than he was the night before. This is starting to be a worrying trend. What will he look like in ten more years, at this rate? His hair is tousled, and he is wearing, for the first time since my arrival in Minnow Bay, a coat.

"Hi," I say, ridiculously.

"What are you still doing here?" he asks.

Relief floods me at this question. He was counting on my leaving today as much as I was. This is not going to be as awkward as I had first assumed. "Trying to escape Minnow Bay has proven harder than I first thought," I tell him. "Didn't you hear from Hutch?"

"Hear what?" he asks, looking genuinely confused.

"Hear about my tire. I must have driven over a nail on Friday. Maybe at your place? I had a flat waiting for me when I went to leave this morning."

"Oh. I'm sorry to hear it. But what does this have to do with my dad?"

"His Duluth trip? He was going to buy me a new tire when he went up there for his Sunday run, but he couldn't go? Because of the storm? I can't believe you didn't get this via the Minnow Bay News Dispatch."

There is a long, confused silence.

"So he's going to go tomorrow," I try.

"Go where?"

"To Duluth. To Sears, to buy me a new tire." What is so mysterious about this?

Ben scratches his five-o'clock shadow. I remember how it felt on my cheek last night. I try to remember anything but. "Well," he says, "I very much doubt that."

"What? Why?"

"Because the bar is open Mondays from eleven to eleven. And he will be running it."

"Him? By himself? Not someone else, like staff?"

"He doesn't have any staff. Not in the winter."

"Huh."

"Huh."

"Maybe he's going to go in the morning," I say, though I'm not sure why I'm arguing about this. Colleen's got the logistics all figured out in her own way, knowing her.

There's another long, weird pause. Then Ben shrugs and says, "Maybe."

"Anyway," I say, feeling embarrassed though I'm not sure why, "that's why I'm still here."

"A flat tire?" he asks. "No other reason?"

"Yes," I say, sensing the uncertain territory we've wandered into. "Otherwise I'd be back in Chicago by now. But, ah . . . hey, since you're here anyway, I can give you the paperwork you need. Save on FedEx bills."

There is a long, heavy silence. Have I said the wrong thing? No. He's the one who was in such a hurry for the divorce, as I recall. All kissing aside, that shouldn't have changed overnight.

"You have another copy?" he asks at last. "Besides the one you ripped up?"

I nod. "Your lawyer sent me one to keep. It's in my room, I'll go get it."

"You don't have to get it right now," he says. "You look like you're in the middle of something."

"What do you mean?" I ask.

He gestures to my hair, then pats his own head. I turn to the dining room buffet where the mirror now hangs. There is a huge swath of August-sky-blue paint in my hair.

"Oh my gosh. Why didn't Simone tell me?"

"Simone Wajakowski?"

"We were painting together. In that studio behind the gallery."

"Oh. That makes sense. Maybe she just thought it was a fashion statement."

"Blue hair?"

"You've seen Simone's clothes?" he says lightly. "She sees color in a way none of us can quite understand."

A little smile plays on my lips. "It may prove to be evidence of latent genius," I tell him, thinking of the riotous colors of her work, her wardrobe.

"I hope so," says Ben. "She's a good kid."

I think of what paroxysms such a comment would give Simone if she were here to hear it. Probably best she's not.

"Ben?" I say.

"Hm?"

"What are you doing here?"

"Oh. That. I came to see the painting."

The color drains out of my face, and I feel powerfully self-conscious. "You did?"

"Yes. Colleen couldn't stop raving about it to my brother this morning. Said everyone should come over and see it tonight before she took it to be insured."

"That's very sweet of her." And crafty, I think.

"She's not wrong. It *is* beautiful."

I color deeply. "Thank you," I say, more embarrassed by his compliment than I would be if he hated it.

"I wasn't sure if you'd be gone," he adds. "I didn't know about the, er, tire situation." He takes two steps closer to me. I realize now how many steps I've taken toward him. Now, again, we are too close together.

"I have a boyfriend, in Chicago," I blurt, before I accidentally kiss him again.

Now it is Ben who colors.

"It never came up before—I probably should have stuck it into the conversation at some point, but, things were a little fraught . . ."

"No, of course. That makes sense." Then he takes one more, tiny step closer. "But last night . . ."

"I know," I say, nodding. "Last night."

"It was . . ." Ben presses his lips together. Those lips.

"It was a mistake," I say, too quickly, too loudly.

His face transforms. It is a slate wiped clean. "Okay. A mistake."

I can think of nothing to say back. I want to explain, at great length, the series of events and misunderstandings that led to our kissing last night. But I don't know how to start.

Ben takes a mighty step backward. "I think, if you really don't mind, I will take that paperwork now."

I retreat in turn. "Right. Of course." I want to die a little. "I'll just go get it right now."

I turn to head for the stairs. My steps falter a little. Something inside me is flashing, a beacon of something, telling me to do something else.

Do something differently. I don't know what something it should be. Give up my dreams of the museum? Betray Mitchell, the one gallerist who believed in me from the beginning? Burn the only bridge that leads back to my life before? I start for the stairs. One foot in front of the other. Get the paperwork. Say good-bye. Go to bed. Get up and get the hell out of here.

I close myself in my room. Lean against the door. *Get the paperwork. Go home.*

Instead I stand there perfectly still, wishing there was another way.

I don't know how long I stand there frozen before I hear a mighty racket in the foyer. I turn and step out into the hallway, head for the stairs. Before I can reach the first landing, a loud voice calls up to me. "Lily?" It is Colleen, breathless, shouting. "Lily, are you in here? You must be in here, we've looked everywhere else. Come quick, Lily!"

She starts up the stairs. "There you are. Oh, thank goodness. Well, wait, no. This is bad."

"Slow down, Colleen," I say patiently.

"If you're here, and your car isn't. Oh, this is bad."

"What do you mean my car isn't?" I say warily. "My car is in the parking lot in front of the inn with a flat tire."

"No, it's not. It was, but—oh, hi, Ben!" Ben has come up the stairs, most likely to see what Colleen is caterwauling about. "Guess what? Lily's car is being stolen. Right this second!"

Thirteen

My car isn't being stolen. It is being towed. To a garage. Where they sell tires.

Ben explains, on a patient sigh, that he texted his brother Erick, part-time mechanic and tow truck driver, when I went up to my room. Told him about my predicament and how eager I was to leave town. One of Erick's guys was in the truck plowing out a parking lot two doors down, so he came right away, hitched up the car, and that's what Colleen mistook for grand theft auto.

Colleen has the good manners to look sheepish. "They sell tires at Hutchinson Auto?" she asks. "But when I needed to replace the tires on my truck, I had to drive to the Sears in Duluth."

"Probably because it wasn't urgent, or you needed a certain kind of tires. Erick only has a small selection of patch jobs, but that probably includes something that will work on Lily's car in an emergency."

I look from Colleen to Ben and back. She is giving him a crazy buggy-eyed glare as though she's trying to bend his brain like a spoon. Ben is looking at her like she's a moron and shaking his head.

Then, in his stone-cold way, he tells her, "Perhaps you don't understand, Colleen. Lily is *very eager* to get back to Chicago. Like, *emergency* eager."

I say nothing. Colleen says, "It doesn't sound very safe to drive all the way to Chicago on a secondhand tire."

"Probably safer than her driving on the imaginary one Hutch was going to get her tomorrow from Duluth. While he worked at the bar at the same time."

Colleen falters for a beat, and then says, "Shit. He said he was going to go the minute he could get up there after the storm. I didn't think about the bar."

"Maybe I could run the bar for him?" I say dryly. I feel like I've wandered into a Stoppard play.

"Ooh, good idea," says Colleen, oblivious. "What do you think, Ben?"

"Great idea," he replies, matching my tone. "Or better yet, I'll run the bar, since I'm his son and all, and Lily can teach my AP comp sci classes at school."

Colleen tilts her head. "You aren't being very helpful, Mr. Hutchinson. Maybe if I had a word with your mom . . ."

Ben holds up a hand. "We don't need to go nuclear. Believe me, I want Lily to get home as badly as anyone," he says. "Did you know she has a boyfriend who is expecting her back?"

"I'm right here," I say with a little wave. "I'm sorry I didn't explain, Ben. It's a long story."

"I'm getting the idea that most of the things you do have a long story to go with them."

"And I'm getting the idea that your Dr. Jekyll and Mr. Hyde thing can really give a girl whiplash."

"Now, now," Colleen says. "Lily, Ben did a nice thing for you, getting your tire situation taken care of. Thanks to him, you can leave first thing tomorrow. And Ben, Lily really does have extenuating circumstances. We can fill you in over dinner at the bistro—"

"NO," Ben and I say at the same exact moment.

Colleen shrugs dramatically, as if to say, *See, you guys are of one mind.*

"Here, Ben," I say, thrusting over the annulment renewal paperwork. Then I turn to Colleen. "I'm hungry and I want French fries."

"Thanks," he says, also to Colleen. "Enjoy your fries. I'm going to go get a beer."

"Not at the bistro," I suggest.

"Agreed."

"Good."

"Good."

"Oh, for heaven's sakes," says Colleen merrily. "Like an old married couple. Well, it's wine o'clock, honey," she says to me like this hasn't been the most uncomfortable and confusing exchange her inn has ever seen. "Let's get uncorking!"

A glass of really good Zinfandel heals a lot of the wounds from the uncomfortable encounter, or "Ben-counter" as Jenny is gleefully calling it. Perfectly steamed and sauced mussels and a shared tin of crispy fries with sriracha aioli heals the rest. By the end of the meal we are all laughing over the flat tire, the tow truck, and Ben's ruffled feathers. That's all they are, I'm quite sure. It was only a few days ago that he was barking at me about divorce from his front yard while wielding a hatchet. A little nostalgic smooching in the gentle snowfall doesn't change the fundamental fact that this guy does not like me.

Fortified, I pass the rest of dinner telling the girls about my life in Chicago, such as it is. I tell them about Red or Dead, which they think is a brilliant and ballsy business concept, and about Renee's white-shoe firm where I can often be found sullying the otherwise impeccable waiting room among Chicago's wealthiest and most disgruntled spouses, and about the pop-up craft fairs where I tried, usually unsuccessfully, to sell my art before landing a gallery. I tell them about the great Affair of the Thirty Thousand Dollar Potatoes—the one time Mitchell ever had a genuinely emotional reaction to anything, the only time I've seen his calm shattered. He brought in, from D.C. at no small expense, an extremely high-profile experiential sculptor, who worked by throwing huge clay pots, carving pornographic images into them in relief, and then smashing them with a sledgehammer in order to make mosaics from the resulting shards. Mitchell commissioned this guy, again at no small expense, for a show of six works, which the artist refused to show him in advance and installed in the gallery under the cover of darkness early on the morning before the opening. But instead of mosaics, the works were six different arrangements of grocery store baking potatoes, held together in various vaguely sexual poses with toothpicks. The title of the collection was "No Smoking on Television."

When Jenny hears this she claps her hands together and says, "Of course!"

"You read about it?"

"I did. Unlike you, I cannot keep off the art blogs."

"Some of the critics loved the potatoes. Especially when they sprouted."

"Yet Mitchell was still upset?" Jenny asks, faux innocently.

"The artist wouldn't shellack them. Part of his rider—no use of petrochemicals. The potatoes molded quickly under the lights. Returned to the earth from whence they cameth. The artist actually used the word 'cameth' in his statement. Mitchell took a bath on the affair, and the artist, once back in D.C., immediately went back to the clay-pot thing, making his regular gallerist a fortune."

Jenny nods her head knowingly. "Art."

Colleen shakes her head less knowingly. "Is it any wonder no one thinks the emperor is wearing any clothes?"

"Half the time, he's not," I say.

"I'm seeing early interest in your works," Jenny says out of nowhere. "You, at least, don't seem to be standing in front of a crowd naked."

I color. "I feel like I am most of the time."

"That's your job," she says. "Mine is to disabuse you of that notion. I had three people in today to look at your work."

"What? Really?"

"Exclusive showings. Demanded by important local buyers. Retired bankers, all. They always want to think they're the first to know."

My stomach clenches. I was in the back studio all day painting a few inches of dark-bright-gray-neon-blue sky, and meanwhile a few hundred feet away, my work was being appraised by a stream of collectors. I try not to ask what they said.

"They were impressed," Jenny says into the void.

"Don't tell me anything," I say, waving my hands in front of my ears. "I can only survive this business if I don't ever think about the actual *business*. I have to just trust people to take care of it for me."

Jenny looks to Colleen. They share something, one of their secret looks. But neither says a word to me. "What?" I demand.

"Oh, nothing," says Jenny. "Just . . . perhaps that's how you got into this situation in the first place."

"I'm not in a situation," I say, trying to sound unaffected. "I was, and then I caught a few lucky breaks, and now I'm not. Situation, unsituated."

"Oh! Well, then," says Colleen good-naturedly. "In that case, would you prefer to pay your hotel bill in cash?"

"Your point has been taken," I say. "But you've been in no hurry to get me out."

Colleen shrugs. "It's the only way I can feel semi-honest about keeping your five-figure painting. The more nights you stay, the less I feel like I ripped you off." The bistro bill arrives just then, and Colleen snatches it up, slides a card in the wallet, and hands it right back to the server. "Speaking of."

"I hope you're running a tab," I say. "At the rate I'm moving, I very well may use up my surplus."

Again, Colleen and Jenny exchange meaningful glances. They are starting to make me nervous, and I'm about to press them to disclose when my cell rings. I look at the screen.

"Oh, crap! It's Mitchell. I forgot to tell him I wasn't coming tonight. He must be worried sick."

"Must be," says Jenny. Even though I have already hit the answer button, there is no missing her sarcasm.

"Mitchell!" I say into the phone, while excusing myself from the table and heading for a quiet hallway by the bathrooms. "I'm so sorry I didn't call."

"Hm? Oh, did you say you would?"

"I said I was going to be back in Chicago last night, remember? I got held up."

"Where?"

"In Minnow Bay. I got a flat tire."

"My goodness. That town sounds like a living nightmare," he says.

Strangely, I bristle at that. "Well, I'll be back on the road tomorrow," I tell him, ignoring the twinge. "Leaving before noon, hopefully. Should we have dinner?"

"On a Tuesday night?" he asks, like I just told him to tattoo my name on his neck.

"Uh . . ."

"Sure, Lily, that would be lovely. I can't wait to see you. Special weekday date. Why not?"

Does he always talk to me this way? Like the simplest request is asking for the moon? I shake my head. The wine seems to be making me touchy. "What's up, then?" I say. "If that's not why you called?"

"Just some news I couldn't wait to share."

My mind flashes back to the museum—it hasn't been far from my thoughts all day. "The exhibition company?"

"What exhibition company? Oh, right, right. Your thing. You've got to learn some patience, Lily. I'll get it all carved in stone in due time. No, this is about my upstairs neighbor. The ancient blowhard with the stomping problem?"

Mitchell has, to his own mind, the world's loudest upstairs neighbors in his chic North Shore condo building. It's actually a little old man who lives alone, and granted, he does stomp a bit, but Mitchell also complains that the guy's toilet flushes too loudly, and I don't think that's actually a thing.

"What about him?"

"He's dead!" Mitchell announces gleefully. "Terrible, of course. But his apartment is up for grabs!"

"Oh, wow. That's too bad. All those grandkids."

"No, no, don't you see, Lily? His apartment is directly over mine. It's perfect!"

I pause, confused. Then I think I start to understand. "Mitchell, I'm touched you thought of me, but there's no way I can afford your building, even with all the good news you told me this morning."

There is silence on the line. Finally Mitchell laughs, and his laugh is so smooth and charming, it almost feels greasy. "You're adorable, Lily, but you can barely afford a cardboard box in the Chicago real estate market. Besides, I already bought it. It's a dream come true. I'm finally getting my duplex!"

"Oh! Oh." Slowly, slowly my brain catches up. Damn you, Zinfandel. "Wonderful news. I'm so happy for you."

"Be happy for *us*," he says grandly. "This changes everything, you know."

"It does?"

"Of course it does," he says. "Have you been drinking? Never mind, we can talk about it when you get back. When will that be?"

I'm pretty sure I told him five minutes ago, but I repeat myself. "Hoping for tomorrow late. Dinner?"

"Of course. Come over to my place. We can talk about remodeling plans. What do you think of his and hers walk-in closets?"

My eyes widen in surprise. "Sounds lovely," I say. "Mitchell, I . . ." I'm cut off by a beeping sound coming through the phone.

"Yes—me too," he says before I can finish my thought. "Other line—I've got to take it!"

"Ok, well, uh—" I mumble before I realize I'm on a dead line.

When I get back to the table, I am still staring in confusion at my phone. But as I look up I get that icky, you-are-being-talked-about feeling you have when you realize that an animated conversation has ended abruptly at the exact moment you came into earshot. I try to dismiss it.

"Sorry," I say into the silence, but there is a question mark in my voice. "He just . . ." I struggle as I try to decide on the fly if I should tell the girls about this surprising turn of events with Mitchell, or demand to know what they were just talking about, or what. "It was just, um, a check-in," I finish.

Colleen smiles so broadly I question my momentary distrust. "Was it about the museum show?" she asks. "That is so exciting. Jenny and I were just saying we would drive down when it opens and surprise you. But I can't do surprises, obviously. So can we come?"

I laugh, filled with relief. They were only talking about the museum showing. "I would like nothing better. But it wasn't about the museum. I'm not really sure what it was about, actually." I furrow my brow.

"Maybe he just misses you?"

"Maybe." Though he said not a word about missing me. But he did just ask me to live with him, didn't he? Which should make me happy, but actually only makes me terribly suspicious. When I was evicted, Mitchell wouldn't hear of me moving in. Now that he is taking on a second mortgage, he suddenly wants a roommate? Or is it about the museum breakthrough? Or . . . could it be as innocuous as missing me while I'm here, and realizing he wants us to be together more?

"You look like you might enjoy one last glass of wine," Jenny says, and pours out the rest of the bottle evenly among the three of us.

I nod gratefully as she does. "Do you guys ever have that weird feeling where you can't tell if someone genuinely cares about you or if you are being used?"

Jenny and Colleen pause for a moment, both with glasses aloft. Then they both answer at once, "No."

"So it's just me?" I say sadly into my own wine.

"'Fraid so," says Colleen. "Oh, speaking of being used, though. Can I prevail on you to drive me to an appointment tomorrow? Early, while they're working on your tire at the garage. We'll take my truck. I need a tiny little procedure, but they suggested I get someone else to drive me home just in case I need to take some pain medication. No big deal."

"Are you okay?" I say, concerned, forgetting Mitchell's confusing phone call instantly.

"Perfectly fine. It's basically nothing bigger than a mole removal."

"And I have to do another showing in the morning," says Jenny. "Or I'd take her."

"Of course," I say. "I'm happy to help. But you're sure you're okay?"

"Perfectly sure. And now I'll have a friend along so I'll be even more okay."

"Well, I'm glad to do it," I say. Because, yes, I do think of Colleen as a friend, and it's nice that she does as well. Jenny, I am not so sure about. The gallery business has me a little turned around. Is she a predator, as Mitchell suggests? Or a tender-hearted sucker for drowning artists? Or just a businesswoman, running a nice gallery that caters to rich vacationers, trying to make a good living doing what she loves? I want to trust her. But I don't. Not yet.

Colleen, though, with her quiet disapproval of Ben's bad behavior, coupled with her complete acceptance of mine, has won me over completely. Add in her generosity in letting me stay at the inn, her sweet sunny spirit, and her uncanny ability to take everyone she meets exactly as they are, and I realize I will be quite sad to say good-bye tomorrow. Back home, even I have to admit that I am surrounded by confusing relationships with people who push and pull with no discernible rhyme or reason. Here in Minnow Bay, the women I meet only seem to want me closer.

It's enough to make me fantasize about a different kind of life.

One that feels entirely out of reach.

Fourteen

It is beginning to get through my thick skull that Colleen is trickier than she first appears. My big clue? The fact that we've been driving for an hour and are not yet at her doctor's office. Another hint? In that hour's time, we've passed a Farm and Fleet with the following emblazoned on the front:

GROCERIES PHARMACY BAIT FEED TIRES

Tires. And we are nowhere near Duluth. Rather, we've gone in the opposite direction, and I've learned a bit about the geography of Minnow Bay, and the North Woods. While remote in many ways, I believe the case has been somewhat overstated for Colleen's own interests. Namely: matchmaking.

And another misrepresentation—the routine nature of this medical appointment. I know, because we do not arrive at a doctor's office when we finally reach true civilization after an hour and a half of driving. We arrive at a hospital.

"This is it!" Colleen chirps merrily. "They validate parking. Just go to the ramp."

Though Colleen seems in perfectly good health, she did insist I drive both ways, and now, from the driver's seat, I look at her carefully, studying her for signs of . . . what? Dying-ness?

"Colleen . . ." I say, warily. "What exactly is going on here?"

"What do you mean?"

"I mean, why are we at the hospital? They don't do mole removals at the hospital."

"Did I say it was a mole removal?" she asks innocently.

I think back. No, technically, she said it was *like* a mole removal. Apparently the "like" was literal, and not the usual verbal tic. "I suppose not," I admit. "What is it, exactly, we're doing here?"

"Oh, it's just a hysterosalpingography. No biggie."

"A hystero what now?" I can't even remember the word she just said two seconds ago. "That sounds horrifying. Plus, we're at a hospital. How is that not a biggie?"

"It's a hospital *and* clinic," she says, gesturing to the signage above the building.

"What is it exactly you're having done?"

"A hysterosalpingography. I told you."

"And what is a hystero-sal-ping-og-raphy?" I stutter.

"It's a test for infertile women," she says nonchalantly.

Silently, I negotiate the twists and turns of the parking garage. "I see," I say when I think to speak. The closet in her attic quarters blooms into my mind. But now instead of yellow and green pastels, it takes on a dark, murky feel, as though someone has cried all the color out of each little onesie.

"They shoot some dye in my hoo-hah, I think. Then they take pictures of where the dye goes. To find out why I can't get pregnant."

"I'm sorry," I say. I feel intrusive, and want to back away from this. Want her to stop talking. "It's none of my business."

"If I didn't want to tell you, I wouldn't have made you drive me here. It's no state secret: I can't conceive. I need to find out why."

I put the car in park. "I'm sorry," I say again. Out of the corner of my eye I look at her face. It's neutral. Bland, even. Not the look of a woman brought low by the trials of infertility. Or is this *exactly* what that looks like?

"Thank you," Colleen says, and unbuckles herself. "Just FYI, Jenny doesn't know."

"What?"

"I told her it *was* a mole removal. She doesn't get babies; she doesn't have the mom muscles. Or not yet, at least. Hurry up, my appointment is in ten minutes."

I hustle to pull on my hat and gloves and follow her to the parking elevator. "So it *is* actually a state secret?"

"Well. Yes. A little bit." She is moving at the speed of light, whether to avoid my questions or lose me in the twisting pathways, I'm not sure.

"Slow down! I'm totally confused."

"I told you, appointment in ten minutes. Oops, no, five. Hustle up."

I race after Colleen, who clearly has spent her fair share of time in this clinic/hospital. She knows exactly where to go, to a waiting room absolutely jam-packed with stressed-looking couples, holding hands and whispering to each other. I trail behind, slack-jawed.

"This doesn't make any sense."

"Why?" she asks as she waves hello to the receptionist, swipes an ID card at a computer kiosk, signs something with the tip of her finger.

I pause, trying to pluck the right words from a garden of thorns.

"Because I'm single?" she asks, doing it for me. "Single women have kids." She starts circling the waiting room.

"Slow down," I tell her. "Sit down. Start from the beginning. Talk to me like I just joined this conversation a week ago."

I hear the words out of my mouth and furrow my brow. "I did only join this conversation a week ago," I say more for my benefit than hers. In that time we've talked a lot, spent a lot of time together. In that time, without my noticing, we've become friends.

My new friend stops in her tracks and spins around on me. She drops the card she was holding into her handbag and lets it hang off her shoulder. Takes my right hand in her left and my left in her right. We are a two-woman game of ring around the rosy. Then she squeezes my hands hard and her bland face falls away.

"I'm scared," she says. "I don't feel good about this."

I open my mouth to ask one thousand questions at once. Why are you doing it? What is it that scares you? How did you get here? How can I help? But all that comes out is, "Okay. I'm here."

Her eyes fog over with tears. "It's a very lonely thing, infertility."

I am surprised when she says this. I know nothing about infertility but I know about Minnow Bay and I know it is very hard to be lonely there. She could have chosen among so many old friends and neighbors to come up here with her, instead of me, a woman she's only known for a week. The town is full of people who love her and would want to help in any way they could.

But then I think of the special loneliness I feel whenever a certain special sort of mom-moment comes up. An event, a moment, a problem, that *before,* no matter how old you were, you would bring only to your mother. And then *after,* you only hold inside.

This, I have to imagine, is a mom-thing.

"Colleen O'Donnell?" calls a CNA in a purple outfit before we can even sit down. "Colleen?"

In an instant, Colleen's face wipes back to neutral. She lets go of one hand but not the other, yanking me to the exam threshold where the CNA stands. "Hi, Janet," she says. "This is my friend Lily. She's going to be on call in case the doctor needs supervision."

Janet laughs good-naturedly. "Sounds like a good plan," she jokes. "Do you need to empty your bladder?"

Just like that, Colleen vanishes into the bowels of the clinic without another word. I wait, uncomfortable and confused, in the insipid pink waiting room. The seats are that vinyl-fabric hybrid that you cannot slouch in without falling to the ground, so I sit up straight and put my feet flat on the floor like I am a Catholic school student trying not to be called on.

To my left and right and straight ahead are couples, waiting, clutching hands, whispering. On the table next to me I find, perversely, a magazine called *Modern Pregnancy.* On my phone, I type "H-Y-S-T" because that is Latin for lady parts, as far as I can remember, and Google autofills for me with, among other things, "HSG test for infertility." That's got to be it. Oh, Google. If you weren't so helpful, I'd be creeped out right now. I tap and tap until I get to a reputable website, and start reading.

As near as I can understand after reading two articles and watching a slightly horrifying video, an HSG is when they inject you with some dye that shows up on an X-ray. Then they take a bunch of pictures to follow the dye backward to the ovaries and see if it gets where it's supposed to go. If it gets stopped at the fallopian tubes, it turns back, and that means tubal blocks. And then, depending on where the tubal block is, that may mean conceiving the old-fashioned way is out of the question.

The site helpfully explains that this is not a first step for diagnosing infertility. Not even close. In fact, if this is accurate, before I met Colleen, she might have spent a year, maybe two, trying other methods of conception. And all of this without a prospective father by her side. I am perplexed. Why would she put herself through this? Why would she want to be a single mother?

Will she tell me about all that, I wonder, when she gets done with her appointment? And, if she doesn't, am I allowed to ask?

A woman shifts her position on her own hard waiting room sofa. She leans into me, her husband engrossed in a *Sports Illustrated.* "The wait times here are awful," she says to me.

I nod, as though I have the first idea.

"It's not so bad," she goes on. "The HSG."

I look at her in surprise.

"Your phone. I'm sorry. I don't mean to pry. It's just that we're all in this together, you know?"

I don't, but I can tell that wouldn't be a kind thing to say. "Mmmhmm." Then, after a moment's thought, I add, "Did you have one? An HSG?"

"Oh, yes. Yes, actually it came up clear. No blockage. Well, there was blockage on my left side. I thought, great! One whole pathway for eggs to come down, still half-working! But it turns out the left side is the only one making viable eggs. The other side makes miscarriages. I mean, come on, right? And then I spent a year figuring that out. Talk about heartbreak hotel. Now I'm ancient but they're still going to attempt to harvest."

"To harvest?"

"Can't you tell? Look at these jowls. I'm so full of estrogen just looking at a muffin adds five pounds to my face. I'm going to need a chin bra soon." She laughs anxiously. More loneliness, I think.

"Anyway, today's the day. Wish me luck."

"Good luck," I say almost automatically. Then I pause. "No, really. It's . . . it sounds like it's been so hard."

She rolls her lips together. I see tension in her eyes, her shoulders. I wonder if she too has a closet full of dreams unfulfilled. "It's better when I come in here," she says. "I waited so long, and I feel like it's all my fault most of the time. It's helpful knowing I'm not the only one, you know?"

I set my phone on my lap and reach for her hand. "You're not," I tell her, and keep on waiting for Colleen.

An hour later, she reappears on Janet's arm. Janet deposits my friend next to me and tells me they gave her a mild sedative to prevent uterine cramping during the test. I say, "How did it go?" and Janet replies, "You'll have to ask her," and walks away just like that.

I look at Colleen's face. It is soft and dull and uninformative. Rather than press her for information, I lead her, in quiet silence, back to her car. Help her into the backseat, where she can sit with her legs up, her back against the window. She is quiet. Her eyes are blank.

But then I get in, and buckle my seat belt, and turn the key in the ignition, and softly, almost inaudibly, the tears begin. I look into the rearview mirror as I back out, then quickly look right and left, pretending I didn't see.

"It's not going to happen," Colleen tells me after about thirty seconds. She is not weeping or wailing. But the tears are clogging her throat, and her words are thick.

"What do you mean?"

"Tubal blockage. Or some such bullshit." I don't think I've ever heard her use a curse word before. "It's the end of the road. Literally."

"Are you sure? Don't you need a second opinion?"

"I *need* to stop getting injected and poked and tested," she says. "I'm not up to this anymore."

"Oh, honey," I say, because I'm not sure what else to say. I think of the woman in the waiting room, a year further into the process than Colleen and still quite hopeful under it all. "Don't make any decisions right now." The sentence has an echo to it I can't place at first. And then I remember. I am sitting with my mother in her oncologist's office after she laid out all the possible treatments for what she termed as "palliative care." "Don't make any decisions right now" is what doctors say to patients who are screwed.

"I'm not making any decisions," says Colleen now. "I mean, I already made my decision, last week. If this test went one way, I was going to keep trying. If it went the other, then I was going to start adopting."

"And it went the adopting way?" I ask, catching her eyes in the mirror.

She nods. "I don't know why I'm crying. It's six of one, half a dozen of the other."

I think of the packed waiting room and the parade of couples, all trying to do what she wanted to do. "You're crying because you're human, and disappointment is human."

"What is it about me that makes me want to have *my own* child so badly?"

"It's not just you. The clinic was packed with other people with the same dream."

"Other *couples.* Not other people."

"That's true," I admit. In the time I was there, I didn't see another single woman in the clinic. Don't single women try *not* to get pregnant? I know that's been my main aim in life, at least in the sex department.

"And that's the thing," she goes on, her voice gaining strength. "As hard as this rigamarole has been, it's harder still because it's not the *right* way to do things. The doctors think I'm a lunatic. They tell me to come back when I'm married."

"What? Not really!" I am ready to have any such doctors disbarred, or whatever you do when you hate a doctor.

"Not really. Not in those words. But they do suggest that parenting is hard enough when there are two of you, and you need a partner to survive the rigors of IVF, and so on and so forth."

I consider my next words carefully. "It sounds like you agree."

"I guess even a little taste of infertility treatment is all I need to be dissuaded," she says sadly. "I feel like such a quitter."

I look at her again in the rear view mirror. She does not look like a quitter to me.

"Colleen, can I ask you a rude question?"

"Of course."

"Why do you want to get pregnant? You're single."

She sighs heavily. "Exactly. Exactly, exactly, exactly."

I move my eyes straight ahead, as though my mind is one hundred percent on driving. It is not.

"You're going to wait me out?" she says, when I don't say anything.

"I'm interested. I want to know, genuinely."

She sniffs. "I'm not sure I want to talk about it."

"Okay," I say. "No problem." But it *is* a problem, to me. She is still brokenhearted and I still want to help her. I want to know how to help.

We drive quietly in her teary silence. I turn on the radio, find a classical station. They break from music, do the weather. More precipitation, they warn in those cozy public-radio voices. Up to a foot.

As if on cue, it starts to snow. I keep driving the speed limit, but now the wipers are on intermittently and the blacktop is turning white.

Five miles go by in silence. Then ten. The flurry is moving with us, not accumulating. Each mile is new snow, always crystalline, always transformative. I sneak another peek at Colleen. She is sleeping. The sedative, the crying, or both. I try to put together everything I know. She wants to have a baby. She wants the baby more than the husband you're supposed to get in order to get the baby.

That's not so crazy. Or maybe it is? But it's what she wanted. Wanted a lot, from what I can tell.

I haven't given a lot of thought to babies. I have thought I might like to be a mother, when it's come up in conversation. Or rather, that I might be good at it. But when Mitchell told me he was never going to have children, it wasn't much of a blip on my radar. I figured either he'd change his mind, I'd change mine, or we'd never get married. Honestly, I never thought Mitchell would marry me in a million years, so it was largely a moot point.

Colleen, though, knew what she wanted, and didn't care about getting someone else on board to get it. That's beautiful. That's brave. I look over at her again. She is drooling on the seat belt. I grab my phone and ask Siri for the number to the Cho Gallery. Siri obliges and I call Jenny.

"Jenny?" I whisper into the phone.

"Huh? Speak up? Is that Lily?"

"I can't talk much louder. Colleen is sleeping in the backseat."

"What? Why is she—oh, right. Good news or bad news?"

"About the mole?" I ask, thinking quickly.

"What mole? About the fallopian tubes."

My mouth falls open. "You know?"

"Of course I know. God, she must think I'm a moron. When, in fact, I'm actually a snoop."

"Does everyone know?" I ask, my Minnow Bay paranoia carrying me away.

"Of course not. This is private."

"But not so private you didn't find out," I say, gazing out on the snowy, empty highway.

"What can I say?" replies Jenny. "She's my oldest, dearest friend. I can't seem to leave her alone."

I think of the way I pester Renee. Ask her nosy questions all the time. Refuse to go away though she shows absolutely no signs of wanting me around. I nod in understanding. "She thinks you don't get it."

"I don't get it. But you didn't answer, good news or bad?"

"Bad."

Jenny swears for about two straight minutes.

"It doesn't seem fair," I say, when she's wrapped up her tirade with a final drawn-out F-word.

"It's not fair," she says. "She's already shelled out a fortune on this nonsense. Do you know how much good sperm costs these days?"

I cough politely. "No idea."

"A lot."

I think once more of the closet full of baby stuff in Colleen's apartment. I didn't know what it was when I first saw it but now I know: it is an accumulation of hope. "How long has she been at this?"

"Two years. She told me about it in the beginning, but then said she changed her mind. Big fat liar. I didn't believe her for a second. And even if I did, I see her almost every day. And once a month I see her brokenhearted."

"Huh. Once a month for two straight years," I say, thinking of the disappointments stacking up. Does she test every month on one of those pee sticks? Wait to get her period? Take her temperature daily, three times a day, to find out when she's ovulating? Rush into a clinic when she's ready? How does this process work? How does she find out when it doesn't?

I remember my one and only pregnancy scare, back in college, back with Nic. Of course, I was so into him then, it wasn't really a scare. It was more like a global shift in thinking, a three-minute wait time, and then a resumption of my original way of thinking. First comes love, then comes marriage.

Except not for Colleen. She already had her global shift in thinking, two years ago, and stuck with it.

And what now? Does she stay in her apartment all day crying once a month? Put in a tampon, pull up her pants, and give herself a pep talk? Scream in anger and throw the test across the room?

"It doesn't seem fair," I say again.

"Right?" says Jenny. "It's utter bullshit. And for what? She should have gotten a dog."

I smile sadly. "I can't imagine why she stopped filling you in," I say lightly.

"Shit, you're right," she says, contrite. "I've got to do better. Pity party tonight? My place?"

I want to do that more than anything, but I'm supposed to be heading to Chicago in an hour. To talk to Mitchell about his sudden grand apartment plans. But do I really want to know what they are? Maybe it would be better for us to live apart, like he said before. Maybe he needs some time to think this through.

Besides, he doesn't really want to see me on a Tuesday night. He wants to finish reading *TIME* magazine with a glass of high-end brandy and delivery sushi. Ugh, do I even still like this person? I have nothing kind to say about him lately.

But. The museum exhibition. The misunderstandings. The offer to live together. The ugly fact that after two years of dating this man with little to no emotional reward, this is the absolutely one hundred percent wrong time to decide to kick him to the curb. In fact, this is the first time in a long time he's shown much of an interest.

Maybe absence makes the heart grow fonder.

In which case, no reason to discontinue the absence prematurely.

"I'm in," I say. "If she's up for it. One more night in Minnow Bay before I blow this pop stand."

Jenny laughs. Honestly. "We'll see," she says. "I like what you're working on in the studio. Why don't you finish that up before you head out."

I shake my head though she can't see it. "No offense, Jenny, but I know you're full of it. There's nothing to like. It's just a blue canvas." If only that were true. If only it weren't the manifestation of the first creative spark I've had in months.

"Maybe," she says cryptically. "Maybe it represents something much bigger."

She can't know, I think. I haven't breathed a word to anyone about my block. Ah. Anyone but Simone. Asked and answered.

"It's just a blue canvas," I say again, knowing now that she knows

I'm lying. "But I would like to keep pursuing it. Do you mind if I borrow some more studio hours later today?"

"Not at all. I'll have a key made for you and put it under your door at the inn."

"Thank you," I say. I am starting to understand what that blue sky is all about, and itching to get it on paper.

"Of course. Let her sleep as long as you can, okay?" says Jenny.

I look at the GPS mounted on Colleen's truck dash. I'm five miles from Minnow Bay now. To the north, if I turn now, I can sightsee around the local chain of lakes. Moose Lake, Lake Orion, Lake Norma, Apple Pie Lake. The names alone are irresistible.

I have my Canon in the backseat just in case. Maybe I'll see something. Something I want to paint.

"Okay," I tell her.

"Take care of my best friend, will ya?"

"I promise. But Jenny?"

"Hm?"

"I have to leave in the morning."

"I know. First thing tomorrow. Without a doubt."

Fifteen

The next morning starts with a mild hangover and a honking horn.

The first is all Jenny's fault. The second, Colleen's.

I hear banging on my door about sixty seconds after the honking starts, and when I open up, wrapped in my quilt, feet going to ice in the cold morning air, Colleen is standing there in flannel plaid jammies looking just as disheveled as I feel. "I'm so sorry! I totally forgot to tell you that Ben is taking you to the mechanic this morning."

I raise my chin at her, ready to complain, but before I lay in, I notice her eyes, as muddy as mine must be from too much wine, plus reddened by tears. "Okay," I say. "Tell him I'll be right down."

"Hurry, okay? He needs to get to school on time."

I rush to get dressed, picking yesterday's pants up off the floor. I wish I could just stay in this quilt. Instead I pull on a men's sweater that appeared in my room yesterday after I mentioned the permanent chill setting into my bones. It is well-worn wool, at once soft and scratchy, in the prettiest shade of navy blue. I jam my feet into boots and race down the stairs.

Ben's SUV, a big boxy thing that is meant for getting up snowy driveways and out of muddy ditches, has been scraped of snow only in the most perfunctory of ways. There are portholes in the front dash and side windows, but the back is still almost impenetrable. He could probably strangle me in the backseat on Lake Street and no one would see a thing. If they did, they'd probably take his side anyway.

"Hi," I say as I slide into the passenger seat. "Hi."

He looks at me, his lips set in a deep frown. "What happened to your hair?"

I reach up and find it is sticking up in stalks. The reality of bed-head. "Oy. They didn't tell me you were coming. I just woke up." I look in the mirror of the sun visor, and then avert my eyes in horror. "I'm surprised Colleen let me see you like this."

"Me too. They're trying to set us up," he says matter-of-factly.

I nod. "I know. They're not coy about it. I think they worry about you. They say you're a hermit."

He sighs wearily. "Buckle up."

I do. He pulls out of the inn's Lake Street parking, then drives forward in silence. Across River Street, he turns onto First Street, then crosses Aspen Avenue. Then he pulls to the left and puts the truck in park.

"What is it? What's wrong?" I ask, confused about why he stopped the truck.

"We're here."

I crane my head around. "You've got to be kidding me. Colleen made you pick me up and drive me three blocks?"

"Like I said," he starts. "They're trying to set us up."

I shake my head in befuddlement. "I'm sorry," I say in defeat. "This is a strange town."

"S'okay," he tells me. "It's on my way to work." He raises his eyes from his lap, holding my gaze for a moment. His lips part. He's telling me something in this look, this silence. Trouble is, I have no idea what.

"You know. The girls. They're not wrong," he begins.

I frown. About what? About setting us up? About him being a hermit? I shake my head.

"But they know I'm leaving," I say. "They know about my boyfriend."

He exhales deeply. "I don't understand it," he says. "I don't understand you."

I force a laugh to lighten the mood. "What's to understand? I'm a stereotypical scatterbrained artist with money problems, who accidentally stayed married to a stranger for ten years, and came up here to get unmarried."

Ben shakes his head. "If that's all true, then why are you still here?"

Uncomfortable, I drop my eyes to the spot where his upturned hand wraps around the gearshift on the steering column. His bare wrists strike me as strangely beautiful, maybe because it's so cold in this town, and bare hands are such a rarity. Or maybe because they're obviously so strong. With the truck in park, his arm is raised enough to drop the sleeve of his coat down, showing a stripe of tanned skin between where his gloves must normally end and his sleeves start. I can just see the underside of his wrist. Three veins show through the sinew, then disappear under the callus of his palm.

"Ben," I say. "I . . ." When we kissed, that night in the snow, that same hand I'm looking at now was in my hair. I can remember what that wrist felt like against the nape of my neck. Without thinking, I raise my own hand to the spot where my chin turns into jaw. His hands are so big. My lips feel very dry.

He moves his hand from the shifter, wipes it on his jeans. I realize how warm it is inside his truck. That's all it is. Too warm.

I reach for the door handle. Something oppressive is sitting on my chest. It's not attraction, exactly, unless we are using the physics definition. It is a force stopping me from getting out of this truck.

"Lily," Ben says. I turn around, face him. What would I do if it weren't for my other life? If it weren't for the dreams and history waiting for me back home?

His hand slowly loosens on his leg. I think he is reaching for me. I find I am no longer breathing.

There is a knock on the glass beside me.

We both jump. I turn quickly and see nothing but a blind of white in the window. When I buzz it down, clumps of uncleared snow tumble in on me.

"You must be Lily," says a younger, blonder version of Ben Hutchinson as he uses a free hand to scoop snow out of the window frame so I can lower the window the rest of the way. Then he leans around me, and says, "Hey, bro." His eyebrows wiggle at Ben a little bit. It's not a warm greeting. I feel I've been assessed and come up lacking. Or maybe Ben has?

"And you're Erick, I presume?" I ask.

"Yep," is all he says back. The word has three syllables at least.

"Thanks for your help on the tow and everything. I'm looking forward to getting on the road today." I move to get out of the truck, but Erick holds a hand up.

"Don't thank me yet. I got the new tire on, but when I went to park it in the lot, it wouldn't turn over. Gave it a jump and the oil light came right on, bam. When's the last time you had the oil changed?"

I say nothing, because I have no idea. All I hear is ringing in my ears. I am never getting home.

"Don'tcha check the levels?"

I stare blankly.

Erick sighs. "There's a Jiffy Lube sticker on the windshield that says you were due for a change five thousand miles ago. Sound right?"

I bite my lip.

"Gunky oil, gunky engine. Probably no problem in balmy Illinois. But up here, so damn cold everything turns to sludge. You don't turn it over a couple a days, warm it up, thin it out, and here we are."

Desperately, I turn to Ben. I know nothing about cars. The words Erick just strung together do not mean anything to me. Oil changes, yes. That is something I know about. But knowing and doing . . . these are very different things.

Ben saves me. "Come on, Erick. Bad oil, it should still turn over."

"You stick to computers. I'll do cars."

"But an overnight in the garage didn't warm it up?"

"We had to leave the bays open last night," he tells Ben. I feel like I'm being talked over, but then, I can hardly complain about sexism when I don't know what the hell they're talking about. "Fume problem."

"Yeah, I bet there's a fume problem." Ben says dryly. "Christ, Erick. You work on the county sheriff's car. He could pull in at any moment. Did you ever think of that?"

"Lay off, Mr. Upstanding."

Ben sighs deeply, like an old man. "What you do to your mother."

"Me? At least I'm not a hermit living in squalor."

"How much," I interject, "to fix it?"

Erick rolls his eyes at his brother. "Can't throw money at this problem, much as I'd like to let you. Need a day where it gets over ten degrees. And an oil change; that you *can* pay me for. But I'm not doing anything until you promise never ever to keep driving when the oil light comes on again. Tell her, Ben."

"That's bad," Ben says. "He's right."

"And no matter what the manual says, a car gets over ten years old, you gotta baby the oil situation in cold weather. And top it off between changes. Levels were really low. No one teach you to take care of your car?"

Damn it if I don't start to cry. I scrunch my face inward, try to hold in the tears. *I will not cry in front of any Hutchinson boys,* I silently vow.

But Erick sees my squinched-up face and knows what it means. "Lady, it could have been so much worse. Another day and you'd have burned out the engine. Coulda happened on the way home. Coulda froze to death."

I squinch harder.

"Come on, now, Erick," says Ben. "This isn't the Arctic Circle."

"Happens," Erick says.

"I just . . ." I try, through stifled tears. "I'm such a . . ." I don't know how to finish that sentence. "I can't do . . ." *anything right,* I want to say, but I'm too embarrassed to even say that.

Over my stammers, Erick raises his eyebrows high. He leans into the car. "Ben, you got this, man?" he asks. "I've gotta, um, do something else that's not talking to a crying lady."

"I'm not crying!" I manage to shout. Erick only raises his eyebrows.

From behind me Ben says, "I should come take a look."

"Be my guest," Erick says with a shrug. "It's not rocket science." He looks at me and then adds, ". . . for most people."

I blow my nose loudly into a tissue I find in my purse.

"Erick, come on. She's got to get home today," says Ben. "You guys can't warm it up in there for a couple of hours and—"

"No," I say to Ben, stilling him with a hand waved in his direction. "It's okay." I take a deep breath. "Erick, you do whatever it is you need to do, whenever you need to do it, and call the inn when it's done. Ben, look at the time." I gesture to the dashboard clock. "You need to get to school. I can walk back from here." I slide out of the truck before anyone can protest, forcing Erick out of the path of the swinging door. "Thanks for the help," I say as I walk off into the cold, leaving the Hutchinson boys behind me in confusion. "Both of you. I'll be fine."

Two weeks ago, when I told Renee I had been evicted, I told her the universe was trying to tell me something. She laughed and said the universe was trying to tell me to pay my bills. She was right. Evictions, legal snafus, broken-down cars—these aren't bizarre twists of fate guiding my path. These are the natural consequences of my complete failure to get my life together.

I think of Colleen, my age, motherless like me, unlucky in love and now in health too, but nevertheless running her own business, starting her own family, knowing what she wants and figuring out how to get it. Not frozen in a time ten years past when everything seemed perfect. Not trapped by the whims of a muse who may or may not ever come back. Something tells me she even changes the oil in her car *before* the light comes on.

Well, if Colleen can do that, so can I. Right?

A blast of wind picks me up from behind, pushes me forward. The sky is bright, the air is sweet and cold, the snow is freshly shoveled, the path under my feet is clear.

The problem is, it leads me only as far as the inn.

On the way back, dreading explaining to Colleen that I have to extend my stay yet longer, I stop in the first storefront I pass. It's the diner, an all-day-breakfast sort of joint, and I take a booth by a window and order bacon and eggs, coffee, and a pen. Then I take out my phone, call up my banking app, and look at the facts. To my great surprise, they are heartening. I'm in debt but not in declare-bankruptcy debt. If Jenny is even half-right about the value of the paintings she is selling for me, I could one day be out of debt.

On a napkin I start a running tally of numbers. I could make, when the conditions are perfect and the stars are aligned and I'm not procrastinating like my life depends on it, two paintings a month. That means, if I stop dicking around and get back my mojo, I could support myself painting, for real, no living in dumps, no using my credit cards for groceries, no deferring car maintenance and doctors' visits and teeth cleanings. I wouldn't be rich, but I would be an actual adult.

And, I could be a professional artist for a living.

That is an amazing gift, and I am squandering it.

Well, no more.

If I had my car, I would hop in it with the same energy I had the day I graduated from college. Just like then, I would point it straight toward Chicago, toward my old neighborhood, toward the first apartment with a FOR RENT sign out front. I would start this adult life I have sketched out on this diner napkin immediately, while I can envision it, while I still have a life to go back to. I would deal with Mitchell face-to-face, in a professional manner, with a calculator in hand. I would shake Renee and tell her I want the old Renee back. I would tell my stepbrother I love him but the bitterness has to stop, now. There would be no more elaborate flights of fancy to storybook small towns. No more fecklessness. No more depending on charity from near strangers. No more kissing men I barely know by snowy rivers.

But I don't have a car. So the adult life is going to have to start here. In said storybook small town. With said near strangers. In close proximity to said kissing partner.

And there's absolutely nothing I can do about that.

My first stop after the diner is the local bank. It's a tiny little credit union two doors from the inn, but they have online banking, so I open up an account, deposit the advance from Jenny, and immediately pay my minimum monthly payments on my credit cards. I call my old landlord and leave the scariest message I can muster demanding the swift return of my security deposit and dropping the name of Renee's firm. I send texts to Renee and a few other friends at home who should be—though they aren't letting on if they are—worrying about my whereabouts, to tell them I'll be gone for a while. I punch in a similar message for Mitchell but don't quite hit send. Him, I probably better talk to in person. Later.

Then I go to the gallery. I'm way, way too disheveled at the moment to be seen inside, but I have a key to the studio now, and a camera full of exciting new pictures from my drive yesterday. One in particular has my heart in knots. It's of an old decrepit boathouse that fell in on itself from the weight of ice—maybe this season's, maybe an icy season long past. I want to paint it with a palette of grays that speak of the middle layer of feathers on a nuthatch, a bird I see everywhere on feeders here in town despite the punishing weather. I want there to be some sparkling Carolina blue, some frosty white, and then the boathouse will be nothing but sunlit gray. I want to show the most brilliant hue of gray I can, the iciest white, the most shimmering blue. A few bold stripes of the straight, naked-from-the-waist-down pines, and underneath, three blocks of brilliant color and that is all.

I spend an hour sketching, then two, before I start to get squinty and realize I need a break. I put back on layer upon layer and turn off the pellet stove and, when nothing is exposed but my eyes and the top of my nose, I go back out into the chill for a walk.

The sun is midway through its path, about forty-five degrees above the horizon, making for a sunny side of the street bustling with what I now recognize as the Minnow Bay lunchtime crowd. The snow that fell yesterday was just enough to refresh the whiteness of everything, and trees, railings, street signs—everything has a layer of crushed diamonds atop. At foot speed I look into the windows of a bookstore and see a display of comfort-food cookbooks under a chalkboard sign that reads, COMPLETE HIBERNATION HEADQUARTERS. A yarn store appears after that; it is chock-full of hand-stitched sweaters that look like heaven to wear, and the tops of the windows are draped with long variegated scarves that look like streamers. I go in because one is the dusty lime–to–Kelly green progression of late summer grass I want to capture in my August painting, and find out the scarf is not for sale, but the yarn it's formed from, at just six dollars a ball, is. Yarn in hand, I pass a pastry shop, a closed-for-the-season store that apparently sells nothing but popcorn, and the outfitters where I got these mittens that are currently keeping my hands so blissfully warm. I pass a library, a shuttered gardening store, a realty agency, a church, and a pharmacy. I keep walking for a long time, until I come to the boxy brick high school. Then, ignoring that strange physics I feel for Ben Hutchinson, I turn around and walk back.

When I get to the inn, a cold mess of confusion, Colleen is standing in the foyer, looking posed, hair casually swept up, brown riding boots on, sweater loosely belted about the waist. "Oh," she says as I push the door closed to the chill behind me. "It's just you."

"Who were you expecting?" I ask as I start to pile my woolens on the coatrack.

"New guests. Skiers. The Nordic racing crowd is starting to come in."

"Nordic racing?"

"Mmhmm. Also known as my only paying customers from January through March." She pauses. "Well, I get some skate-skiers too, but not as many since there's less grooming for them in this county."

I nod as though I know what skate-skiing is. "I was beginning to wonder how you stay open in the winter."

"Mostly my business plan involves not accepting art as payment for weeklong stays."

Has it been a week? "It was your idea. Anyway, how much art would you charge for two extra weeks in a broom closet?"

Colleen's eyes brighten. "You're going to stay?"

I nod. "I think I am. You've inspired me with your whole baby-making thing. To take a closer look at what I want, and how I mean to get it. I think the search starts here."

She turns her face and looks at me sideways. "You sure this has nothing to do with the fact that your car won't start?"

I throw up my hands. "Six of one, a half-dozen of the other," I admit. "But, really, what you told me last night blew my mind."

Yesterday, when her sedative had worn off, I stopped driving in circles and brought Colleen straight to Jenny's gallery. There, lazing on those low chairs among the interesting, inspiring inventory, clutching cocoa and molasses cookies, Colleen told us the full story. How she and her ex-boyfriend Mason had, and I quote, "pulled the goalie" a couple years into the relationship, knowing that Mason's National Guard unit would probably soon be called up and worrying they would miss a window. And then, eight months later he shipped out, but there was no baby, so he had left some, ahem, deposits. And then when he came back on leave, there was still no baby. And then Colleen had wanted to start a medical workup, and Mason hadn't, and they'd broken up over it, and he'd re-upped.

She was matter-of-fact about all of this part last night. I get the impression that Mason was more important to her than she lets on, partly from the way Jenny suddenly produced another round of cookies when his name came into the conversation. But also, partly because Colleen said so very little about him. I am noticing that the less she says, the more it matters. And the same, I find, goes for Ben. Now I wonder, was Mason the same way? Is that part of why they fell in love?

What Colleen did tell me last night was that after a year of licking her wounds over not conceiving the old-fashioned way, she'd decided to do it herself. First there was what she called “gene shopping,” where she looked for the perfect donor. That part, she told me, had been the best—full of hope and enthusiasm. That is when she’d bought the books, and stuffed the closet full of baby gear, and started researching baby names. Then DIY insemination went nowhere, so doctors got involved, and then blood tests were done, and results waited for, and more invasive tests done, and Clomid injections started, and so on and so forth, until two more years had gone by without a pregnancy.

And, in the time that had passed waiting, she told me, she knew one woman at her gynecologist’s office who had had two sets of twins.

“It was about the woman with the twins,” I tell her now. “You said you were done waiting to find out why things weren’t happening the way you thought they were supposed to. Instead you were going to change your mind about the way things were supposed to happen.”

Colleen smiles at that. “Did I say that, really? I’m awfully wise.”

“Yes, you are. This morning, the car wouldn’t start, and I decided I was done trying to make things happen the way I thought they were supposed to.”

“Oh, wow. Well, welcome to the club. You can stay as long as you like.”

“Are you sure? Do you have room, with the Nordic racers and all?”

“Plenty, for the time being, as long as you don’t mind being bumped to steerage. What are you going to do while you’re here? Now that you aren’t trying so hard to leave?”

“I’m still going to leave,” I tell her gently. “But first I’m going to paint. And try not to make out with Ben Hutchinson. And pay some of my bills. And go with you to the adoption lawyer. And eat a lot of steak frites.”

“Sounds like you’ll be busy.”

I smile at her and nod. Ten years in a holding pattern, ended by a car that won’t start and a new friend who won’t give up. “There’s not a second to lose.”

PART III

Study From Life

SIX MONTHS EARLIER

"I think I have painter's block."

Renee and I are in the Whistler room on the second floor of the Art Institute, clutching our smuggled-in iced coffees as though our lives depend on them. Outside, Chicago seethes in the high nineties. I feel winter will never come again. We will be hot, humid, plagued by mosquitos forever.

"I thought you didn't believe in blocks," Renee says idly. She has her phone out in the non-coffee hand and doesn't seem to be looking at the art.

"I don't," I agree. "Doesn't mean I don't have one."

"Hm." She scrolls past something online. "That's interesting," she says after a beat. "What does Mitchell say?"

I start. "Why would I talk to Mitchell about this?"

Renee lowers her phone and narrows her eyes at me.

"He cannot know, Renee," I tell her, shaking my head.

"He cannot *not* know. What are you bringing him right now?"

I twist up my mouth. The answer is nothing good. "Well. You know . . ." my voice trails off while I concoct some facsimile of the truth. "I am just working out that one idea. I'm calling it a series, and he seems to be going for it."

"This is the view out your apartment window again?"

I nod, a little embarrassed. I've been painting this same subject for a month now. Honestly, I think I've been painting the same *painting* for a month now. "He doesn't seem to have noticed."

Renee stops milling in front of Mary Cassatt's infinitely pleasing impressionist portrait, *On a Balcony*. In it, a pleasantly stout woman is reading a paper in her day dress, sitting comfortably, even slouched a bit, in a wrought metal chair in a close garden overrun with roses. Renee sighs heavily. "Isn't it heavenly?"

I agree that it is. Perhaps this is some latent sexism speaking, but I have always thought Mary Cassatt was such a *tender* painter, choosing—or perhaps just seeing—in her subjects only the moments most incredibly weighted down with feeling.

"I think it's the pink ones. That's what's otherworldly about it."

"Pink what?" Renee asks.

"Pink roses? The one on her dress plus the two behind the newspaper? Like a spotlight of her attention?"

"Oh, yes. I guess the roses are nice. But I was actually thinking of the way she is sitting someplace quiet and just reading a paper all by herself. I bet that woman does not have any children. Maybe not a husband either."

"I always thought she might be pregnant. Look how the dress doesn't have a waistline. And she's full in the face."

"Ugh. Don't ruin it for me."

"It's just an idea."

"Typical Cassatt," Renee says bitterly. "Romanticizing everything about motherhood because she didn't have kids of her own."

"Tough times in the Larsen household?" I ask her.

She sighs deeply. Her face looks a little dark. A little pained. For a moment I wonder if I've said something terribly wrong. Then she shakes her head and says, "Stop trying to change the subject from your so-called painter's block. Artists make work. You wanna be an artist? You gotta paint."

"I am painting," I say in my own defense. "Just very badly."

"What do you think brought this on? Is it something that happened at the showing?"

I shrug. I never thought of that. Last month, Mitchell gave me a little reception for my latest series. Everyone was very nice to me. But it was all strangers—my friends have grown tired of my endless shows and openings, and I felt very alone and on display.

"I kind of wish you had been there," I venture. "Everyone was so ridiculous. You would have loved making fun of the scenesters."

Renee shakes her head at me. "I'm just so busy at work," she says defensively. "You know that."

"I know. I'm not mad or anything. It was just a weird vibe. Everyone wanted to hear what I had to say until I said it. Then they seemed disappointed."

"What did you say, exactly?"

I shrug. "People were sort of theorizing that my work was a statement about our generation. Something about me seeing everything as though it were on the screen of a smartphone. I can barely work my smartphone. I said my work had nothing to do with smartphones."

"That's true," Renee says. "You can barely work your smartphone."

"Do you think that was what it was like for Mary?" I ask, gesturing to the woman in the painting. "Everyone buzzing about how she painted a woman reading a newspaper instead of doing needlepoint—what a statement! When maybe this is actually about something completely different?"

"I think having people trying to interpret your art, even poorly, is a wonderful compliment." Renee wanders away from the Cassatt and casually takes in the American landscapes that surround it. "Icebound," she reads from the placard next to a painting by John Henry Twachtman. "God, doesn't that look nice too?"

"They should call this the Hall of Wish Fulfillment," I say, looking at the sight of ice floes closing up a rocky emerald stream. "With the Whistler seascapes, and the bronze Diana who doesn't need to wear a bra when she goes hunting."

"And then there's her," Renee says, gesturing to the full-size nude by John Singer Sargent. "I would kill for that ass."

The Sargent, titled *Study from Life,* was one of those standard-bearers of my art education, crammed down our throats like Grant Wood and Jasper Johns. In it, an impossibly tall Egyptian woman stands with her weight on her right foot as she turns to look over her left shoulder, all while braiding her nipple-length hair. In college I thought it was preposterous—who stands like that? But here in the gallery I see the perfection of the work for the first time.

"She is really beautiful." I nod, my eyes tracking the lines of her calves, the shading of her twisted back. "Do you remember when we took our first life drawing class freshman year? How hairy that lady was? How we tried to grow out our armpit hair and it looked like a fourteen-year-old boy's first beard?"

Renee doesn't seem to hear me at first. Then she says, "Not really, Lils. That was a long time ago. Practically another lifetime."

"Well, I mean," I stammer. "It was only ten years ago. It would have been a pretty short lifetime. Anyway the sensation of itchy growing-in armpit hair stays with a person forever."

"Hm," she says, not listening. Her phone dings. "I think I better get back to work."

"Already? We've only been here for twenty minutes!"

"You wanted the artist's life," Renee says suddenly, out of nowhere. "But some of us did not. Some of us have real jobs."

I shut up. It's not out of nowhere. Renee is busy. She works hard. She doesn't want to hear about my so-called block. "Of course," I say after a moment. "But I hope you don't mind if I stay here. Just a little longer. There are a few more things I still want to see."

Sixteen

I spend the next week in Minnow Bay painting. Each beautiful frosty morning, I fire up the stove in the studio, and then go back to the inn for granola or oatmeal in Colleen's kitchen, keeping her company while she preps breakfast for four ravenous cross-country ski racers staying in two rooms on the second floor, directly below my new room. Then, when I get back, the studio is warm and I am too. And ready to work. What has been like pulling teeth in Chicago is like rolling down a hill in Minnow Bay. Dreaming of the steamy summer in this painting, imagining the heat of an August sun, the glare of a cloudless day, and the yellows of a overheated earth, and sketching for a new series, keeps me engrossed. I forget the time until someone comes and gets me and shakes me out of the trance. This being Friday, that someone is Simone, racing here between early release at the high school and her shift at the café. She opens the door with a clatter and says, "Oh *God,* what are you doing?" when she walks in, and I realize I have been standing with my face exactly perpendicular to my painting on the left side, trying to figure out what the sky still needs.

"I'm working," I say, rubbing the ache out of my neck.

"You are such a weirdo."

I stand back from the painting and look at her outfit and know I am in good company. She is wearing black-and-white zebra-print parachute pants and a sequined yellow crop top. Said top was once was a full-length knit sweater, and has a jagged edge where it was unwillingly and aggressively abbreviated.

"Simone, what are you wearing?"

"I could ask the same of you."

I look down. I am wearing a man's button-down from Goodwill as a smock, and black leggings, and warm boots. There is nothing noteworthy about my outfit in the slightest.

"Okay," I sigh, defeated. "What do you think?" I gesture to the painting, which is almost half-done.

"It's ugly. What do you think of mine?"

She opens her unusually large sketchbook, flips through a few pages, and turns to a watercolor I've never seen before. "I did it this week."

"Oh, Simone. Honey."

It is Ben Hutchinson, of course. So far I've seen nothing from her but different brightly hued interpretations of Ben Hutchinson. But this time it isn't just his portrait. This time it is his face, imposed on the body of Michelangelo's David.

Michelangelo's *naked* David.

"This just isn't appropriate," I tell her as gently as I can.

"Yeah, I'm gonna burn it. But look at the lines."

I do look. It's a copy of a great work, and though quite representative, it brings nothing interesting or new to the party. It's junk and she knows it. "Simone, why did you paint this?"

"I don't know. I told you I'm stuck."

"So you decided to just reproduce something the whole world already has burned into its retinas?"

"I needed a reference point. I don't actually know what Mr. Hutchinson looks like naked. Unlike some people."

I blush. "I haven't seen him naked," I say.

"Not even back in Vegas?" Over the last week I have, against my better judgment, told Simone the full story of our marriage. My side of it, at least.

". . . in ten years," I amend.

"Maybe if you describe your memories to me in great detail I could be reinspired."

"No. Just, absolutely no." I sigh. "Painting someone in the nude without their permission is a terrible violation of their privacy. Painting them in the nude poorly is a violation of their privacy and their taste."

"But you have to have nudes in your portfolio to submit to art school," she whines. "How am I supposed to get someone to pose nude for me in this town?"

I look at her, unmoved. "You can do me. Hang on, I have to make a note on where I'm at." I move to my sketchpad. "Can you crank up the stove? Start by burning that painting."

"I do not want to see you naked," Simone says, though she does obediently feed the horrible Ben/David into the fire, to my great relief.

"I know you don't. That is never, ever the point."

"Tell that to Picasso."

"Yeah, okay. Let's just give him the whole 'genius who changed the world forever' pass and then not worry about how the rules apply to him. For you, a sixteen-year-old girl trying to apply to art school, what matters isn't *who* you paint. What matters is what you *see*."

"I see someone who is too old to pose naked. God, put that smock back on. What happened to you? Is that back fat?"

"You're in love with Ben Hutchinson, right?" I ask her, as I hang the smock on a hook just to the right of my easel. Under it I am wearing a camisole, white, paint dabbled.

"You know that I am," she replies.

"Great." I pull off my camisole, revealing a highly functional wireless black cotton bra. Simone pretends to shield her eyes in horror. "Now, for the sake of argument, let's just say you actually know what the hell love is, and let's also say you're under the impression that I've stolen him from you."

"You have. And I do."

"You're excellent at playing along," I tell her. "Now, how does the woman who stole the man you love look to you?" I unhook my bra. Like every art student ever, I posed nude for extra money in school. I have zero self-consciousness about it.

"Your boobs are droopy," she tells me.

I raise my eyebrows "If that's what you see, start sketching."

Simone sighs deeply. "You're the worst. You're actually kind of pretty and sort of talented and now you're, like, a deep thinker too." I'm amused by this assessment. I may be confident in the studio, today, after a good day of work. But what if Renee heard me described that way? She'd pee herself laughing.

"Why aren't you embarrassed to be naked?" Simone asks.

"I'm not naked. I have my pants on."

"Please leave them that way."

"I promise. Waist up is enough for art school. Plus, it's still pretty cold in here."

"Just tell me you're a little self-conscious," she pleads.

"Not even a little. When you paint a fruit bowl, you might look hard at each apple, and turn each one over, and look at the shape and the color and find bruises and lumps and see everything there is to see. That's your job, to see everything. But the apple is just busy being an apple. That's the apple's job. What you *see* has nothing to do with what the apple *is*."

"Your apples look more like pears," she says.

"There will be a day when being naked doesn't make you ashamed," I tell her, and say a silent prayer that it will be true. "Now shut up and sketch." I take a seat on a high stool, arms in my lap, shoulders curled slightly from the cold.

Simone stares at me critically, and then finally starts drawing, furiously, her hand moving over the page and turning black with smudging. Despite my lecture, I start to wonder at what she sees that I don't. Not in me, of course. I know what I look like. I have my mother's small, soft bone structure and her easily flushed skin. I have a large top lip that keeps me from wearing lipstick because it would feel too overtly sexual. There are exaggerated arches in my eyebrows from overzealous tweezing last week during an episode of *Extreme Cheapskates* at the inn. My eyes are dark, dark brown.

But what does she see in Ben Hutchinson? She says she's loved him since she first saw him. I can understand that from one respect: he is handsome, without a doubt. His face is angles and shadows. His mouth is set sternly but there are smile lines by his eyes. His body has that triangle-on-its-tip shape, shoulders to hips, that I don't remember from Vegas. It is probably earned from shoveling snow and chopping wood. He is tall, and because I am not, I feel yippy around him, like a Chihuahua chasing a bicycle.

Simone is easily six inches taller than me. I suppose when she sees her teacher, she sets her chin up just an inch so she can half lower her eyes at him, the universal language of come hither. When I see him I tend to stare at his chest.

In Las Vegas, that night with Ben, I was self-conscious to be naked. I was not an apple, busy being an apple. I was a *woman,* and I knew I was being seen. I had a flatter tummy then, and he put his hand on it, and I sucked it in. He ran his fingers up the side of my torso, and I held my breath. He set his lips to the spot where breast met body and I tried to puff myself up, to move my flesh around into just the right organization by sheer force of will. Would I feel that way now, ten years wiser, if I were in his bed again?

"You're blushing," says Simone. "It's annoying."

I startle and color even more deeply. "No I'm not."

"Look at your cleavage."

I don't have much cleavage, but I look down to the place where it would be if I did. I'm a speckled red hen down there. "Yikes."

"I hope it's because you can feel my critical gaze."

"Thanks, but no." I tip my head back, embarrassed by my train of thoughts, but also unnerved.

"Were you thinking about him?" she asks, setting down her pencil.

I pinch my lips together. "I guess I was."

She sighs deeply.

"I'm sorry, Simone."

"Apologize to your so-called boyfriend back in Chicago. Home-wrecker."

"Technically in this scenario Ben would be the home-wrecker. But no homes are currently being wrecked. I have nothing to apologize for, or at least nothing much. I know you don't believe me, Simone, but this is what it means to be a woman. Life gets confusing, and you keep trying to do the right thing."

"Since when is the right thing stealing the love of my life?"

I am about to attempt, yet again, to squelch this notion when I hear the studio door opening.

Simone and I both freeze, and my heart stops a bit. I am sitting on a stool topless and my smock is too far to reach. She could reach it easily, throw it to me, but instead she turns to the door. "Shield your eyes!" she shouts toward the incomer, as though my naked chest is the mammary equivalent of Medusa's face.

"Shield my eyes?" asks Jenny. I exhale dramatically and unwind my arms, which seem to have wrapped themselves around my front on their own. "Oh! Life painting 101 going on in here?"

"Jenny. It's you. Thank God," I say instead of answering. "I thought based on the way things seem to go around here that you would be Ben."

"Thought, or hoped?" she asks. "Nice rack."

"Thanks," I say, crawling off the stool and pulling on my bra. "Simone needs to work on life painting for her art school portfolio."

"Art school?" Jenny looks thrilled at this. And surprised.

Simone nods. "Lily thinks I shouldn't imagine people naked without their permission."

Jenny laughs. "While I think that's a good goal, it may not be entirely achievable."

I nod ruefully, thinking of Ben again. Then I laugh to myself. "When the door opened, I was sure you were going to be a Hutchinson. There are so many of them in this town. I was certain I was about to be standing naked in front of Ben."

Jenny snorts. "This isn't a romantic comedy. How come you always have so much paint in your hair?" she asks as I pull the button-down smock back over my camisole.

"How come you're always so dressed up?" I volley back. She is wearing a beautiful pair of leather jeans with a soft thin cashmere tunic over the top.

"Did you forget? Carla's surprise party? We've got to go straight over there or we're going to miss the shouting and jumping part."

"What surprise party?" I ask, flummoxed.

"The one I told you about yesterday," says Simone.

"Simone! I didn't even see you yesterday."

She shrugs. "Surprise."

Jenny shoots her a warning look, but I can see she's not genuinely mad. "Well, too late to do anything now. If we don't get over there, quicklike, we're going to be the jerks that meet her on the way in and spoil everything. Hustle up."

I grab our jackets while Jenny stifles the fire and Simone quickly stashes the paints. Together we race across the street, the lapels of our coats flapping as we scurry through the icy winds. I look a mess, I'm sure, but it doesn't seem that important considering I don't even know the person whose birthday I will be jumping and shouting about.

"Who is Carla, again?" I ask just as we're about to open the doors of the brew pub.

Jenny laughs but doesn't answer me. "Simone, you're pretty cruel, you know that?"

"What?" I ask. "Wait, who is this? What's going on?"

"I figured if Ben sees her looking like an escapee from the mental institution," Simone replies, gesturing to my wild paint-streaked hair and half-buttoned smock, "he'll realize there are other fish in the sea. Younger, cooler fish."

Jenny shakes her head indulgently. "It's not going to work, my young, cool friend," she tells her. "He's been bitten by the love bug."

"Wait. Stop, both of you!" I finally shout, and both of them freeze, startled. "He hasn't been bitten by anything except maybe the bug up his butt," I say first to Jenny. Then to Simone, "Now, whose surprise party is this that I'm walking into?"

At last Jenny and Simone do stop and turn to me, hands on doors. A wicked smile crosses Simone's face. "Well, Carla Hutchinson, of course."

I look to Jenny, desperate. "Not . . ."

She nods just a bit ruefully. "Ben's mother. Hope you're ready to meet the fam!"

Seventeen

I am not, to put it mildly, ready to meet the fam. All my crowing about having no self-consciousness in service of art flies right out the window when the heavy leather door opens and I am faced with a sea of people, most of whom I've never met, who fall silent the second I walk through the door.

And I mean *silent.* I mean, all heads swivel toward me. My mouth goes dry and I reach up to touch my hair. How bad is it? I should have at least looked in a mirror. But then some kind of recognition starts to creep over the faces of the partygoers.

"It's not her!" calls someone and then everyone goes back to their conversations. I put my face in my hands.

"You need a drink," says Jenny, but instead of following her to the bar I beeline for the bathroom. I don't see anyone else I know yet, so I'm going to use this temporary reprieve to make myself as presentable as possible. Or sneak out the back.

There's someone in the one-stall ladies' room. Feeling a little panicky, I slip into the other option and flip on the lights. In the mirror I see my hair is wilder than usual, completely undeterred by the purple headband I have on, and flecked with green paint. I also have a gummy stripe of dried zinc yellow marching from forehead to eyelid, stopping by way of my eyebrow. I must have also wiped my rinsewater hands on my leggings one too many times because the thighs are covered with gray finger trails, and this smock will not pass as a shirt again until it's been washed. Twice. Maybe I can turn it inside out. Or maybe the back door is really the best plan.

Or maybe I should not care about this any more than I did before I knew who the party was for. For years I've been busy cleaning myself up to be good enough for Mitchell. I've been twisting myself up in knots to keep my friendship with Renee. In Minnow Bay, I've been doing nothing more than being myself, and it's been kind of wonderful. Why would I stop that now? I said I wasn't interested in Ben, so I shouldn't care what his mother or endless stream of brothers or fathers or cousins think of me. I shouldn't care if I look pretty or not. I shouldn't care that my breath smells like coffee and the venison jerky I found in a desk drawer in the studio earlier this afternoon.

The door opens. I guess I didn't lock it in my haste. I spin around ready to apologize.

It's Ben.

"GOD DAMMIT," I shout.

His eyes fly open wide, his jaw drops, and he backs out and slams the door.

Shit. I splash some water on my eerie yellow eyebrow and turn around and reach for the door.

"I'm sorry," I say before I even see him. I am standing in the men's bathroom with the door open wide and some yellow paint water is dripping into my eye. "It's my fault," I tell Ben's chest. I can't look him in the eye. "I . . . the women's room was . . . so I . . . Look at me, and I needed to . . . And I smell like deer meat." I cover my eyes with my hands.

"Lily, are you okay?" he asks. "Are you having a stroke?"

I put my hands down by my sides and sigh heavily. "Here I am,"

I say, gesturing from hair to thighs. "This is me reinventing myself, getting my life together. Ta da!"

"Come out from the bathroom," he says gently.

I try not to sniffle as he guides me into the narrow, dark hallway between bathrooms.

"What's wrong?" he asks.

I shake my head furiously, not sure if I should laugh or cry. Why do I care so much about this virtual stranger?

"Hey, hey, what's going on?" he asks. "I'm worried about you."

I breathe in deeply and then try to tell him. "I'm trying to turn over a new leaf. Work harder, pay my bills on time, be an adult, mend my relationships, spend my time and energy on my art."

"That all sounds really good."

"And stay away from you."

"Huh," is all he says. "Based on our previous interactions, you'd think I'd be fine with that. But I'm not. The problem is, I can't stop thinking about you."

"Oh," I say. "Well."

"I hate parties," he tells me. "My mom knows that. She would have completely understood if I stayed home. But I knew you would be here tonight," he says. "I knew Jenny and Colleen wouldn't miss this opportunity."

I sigh. "So you saw it coming? I don't quite have all their schemes figured out."

"Ever watch *Three's Company*? *I Love Lucy*?"

I shake my head no.

"Well, that explains it," he says. "You'll get the hang of it here. Maybe you'll even come to like it."

"I do like it," I admit. "It's just that it's working very counter to my plan."

"Like, your plan to stay away from me?"

I nod jerkily. "Exactly. I have to stay away from you, because otherwise I'll spend all my time thinking about what you think about me, and what kissing you is like, and whether you're the same man I met in Vegas or someone totally different. I mean, look at me now, trying to wash paint out of my eyebrows in the men's bathroom! Why should I care if there's paint in my eyebrows? There's always paint in my eyebrows. I'm a painter. That's where the paint goes. And I forgot to stop for lunch. So my breath smells like venison jerky. Who cares?"

"I don't care," he says quietly. The hallway suddenly becomes very still.

I gingerly direct my gaze to his. "Are you going to kiss me again?"

"I want to. Do you want me to?"

"No," I lie. "I'm in a relationship. It's not a great relationship, but it's a relationship nonetheless. Also I am getting my life together. And letting go of the past. You are the past. The distant past. The sexy distant past."

His lips set in a straight line but he nods. "Okay. So then, to be clear, no kissing?"

"Right."

"It seems like you would rather be kissing."

"I would."

"I would also rather be kissing," he tells me.

I sigh heavily again. "Come on, man."

He runs his hand over his jaw. "It's hard not to take this personally," he tells me.

"Well, don't. Or do, and learn from this."

"Um?"

"Next time a nice person shows up at your house and tells you she's married to you, don't be a dick about it."

"Okay. Good note. Do you think I'm married to anyone else without my knowledge?" he asks.

"Well! You could be. You married me."

"I really liked you," he says.

"Please," I tell him. "At the time, I wanted to believe that. I did believe that. Now I'm all, girl, please. You liked wearing nice suits, and picking up girls in Vegas, and being outrageous."

"I did like all those things, but I didn't marry anyone else, did I?"

I shrug. "You tell me."

"I didn't. I shouldn't have married you either."

"Oh, here we go," I say, thinking Ben's Mr. Hyde routine is about to unleash itself. But it doesn't.

"I shouldn't have married you in an all-night drag casino and pancake house. I should have surprised you in Chicago a week later and swept you off your feet. I should have sent you two dozen roses and a plane ticket. I should have said to myself, 'Hey, dumb ass, this one is interesting, and beautiful, and good, and gives you a run for your money. Go after her.' But instead I married you one night and went back to my stupid life in stupid Silicon Valley the next. And that is what I did wrong."

The words fall out of my brain. After a while I remember to breathe. Then I say, "You make me want to break up with my boyfriend."

"Please do."

"It might ruin my career," I tell him, thinking of that exhibition offer going up like a puff of smoke.

"I sincerely doubt it," he says. "But I'm sorry if it does."

"I came to Minnow Bay to disentangle myself from you," I say.

"I don't want to be disentangled," he says. "And I like you with paint in your eyebrows." With that he takes the pad of his thumb and wipes a drop of the paint-water from under my brow, stopping it before it can roll into my eye.

"Let's kiss now," I say. "Just a little."

"Yeah," he agrees. "Let's."

So we do.

And that is all we do. One soft and slow kiss, one little start to something that wants to be something else, and then we stop for all the right reasons, and his mother arrives and we all crouch behind our chairs and then jump out and yell surprise and she pretends to be surprised though clearly she is not, and then there is a loud and raucous Minnow Bay party in which Ben and I look at each other too much and touch not enough.

Three of his brothers are there and they size me up quite openly, as do a couple of cousins. Mason, as in Colleen's ex Mason, is not there, so I assume he is deployed. Colleen is absent too. She is at home working on a scrapbook about her life for the meeting with the adoption lawyer Monday. Jenny leaves early too, pleading a headache. I get home at midnight—too late to call Mitchell—and barely get my shoes off before I drop to sleep exhausted on the big soft four-poster bed.

In the morning I head down to breakfast and find Colleen and Jenny there with four cross-country skiers and a huge breakfast of dried cherry and walnut pancakes with perfectly crispy maple sausages. The seven of us cram around the table and participate politely in a few discussions over the speed of the snow (fast) and the grooming of the trails (expert) and the nip in the morning air (which is minus two degrees Fahrenheit and more of a Rottweiler bite than a nip). Then I announce to the table, "I'm think I'm breaking up with Mitchell."

"Oh, praise the lord," says Jenny. "Finally. We were starting to think you had brain damage."

"Who is Mitchell?" asks one of the skiers politely. He is a burly man with a little potbelly and an impressive winter beard.

"He's my boyfriend back in Chicago," I tell him. "And my art gallerist. But I think he might be taking advantage of me a little. Or at the very least, he's an opportunist."

"I don't like him," Jenny supplements.

"She's never met him," I tell the skiers.

"I don't like him either," says Colleen.

"Also never met him."

"I have a good sense about people," Colleen says with finality. "By the by, did you all sleep well last night? Anything I can bring up to your rooms while you're on the trails today?"

"Do you have any decaf green tea?" asks a woman, the only one with the skiers. She's the wife of Mr. Beard, and she looks crazily fit and obsessively preserved. "The regular stuff makes me a bit jumpy but I can't survive without my polyphenols."

"I do," says Colleen, as though the words she just heard were not ridiculous. "I'll bring up some loose-leaf tea and an infuser so you can pour yourself a nice hot cup whenever you get back in."

"Oh *thank* you," says Mrs. Beard. "So this Mitchell guy, he's in Chicago?"

"Uh huh," I tell her, still wondering what polyphenols are.

"So then, you're driving back to break it off today?"

I pause, momentarily stumped. "Well, I hadn't planned on it," I admit. "Actually I hadn't really thought that far. I don't suppose doing it over the phone would be appropriate."

"You could send a text," says Jenny helpfully, mouth full of pancake. "Maybe we could make a GIF of you waving bye-bye?"

"How long were you dating him?" asks Mr. Beard's older brother, a much smaller, much less hairy fellow who is here with his husband Don.

"Ah, um . . . two years, I guess?"

Don sets down his silverware with a clatter. "I think you better dump him in person."

"Trust me," says Jenny. "A text is all he deserves."

"It's bad karma to dump anyone in a text," says Mrs. Beard.

"I agree," says Brother Beard.

"Forget karma," says Don. "It's bad business. He's basically your meal ticket, right? You need to be there to mitigate the damage."

"You're right," I say sadly. "But I can't go down there today."

"Sure you can," says Jenny around a mouthful of sausage. "You can take my car."

"Oh, ho! Now that I want to break up with Mitchell, suddenly you're rushing me back to Chicago?"

She smiles wickedly and waggles her eyebrows. "Pretty much."

"The problem is, I promised to work with Simone tomorrow, so she can get her art school applications in by next week."

"Art school?" exclaims Colleen excitedly. "That's incredible!"

"Right?" says Jenny.

I pause in my thoughts. "I thought you guys knew she wanted to be an artist."

"Oh, yes. But we never thought she would actually try. There's so much pressure on her to go into the family business, but I'm afraid she'll never be happy if she doesn't see what else is out there." Colleen beams at me. "You have no idea what you've done for her, by encouraging her to try this out."

I shrug sheepishly. "I hope her parents don't hate me."

"They're loving parents. They only want her to be happy. They just don't know what will bring her happiness."

Funny, I think. That's almost exactly what my mother said to me when I told her I was applying to art school. My heart gives a pull and I remember what Colleen and I talked about a couple nights ago. About her plans for adoption.

"So go to Chicago on Monday," says Mrs. Beard, dragging my focus back to Mitchell. Unpleasantly.

"Monday I am going to an, uh, appointment with a friend here in town."

"There's not much point in trying to be discreet anymore," says Colleen with an eye roll. "The cat's out of the bag. She's coming with me to the adoption lawyer."

"Oooh!" says Brother Beard. "Good for you! Matt here is adopted. And he turned out great!"

Matt, aka Mr. Beard, nods. "That's why I'm the brains of the family."

"And I'm the brawn," says Brother Beard. They both share a laugh. I find them cute. Just two brothers and their partners, going skiing together and eating lots of pancakes. Bros for life.

"You'll make a wonderful mother," says Don. "And really change a life forever."

"I hope so," says Colleen, and she is beaming.

"I had no idea you were even married," says Mrs. Beard.

"Well, that's because I'm not," Colleen replies casually.

"Oh!" says Mrs. Beard. You can see her brain is melting a bit at this, but she doesn't elaborate.

"That's what I said," says Jenny. "I said, 'Oh! What a terrible idea!'"

Colleen rolls her eyes again. "And I ignored you. Again and again."

"Well, I can see her point," says Mrs. Beard. "My sister has kids. It does seem like a lot of work. And she's got a husband to help out."

I think of a bunch of snarky things to say to that. "How lucky for her," to start, and "Your sister has kids? I guess you're an authority!" and so forth. Jenny seems similarily inspired based on the light flush coming up on her cheeks, but Colleen puts a hand up. "The thing my friends tell me about having children is that it is insanely hard and there is no way to prepare for it. I'm going to need all the help I can get. But wonderful children are raised by single mothers every day, so I'm encouraged and optimistic. Does anyone need more coffee?"

"She's very diplomatic," I tell Jenny sotto voce as Colleen rises for the kitchen.

Mrs. Beard nods. "Well, she convinced me."

Brother Beard nods too. "Maybe we should adopt, honey," he says to Don with a little playful smile.

"Do you know how many impromptu ski trips new parents get to take every year?" Don asks. "Zero. Zero impromptu ski trips."

"Never mind, then," says Brother Beard jovially, and then he turns back to me. "So the boyfriend. Can it wait?"

"No!" says Jenny. "It's kind of urgent. There's something she needs to do once she's single."

"Something?" asks Don. "Or someone?"

"Exactly," says Jenny. "And you should see this guy. Six foot something, prime physical specimen—"

"It can wait," I say before things take an un-breakfastly turn. "Certainly it can wait until Tuesday. I've been gone for almost three weeks now without more than a couple of phone calls between us, so I don't think it will come as much of a shock."

"You never know," says Don. "Some people don't notice the world changing around them, you know? They don't see other people moving on, moving away . . ."

Colleen comes back in then with a fresh carafe of coffee and says gently, "I think she knows."

I nod. "Yep." I *am* that person.

"Go easy on him," says Brother Beard. "People like that deserve our sympathy."

Colleen refreshes my cup as she says, "And our kindness."

I smile gratefully. Kindness is in no short supply here in Minnow Bay. It will not be easy to go home.

Eighteen

I have never been to a town so small it didn't have at least one lawyer's office, and Minnow Bay is no exception. In a converted Victorian with a shingle—an actual shingle—hanging from one of the pillars of the porch, works June Jorgens, Family Law. Colleen tells me she handled Jenny's divorce, which gives me a double take, and also that she does the wills of everyone in town, and beyond that, she also serves as an assistant county attorney for the sheriff's office.

"And she also breeds layers."

"Excuse me?" I ask as we pull open the front door.

"Hens. Laying hens."

"Your lawyer raises chickens?"

"Just the hens, and just until they're ready to lay. Then she sells them."

"What about the boys? I mean, the roosters. Does she sell them too?"

"The roosters go out to, ah, the farm."

"A farm near here?"

"No, the euphemistic farm."

"Oh. Right. I see," I say. But I am thinking, *This is the person you chose to be your adoption lawyer?*

This question persists when June Jorgens's secretary ushers us into the "conference room," which, based on the built-in china hutches in two corners, was once a dining room. The table is a pretty rectangle with rounded corners, and the chairs are ornate carved things with velvet seats. The room is nice enough but really warm, and the lighting is weird. I take off my wool sweater and think to put it on top of a serving hutch behind me, but just in time I realize what the weird lighting actually is.

Incubators. Chicken incubators.

"This is what I get for letting Rosemary and Cinnamon come inside during the winter," says a small, round-shaped woman in a cranberry colored sweater dress as she bustles into the room. "June Jorgens." She extends a hand to me. "You must be Lily Stewart?"

"I am," I say, pivoting to shake her hand. "Rosemary and Cinnamon are chickens, I gather?"

"And best friends." June squeezes past me to the window, which is covered in white lace, and pushes the curtain aside. "Cinnamon is the red one," she gestures to a proud ruddy bird pecking in the snow. "Rosemary is my best breeder; she's probably having a sit down in the coop. I thought I'd see what happened to her egg production if she got to sleep inside and then Cinnamon had a fit of jealousy so I brought her in too. And then they both got their seasons screwy, messed about with the rooster, and now I've got a head start on this year's chicks. Wanna hold one?" she asks with a smile. "They're in those hutches behind you."

"I do, very much. Is that inappropriate? I am not sure about chicken manners in a professional setting."

"I'm afraid I've never been much for professional settings myself. Cuddle away, but first you need clean hands. Go wash up, and I'll get some starting details from Colleen."

June points me toward the hall and, as I make my way through to a tiny bathroom with a cut glass doorknob, I hear her asking Colleen how the hell is she, and what, is she crazy trying to adopt by herself? It all sounds very good-natured, almost motherly, though June is probably younger than either of us. Despite my misgivings, I find I like her and her henhouse of law.

When I come back scrubbed from fingertip to elbow, June is in the midst of a detailed conversation with Colleen about adopting countries. The pros and cons of each. June may be a jack of all trades but she sure does know her stuff, I think, as I listen to her rattle off nuanced details about various nations and their intricate adoption policies. My head feels a little swimmy from this, but Colleen is taking notes and nodding actively. June interrupts herself when she sees me hovering awkwardly by the incubator, telling me, "Just be gentle, Lily, cup your hands, that's right," and watches carefully as I scoop up a powder-soft little yellow peeper, who sort of half pecks and half nestles into my hands. The chick is easy to hold and I keep her cupped in my hands as I sit down next to Colleen and try to be helpful.

"Ultimately," June is saying, "no one but you can make these decisions. Your timeline, your, ah, ability to interact in the home country, the budget—this is what steers the choice. And you have to protect yourself and heed the recommendations of the state department."

"This all sounds really intimidating," says Colleen.

June shrugs. "Foreign adoptions are commonplace and beautiful, Colleen. Your life will be changed for the good forever." Colleen sighs in anticipation. June presses on. "Things rarely get hairy. But when they do, they get very, very hairy. That's why you need both agencies and lawyers."

She leans back, crosses her legs. "And I'm sure you know these things are tricky to initiate. There are many, many hoops you'll need to jump through, and a shocking number of palms you may need to grease. There are residence rules that mean you may have to relocate for weeks or months to the home country. This is a big endeavor that will have to be your number-one priority for months or possibly years."

"Whoa," I say, a little overwhelmed myself.

"But it's worth it," says Colleen, and she looks a little choked up at just the thought. "When you bring the baby home?"

June nods. "My old law partner, the one I bought the firm from before he retired?" Colleen nods. "He told me many lovely stories of adoptions completed. To see the kids grow up, happy, healthy, loved, and at home in Minnow Bay, is a wonderful thing indeed. In-country, international, he told me it was his absolute favorite kind of client. And I can see that now, even though I've only done a handful. The day the parents find out there's a child for them . . . it's the happiest day of their lives." I think of the pinks and yellows of such a moment, such a discovery. Like waking up thinking you'd slept past the sunrise, only to throw open the curtains and see it has only just begun.

"There's an infertility blogger I read sometimes," Colleen says. "She went through everything I've done and much more. Then she decided to adopt from Haiti, and it was so incredibly successful, she adopted three more times."

"Let's just start with one, shall we?" says June. "A family of two is still a wonderful family."

Colleen nods wordlessly. The chick peeps at me and I hand her to my friend, who accepts her gratefully, turning her wet eyes to the little bird's.

"That's going to be a hell of a hen if she makes it through," says June, turning her attention toward the bundle in Colleen's hands. "In fact, I'm actually thinking of naming her."

"Marnie," says Colleen.

"Pretty, but I was thinking Ginger, actually. I usually keep with an herbs-and-spices theme, you know."

"No, Marnie is what I want to name my daughter," says Colleen. "When we get through all of this. It was my mother's name."

God help me, I have to try hard now not to cry. Suddenly I want to adopt too, just so I have a daughter to name Sylvia. I take in a deep breath and say, "I'm think I'm going to need another chick."

"Me too," says June, unearthing a bottle of Purell from a buffet drawer. We take a short chicken break.

A few minutes later, composed again, Colleen asks the question I've been dying to know throughout.

"How much do I need to have liquid for this?"

There is a long silence. It seems to me only June is breathing.

"Depends on your timeline," June says at last. "If you've got a long horizon, you can put away a few hundred a month, save up for it, with the added bonus that the slower the country, the cheaper the adoption. If you're thinking you want to adopt within the next couple years, well . . . you can expect to spend around $5,000 for the application process, home study, and postadoption support, which, by the way, is worth every penny."

Colleen exhales loudly. "Oh, thank goodness. I was afraid you were going to say it was prohibitively expensive. I've already saved up three times that amount for this very reason."

June is silent for another long moment. "Now, Colleen. There are also some service fees. Program fees, translations, donations to the country—sometimes those are called in-country fees or humanitarian support. Can range from a few thousand to ten thousand, depending on the country."

Colleen looks a bit more hesitant but tries to summon her optimism. "It's okay. Surely I can scare up a little more cash. Friends and family."

This time the silence lasts longer. June's face is grave.

"It gets worse, doesn't it?" Colleen asks June.

She nods. "You have to pay the broker; that will run you five grand. And then another five at least for the travel, and another five or so for the consulate, immigration, and the actual adoption paperwork."

"Thirty thousand dollars?" she asks in horror. My mouth flies open. Even the chicks seem to peep in outrage.

June nods sadly.

"I don't have that kind of money," she says quietly.

"Not many people do," says June. "Especially not single people. That's why I like my chickens."

Colleen looks back at her little chick, who seems to be sleeping and peeing at the same time, in her hand. "But I . . . I don't want a chicken," says Colleen as she reaches for a tissue from the box June keeps on the table.

"I know you don't," says June. "I'm sorry. There are some grants and loans out there. But I'll be honest, you'll see a lot of competition from married couples for them. Many families decide to take cash advances on their credit cards, or second mortgages, or ask for money from friends and family. But bear in mind that many countries have a minimum net worth per family. If you don't meet it after the fees are factored out, they don't even consider you."

Colleen inhales deeply.

"There's a lot to think over, Colleen. As a lawyer I can guide you, but as a friend I want to caution you from getting too close to the bone. Expenses don't end when you get your adoption finalized. Kids are expensive, even more so when you're the only caretaker and breadwinner. If you dig yourself into a hole, it could be very hard to get out. And a foreclosure on your home is, in your case, also a foreclosure on your business. Not good."

Colleen nods solemnly.

"Take some time to think about it," says June.

"I can think about it all I want," my friend says. "But I don't have thirty thousand dollars to spare. Not even close." Her voice is the saddest thing I've ever heard. Crackly from the tears she's not crying. Defeated from this final, probably permanent setback. I put back my chick so I can throw an arm around her.

"Do you want to take Ginger home with you?" June asks. I can see she too is at a loss.

Colleen shakes her head without speaking. Finally she says, "I never wanted a chicken. I just wanted a child."

It is the last thing she says to anyone that day.

I watch Colleen as she silently walks back to the inn. At first I try to talk to her, but she shakes her head at me sadly and steps away. She wants to be alone, without a doubt. I can understand that.

Still, the protective nature in me forces me to follow her at a big distance, quietly, until I'm sure she's back to the inn. Then I text Jenny. *Adoption meeting n/g,* I tell her. *Wants to be alone. Check in later?*

I head back down Lake Street. The other guests of the inn all headed out for a big skiing something-or-other today. They had Colleen pack them box lunches. So she'll have her space for a while. As long as I stay away.

But I don't have many other places to go, this far from home. I walk past the bookstore and the craft shop and past Jenny's gallery, but there I hesitate. The lights are blazing inside and there's no missing my works in pride of place just by the window. In fact, someone I've never met before is standing in front of one of them gesturing animatedly to Jenny. I shuffle away fast before she spots me and calls me in to say something profound to this potential buyer. This is something Mitchell has always frowned on—making the artist too accessible to the shopping public—but something tells me Jenny falls on the other end of that spectrum. For better or for worse.

Still, I manage to linger long enough in the window to confirm my fear—that there are no "Sold" placards by my works. Not one. It's not a good feeling.

I wind past the bistro and the diner and over the little river bridge and walk several more blocks and look around me. It's a lovely little wander, and I start maneuvering down side streets. The houses in town are each more charming than the one before. Many still have holiday decorations up. They are mostly bungalows, and farmhouses, about a hundred years old each, all lovingly taken care of. The city girl in me marvels at front porch after front porch, each neatly shoveled, many positively loaded down with skis and snowshoes and sleds.

Finally, though I have been trying desperately not to, I glance at my watch. Perfect. Colleen and Jenny have not been subtle about dropping little tidbits, like when Ben Hutchinson has his prep period at the high school, and up to now I thought I was doing a good job ignoring such tidbits. But now I find that it has all penetrated my thick skull, and I'm glad of it. I need someone to talk to. And I want to talk to Ben.

At the high school, I easily remember the way to Ben's classroom. And that first day I visited it. How taken aback he was by my news, and how gracious he seemed in that moment. And then how quickly he turned against me. The memory gives me pause. He was so swept up in paranoia and suspicion that night. Is this a man I should really confide in?

But, unmistakably, there is something real behind my powerful attraction. Behind our ill-advised kissing. There is a private dignity with which he seems to conduct his life. In the weeks I've been here I've seen him treat many, many people—even me, most of the time—with respect and kindness. I remember that kindness in Las Vegas, but now that I know him better, I see it's more than hundred-dollar tips and extravagant dinners. He gave up his old life to be closer to his family when they needed him. He endures and appropriately attempts to deflect Simone's incessant crushing. He footed the entire bar tab at his mother's surprise party without saying a word to anyone about it. He had my car towed for me and then drove me to the mechanic even when it was only three blocks away, just because Colleen asked him to.

Or maybe because he wanted to see me.

I honestly don't know what to think.

And I don't trust myself to make any judgments on this. After all, I still can't even figure out what Mitchell is up to, if he's up to anything at all. I can't decide if Renee loves me in her own way or is trying to get rid of me. I can't really figure much of anything out.

I knock on Ben's classroom door.

When he opens it, he is sitting in a rolly chair.

"Did you roll all the way to the door in that chair rather than stand up?" I ask him.

"I did," he tells me proudly. "I never stand up during prep period as a rule."

For a flash of a second, I want to say something playful and sexy about things you can do standing up. Instead I say, "Colleen is sad. I'm mixed up. Jenny is immune to reality. Do you have time to talk?"

Ben tilts his head thoughtfully. "I do. Right this way," and then he rolls himself in a single go all the way back to his desk. "What's up?"

"I don't even know where to start," I start.

"Best to worst. Jenny's lack of grasp on reality. That doesn't sound very serious. Or newsworthy."

"She thinks my paintings are worth six times what they're actually worth, and she's stuck them in her gallery with outrageous prices on them, and they will never sell."

Ben laughs. He just laughs at me. "Okay, that one feels like not a big deal. Like, she'll figure it out eventually and reprice them, right?"

"I guess. But I was . . . this sounds stupid, but I guess . . ." I let my voice trickle away into silence.

"You were hoping she was right about the price?"

"Well, yeah. Mitchell said overestimating a work's value is a common ploy when a gallery is trying to poach you. But I was hoping Mitchell was the one feeding me a ploy."

"Mitchell is the boyfriend?" he verifies.

"Yes."

"And the gallerist."

"That's right."

"That seems like a bad setup."

"In the best of worlds," I agree. "There's also a possibility he's been robbing me of my true earnings for the last two years, and the faintest chance he made up a completely bullshit scenario where all my dreams come true just to get me to move in with him so he can afford a duplex."

I startle myself at these words. Now that they're out there, they feel disturbingly true.

Ben, too, looks taken aback. "This is the guy you blew me off for?"

"No, I blew you off because you had me investigated and accused me of terrible things and I just happened to be dating this guy at the same time."

"You say to-may-to."

"Yes, I do. Because that is how it is pronounced. Anyway, I'm dumping Mitchell as soon as I get a chance to go back to Chicago. I think. Well, I'm pretty sure. Almost positive. As sure as I am about anything, which is not that sure."

"Fair enough. And when will that trip to Chicago be, exactly?" he prods. "I'm asking for a friend."

"Well, that's the thing. I was going to go back tomorrow. But I'm worried about Colleen. We've become pretty close, and something happened to her today that may have broken her heart. I'm not sure I can leave her. It would feel like bailing on a friend."

Now Ben looks truly concerned. "Okay, so we're getting to the top of the list. What's going on with Colleen?"

"She wants to adopt a baby."

"Whoa. That's huge."

My jaw drops. "I can't believe you hadn't heard that yet. Or read it in the Minnow Bay Gossip E-mail Blast."

"I don't think there's one of those. Yet." He picks up a pencil from his desk and licks the tip as though about to make a note to himself. I roll my eyes.

"Well, you know she dated Mason, right?"

"Of course I know," Ben says. "He's my cousin. And they were engaged, actually," he adds, so I know he's at least a little up to speed.

"Are you and Mason close? Do you talk a lot?"

"When he's not deployed, we do. I don't socialize a lot other than with Mason and my brother Drew. Perhaps you've heard?"

I want to ask him about his strange insulated life, but there's something tender and raw there, like the place a splinter has only recently been. "Did he ever tell you that they wanted a kid together?"

"Of course. I just thought . . ." His voice trails off. "Since they broke up . . ."

I sigh. "As far as I can tell, that kind of wanting doesn't go away just because the sperm donor does."

Ben shakes his head. "I suppose it doesn't."

Against my better judgment, I blurt out, "Do you?"

"Do I what?"

"Want kids? I'm asking for a friend."

"Oh. Oh yeah, definitely. One or a gaggle, I'm not sure which."

I smile. This is the right answer, I suddenly realize. "Me too. But I always assumed it would be in a sort of man-woman team-conception situation. And I didn't worry about timing because I thought if I waited too long or didn't have the workings, me and said man would adopt."

"I've never thought about it much, but that makes sense."

"Women think about these things. We get told all the time that our lady parts are a ticking clock. It's rattling."

"I suppose so."

"But here's the catch: adopting as a single woman takes years, is prohibited in half the countries that do foreign adoptions, and costs one billion dollars. And getting a young child domestically is as likely as winning the lottery."

"Really?" he says. "This is news to me."

"Really. I just came from June Jorgens's office."

"Ooh. I heard she got some winter chicks."

I drop my chin and levy him a dubious look. "So *that* made the bulletin?"

He shrugs. "Also in the bulletin," he adds, "I heard you are helping Simone apply for art school. And you took Colleen to a medical procedure—apparently something gynecological—and took care of her after like she was a sister. And you've quietly connected Jenny to three up-and-coming artists from Chicago who are looking for galleries." He clears his throat. "And you got me—famous town recluse Ben Hutchinson—to go to a party."

"It was your mother's birthday party."

"Sure it was. Did Jenny and Colleen tell you the last time I was out in a social setting in Minnow Bay?"

"No."

"Try the mid-nineties."

Just about everything this guy says is a surprise to me. "So you're an actual hermit? Not the exaggerated kind of hermit that Jenny had me thinking of?"

Ben sighs. "I'm not proud of it, but since you're thinking of breaking up with your boyfriend for me, I should probably give it to you straight. It's been nothing but work, home, and the café since I moved back to town five years ago. And only the café because the electricity in my house is iffy. That night after we fought, that was the first time I've set foot in my own dad's bar since I moved back."

"Jeez. What exactly happened to you in California?"

He shrugs. "I lost myself."

"And yourself was in a broken-down cabin in Minnow Bay?"

He pauses. "Up until recently. Yeah." He gives me a meaningful look.

I feel momentarily stymied. Then I blurt, "I'm not breaking up with my boyfriend *for* you. If I do break up with him."

"Which you should."

"Which I probably should. Still, it's important that you understand that."

Ben nods. "Okay. Got it."

"And your house is a dump. It's about to fall down around your ears."

"Well, that's uncalled for."

"I'm starting to care about you, Ben," I hear myself say. "And I don't think it's good to be living like that. I mean, to care so little for yourself that you can't invest in a comfortable home . . . It's one thing if you're broke. But I have to assume that Minnow Bay High pays you enough to get a decent furnace."

"Minnow Bay High doesn't pay me anything," he says softly.

I start. "What? You're a volunteer?"

"Please don't tell anyone. It's between me and the principal."

"But I don't understand. Why would you work for free?"

Ben pauses for a moment. I feel like he's going to sidestep me. Then he says, "Because I can. Because these kids deserve a good STEM education. And, for that matter, they also deserve having an artist in residence. Someone who does internships. Teaches master classes from time to time." He looks at me searchingly, as though he is daring me to imagine a whole life in Minnow Bay. And God help me, I do.

"I have to go back to Chicago," I say almost out of habit. Ben says nothing. There is a too-long quiet between us. Not companionable. Uncomfortable.

"I'm not broke, Lily," he finally says. "I could afford to fix up the cabin . . . if I had a reason to."

I know what he is saying but I pretend to misunderstand.

"Well, I am broke. And, coming full circle, since Jenny was wrong about the paintings, and Mitchell will definitely fire me when I break up with him, I am going to be pretty broke for the foreseeable future." I hear the false lightness in my voice. There's no covering it up.

He tilts his head at me. "Have you ever heard the phrase, it's only money?"

"Are you kidding? I *invented* that phrase. But now I don't know. I mean, try telling that to Colleen today, when she found out what it would cost to adopt. It's not only money for her."

Ben nods quietly. "I guess it isn't. But I do know how to cheer her up."

"You do?"

"Uh huh. But first, tell me how you do on ice skates."

Nineteen

What a question. How do I do on ice skates? I do like every other non-hockey player from the suburbs of Chicago does: every time I lace up it's like I've never done it before. Then I go around in a circle about ten times, fall about five, and pretty much feel okay and enjoy the rest of my time out on the ice. Then I go home and don't do it again for three years.

Apparently my three years is up. But there's an extra wrinkle to ice skating in Minnow Bay, Wisconsin: they do it outside. This dawns on me very, very slowly, that there is no ice arena in a town the size of a mall parking lot.

I meet up with Ben after school, and get in his car, and he says, "Did you bring skates?" and I say, "What, isn't there skate rental?" and he laughs himself silly. I mean really. He just laughs and laughs. I have to sit quietly in the passenger seat and wait for it to die down.

Finally he shakes his head and says, "Never mind. We're only grooming for now," and drives me through town in the opposite direction of Lemon Lake, past a few side streets and then by a pretty little park with a gazebo and a snow-covered play structure. And across the road from that, there is a large clearing, no houses and no trees, and a sidewalk that leads to a tall iron bridge over the snow.

"Is it a pond?" I ask, because the snow has fallen so deep that there's no telling what's underneath it. "A skating pond?"

"Yep," he says. "Cute as a button once it's cleared, but until then, we've got our work cut out for us."

"But what do you mean, cleared? As in, we have to shovel the snow?"

More laughing. "Shoveling would be crazy. No, we've got to think smarter, not harder."

I gesture to the car's temperature display. "It's four degrees outside. Smarter would be to go home and watch people ice skate on TV."

Ben smiles with a good-natured twinkle. He *is* good natured, right? Except when he's looking at me in that dead serious way of his that makes me feel not just naked but skinless. "That wouldn't be as fun." He hops out of the truck and slams the driver-side door shut, leaving me in the warmth of the car trying to figure out what is going on here. I can't, and it looks cold out there, so I just sit tight. After a few moments my door opens and Ben peers inside.

"Everything okay in here?"

"I'm just trying to understand why I'm looking at approximately thirty tons of snow and how you expect to move it."

He nods. "That's fair. Climb out and I'll break it down for you." He offers me his hand out of the car. I touch it and there is electricity even glove to glove. I pretend not to feel it and put my hands on my hips, then cross them over my chest, then back to my hips awkwardly. "The snow isn't really our major concern," he tells me.

"Oh no?" I ask, and pointedly look down to the spot where I am standing, where the snow is up to my knees.

"Nope, the ice is. You see, we've got to test the ice, and then, if it's strong enough, which I'm *fairly* certain it is, we go into that shed over there"—he gestures to a small abandoned-looking shed—"and get out the snow tractor."

"Snow tractor?"

"Basically an ATV with a plow blade."

"Like a riding lawn mower?"

"For snow."

"You can't go out on the ice in a riding lawn mower. For snow. Someone could die. It could be you."

"Well, you may be right. That's why we test first."

"And how exactly do we test?"

"By walking on the ice."

"With our feet?"

"Yes, walking with our feet," he says casually, as he opens his trunk and pulls out a pair of silver foil blankets tied in a bundle, a thermos of something, two lengths of rope with knots and carabiners, and two bright orange vests with lots of useful-looking loops.

"And if the ice isn't strong enough for our body weight?"

"Then we'll be glad I brought so much rope."

"This is not a good idea. This is not a job for two nice but highly citified people who want to cheer up a friend. Think of her face when she learns we've drowned in the freezing water."

"The pond is barely eight feet deep."

"I can drown in three feet. Try me."

"I'll take your word for it. It's been subzero for almost five days in a row. It's January. I have this ice auger I borrowed from the fire department, and these flags for us to carry, and we go around together, staying close to each other, and we test the ice's thickness, and then put the flags in anywhere it's safe. Hopefully it's thick enough not just to stand on, but to plow as well. If one of us falls in, the other fishes him—or her—out and goes to the clinic. The keys are in the truck."

I stare at him agog. "This is a terrible idea. You see that, right? The reason the fire department has the ice auger is because this is a job for said fire department."

"Actually, I'm a volunteer fireman."

It is all I can do not to smack my forehead like a sitcom actor. "Of course you are. And what qualifications does that entail, exactly?"

"Oh, they run a background check. I think. As I remember, I had to do a mental health questionnaire and a safety class. Most of the strong healthy people ages twenty-five to forty in Minnow Bay are on the squad. Some are much, much older. But you have to be at least able to lift a forty-pound bag."

"You can lift a forty-pound bag and this qualifies you to wander out onto untested ice and possibly plunge to your death?"

"Possibly plunge. Definitely not to my death. Rope, remember?"

"How exactly did you pass that mental health questionnaire?"

I get a good laugh for this, and I am satisfied.

"I can see your reservations," he says. "But I've done this before. I may have spent fifteen years getting soft in the valley and five more hiding in my cabin, but before that I was a real Minnow Bay kid. And it used to be that this pond got groomed for skating every year by the city."

"Really?" This makes me feel somewhat better. "Why did they stop?"

"Oh, it's hard to say. It might have had something to do with that poor drunken teen couple who fell through and drowned some years back."

I jerk my head up at him. He's smiling.

"That's not funny," I say, though it is a little. In a dark way.

"I can't help it. You make this face when I say something outrageous. It's so funny. Like you're horrified, yet not surprised at all."

"I think it's because I expect you to be an utter lunatic."

"I wasn't the one who ripped up our divorce papers like a madwoman."

"No, you were the one brandishing the hatchet like an axe murderer."

"And I *still* didn't hack you into pieces. Not even a little. Don't I get any credit for that?"

I laugh and shake my head. "No. No you don't. I may have settled for less than I deserve in the past, but I still don't give out any gold stars for refraining from axe murder."

"It sounds like you're going to be very high maintenance," he says with a wink.

"Sounds like you're going to have lots of opportunities to see my horrified face," I tell him back. "Now, tell me why they really stopped grooming the pond."

"Because of furloughs. Tough times during the recession. The town had to close one ice rink—either this one for public figure skating, or the one behind the high school, which is for the hockey teams. And, considering the Stormin' Sturgeonettes hockey team won State three out of the last ten years . . ."

I nod. "That is a much better explanation."

"Plus it has the advantage of being true," he says. "Okay, let's get out there and start flagging. You can start by putting a green flag right where you're standing. Careful, the tip is sharp, it cuts right through, you don't have to push too hard . . ."

"Is this to remind us of where the edge of the pond is?" I ask as I pull a green flag out of Ben's leather satchel and plunge it into the ground.

Ben shakes his head mischievously. "Nope. See that?" He points to the spot directly in front of where he parked his car. "That was the edge. We've been standing on the ice for the last ten minutes. Seems strong enough to me."

A very cold but strangely exhilarating hour later, we have flagged a nice large pond, and with the exception of two spots near the edge, the ice is thick enough not just for two adults but for the plow. By now, full dark has fallen over the pond and the pretty gas lamp–style park lights make a beautiful ring around the perimeter.

Ben sends me back to the truck to watch him plow. I want to go with him—after all, there is a cab with heavy plastic sheeting to keep warmth in, and the tractor looks fun. But he wisely points out that we are human and even humans with ice augers make mistakes. So my job is to watch with phone in hand from his truck and call 911 if worse comes to worst. Then he has to spend five minutes reassuring me that this is only a precaution and no one has ever fallen through the ice on the snow tractor. And then he has to spend five more minutes showing me how the plastic-coated cab of the tractor breaks away if you just push firmly on it, so that in the event of an emergency, he could easily get loose. Then he leans in to kiss me on the cheek and I turn my head and that's another five minutes. Then, and only then, do I go back to the truck to watch him plow.

The slow, methodical circles he drives are hypnotizing. I start to imagine the end result of all this hard work. It's going to be surreally beautiful, when the ice is cleared and the drifts of snow around it are waist high and the pretty iron bridge is rising high out of two puddles of white and skaters can slide underneath. Ben and I were making a mental list of who to invite skating for Colleen's cheer-up party, and we ended up thinking it would make the most sense just to invite Simone and Jenny, thereby informing the entire town. The forecast is for a slight warm-up tomorrow and only light snow between now and Thursday, so we plan the party for Thursday night. I look out the windshield and start imagining a few small touches to bring more magic to the scene. Luminaria, maybe, on the edge of the ice? Dozens of them, flickering against the snow to their own private rhythms.

Now I'm wondering if there's a good fresh X-Acto knife in the art studio. I could make snowflakes on the luminaria. Or mehendi designs, inspired by henna tattoos . . . or I could do the same designs on tissue paper, decoupage them around mason jars, drop candles inside, and hang them from the big willow tree that hangs over half the pond . . .

I have always loved paper cutting—I find it enormously relaxing compared to the hunched-over eyeball-straining work of my paintings. When Renee was expecting her first daughter, she told me the nursery theme was going to be "prima ballerinas," which I felt was maybe a *hair* oppressive for someone we hadn't even met yet, but even so, I wanted to get on board. So I cut out from heavy pastel card stock these soft and round jungle animals—hippos, rhinos, okapi, and elephants—in various states of arabesque and plié, and hung them from the finest fishing line until they were dancing a *Swan Lake* of their own. And, since the baby was a winter baby, I made them snowy tutus—layer upon layer of precision-cut paper snowflakes with the creases gingerly steamed out and then the paper positioned around the animals' waists. For their crowns, tiny dried lavender and baby's breath woven into miniature circles befitting their grand wearers' status.

It was a prissy, painstaking labor of love and I enjoyed every second of it. Renee dotingly hung it above the changing table and for months baby Natalie goggled at it as she had her diaper changed or during her little after-bath massage. I remember standing aside uselessly, goggling myself at Renee's strange competence with the baby—where did she learn to be such a wonderful mother?—and at the same time trying not to wonder what kind of mother I would have been to Nic's babies.

I know now, years upon years later, that I would have been no kind of mother then, and Nic is not what I wanted in a husband anyway, and the fairy tale that Renee had, that I tried so desperately not to envy her for, was not a fairy tale at all. At least not my kind of fairy tale.

Twinkling park lights, red, windburned cheeks, listening to an old Gillian Welch album and dreaming up frivolous art projects in a warm truck, as a man you are falling for competently clears a pond so everyone in town can enjoy one magical night of ice skating . . .

That is my fairy tale.

My mouth goes dry. *This* is my fairy tale.

I pick up my phone. I am *never* going back to Chicago. My fairy tale is right here.

I have to tell Renee. And Mitchell. And my brother.

It's time, I think, to say good-bye to that old life forever.

And that is when everything starts to go to hell.

Twenty

The phone rings only once before Renee picks up. "Hello?"

"Renee? It's me. I'm calling because—"

"Where the fuck are you?" she screams into the phone.

I spend a second being taken aback. "What? Are you okay?"

"Just answer the question." Her voice sounds raspy. Thick. Mad.

"I'm in Minnow Bay," I tell her, a little scared.

"You cannot be serious. How hard can it be to get a freaking divorce from a man you barely know? God, Lily, what is *wrong* with you? Why won't you just come home?"

I am rendered speechless. Rather than answer, I just stare out the window at Ben driving the tractor.

"Lily? Are you even listening?"

"Hm?"

And then she bursts into tears.

There are three times in my fifteen-year friendship with Renee that I have heard her cry. The first time was a month after we met, late at night after we drank too much cheap vodka mixed with Hawaiian Punch at a frosh party and she cried after throwing up on her new bought-just-for-art-school extra-long twin comforter. Once she cried from stress the night before she took the bar. And the last time was when she told me she was pregnant again when baby Natalie was only fourteen months old. Three of her grandparents have died in the time I have known her and there were no tears for any of them. She failed the bar on the first attempt and had to take it a second time—no tears over that. And one time in college a horrible professor told her she would never amount to anything and should give up art, in front of the entire seminar, and that didn't make her cry. It made me weep like a baby, and then drop the class in protest and write a mean instructor review, but it didn't make Renee cry.

Now she is crying. "Nic left me," she says, her voice full of pain and mucus. "He called me a cold, unfeeling bitch."

"What?" I say, suddenly violently mad. "Are you kidding me?" I will go down there and I will show Nic just how "unfeeling" a woman can be.

"Well, he did say I was cold. He said I wasn't invested in him or the girls. He told me I wasn't the woman he married." There's a little more wailing.

My rage flickers out as quickly as it came. "Oh. Oh, Renee. I'm so sorry. But just to be clear, he didn't call you a bitch?"

"Of course not," she says, her voice becoming more clear. "He doesn't have the balls. He said he loves me but I've changed. He wants to go to marriage counseling. Marriage counseling! Like we're some ugly middle-aged couple who never have sex anymore."

I recall a few times hearing about how Renee and Nic never have sex anymore. "Maybe it would be kind of a good idea? Just to get back on the same page and reconnect a bit?"

Renee snorts through her tears. "I don't want to reconnect. This whole tantrum of his has made me realize I never loved him. It's all been one huge disappointment."

This stops me cold. "What? No, honey, you don't mean that."

"Don't I? Think about it, Lily. I was about to graduate from college, I was scared of being alone, and he was just so convenient, you know?

I was looking for someone secure, who would stand by me as I went through law school. Someone I could count on to never outshine me. I knew he wasn't a cheater or a letch. And he was right *there*."

A hurt rises up in my chest that feels almost unbearable. I try to put it elsewhere—after all, this is not about me. It is about Nic and Renee.

Even still, as I go looking for the right words to say in response, only pointed questions appear in my mind. *He was convenient because he had been my boyfriend for the three years previous?* I want to ask. *He was "right there" because he had just broken up with me? You "knew he wasn't a cheater" because he had been faithful even to* me? Everything I want to say is hysterical and self-centered.

"I . . ." I say, because I've been silent for far too long, and I am praying something reasonable will come out. "I didn't know that you felt that way?" I attempt.

"Of course you didn't," says Renee, and then there are some more weeping sounds. "You've always been such an amazing friend to me, Lily, and you've always been on my side, and now that I need you, you're a million miles away on some kind of weird spirit quest, and my whole life is falling apart."

"I'm not a million miles away," I try. "I'm in Wisconsin."

"So you can come home, then?" she asks weepily. "I have to figure out what to do. I need you."

I swallow hard. All the times—there have been so many of them—Renee has been there for me are playing in my head. I'm usually the one having drama, needing guidance, not knowing how to negotiate some new self-created catastrophe, and she's the one who talks me out of doing stupid things and taking unnecessary risks and letting important things slip through my fingers. Right up to ten minutes before I left for Minnow Bay this was the case. She was the one who found Ben, who told me how to handle the situation, got me out of my panic and paralysis. Without her, I probably wouldn't even be up here. I wouldn't have met Jenny and Simone and Colleen and Ben. I wouldn't be sitting in this truck looking at my fairy tale through the windshield, thinking of how fast I'll have to abandon it.

"Of course I can come home. The weather looks clear. I'll get some coffee and leave as soon as I can."

"Oh, thank you," says Renee. "Thank you thank you thank you, Lily. You're my best friend in the world, you know that? We fight, but still, we'll always be there for each other. No matter what happens, just like we promised each other freshman year."

Freshman year. When, after six months of clinging to each other as we navigated homesickness and aimlessness and artistic terror, my mother was diagnosed with terminal cancer, and instead of packing up and going to her, I lay down in my lofted bed and stayed there for three days. And on that third day, Renee came home from class, climbed up the loft ladder, grabbed my ankles, and actually tipped me out of the bed so that I had to hang on to the edge to soften my fall.

"You're all packed up," she said, when my dismount was complete. "The registrar is calling your professors now. You will be able to come back whenever, but probably next semester is most realistic."

I lay there on the floor for a few more minutes. I was crying in such an empty way, it wasn't even a good cry, it was just a half-assed attempt based in self-pity. It was crying for lack of a better plan.

As though I were a child, Renee washed my face with a warm washcloth and changed me out of stale pajama pants into a clean pair of jeans—jeans she must have washed for me, because God knew I hadn't done laundry in weeks. "Get up," she said when she was done. "Stop wasting time."

"My life is here," I said then, stupidly, selfishly, because I was eighteen and I thought my life was in any particular place at all, and that I had a life to geolocate in the first place. "I can't just leave."

"Fine," she said. She crossed her arms over her chest and nodded. "Then we'll just go out to dinner. You've got to get out of this room. Get your purse."

But of course when she got me into the car—a car she had somehow obtained, though freshmen weren't allowed cars on campus—she pointed it west and didn't stop driving until we were in my home suburb. I sat, catatonically, knowing what was happening, knowing it was the right thing, and hating it all the while.

In the parking lot of a nearby grocery store, she flicked my face right on the temple, hard, as I remember, and said, "I need directions to your mom's house."

Instead of giving them to her I begged her to turn around. "I can't face her. She'll see I'm too weak to help her. I'll only make her feel worse."

"Worse than having terminal cancer?"

I burst into tears instead of answering.

After a moment, Renee said, "You're right. You're useless. Which ends now. Time to nut up and go show her you'll be okay."

I sniveled and shook my head. "But I won't be okay. I'm going to be all alone when she's gone."

And Renee, in her way, turned off the radio and said to me, "Don't be a stupid fucking idiot. You won't be alone. You'll always have me, moron. And I'll always have you, whether I like it or not. We're family now. And family is yours for life. Now, give me your address."

"Just like freshman year," I say now, a million miles away from that terrible day. But not with any kind of enthusiasm.

As soon as Renee hangs up, I look over at Ben and see that he is parking the snowplow back in the shed. I dash a note off and put it on the dashboard and then race back the couple of blocks to the inn on foot. I thunder up the stairs noisily enough that Colleen appears at my door, Jenny trailing behind her.

"We were looking for you," says Colleen. "Everywhere. Where have you been?"

"I was—" I'm about to tell them about Ben and the lake when I realize, Colleen will still get her surprise even though I won't be here to have it with her. It makes me feel a little better about leaving. "I can't tell you, actually. You'll find out tomorrow."

"What are you doing?" asks Jenny.

"I'm packing," I tell her. "I'm sorry to do this, but I have to go back to Chicago right now."

"Now?" Jenny says, horrified. "Not now! Tonight?"

"Tonight. It's an emergency."

"Oh my goodness, what's wrong?" asks Colleen, crossing to my bed and grabbing clothes from the closet to fold for me.

"It's Renee," I tell them, "I think she's leaving Nic. Or he's leaving her? I'm not a hundred percent sure. I only know that she needs me."

"Renee, the lawyer who wouldn't lend you two hundred bucks?" asks Colleen, her folding speed slowing tremendously.

"Renee, the lawyer who has been my best friend since freshman year," I say.

"And Nic is the guy who left you for your best friend?" says Jenny.

"Yes," I say, because there's no shine to put on that particular nugget.

"And this constitutes an emergency how?"

"Does a divorce not constitute an emergency?"

Jenny shrugs in her Jenny way. "Mine didn't. Well, it was hard to get enough Champagne on such short notice. . . ."

Colleen waves her off. "Are you really the only one she can go to with this?"

I drop the pile of bathroom ephemera I'm scooping up back to the counter with a clatter. When I turn around I see Jenny and Colleen, who are both standing in my room with hands on hips now, looking formidable, looking like they mean to keep me here by force. "Ladies," I tell them. "I appreciate your kindness and friendship, and the zeal with which you have encouraged me to extend my visit to Minnow Bay. However, and I say this with love, this is none of your business."

Jenny doesn't bat an eye. "Lily, and I also say this with love, it is entirely my business."

"We care about you," says Colleen. "And it doesn't seem like Renee has treated you very nicely in the past."

"And furthermore," says Jenny, "I've invested in you. I went into the studio today, when I was looking for you, and I saw what you are working on. *The August Drought,*" she says, and immediately I realize that that will be the name of this painting, if I ever get it done. "It's going to be your most important work. It's so full of anticipation. Of the agony of waiting. It's painful and beautiful at once."

Colleen nods. "It hurts me to look at it," she says, and her eyes are a little wet. "It's my last three years, on rice paper."

I look down, a little sadly, a little ashamed. "I'm sorry," I say to Colleen, for surely she has now seen what I added in only yesterday, in a window of the outbuilding, no bigger than my pinkie nail, on a gessoed canvas more than four feet tall. A young genderless child, the very image of Colleen, looking out impatiently. Waiting, desperately, for that hot sticky blue sky to make rain. "I hope it's okay."

She shakes her head. "No. No, it's exactly right. You got it exactly, perfectly right."

"I don't exactly choose what I paint," I say feebly.

"And we don't exactly choose what we want," says Jenny. "Don't you want to tell Renee that you can't be there for her now?"

I swallow hard. "I don't know," I say. "Yes," I add. "But I'm not going to."

Jenny sighs. Colleen goes back to packing my bags. "You're a better friend than I am," says Colleen. "From where I sit, it seems like you're driving through the black winter night to support a person who left you to twist in the wind through your loneliest moment."

I smile sadly, but internally, my heart plummets, knowing that I am actually doing the very same thing to Colleen right now. "This is something I have to do," I try. "It's a promise we made long ago."

"But if you go back there, you're never coming back to Minnow Bay," says Jenny.

"What?" I ask. "Of course I am! I may even want to move here, find a place, see where things go with Ben—"

"Ben is leaving," says Jenny. "Moving back to California."

"What?" I ask again, shocked. "No. No, that can't be true." I think of him on the snow plow. Of the lights on the river. Of the class of fourteen-year-old hackers. "He doesn't belong in California."

Colleen nods sadly. "And the end of the school year," she says. "He's going to fix up that terrible dump just enough to sell it and leave again. He gave notice at the high school the week before you arrived."

"But . . . how can that be? What about his family? He loves it here!"

Jenny nods. "He does. He truly does. But Minnow Bay is falling apart. I think it breaks his heart to watch it happen."

"Falling apart? Are you nuts? This is the most amazing little town I've ever been to. It has a thriving art gallery. Three incredible restaurants. An amazing school. The most beautiful little inn with the most amazing owner . . ."

Colleen looks down, unable to meet my eye.

"Right?" I say.

Colleen sighs deeply. "This winter is probably going to be the end for the Minnow Bay Inn. Usually summer gets me through, but last year was rough. Bad combination of road construction and flooding downstate during the art fest. Forced us to cancel the event that usually fills the town to the gills. Combined, it nearly killed us all."

I look to Jenny, expecting her to set the record straight, but she only nods. "Same story with the gallery. We just can't keep going year round anymore. Don't you see how empty the stores are all month long? The city council is recommending local businesses move to a summer-only model. But that leaves the town unemployed more than half of the year."

I stare at them, speechless.

Colleen shrugs. "Up until today, I have been trying to save every penny I have for the baby, to conceive, to adopt—I didn't know how futile it would be," she tells me. She is so matter-of-fact. While my heart breaks all over again to think of it. "Now I can use that to start over in Duluth or Green Bay—wherever I can get a hospitality job—while I wait for a buyer for the inn."

"You can't do that," I nearly shout. "You can't sell the inn! Ben can't leave. You can't close the gallery. What are you guys even talking about?"

"Well, there's a bit of good news there," Jenny smiles sadly. "I won't have to now, thanks to you. Your paintings are going to cover my winter expenses and then some when they all sell."

If any of them sell. I stop packing and try not to make eye contact.

Colleen nods. "And you've done so much beyond that, don't you see? You've been such an amazing friend while I was finding out about . . . about all the *disappointments* I have had in the last few weeks. You've given Simone a beautiful future by encouraging her passions and showing her a life outside of her imagination. You brought much-needed business to Erick's garage. Dragged Ben out of his shell. You've even gotten him to invest in the town again . . ."

"What do you mean?" I ask. "Invest in the town? What do you mean?"

"Lily. Come on. Think about it. Here's this dot-com millionnaire living in a fishing shack miles out of town, working as a high school teacher, chopping his own wood for heat—did you think he blew all that money he made in tech on drugs and iPhones?"

"Well, vacations and women, actually. But yes."

Jenny shakes her head at me like I'm the world's biggest moron. "It's him who was propping us up during the recession. He doesn't think any of us knew, but for three straight years he was paying the rent on the bistro so they could afford to expand to lunch. Rehabbing the yoga studio so they could add children's classes. Setting up online sales for the bookstore so they didn't get creamed by Amazon. Making capital investments in the café so they could hire help. Matter of fact, it was a grant he invented out of nowhere that turned my back-alley garage into a studio for resident artists. And his software company is the main underwriter for the entire summer art festival."

My jaw drops. "Holy shit."

"That's why he lives in that dump, Lily, out by the water. Because the money he thought he would spend making it beautiful has all gotten poured into his beloved Minnow Bay. He moved here to be a well for a town parched with thirst. But even the deepest wells run dry over time."

I put my face in my hands and start to cry. "I had no idea," I say. "You guys never said anything."

"Surely you saw some things weren't right," says Colleen.

"I saw a beautiful little town with the most amazing people, people who care deeply about each other, who support each other and treat newcomers like family. And, until earlier today, I thought Ben was a grouchy loner hoarding the last of his fortune for dear life."

"He is. Except for the hoarding part. But it changed when you got here. Then suddenly he wasn't such a hermit anymore."

"And that's why you wanted me to stay?" I say, feeling the other shoe descending fast. "To keep Ben here?"

Colleen shakes her head adamantly. "We wanted you to stay because we like you. We forced you to stay because we thought maybe you could keep Minnow Bay alive a little longer."

I blink. "What do you mean forced me?"

"Surely you knew what we were up to," says Colleen. "With the mysteriously flat tire, and the nonsense over driving to Duluth, and the car that wouldn't start because it needed an *oil change,* of all things, and the dropped texts, and the bogus birthday party . . ."

"Wait, what now?"

Jenny laughs a bitter little laugh. "I told you she wasn't playing along, Colly. She really had no idea."

"What did you do to my car?" I ask.

"Nothing," says Jenny. "Well, I punctured your tire with Colleen's ice pick." She gestures a thumb at Colleen. "She's the one who came up with the bullshit story about there being no tires in Minnow Bay. And then the whole 'Hutch is going to Duluth' scheme was all her, which was pure genius, really," she says to Colleen.

I look to Colleen in horror.

"Jenny," she says with caution in her voice.

"And then I strong-armed Erick to tell you the car wouldn't start, that day after Ben spoiled the tire ruse. He was all set on being honest. I practically threatened him at knifepoint."

My jaw drops open. "*Jenny,*" says Colleen louder.

But Jenny ignores her. "And Colleen organized the fake birthday party for Ben's mom."

"Fake birthday party?"

"Carla hates surprises. She was in on it from the start. We wanted an excuse for you to spend some real time with Ben, and meet the family, and see how wonderful this place can be. . . ."

"You did *what*?"

"It sounds sinister, but it's not," says Colleen. "It was out of hope. For you and for Minnow Bay."

I shake my head. "I can't believe you, Colleen."

"In my defense, Jenny was the one who deleted those text messages on your phone. I told her that was a bridge too far."

"You did what?" I say again, this time with added fury.

"If he really loved you, he'd pick up the phone," said Jenny. "He doesn't care about you, you know that, right?"

"He—I—That is not okay!" I stammer. "You can't delete a person's text messages!"

"I didn't delete anything real. Just bullshit about the museum thing," she says.

"What?" I shout again. I am starting to shake a little.

"It was all bullshit, Lily, I'm so sorry to tell you. It sounded so fishy that I checked with the exhibition company. They went with a different artist. Decided weeks ago. Mitchell was stringing you along, to keep you from firing him. He was defrauding you, Lily. Really, he still is."

"But . . ."

"I should have told you right away, but I hardly knew you then," says Jenny. "I wasn't sure how you would take it. And then when I got to know you more, I was worried about breaking your heart," she said. "So I deleted the messages so you wouldn't get led on further."

"But . . . how . . ."

"You leave your phone on the dresser every day when you go to paint," says Colleen. "She came in when I did towel service. I'm sorry—but you try arguing with her. Especially when so much is at stake . . ."

"But," I say, and now I am crying. The Smart. The Chazen. MAM and Weisman and St. Paul and Carleton . . . I had already pictured my paintings in each one of those halls, under all those hundreds of thousands of eyes, being written up by important publications, being truly *seen* for the first time in my life as an artist. . . . "It was all bullshit?"

Jenny nods. She looks chastened. She knows now how upset I am.

"And you guys knew the whole time?"

Colleen looks very very contrite, but she nods.

I say nothing for a long time because I am afraid I will betray myself with a storm of sobs and wails and childlike tears. Finally I say, "I need some time alone."

"Just tell us what we can do," says Colleen. "We know this is bad. We knew it was wrong the whole time. We just . . . we thought you were playing along. We didn't know you as well then."

Apparently not. If they'd known me, maybe they would have known I wasn't worth keeping around anyway. I'm not a museum-caliber artist. I haven't painted anything good in months. I can't even keep Ben Hutchinson in town. He's been secretly planning his exit this whole time.

"I don't want you to do anything," I say honestly. "I think we've all done quite enough. Don't you?"

As quickly as I can, I finish packing. Unbidden, Colleen calls Erick and he brings my car back to the inn despite the hour. By now it is nearly 9:00 P.M. I know leaving so late is insanity, but staying would be just as insane. I have to get out of here. Loading the car, with the extra canvases gone, takes only a moment, and then Jenny takes me by the hand, as though everything she just told me does not make me want to wrench it away. "I have something for you. Something that probably ensures you will never be coming back. But it belongs to you nonetheless." And then she hands me a check.

I look at it in shock. "What the hell?" I blurt, when I see the large number it's made out for.

"I sold your works," she says, with a sad half-smile. "That's what I wanted to tell you today."

"All of them?"

"Just two. Another of the stable and one from the urban duet."

"This is for just two paintings?" I say in shock.

"Less my commission, yes. I'll get you a full statement soon, but I wanted the moment of handing you the check right away. Like the Publishers Clearing House, you know."

"Yes," I say, because this feels exactly like that, except if I were extremely mad at Ed McMahon. "Are you sure this is the right amount?"

"I'm positive. You deserve every penny, Lily. You're the real deal," she says. "We may have . . . exaggerated some things and not been totally honest about some others. But about your talent, I have told you nothing but the truth."

Tears spring up in my eyes. I want to cry in gratitude, in surprise, in joy. Instead I think of the big scam I've just been party to and the joy completely dries up. "Thank you," I say as coldly as I can. "I appreciate it."

"Congratulations," says Jenny softly. "I'll mail a check when the other one sells."

"I might be back," I say, not meaning it in the slightest. "To finish the new one, I mean."

"Okay," says Jenny, though I can tell she doesn't believe me. "I'll see you, then."

"Good-bye," says Colleen, and gives me a weird forced-upon-me hug through the driver's-side window that shows that she too thinks I am gone forever.

I think of how, just an hour ago, I would have been eager to prove them wrong. How I was looking forward to making this trip in the other direction, as soon as humanly possible—maybe a week or two would be all it took to get Renee on her feet. Now I do not know where I will be living, I only know that I am not coming back here.

"I know you're angry at us," says Colleen. "I get that. But be careful back home. Don't let them walk all over you."

I give a weary childish sigh. I know what they think, that I am too weak-willed and complacent to break up with Mitchell or tell Renee to lay off. That I will rush back to my old life at the first possible opportunity, regardless of what awaits me there.

But I've changed, in the last hour. I'm coming to figure out who I can trust.

And, apparently, I cannot trust anyone.

"I think," I say coldly, "that it's time for me to put my days of being manipulated behind me. If such a thing is possible."

"Where will you go?" Jenny asks.

I shake my head and then take one last look at the pretty snow-clung brick facade of the Minnow Bay Inn. "I only know where I won't be," I tell her. Then I roll up the window to stop the icy wind coming in, and put the car into drive, and prepare to leave Minnow Bay forever.

There's just one more stop I need to make.

When I pull into Ben's house on Lemon Lake, it seems like no one is home. Actually, it seems like no one is home on the entire lake. The houses are totally dark, the streetlights are sodium dim, the moon isn't out, and the only clue to the whereabouts of Ben's driveway is a tiny silver bike reflector on the mailbox in front of it. I rumble up the gravel driveway and shine my headlights on the house, which is completely dark, and then, just as I am about to give up and leave, I spot a little glowing illumination coming from, of all places, Ben's roof.

I cut the lights, pull my coat around me, and head to the house.

"Up here," he calls, and I see a big aluminum ladder propped against the garage.

For a second I think about ignoring him. I could pretend I didn't hear him, knock, go back to the car, and leave forever.

Or, perhaps more fun, I could "accidentally" knock the ladder out of position, trapping him up there. The woman who came here and tore up the divorce papers weeks ago might do that.

I am not really that woman.

Instead I walk to the ladder, tip my head up to where that tiny little light is coming from, and say, "Is it icy?"

"I raked it yesterday. Safe as long as you watch your step."

The gable of the roof is perpendicular to the lake, and the ladder is set halfway between edge and peak on the lake-facing side. I make my way slowly up the ladder, glad for my serious boots and questioning the merit of my felt mittens yet again. When I come to the top of the roof and get myself to standing, mountain-goat style, I find Ben sitting on what is clearly a homemade addition—a small teak bench set into the roof, with a PVC pipe handrail leading straight to it.

"You can't winterproof your house, but you can build a winterized bench on the roof of your garage?" I ask.

"You must remember how I feel about stars," he says. "It gets so nice and dark up here."

It is so incredibly dark. When I am seated on the bench, padded with one of those impossibly thick army-surplus blankets, and my heartbeat settles a little from the climb, Ben turns out his lantern and we both look up. It is like nothing I've ever seen before. The sky is brighter than any cityscape I've ever seen. There is an arch of creamy glow in the sky that I know from planetarium visits to be the Milky Way. It stretches across the entire sky, above, behind, in front, and through it, stars on top of stars, on top of stars.

Without knowing exactly how I can feel inspired amid all that has happened today, I let a deep sigh escape.

"You might see the northern lights. If you stay up here long enough."

"I'm leaving," I tell him quietly.

"I know. I found your note when I came back from plowing the ice."

"And I'm not coming back,"

"I know that too. Colleen texted me already."

"The Good Old Minnow Bay Bulletin Service," I say, not turning away from the stars.

"You know, they didn't mean to hurt you. They thought you were sort of in on it, the whole time. You didn't put up much of a fight."

"I'm not much of a fighter," I say. "I trust people so easily."

"That doesn't mean they never deserve your trust. Colleen and Jenny are not bad people. They're actually wonderful people."

"I know," I say. "But it doesn't help."

He says nothing for a time.

"When were you going to tell me you were moving?" I ask.

Again I get silence.

"Were you waiting for me to fall in love with you?"

The longest silence yet. Then, finally, quietly, he says, "Yes."

"I think I was," I tell him.

He swallows. At some point in the last few moments I've turned to him, and now I see his windburned face set in a deep frown, his eyebrows furrowed. "I was hoping you'd come with me," he says. "We'd go back, and I'd start another company, and we could buy a beautiful apartment in the suburbs, and you could paint whenever you wanted."

My heart contracts. That sounds exactly perfect for a version of myself that no longer exists. "But that's not what I want."

He sighs. "I know that now."

My eyes start to sting. The cold. "I wanted something that wasn't real," I say, thinking of Minnow Bay's incredible main street. It's friendly, cold-proof people.

"It was real. It just isn't lasting."

"What I want would last."

We sit quietly for a little longer.

"I have to go now."

"Just stay tonight," he says, turning to me, suddenly with hands on my shoulders, his face a foot from mine and yet so incredibly close. "Please."

I want to. I want that so much. "I can't," I tell him. "Despite . . ." I grope around for the words to describe the manipulation, the confusion, the disappointment I feel, and then give up, ". . . *everything.* There's a part of me that wishes I could stay. But, for better or for worse, I told Renee I'd be there for her in the morning. I think she needs me to watch the girls while she consults her lawyer."

"Oh, come on," Ben says, suddenly angry. "What about a nanny? What about the husband? The one you almost married? What about anyone else in the world but *you*?"

"It has to be me."

"It doesn't have to be you. Don't you see? Can't you see through any of this manipulation?"

I bite my lip, hurt. "Apparently not, Ben. If I could, I wouldn't still be here."

"No, you'd be back in Chicago with your so-called boyfriend and the best friend who treats you like shit and the brother who won't take your phone calls unless he needs money."

I press my eyes into my hands. It all hurts so much. I feel so incredibly lost.

"I know you think you can't trust us, Lily. But the people here, we care about you. Colleen, Jenny, Simone, Drew—"

"Drew?"

"My older brother. You met him at my mom's party."

"Your brother? What the hell does he have to do with this?"

"He's the one who bought your paintings, Lily. Don't you see? People who barely know you believe in you, and I believe in—"

"Stop," I say, and wave my hands in front of my face like his words are ravens aiming directly for my eyes. My mouth goes dry. I want to cry and barf at the same time.

"A Hutchinson bought my paintings?"

"Yes," he says. "I don't know why Jenny didn't tell . . ." His voice drifts off as he starts to understand exactly why Jenny didn't explain that no, my paintings didn't sell because I'm talented or I'm worth what she said I'm worth or because some collector saw investment potential or just fell in love with the works and they'll soon be hanging in a carefully decorated lake home and admired for exactly what they were intended to be. No, Jenny forced them on yet another obedient Hutchinson who obliged as one more attempt to preserve the smoke and mirrors that my last month has been comprised of.

So that's good. Because now I can do what I need to do with absolutely no lingering regrets.

"Give this to Colleen for me, will you?" I say, and stand up, carefully, because no matter what Ben tells me, everything, everywhere I look, seems so tenuously icy.

Ben takes the envelope I hastily stuffed together in the car. "What is it?"

"Just give it to her," I repeat. "And help me down this ladder. I'm leaving now."

"I want you to stay," he says. "Please. Lily. Stay."

I shake my head, make my way to the ladder, accepting his help, wishing I didn't so badly want to say yes, and knowing that I have let everything go way too far. At the edge of the roof, once my legs are kicked over and solid on the ladder, I wrench free of his hands.

"It's better I'm leaving," I tell him. "After I'm gone, you can watch for those northern lights for as long as you like. For the rest of your life, if you want."

Twenty-one

I am angry, truly angry, at the citizens of Minnow Bay for only about an hour. Somewhere around the time I have to stop to pee and buy more syrupy fast-food coffee, I stop being mad at them and turn the blame directly where it belongs, onto myself. I came to Minnow Bay looking desperately to get unstuck from any number of things, but no matter what I might have told myself, the very last thing on that list was my marriage to Ben. I came because I didn't know how to keep an apartment, break up with a jerk, stand up to a friend, or be a sister to my brother. I still don't know how to do any of those things, but I know now the answer isn't running away, or throwing a tantrum, or buying a really soft pair of mittens.

Back in Chicago, in my real life, such as it is, I can decide to learn how to do those things. Or I can move in with Mitchell, take care of Renee, and try to cram myself back into as close a facsimile of a time long past as possible.

And what makes me so angry is that I'm having trouble deciding on which thing to do.

I don't love Mitchell, not even a little bit. I was telling the truth when

I said I was falling in love with Ben, so that is how I know for sure about Mitchell. Maybe before I went to Minnow Bay I could have convinced myself that what we had was something love-like. Now I can be absolutely positive it is not.

And I know too now that my creative "block" in painting was a similar invention of mine, as useful to me as the idea that I might one day feel love for Mitchell, and just as improbable. I was not waiting on perfect light or ideal material or some kind of painterly lightning bolt of inspiration to strike me from the sky. If I could work in a sixty-degree garage in an alleyway in the middle of darkest Wisconsin winter, painting from a sketch made by a stranger five years earlier, I can work anywhere. The real reason I wasn't painting was because I didn't believe in myself anymore. When, for ever so short a time, I did, I painted again.

And the most infuriating thing of all? The thing that hurt me most in Chicago, that hurts most now, that fundamental understanding I seem to be incapable of having? That my best friend is a shitty one, and my attempt at replacing her was utterly unsuccessful, and that the reason for all of this is that my magical-unicorn-ride idea of friendships has been, all this time, unrealistic, childish, and just plain stupid.

Apparently, my friendships aren't the "always there for each other, push you forward when it hurts, hold you back when you're about to step into traffic, move next door to each other and talk on the phone every day and cry and laugh and get old and play cribbage together" bullshit I was promised since I read my first Baby-Sitters Club book at age seven.

Apparently, my friendships are conditional. And deceptive. And fleeting.

I look straight ahead, into that wintry dark that creeps into the edges of my headlights, that threatens to overtake me from behind, that seems utterly inescapable and, for the first time, I truly understand: you cannot, it turns out, build your entire life around your friends' lives. You must have a life of your own. And believing otherwise will only land you with a nasty surprise ten years down the road.

When the bachelorette party is long over and everyone else's life has moved on and yours is only standing perfectly, totally still.

In Chicago I go straight to Renee's house. It is six in the morning when I arrive—I had to stop and sleep for a couple of hours near Rockford—and I don't want to ring the doorbell in case she cried herself to sleep in the late hours the night before. I'm mad at her, but I'm not a total asshole. Instead I park in front of her house—my God, it seems even bigger than usual, and yet more outrageous that she couldn't squeeze me in there for a couple of days—and wait until I see some signs of life.

Some number of minutes later I am asleep with my face on the steering wheel and Renee is knocking on my window at the same time as she is yanking on my door.

I nearly tumble out, catch myself, blink my eyes hard, and wrap her in a hug. It's like a reflex, like opening your mouth when you put on mascara. I see her, I hug her, I try not to cry. She hugs back, a real one, the first I've gotten from her in a long time, and says, "You really did it. You drove through the night."

I nod. I'm feeling sleep addled. I'm supposed to be mad, I remind myself. I'm not.

Renee shakes her head at me. Disappointment? Relief? "I don't know what to say."

"Are you okay?" I ask her.

"I am. I'm really okay," she says. "I'm good, actually."

I look at her blankly. My car door is standing open, and I must have left the keys in the ignition because the car is dinging at me. "Ding, ding, ding," it says, like a wakeup call gone unanswered.

Renee takes my arm and pulls me out of the car, pushes the door closed behind me. She grabs my hand, presses it tight in her fingers. "You know Nic and I are never going to split up," she says matter-of-factly. "We have two amazing daughters together, and an obscene mortgage, and fifty thousand dollars in credit card debt holding us together even if just being married wasn't enough."

My mouth falls open.

"And you drove all night long just to be here for me, even though you knew all those things."

I shake my head at her wildly. "I did *not* know all those things, Renee." Fifty thousand dollars in debt? The vast number knocks my brain out of my ear.

Renee laughs. She laughs! "What did you think, Lily? Did you think I like working ninety-hour weeks and dressing exclusively in my aunt's hand-me-down Ann Taylor Loft?" She pauses for a second but obviously not so I can respond, which is good, because I'm stunned speechless. "I just don't know what else to do. And neither does Nic. And there you are, no student loans, no kids, no tuition, no responsibility, just fucking up any old way you want to with no repercussions, and *making your art* all the time, and then not making it because apparently even that was too hard, and taking extended sabbaticals to nowhere-freaking-Wisconsin with all your possessions tossed into a fifteen-year-old car you own free and clear."

I stare at her wide-eyed.

"And Nic really *loved* you, you know that? He told me you were better in bed than me. And to then have you ask to move in? Can you imagine that, you living your carefree life, floating like a helium balloon around this house while we stagger under all this *stuff*?"

I still stand there. I feel groggy, from driving, from sleep, from not understanding anything I thought I so clearly understood just a few minutes ago.

"It's just been hard to love you," Renee tells me, and now she is crying. "And I do. I do love you. And Nic does. Not like that. Though, I don't know that for sure. The girls love you. You're Natalie's hero. But it's just been so freaking hard to be your friend. That's why I was trying to hurt you, Lily. That's why I've said so many awful things." And then she sobs for the second time in ten years, and two days.

"I didn't know," I say dumbly. "I had no idea. How was I supposed to know?" But of course now I start to think of the things I've misunderstood. The clothes. The permanent state of hurry. The dark circles under her eyes.

"Nic and I have been in separate bedrooms for the last year. That's why I never have you over anymore. And he said to me, last night, before you called, he said I wasn't the woman he married, and he asked me why I couldn't be more like you."

I stand completely still, completely quiet, completely and utterly stunned.

"And that's why," she says. "You see, don't you? I'm not the woman he married. I'm not the friend you lived with freshman year. I can't afford to be, not anymore. I had to give that all up."

I start to see it all now. The last ten years, completely rewritten in an instant. All the drinks dates laughing about my stupid boyfriends and my incompetence with money and my dead-end jobs. All the times I showed up with lattes at her office at 4:00 P.M. and she dropped whatever she was doing to talk for an hour. The real reason the invitations to come over for wine-fueled sleepovers stopped coming, why she stopped attending my art openings, why she stopped taking my phone calls, why she didn't want to lend me two hundred bucks at the blink of an eye.

I see it all.

"I had no idea," I say again.

She shakes her head at me. "I love you, Lily, and you're my best friend, but you can't see things right in front of your own face. And when that inn lady called me last night, and told me what had happened—"

"Wait, what?" I say.

"Colleen O'Donnell? She called me at like, nine P.M. last night just to yell at me. She just wanted to tell me basically how incredible a friend you are and how I am squandering your love and treating you like shit and—"

"You've got to be kidding me." I think, suspiciously, of the envelope, but then remember: 9:00 P.M. I was still sitting on Ben Hutchinson's roof. "Colleen called you? She yelled at you?" That sounds more like Jenny, I think with a sad smile.

"Well, she didn't actually yell. She told me that she had hurt you and you were out of her life and she didn't want me to make the same mistake. She told me you deserved better. And that's when I realized, you had no idea why I was acting like this. You didn't know all the ways you were making things worse. All this time I thought . . . I thought it was because you were too selfish to care."

"I was." I think about all this. "No. Just too stupid to see," I tell her.

Renee takes my hand. She takes it hard, and I feel now it's cold, it's January in Chicago, and we've been standing outside all this time, and she's in her pajamas, and her face is puffy from tears.

"Can we start over?" she asks me now. "With each other the way things actually are, not the way they used to be? Can you be a friend to someone with a drowning marriage and a hopeless fiscal situation and barely enough hours in the day to eat, much less meet up for coffee and boy talk at a moment's notice?"

My throat fills; my voice is thick. "Can you be friends with someone who is living out of her car and cheated on her boyfriend and is in love with a man she slept with once ten years ago?"

Renee actually thinks for a moment before she answers. "Yes. Yes. Of course I can."

"Me too," I say, and now the tears are back and we are both crying. "But before we start over completely, I need to ask one more thing of you."

One after the other, Renee and I clean off the heartbreak and grime of the last twenty-four hours. She pulls out a suit—suddenly her wardrobe of ill-fitting poly-blend business separates make so much more sense—and I pull on a sweater from the top of my suitcase, the very same suitcase Colleen packed for me the entire time I was raging at her for misleading me. It's the men's woolen sweater that appeared, unbidden, in my room at the inn a week or so ago. Was it Mason's? Ben's? It feels all the warmer for its kind intentions.

Both of us hold hot washcloths over our eyes until the red swollen look turns more into a light puff. I look around her master suite bathroom in a new way, seeing now that there is only one toothbrush in the Venetian glass holder, only one Egyptian cotton bath sheet on the heated towel rod.

"We can be like a two-woman support group," I tell her as I take it all in, the loneliness combined with the overspending. "Work together to get our money right."

Renee puts her face in her hands. "I'm going to have to give up so much."

Looking at her in the mirror, I add, "Or, you could just give up worrying about what other people think about you, sell this anchor of a house, and get the girls into public school stat."

She looks back at me. "It might be easier to just file for bankruptcy."

"Might be," I tell her. "But we never were the kind of people who took it easy."

She rolls her eyes but I can see that she's not ruling it out. "Do you have a contract with Mitchell?" she asks me. "I feel like you're going to say you don't, and I'm going to yell at you for being irresponsible, and you're going to mumble something about being an artist and letting the details take care of themselves."

"Consider that entire conversation to have happened already. And then come with me to my car, because I have a box in there labeled 'Papers and Shit' that probably contains everything you need."

It does. She locates the contract, scans it in her leather-appointed home office, and then starts marking up a copy. "Okay," she says. "Here's the passage you need." She circles something in red and makes some more notes. "Now, go get the girls out of bed and ready for school. I'll draft the paperwork."

That one simple instruction Renee gives me is so intensely challenging that I start to understand a little better what her life is really like. Natalie, seven, opens her eyes when I enter her room, shouts, "AUNT LILY!" excitedly, and then turns around and goes back to sleep like a narcoleptic. The five-year-old, Natasha, is already up, dressed in a satin princess gown, and has emptied an entire bowl of expensive organic cereal into a big baking bowl, filled it with milk, and is now trying to pick out only the raisins with her spoon. I rush upstairs and ask Renee what to do about this situation and she doesn't even turn away from the screen, waving one hand and saying, "She only eats raisins now. Breakfast, lunch, dinner, raisins."

Oh my god. Renee, I remember vividly, fed her kids organic quinoa and coconut milk smoothies for their first foods. She breastfed them until they were, like, thirty. If she says Natasha only eats raisins now, I am not going to be able to contradict that.

Instead I go back into Natalie's room, pull the covers off her body, get scolded in a stern seven-year-old voice, and open the blinds and turn on the lights. Nothing happens beyond some grousing and moaning until I tell her I will give her ten dollars if she gets dressed and gets ready for school. She opens her eyes but doesn't move. I can't bid more—I don't have it—so instead I bribe her with a trip to the American Girl Salon for their infamous St. Patty's Day tea. I remember Renee telling me that store is the seventh circle of hell, and me being incredibly curious about it. Now I wonder why on earth I never offered to take her before.

In the kitchen, I eat a bowl of soggy de-raisined cereal and make some coffee. I pour a cup intended for Renee and then have a second thought, and head back up the stairs and in the opposite direction of the home office.

My hands are too full to knock. So I just open the door with a thwack. "NICOLAS LARSEN," I announce as I walk in, like he's a guest on a talk show I'm hosting in his bedroom.

Nic is in a queen-size bed with one pillow, clearly unconscious. He jumps about a mile when he wakes up and realizes I'm standing there. It's very satisfying.

"Good morning, Nic. I brought you coffee and a message."

"What are you doing here?" he asks. He is clearly scared.

"Coffee. Message." I set the coffee on the nightstand. It is black with Splenda, the way Renee takes hers. I remember from our years together he takes his with cream. Too bad.

"Oh, save it," I say as he tries to shuffle his body around, attempting privacy. "We dated for three years. Your morning wood doesn't shock me."

He turns bright red. "I thought you were in Wisconsin."

"I am clearly not in Wisconsin," I tell him. "I am in your bedroom, where you also are, which is odd because your daughters need to get off to school and your wife needs to get off to work and what the hell is wrong with you?"

I have been wanting to yell at someone for the last month straight. Trying to, actually, regardless of the situation. And now, here, at long last, is a person who should actually get yelled at. I am pretty excited. "Damn it, Nic, you stupid jerk! Get out of bed! Look at you! Why are you treating my friend like this?"

"Hang on there, Lily! There are two sides to every story," he says.

"Of course there are, you stupid jerk. That's why you have your own best friends to talk to. As for me, it is only Renee's side that I'm concerned with. And, from where I sit, it's time for you to get your head on straight. Renee is apparently the world's most discreet wife, but now that I know some of what's going on, I'm pissed."

"You don't understand," he says. "She's changed!"

I make a hate-face at him. "Yes, she has changed, but look at you!" At this I lean over and give him a Pillsbury Doughboy–style poke in the tummy. "Your lives have changed because it's been ten years since you got married. And you've gotten in over your heads and you're tempted to give up and, based on the smell in this room, maybe you already have given up. But that is over now. Here is what is going to happen. Are you listening?"

Nic nods, frozen and afraid.

I put a finger up and wag it in his direction. "You are going to stop being lord of the manor, and she is going to go to therapy with you. You two are going to start having sex again, and you are never going to compare her to me again or I will cut off your business." Nic turns green most satisfactorily. "And, most importantly, you are going to start buying raisins without the cereal mixed in because JESUS CHRIST!"

Nic stares at me, confused. He is just a deer in the headlights now.

I know the look because I'm pretty sure it's what I had when Renee told me everything this morning.

"Drink the coffee," I prompt. "Get out of bed. Drive the girls to school. Renee and I have something to do."

Dumbly, Nic gets out of bed. He takes a swig of coffee. He puts on a pair of pants from the floor and stumbles out of the room with the T-shirt he was sleeping in still on. "Natalie?!" I hear him call down the stairs. "Natalie! Natasha! Car. Now!"

I stand at the top of the stairs like an Italian housewife wielding a wooden spoon. When I'm sure he's done what needs doing, I go back for more coffee and take two mugs to Renee's office. "Holy shit, Renee," I say. "Husbands and kids are hard work."

Renee just laughs. It is the laugh of a person who just heard someone discover the world is round a few hundred years too late. "I think I've got this Mitchell thing solved," she says to the computer screen. "The relationship stuff is on you, but here, in section four, there's language that allows you to submit for independent appraisal and auditing of past sales going back two years, and if it's found that he misrepresented his earnings or your fair value, even just by a small percentage, he has to pay for the audits and pay you the money owing with interest as well. If you're not sure about this, and it turns out he hasn't been cheating you, you're going to be out for the auditor and the appraiser. It could be a couple thousand dollars. Not cheap . . . So you want to be sure."

I think of what Jenny told me. And what Mitchell told me. They've both lied a lot, and yet I know in my heart who I can trust.

"I'm sure," I say. "Well, no, I'm not sure. But I'm willing to take the risk."

"Then let's go do this. Here's your letter of notification to terminate his representation. Here's his letter of obligation to provide his accounting to the independent auditor. Here's the notification of independent appraisal. Here's the . . ."

She hands me letter after letter to sign. I marvel that in the time it took me to bribe her kids to get out of bed and dressed, she completely magicked about thirty legal and official-looking documents into being.

"I owe you like one billion dollars in legal fees, don't I?" I ask her when I finish signing.

"The nice thing is, if he really is cheating you, he'll have to pay my legal fees. If he doesn't, you owe me a shit-ton of babysitting. Which I'll need because I just heard you sell me out for marriage counseling."

"Deal," I tell her. "Also, I need to borrow Natalie for an afternoon in March. Don't ask any questions."

Renee looks up at me with that exasperated look in her eye, and for the first time in a long time, I don't see condescension or disapproval or disgust. I see her, doing her damnedest to love me, and most of the time, pulling it off.

Downtown, at Mitchell's gallery, I look at my watch, then at Renee.

"I'm scared," I admit.

"You should be. This is kind of a nuclear option. From what I can tell, Mitchell's definitely been screwing you, but whether or not he's covered it up well remains to be seen."

"It's the right thing to do, right?" I ask Renee. "To stand up for myself, demand what I know is right? I mean, put aside our shitty messes of lives, and our shitty attempts at friendship, and all the ways we've changed in the last ten years, and grown apart, or not grown at all. You're still the woman who dragged me to my mother's bedside. I'm still the woman who made your wedding dreams a reality. We still are people who do the right thing when we're called to, right? Even when it's hard."

"If we weren't, I'd be in Belize right now under an assumed name."

"So there it is. We're storming the castle."

"No," says Renee. "You're storming the castle. I'm sitting in the car. Don't forget this is also your boyfriend. You sleep with this person. You've got to go deal with that too."

I blanch. Unbidden, two years of something—not love, but not outright conflict either—comes to my mind. I think of that apartment he just bought ostensibly for *us.* The way he gave me my first showing.

His silver-tongued way of keeping me around every time I've tried to sneak out.

"Can't we just slip the papers under the door and run for it?"

Renee looks at me hard. "Yes. But should we?"

I do not answer. My vote is pretty clear.

"Get in there!" she says now.

I unbuckle my seat belt. Take the folder of legalese. Drag myself out of the car, into the street, onto the sidewalk, up to the gallery. The door is locked. I peer in and see . . .

"OH MY GOD MITCHELL!" I shout into the glass.

Mitchell is having sex with someone on that ugly chaise he keeps positioned in front of the gallery wall. Well, he's getting a blow job. It's bright outside and dark in there, but anyone capable of cupping her hands around her face to get a look at the art can see plain as day what is happening in there and it is incredibly *gross*.

Mitchell hears me, starts, and puts his dick in his pants. The someone else is a very pretty girl who looks startled and maybe a bit stoned. He rushes to the door. "Lily?" he asks as he's throwing it open. What a strange thing, to hear my name on his lips.

"It's ten A.M. in the freaking morning on a Friday, you weirdo," I say. Because of everything I just saw, for some reason the timing offends me the most.

"It's not what you think."

I put my hands up, and remember what I'm holding. "First of all, I hope it is what I think. I don't want to be with you anymore and this conveniently removes all guilt."

Mitchell's handsome face falls. "You're breaking up with me?"

I look up to the heavens for some kind of lightning bolt to strike. "Mitchell. Yes. Yes, I'm breaking up with you. I've found someone else. And so have you, apparently."

"Who is he?" he asks. I try hard not to look down at his pants. Ick ick ick. And what happened to the, ah, servicing party in this affair? I look behind him but she's gone.

"It's a she, actually," I say, thinking of Jenny's gallery. "And a he."

Because I'm definitely in love with Ben. "And an it." That "it" being a town that isn't all real but isn't all fake either.

"Excuse me?"

I take a deep breath. "Okay, first, you're an asshole. That's a given. But I've been cheating on you with this wonderful man who I'm technically married to, so actually, it's him I've been cheating on, and that has to stop."

"Lily, you're not making any sense. Listen to yourself."

"And secondly, you're also screwing me out of my sales, and here are some documents that my lawyer tells me I need to hand to you and I'm also supposed to tell you our gallery agreement is terminated and you have fifteen days to provide all your sales records as they pertain to me to the auditor whose name is in that envelope. And"—I take a deep breath and prepare the words Renee taught me—"I'm supposed to say 'per the terms of our initial agreement dated January 30th, 2014.' " I shove the envelope into his hands.

"This is insanity," he says. "Pure insanity. You're hurt. I screwed up. I get that."

And lastly, "Thank you, Mitchell, for helping me believe in myself as an artist and sorry about cheating on you. Okay, bye!"

I turn as fast as I can and run, actually run, to Renee's car. "Lily, wait!" calls Mitchell.

I jump into Renee's car. "Peel out or something!"

"What, did you rob him?" Renee asks.

"No! Should I have? No, I just I want to be dramatic."

"Girl, when he looks over those papers, the drama will happen by itself," she tells me, sensibly putting on a blinker and then slowly pulling away from the curb, while Mitchell runs toward the car, calling my name.

"Oh, Renee," I say, watching him recede in my rearview mirror. "It went better than I could have dreamed."

"I'm so glad. And I'm proud of you."

I put my hand over hers on the steering wheel. "Do you want to move to Minnow Bay with me?" I ask her.

She smiles sadly and shakes her head. "I don't know what that town is all about, but it sounds pretty wonderful."

"It is," I tell her.

"Well, let me know how the public schools are," she says with a good-natured laugh, and I know, right then, that as hard as things are for her right now, here in Chicago, she truly does want to see them through. "Are you going back there now?" she asks me.

I stop for a second. "Do you know what?" I say with a slow smile coming over my face. "I think I just might. Not forever, probably. I might have to follow a boy to California. But long enough to finish a painting I started."

Renee looks away from the road and to me, just for a second. Her eyes are large. "You're painting something new?" she asks.

"Something beautiful. Something I believe in with my whole heart."

I am not talking about *August Drought.* That painting needs only a few more brushstrokes here, touch-ups there, and then I will sign it and hand it over to Jenny. I am talking about something else. Something I conceived in my mind on the drive from Minnow Bay to Chicago, and can see as clearly as if it already exists. It is a pond. Frozen over. Freshly cleared of snow. About to be decorated.

Of course, when I was sitting there in Ben's truck, stuck in fantasy and fairy tales and escapism, I saw twinkling fairy lights and elaborate decoupage projects and a rink full of perfectly outfitted skaters, all moving in perfect circles, never falling, never even wobbling as they skated round and round. I saw a man and a woman holding hands, perfect in their steadiness. Unchanging.

Now the thought makes me laugh. It's not just silliness. It's not just trite, overdone hotel-room watercolor art. It's not even real. Ben is a hot-tempered fool. Jenny is a smooth-talking saleswoman. Colleen is a woman lost in longings and unfulfilled desires. And Minnow Bay is going broke and may fall apart before my very eyes.

Or it might, like the rest of us, find some way to persevere. It might shore itself up with a good ski season, and a few idiots ready to spend hours grooming an ice rink, and an artist reinvesting her profits into a good friend's festival, and a dot-com millionnaire getting sweet-talked into staying just a little bit longer, and maybe hiring a few dozen contractors to fix up his crappy lakeside shack to livable conditions.

It might just need, like me, like everyone, a little kindness, a little understanding, a few more months to skate by.

When I get to the commuter train station that will take me back to my car, I give Renee the biggest hug I can muster. She has to go to work and I have to go try to find *home.* Tears rise up and I hold back a sob.

"When are you coming back to visit me?" she asks me and, for the first time in a long time, I can tell she genuinely wants to know.

"Soon," I tell her. "Whenever you need me to take Natalie to the American Girl Spa or Natasha to World of Raisins. In the meantime, stop buying stuff, okay? Maybe talk to a realtor, see if you can unload your place?"

She nods obediently. It feels so strange to be giving her advice.

My train rumbles onto the tracks. I hug her again.

"Renee, thank you for everything," I say, because though we have covered so much ground in the last several hours, and come to understand so much, I know that this good-bye we are saying is more than two best friends spending a few weeks apart. It is a good-bye to the girlhood friendship I hung on to long after I should have let go. "I love you."

The train is loud and I step on.

"I love you too. And I'm sorry," she calls after me.

I turn back and start to shake my head no to her, *No, there is nothing to apologize for,* but then I stop myself. I don't have to be that person anymore, that girl who is never hurt, never angry, has never ever had enough. Instead I nod my head to her and mouth again, "Thank you." The train pulls away. And I finally let Renee disappear from view.

FOURTEEN YEARS EARLIER

"I can't believe we can come here whenever we want." Renee has her arms wide, spinning like Julie Andrews in a dirndl. "This is what I've been waiting for my whole entire life."

"I can't believe you've never been here before," I say. "How long is the drive?"

"Like, maybe eight hours? I don't know. I slept a lot of the way because my parents are too boring to remain conscious around."

"It's very sweet that they both drove down to move you in."

"Sweet, or oppressive? Anyway, they're long gone now. We should be drunk already."

"Are you going to be that kind of roommate?" I ask her warily, though I know by now that she's not. Since we moved in last weekend, we have done nothing, nothing, but talk to each other nonstop. Mouths full of Fruity Pebbles in the early mornings, chattering away. Two A.M. in our lofted beds, still yapping. The whole ride down here on the L, nonstop talking: life histories, family stories, dreams for the future, secret crushes and most embarrassing moments, and the best place to buy cheap ramen in the city.

"Are you going to be the other kind of roommate?" Renee asks me with a challenging smile.

"The lame kind? Maybe so," I admit.

"Don't worry, I can be lame with the best of them. Look, it's our first Friday as college students and we're stone-cold sober and in an art museum. And it was my idea. So I can't be that much trouble."

I look at her wickedly. "Do you think we could sneak booze in here?"

Renee nods twice. "I know we could."

"Were you the bad kid in high school?"

She shrugs. "I was a little bad. My parents think I'm an angel. What about you?"

"I was the nerdy art student."

"So, you're sticking with that persona, huh?" she says with a smile. "Oh my God, is that a real Picasso?" She rushes over to the Daley drawing. Chalk on wood. I always thought it was a little half-assed.

I shrug. "Sadly, it's not a persona. I would be a business major if it were up to me. The good Picassos are way upstairs, by the way."

"I would never be roommates with a business major. Let's go upstairs. Do you know your way around?"

"Slow down. You're going to miss the Chagall windows."

"Who can slow down? We are here to live, Lily! To take it all in! We are artists in the greatest city in the world!"

"It's only Chicago," I say, because in the Midwest we are not allowed to talk about how awesome we have it.

"It's where our whole lives are about to start."

I smile. That is exactly what my mother said this morning on the phone. "I think you are going to be an excellent roommate," I tell Renee, not for the first time.

"You too. You know those sappy stories about people falling in love on the first day of orientation freshman year?"

I shrug shyly, thinking how I've just spent the summer fantasizing about that very thing, only to find the incoming class of our esteemed art school to be less promising in the straight male department than I'd hoped. "Sure."

"Well, we're going to be like that, only with friendship. Which, when you think about it, is way better than getting boyfriends right away, because that means we can sleep around for the next four years before we get pinned down. Then we'll graduate, move into a huge loft apartment right downtown, make great works of art, fall in love with handsome bearded poets and musicians, and have a thousand children each."

"You think so? That sounds pretty great." I can totally see it happening. Exactly like that. Every day like this one. Eighteen forever.

"I have no idea, but I do know one thing for sure. It's going to be an incredible adventure," says Renee in her unbelievably confident way, the way that makes you feel like someone's got your back, from now until forever. "Wait and see. I'm never wrong."

FOURTEEN YEARS LATER, APRIL

"This is it!" Colleen comes thundering down the stairs of the inn. She hasn't walked quietly anywhere since she got the letter last week from her adoption agency in Haiti. Marianna, age four months, with a full head of dark hair, a cleft palate, and eyes to break your heart, is coming to live in Minnow Bay in three short weeks, where she will become Marianna "Marnie" O'Donnell. The expedited adoption, of course, was paid for by the proceeds of the two paintings Jenny sold, the check I signed over to Colleen and tucked in the envelope I asked Ben to give her on the night I left. The three of us girls like to joke that a Hutchinson ended up giving Colleen her baby after all, but the truth is, Colleen took a chance on me, and Jenny believed in me, and I just gave them back what they had already given. *Hope* for something better than what I had. *Belief* that it was within reach.

"Is it about Marianna?" I ask, popping out of my room on the third floor, which Ben, Steve the dog, and I have been renting and shacking up in together while his house gets to a stage he calls "woman-ready." That stage is just having walls in all the rooms and screens on the windows—I'd hardly call that high maintenance, but I sure as hell wasn't moving into that dump.

"No, you idiot," says Colleen lovingly. "Get dressed. Get Ben! This is *it*!" She turns to her phone and starts feverishly dialing.

Ben wanders out of the room, wearing pajama pants and nothing else. We feel like we're in a college dorm sometimes in the inn, with the comings and goings and the shouting and thundering, but then, we're all practically family by now anyway. I sort of half expect Jenny to pop up from the landing, and then thirty seconds later she does, waiving a FedEx envelope in her hot little hands and making what can only be described as an excited hoot.

"Today's the day!"

"What is going on?" I ask, and wrap my robe tighter around myself.

Ben grabs me from behind and turns me around and gives me a huge kiss that I feel in every hair follicle. "Today's the day, baby."

"Will someone please tell me what's going on?"

There are days in Minnow Bay when I think that I should probably have the words "Will Someone Please Tell Me What's Going On?" made into a T-shirt. Even when I'm not being snowed for the purposes of Ben Hutchinson–retention, Minnow Bay continues to mystify and confuse me with its strange rituals and seemingly impromptu parties. I duck into the room and grab a camisole and cardigan to take the place of my robe—I was naked from the waist up for reasons that are neither here nor there except to say that Ben and I are enjoying living together—and splash some water on my face and come downstairs.

The entire population of Minnow Bay is standing in the vestibule of the inn.

They are all in their spring coats and hats. The door keeps opening, and new people keep coming in. Simone, Carla Hutchinson, the woman who runs the bistro, the bookstore owner, the yarn-store clerk, people whose names I've learned and forgotten and people who I've never even met. They are milling about noisily and all of them, apparently, are interested in the contents of the FedEx envelope that Jenny is holding.

Ben, I suddenly realize, is standing in front of the painting I gave

Colleen those months ago. He's smiling broadly at me. He looks like a total computer dork. Band T-shirt over pajama pants, unbuttoned flannel over that, and not having had time to get cleaned up, he's wearing old glasses and sporting a college-kid beard. I'm so in love with him. The last three months have hit me hard.

Jenny hands Ben the package. "Are you sure this is it?" Ben asks, and he looks a little nervous.

Jenny nods. "I peeked," she tells him. I hear the sound of truck doors outside. One by one, the Hutchinson boys are starting to arrive now from further afield.

And then I get it.

My heart starts to tighten, to pound, and I swear my face starts shimmering with excitement.

Ben opens the FedEx envelope with a flourish, reaches inside, pulls out a few official-looking documents, and clears his throat loudly. "Everyone, excuse me, everyone? May I have your attention, please?"

The room quiets, if only slightly.

"SHUT UP YOU GUYS," says Jenny. The inn goes silent.

"Renee?" says Colleen into her speakerphone. "Can you hear us now?"

"I can hear!" Renee hollers from Chicago. "Good luck, Ben!"

Ben inhales deeply, and then looks from me to the crowd. "I'd like to announce a very important moment in my life that starts today. I hold here in my hands the official papers from the state of Nevada, Clark County, dated yesterday, April 19 of this very year. Hereby," he reads, "the court finds in favor of the expedited annulment of the marriage of one Benjamin Hutchinson and Lily Sylvia Stewart, and revokes the marriage certificate of said couple, effective retroactively, for reasons of incapacity and incompetence!"

There's a mighty cheer in the room and I laugh. How can I not, when I finally understand what is coming next.

"And with that," Ben calls over the cheer, "I can now officially tell you all that I am madly in love with a woman who is finally unmarried for the first time in ten years, and I would like her to immediately become married, and to me, and, if she sees fit to do so, I would like her to become married to me as soon as humanly possible!"

I start crying like a moron. There is more cheering. I cry harder.

"So I am going to ask you right now, Lily Sylvia Stewart, now that you have become my lawfully unwedded ex-wife, will you please, please, re-marry me?"

And there, in the Minnow Bay Inn where my life fell apart and was put back together and now will begin anew in ways better than I could have ever dreamed, I wrap my arms around my ex-husband and, in a voice loud enough for the entire town to hear, I say, "Yes."